Wicked by Any Other Name

Wicked by Any Other Name

Linda Wisdom

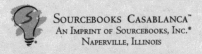

SOURCEBOOKS CASABLANCA™
AN IMPRINT OF SOURCEBOOKS, INC.®
NAPERVILLE, ILLINOIS

Published by Sourcebooks Casablanca, an imprint of Sourcebooks, Inc.
P.O. Box 4410, Naperville, Illinois 60567-4410
(630) 961-3900
FAX: (630) 961-2168
www.sourcebooks.com

Library of Congress Cataloging-in-Publication Data

Wisdom, Linda Randall.
  Wicked by any other name / Linda Wisdom.
     p. cm.
  1. Witches--Fiction. 2. California--Fiction. I. Title.
  PS3573.I774W53 2009
  813'.54--dc22

                                  2008038769

         Printed and bound in the United States of America.
             QW 10 9 8 7 6 5 4 3 2 1

With love to Yasmine Galenorn and Terese Ramin. You two have been with me from the beginning of these books. You made sure I didn't give up in the beginning, and I only hope I've been able to return the favor by always being there for you.

"The only thing we have to fear is fear itself."
—*Franklin D. Roosevelt*

"Are you a good witch, or a bad witch?"
—*Glinda, the Good Witch of the North,*
to Dorothy, The Wizard of Oz

Chapter 1

"CAN YOU BELIEVE THIS ABSOLUTE NONSENSE? I'M BEING sued!" Stasi stormed into Blast from the Past with the force of a Category 5 hurricane. She held up a sheaf of papers that looked suspiciously like ancient papyrus with lines of gilded lettering streaming across it. The large, embossed seal stamped at the bottom made it official. "And in Wizards' Court, no less!"

"Uh, Stasi, love, I have customers." Blair's gaze darted to the four people prowling her shop, who were now looking at Stasi with fascination. Blair's shop specialized in authentic retro items, from a 1940s Madame Alexander doll to a 1950s chrome table and tie-dyed clothing from the 1960s. It was easy for Blair to keep a varied inventory when her sister witches tended to clean out their closets of personal treasures every so often and were happy to have Blair sell them on consignment.

She quickly held up her hands. "Freeze frame, make it so!" She moved swiftly toward one woman who had frozen in the process of returning a tall Warner Bros. Roadrunner glass to the shelf, grabbing the glass just as it slipped from the woman's fingers. She placed it carefully among the other glasses and turned to Stasi.

Stasi's mid-length sunny brown hair flared around her with a life of its own as she stomped to the rear of the shop. She pulled herself up to sit on the waist-high counter and tossed the papyrus down on the polished surface. "This is insane," she snarled, staring at the parchment so hard Blair was amazed it didn't burst into flames. "*Hic!*" A perfectly shaped iridescent bubble escaped her lips.

Blair stared at her best friend in amazement. Anastasia Romanov was known for her sweet, romantic temperament and calm, almost placid, demeanor. Right now she looked ready to go off into a major witchy hissy fit, as evidenced by those angry bubbles. This was not the Stasi she'd known for more than seven hundred years! Stasi hiccupped and two more bubbles floated into the room.

"Now isn't the time to get the hiccups! Take a breath," Blair ordered, running a hand through her dark auburn curls. "And tell me what is going on. Slowly!"

Stasi closed her eyes, hiccupped again (three bubbles this time), and pulled in a deep breath, then another. When she opened them, she looked a bit calmer. And when she hiccupped again, only one tiny bubble slipped out. Blair relaxed a little.

"Carrie Anderson is suing me for alienation of affection. She's claiming it's *my* fault her rotten husband didn't come back." Dark purple sparks shot out over her head.

"Stasi, you need to calm down!" Blair said firmly. She glanced at the front door and promptly set a *stay out* spell on it. The last thing she needed was someone walking in to find customers playing *Statue* and Stasi shooting off magickal sparks. "Everyone knows Carrie's totally delusional about things." Blair glanced at the papyrus. "Why would she sue you for alienation of affection?"

Stasi's golden brown eyes glittered with unshed

tears that had more to do with fury than sorrow. "She's claiming that I did something to the sachet I tucked into her package that made sure her cheating, lower-than-scum husband wouldn't return to her and that by giving her a charm that harmed her marriage I interfered in mortal affairs. The 'cheating and lower-than-scum' description is mine. She's claiming he's the love of her life and she just knows he would have come back to her if I hadn't done something horrible to make sure he wouldn't return. He's, what, her fourth husband? It's a well-known fact that every man she's been with has been driven to cheat on her! And I've never made a claim that the sachets I put in the bags do anything. I make it sound like a joke that they inspire romance, and the customers love it. And it's not as though I can do much more than that, anyway. If I did, Cupid would be on my butt faster than a flea."

"Oh yeah, he's real protective of his job and doesn't like anyone interfering in his field," Blair agreed.

"Like most of the people in town, Carrie knows I'm a witch and she thinks my romance sachet *should* have brought Kevin back to her." Stasi crossed her arms in front of her chest, a full pout on her lips. "So now she's mad at me and wants vengeance. To top it off, she somehow persuaded a top wizard lawyer to file suit against me in Wizards' Court!"

"It can't be done. It has to be prosecuted in Witches' Court." Blair wasn't an attorney, but over the centuries she'd learned more than she liked about witch law.

Stasi shook her head. "Obviously it can, if that bottom-feeding wizard lawyer took the case and filed it. It would be bad enough if she'd hired that one that's

on the late night paranormal channel. Herve Rovenal
will take any case to defend innocent mortals from the
ones who prey on them. But she hired Trevor Barnes!"
Her lip curled as she glared at the parchment again. This
time a thin wisp of smoke curled up from its surface
but was quickly snuffed out—not by Stasi, but by the
parchment itself.

"We can't discuss it here," Blair said. She checked
the black Kit-Kat clock hanging on the wall. "It's almost
closing time anyway. I'll herd these people out once I've
unfrozen them and we'll see what's going on. Okay?"

Stasi nodded. "They'll have another thing coming if
they think I'll put up with this insanity," she muttered,
hopping off the counter. "It's not my fault that Carrie's
husband left her! Kevin used to be a nice guy, and she
treated him like dirt. I'll make her sorry she started this."
She marched to the door, which opened and closed
behind her without her hand touching it or the brass bell
hanging over it making a sound.

Blair quickly unfroze her customers, made a sale to a
bewildered woman, and ushered the rest out before they
realized what was happening.

"Girlfriend's got a problem," Felix, the black Kit-Kat
clock Blair had owned since the 1930s, announced from
his spot high up on the wall. His large eyes swept from
side to side as his tail swung back and forth above a sign
proclaiming him *Not for Sale*.

"No kidding." Blair emptied the old-fashioned cash
register that had once resided in Moonstone Lake's
general store back in the mid-1800s and tucked the
checks, cash, and coins into a bank bag. With the
spell surrounding the bag, no thief would dare try to

steal it unless he wanted his hands covered in nasty itching powder that wouldn't disappear for years. Blair Fitzpatrick took her revenge spells seriously and did the utmost to protect her assets. No shoplifter would get away without some serious pain.

"You're going to tell me all in the morning, right?" Felix asked, always eager to learn any new gossip that cropped up out of his range.

"Good night, Felix." Blair blew him a kiss as she headed for the front door. Judging from the sounds overhead, Stasi was upstairs creating havoc.

Stasi slammed the black iron pot onto the stove so hard it was amazing the appliance didn't buckle under the force.

"If Carrie doesn't watch herself, she'll end up a slug out in her disaster of a garden," she threatened, reaching for the large crock that held the various spoons and spatulas they used for cooking. Her fury caused all the cooking tools to jump out of the crock and fly around the room as a visual display of her temper tantrum. Bogie, her magickal Yorkie/Chihuahua, immediately disappeared into thin air with a faint pop. "Or maybe a chunk of mucus." With a twist of the wrist, she set the oven to preheat.

She headed for the refrigerator, violently pulled out a container that held beef stew, and set it beside the stove none too carefully.

"Or a scab. Yes, she'd make a great scab," she ranted, opening the container and bringing it to the pot. "A scab spewing disgusting mucus."

"*What are you doing?*" Blair raced across the kitchen and pulled the container out of Stasi's hands, almost upending the contents onto the floor.

"What is your problem?" Stasi tried to grab the container back, but Blair held it out of her reach.

"Look at the pot you were going to put it in."

Stasi turned back to the stove. Once she focused on the black pot, which very clearly didn't resemble any modern day cooking vessel, she sagged against the counter and gasped, "Oh no."

"Oh yes." Blair set the container down then carefully moved the pot off the stove. "I don't even want to think what would have happened if you'd used our best spell cauldron for warming up beef stew."

Stasi's pale skin turned even paler as she realized what the consequences could have been. An exploding cauldron would have been the least of her worries. A missing roof—or worse—could easily have happened if mortal products were heated in an object strictly meant for magick.

"I—"

"You're pissed off, and you would have blown us into another realm." Blair turned her around and gently pushed her toward the square oak table and matching chairs with burnt orange cushions. On the wall, the coffee-pot-shaped clock ticked quietly and then perked the hour. "Just sit. I'll do this. What is wrong with you, Stasi? You're *never* like this. We count on you to be the calm one."

"Oh yeah, that's me. Calm, cool, and collected Stasi." She used her fingertip to idly sketch a rune on the table's surface. "Everyone expects me to be the nice one. I'm supposed to be the sweet one. The peacemaker. Not anymore. No more Ms. Nice Witch."

Blair immediately moved to her side and erased the rune from the table.

"You're asking for trouble if you use that one. I'll be the first to say that Carrie's a vindictive bitch, but getting back at her that way isn't a good idea." She turned on the heat under the stew, which now resided in a proper copper-bottomed pot, and then went to work pulling out the makings for dumplings to go with the stew.

Bogie rematerialized and ventured close to the stove in case something tasty should happen to fall his way.

"Where's the parchment?"

"Under the couch."

Blair rolled her eyes. "All right, we'll forget about it during dinner, but I want to look it over later, okay?"

"Fine." Stasi pulled her hair up into a twist that stayed by itself. "But it will only make you mad."

Blair walked over and gave her a quick one-armed hug. "Eurydice won't allow them to get away with this."

Stasi wanted to remind her that with the case under the auspices of the Wizards' Court, the head of the Witches' Council wouldn't have any choice in the matter, but she knew Blair was already aware of that. Plus there was always that little matter from back in 1313 to haunt them the rest of their lives. One of their graduating witch class had cast a nasty curse on a member of the local nobility, causing the entire class to be banished to the outside world, to return to their realm after on hundred years—as long as they behaved. Seven hundred years later, they remained in the outside world. Which was why Stasi and her friends were still on the outs with the Witches' Council.

Stasi wondered what it would take to make the banishment go away. Fellow witch Jazz Tremaine had destroyed a killer of vampires and openly stated that Angelica, the director of the Protectorate and seated on the Vampire Council, was trying to pretty much take over the supernatural world. And that the wizard who'd created her famous bunny slippers, Fluff and Puff, was plotting to drive Jazz insane. Jazz was already on probation at that point after destroying Clive Reeves and his mansion of evil, but it never seemed to inhibit her. She dove right back into another pool of trouble.

Stasi had always been lovingly accused of being Eurydice's pet, since she had rarely gotten into trouble at the academy. But when the head witch had insisted the culprit step forward, Stasi had stuck with her friends and the banishment that followed. While the outside world was not at all how she'd expected it to be, the centuries she spent roaming the world and her friendship with Blair made it all worthwhile.

Now if she could just make this damned lawsuit go away!

Stasi tossed and turned in the elegant four-poster bed that was supposed to be her haven for sleep. Normally she had no trouble sleeping—of course, she had never had a lawsuit hanging over her head before. Her bedroom was decorated in soft pastels, with linens in shades of pale green, powder pink, cloud blue, and hazy lavender—solid colors on sheets and pillowcases, in misty swirls on her quilted duvet and pillow shams. The cream-colored walls were covered with artwork in the same color scheme, and fat pastel candles were scattered on tables and her dresser.

Except tonight she wasn't feeling the peacefulness of her surroundings. After turning her sheets into knots, she finally slipped out of bed, wrapped a soft woolen shawl the color of rich sapphires around her shoulders, and donned a pair of warm slippers before heading for the outside stairs that led to the roof.

Stasi was proud of what she and Blair had done with their building. Its facade spanned about half a block. The downstairs was divided into their two shops, and the upstairs had been totally renovated years ago. There was so much space that each was able to have a large master suite complete with roomy bathrooms, and they shared several guest rooms, an extensive kitchen—since they both enjoyed cooking—and a family room decorated for comfort. They had even set up a couple of rooms in the basement for certain friends who had trouble with the sun. Nick, Jazz's vampire boyfriend, could tolerate cloudy days, but direct sun was still his enemy, and the basement quarters gave him vital protection the few times he stayed there.

Thanks to their building's flat roof, they were able to fix up one corner as a small garden in the spring and summer, with chairs, a table, and a couple of chaise lounges along with a comfy swing.

Stasi settled in the swing and used one foot to push it idly back and forth while she stared out at the woods not far up the hill behind them and imagined she could see over the trees to the small lake for which the town was named.

Stasi knew it wasn't her imagination that something was in the air… literally. It wasn't just the upcoming lunar eclipse coupled with Mercury retrograde—talk about a double whammy! It wasn't even the prospect of dealing with a lawsuit that was fretting her mind. No, there was more going on that she sensed could piggyback on the eclipse and the retrograde, and not in a good way. She wasn't sure exactly what it was, but she hoped whatever it was would wait until after Samhain. She wanted to celebrate, damn it! She didn't want to worry about bad things happening. She was known as the positive one. So why did these qualms niggle the back of her mind and invade her sleep?

"We're a small town with nothing special about us. Nothing here to worry about," she whispered. "We're all like family. We look out for and help each other."

She smiled when a warm weight suddenly materialized on her lap. Bogie climbed up her chest and offered doggy kisses to her chin.

"I wish the Wizards' Court would accept your testimony," she whispered, opening her shawl then wrapping it around the small dog to keep him warm. "You know what Carrie is like. And you'd be a much better witness than Horace. I'd hate to think what he'd say about her other than his reverence for her perfect breasts. I need a plan of attack. Not something that Blair or Jazz cooked up for me. Something I can do on my own. They've gotten me out of jams before, but I can't allow them to help me this time. It's my fight."

Her answer was more kisses, then a soft growl as Bogie perked up and looked out past the edge of the roof. Stasi followed his gaze and saw a black and white streak of fur appear at the edge of the backyard.

"Be nice to him," she whispered. "He doesn't have a wonderful home like you do." She stood up and stepped closer to the edge. "If you're hungry, sweetie, come on up," she called out softly.

The black and white Border collie stepped carefully past the last remaining flowers and climbed the back stairs to the second floor. Stasi met him down there and let him into the kitchen.

Pretty soon the visitor was happily chowing down on the last of the beef stew, while Bogie watched him from a distance. The smaller dog's soft growls didn't deter the larger animal from his meal.

"What's going—oh Stasi!" A sleep-rumpled Blair appeared in the kitchen. "You're feeding that mutt again?"

The Border collie sat down and lifted his paw. His tongue lolled to one side in a large doggy smile.

"He doesn't have a home."

"And he's not getting one here. Look at him. He's not some scrawny stray. He looks pretty well fed to me." Blair dug her fingers into her scalp. "For all we know he has fleas."

The dog whined and offered his paw again, bobbing it up and down for effect.

"Fine." Blair accepted the paw and dropped it just as quickly. "But you're still not sleeping here."

"It's cold outside," Stasi argued on his behalf.

Before Blair could take up the argument, the dog loped over to her, stood on his hind legs, and covered her face with slurpy kisses, then twisted around and managed to nose open the kitchen door, running out and down the steps, barking a thank-you along the way.

"Ugh!" Blair gagged, wiping her mouth on her sleeve. "Dog germs!"

Stasi tried unsuccessfully to hide her smile. "Maybe next time you'll keep your mouth closed." She set the empty dish in the sink and rinsed it out. She filled the teakettle and set it on the stove, then pulled out two earthenware mugs. After rummaging through a substantial collection of tea bags, she selected lemon and dropped them into the mugs while Blair picked up a covered plate and placed it on the table.

"I probably should have brought these out for dessert, but this works even better. Mrs. Benedict dropped off a plate of lemon squares this afternoon," she explained. "She made a point of letting me know she made them and they weren't from 'that place.'"

Stasi shook her head. "Her nose has been out of joint since Fresh Baked Goods opened up last summer. How many years did people tell her she should open a bakery? We all told her she shouldn't give away all her baked goods. But she always said she wanted to create on her own schedule and not have to worry about keeping a shop filled with cookies, pies, and cakes. I think she wishes now she had taken our advice."

"Very true. But it got really ugly when Mr. Chalmers said that their oatmeal raisin cookies were the best he'd ever eaten. He made it worse by going back for more."

Stasi winced at the memory of the day Mrs. Benedict had learned that her devoted beau was unfaithful to her when it came to baked goods. The elderly woman had drawn herself up to her full barely five-foot height and informed the eighty-three-year-old widower who had been courting her for the last fifteen years that he shouldn't expect ever to have another bite of her pot roast and to just forget about Thanksgiving dinner. To date she had kept her word, and he now ate his meals at the local restaurants instead of the widow's cozy cottage. "He cut his own throat with that remark."

"And now he's eating all his meals at Sit 'N Eat and Grady's BBQ Pit."

"He had no choice after he set fire to his kitchen when he tried heating up some baked beans."

Stasi poured hot water over the tea bags, then carried the mugs over to the table. She picked up a lemon square and bit into it, moaning with joy as the tart taste of lemon exploded in her mouth. "Everyone loves the bakery, but all I know is that I tried one of their sugar cookies and ended up with horrible heartburn. Give me Mrs. Benedict's lemon squares any day." She paused and lifted her head, almost sniffing the air. She couldn't put a name to it, but she knew something was very different.

"You feel it too?" Blair asked, stirring her tea with a spoon even though she hadn't added anything to it.

Stasi, who always smiled and was cheerful, looked glum enough to double as the Grinch. "The disorder in the air is probably because of the lawsuit," she said without much conviction. "It's nothing around here. It's all me."

Blair shook her head. "No, I think there's more to it than that. This has been slowly building up for a while and it feels heavier now. More unsettling."

"Well, it can't happen now." Stasi selected another lemon square and ate this one more slowly, savoring the combination of buttery pastry and tangy citrus. "I'm planning on a wonderful Samhain. Jazz, Thea, and Lili promised they'd be here. Maggie might even make it, and she hasn't been able to come for the last three years."

"I'll be surprised if Thea stays more than twenty-four hours. She'd want to spend most of her time up at one of the resorts having massages and spa treatments. And Lili said the hospital is shorthanded again and she doesn't see how she can get away right now."

Stasi pinched off a bit of lemon square and offered it to Bogie, who gobbled it down and gave her his best cute pathetic puppy expression in hopes of getting more.

"We have a lunar eclipse coming, coupled with Mercury retrograde," Blair reminded her. "Along with warnings of early snow storms and a long and cold winter. It's as if everything's happening at once."

"Fresh snow means skiers, which also means tourists in town and even some staying for a few days at the B&B." Stasi hesitated over another lemon square, shrugged "why not?" and picked it up.

"True. I have all those vintage Halloween cards and decorations I need to get out." Blair didn't hesitate taking another square. Mrs. Benedict's baked goods were too excellent to pass up.

"I think we need to check the lake." Stasi threw the end of her shawl over her shoulder and looked toward the kitchen window that faced the woods. The burnt orange and cream print tiers were pulled across the bottom part of the window, but she knew what she would see out there anyway.

"Moonstone Lake isn't going anywhere. What we need to do is find you a good lawyer."

"I would need more than a good lawyer. I'd need an awesome one. Trevor Barnes is considered the best, and he's lost so few cases other attorneys don't even like to go up against him. They always urge their clients to settle."

"Says who? Besides, he's never gone up against any of us." Blair put on her "revenge is good" face. As a witch whose gift was for revenge spells, she knew the art very well. While she never did anything that would fatally harm someone, she did believe in making miscreants suffer greatly for their sins.

"I don't know why I had to be the first." Stasi stared at the now empty plate. "How many lemon squares were there?"

"I dunno. I think Mrs. Benedict brought over a couple dozen." Blair also stared at the plate. "Do you think Bogie snuck up here and ate some?"

Stasi shook her head. "No, we sat here and ate every one." She rubbed her tummy, starting to feel the effects of sugar overload. "I'll get the ginger tea."

"When do I get my day in court?"

Carrie Snyder Ferguson Simpson James Anderson accepted the cup of coffee Mae handed her and took two sips, setting it down on top of the notes Trevor Barnes had spread out on his desk for a case he needed to file that morning. Mae cast a disapproving glance at Carrie, then stared at the cup, which carefully shifted itself to the right and off the papers. Mae smiled at her boss's look of disapproval and disappeared from the office, literally.

Trevor pushed his dark blond hair off his forehead. He'd get a haircut today, he thought. He looked at his new client and narrowed his blue eyes. She was a nightmare, he realized belatedly.

A powerful wizard who dealt with every facet of preternatural law, Trevor Barnes was less used to dealing with the residents of the non-supernatural community. He didn't take many cases where mortals were involved, except those few that caught his interest. He was no longer amazed when humans tried to sue a vampire for breach of contract because the vampire refused to turn them. They refused to consider that it was against vampire law to turn someone for money. But there were many unscrupulous vampires out there, and it was better in Trevor's view if the vamp absconded with the money, leaving the human to deal with his still-mortal condition, rather than abandon a newly turned vampire to fend for itself until an enforcer from the Vampire Protectorate had to be called out to destroy it before it harmed too many others.

He rarely interacted with witches as plaintiffs or defendants since they didn't get on well with wizards and vice versa, and they tended not to cross into each other's jurisdictions. And now he was going to be pushed into dealing with one in court. He had a strong feeling this client wasn't going to settle.

He had been surprised when Carrie Anderson marched into his office two months ago and informed him she wanted to retain him to sue a local witch for alienation of affection. When Trev asked her why she didn't seek justice through the witches' community, she tartly informed him that they protected their own. She wanted justice and knew he would get it for her.

Trev's first instinct was to turn her down, since he really wasn't all that excited about having a mortal for a client, but the idea of suing a witch because she had ruined a woman's love life tempted him. Business had been rather bland lately, with only the usual dry cases that didn't offer him a lick of challenge. It wasn't long before he regretted his decision. It had only taken a bit of research on his client to realize that the woman was pretty much bonkers, and now he was well and truly stuck with her thanks to the Wizards' Code in legal matters.

Carrie was suspicious of everyone, and her past husbands headed the list. Her paranoia about being cheated on drove her first husband to an oil rig in the Atlantic with a vow never to return. Her second husband took off for Alaska with the same promise. Number three did the unthinkable and died of a heart attack, leaving behind several children and a pile of debts that prompted Carrie to waste no time latching on to husband number four. Trev's investigation showed that number four was now ready to bail out. After meeting Carrie, Trev wasn't surprised, except the man had made Carrie's worst nightmare come true. He'd cheated on his wife with "anything goes" Jeanne Tritt and was now happily living in sin.

Carrie tucked a stray ash blond curl behind her ear. Always well-groomed himself, Trev couldn't help but admire the woman's regular features and trim figure attired in a peachy-pink sweater topping soft gray tailored pants. Her brown eyes were shadowed with worry. She chewed off her lipstick as she looked at Trev as if he would be able to solve all her problems in one fell swoop. But he didn't need his wizard senses to alert him that there was something in her eyes and manner that was just a bit off. He wondered if all her ex-husbands were first drawn to her delicate looks, then, once the marriage license was signed, sealed, and delivered, they ended up leaving her because there was something lacking in the woman herself.

An excellent example of beauty being skin deep, because I just bet the interior isn't a match for the exterior.

Carrie started on a familiar tack. "If she did this to me, she's done it to others. She needs to pay for interfering with peoples' lives. The spells on the lingerie I bought there should have brought Kevin home, and it didn't. He's still with that bimbo." She pulled a tissue out of her bag and dabbed at a smudge of mascara at the corner of her eye. It only smeared more.

"Mrs. Anderson, I'm sure Ms. Romanov knows she cannot utilize any spells having to do with romance," Trev used his best soothing voice. "That is Cupid's domain, and he doesn't take it lightly if someone tries to interfere. He would even be within his rights to register a complaint against her."

"She's a witch, isn't she?" Carrie screeched, displaying the anger that, along with her jealousy, Trev was positive had driven her previous husbands away from home. "Everyone knows they'll do what they like. Sure, people in town think she and Blair are sweet and wonderful, but I've read stories about other witches who cast spells on people, horrible dark spells. Who says they're not up there doing that to us, to make us feel we love them!"

"There are rules governing their behavior," he explained patiently. "Punishment is harsh for those who go against laws set down eons ago."

"And she broke them." Carrie's eyes narrowed. "I used to work in a library and I know how to do research, Mr. Barnes. Stasi Romanov isn't what this town thinks she is. At first, I wanted to tell everyone just what a monster she is," Carrie hissed. She didn't back down, even when Trev's expression grew so cold the temperature in the office dropped a good twenty degrees. "But so many people think she's this sweet wonderful woman; I knew they wouldn't believe me. That's when I went into LA and talked to some strange people and discovered she could be sued."

If Trev had been mortal, he would have been downing aspirin by the bottle by now, if not hitting the nearest bar. He only wished the Code didn't stipulate that once you took a case you couldn't dump it. The last time he had wanted to dump a case was when Bernardo, a mountain dragon, was suing a knight for brutality. The case had presented some technicalities that had fascinated him, but his client was so volatile that his court robes had ended up singed, and he couldn't get the smell of smoke out of his hair for months.

He was beginning to think Bernardo was a pip compared to Carrie Snyder Ferguson Simpson James Anderson.

"Wizards' Court handles matters in its own time," he said. "Papers have been filed, Ms. Romanov has been served, and we should be given a court date soon."

"We better." Carrie stood up. "I'm not a patient woman, Mr. Barnes. I want her to lose everything, so she'll leave town."

He likewise stood up, inwardly grateful she was leaving. "Perhaps you need to do some further research into Wizards' Court, Mrs. Anderson. Threats are never a good thing." He walked her to his office door, partly from courtesy but mostly to make sure she was well out of his office. "I'll be in touch."

Trev sighed as he turned back toward his desk.

"Didn't I tell you working with humans would only give you grief?" Mae, his secretary/assistant/surrogate mother/pain-in-the-ass, spoke from her spot behind her highly polished walnut desk, on which a stray sheet of paper never dared to land. He had inherited her six hundred years ago when his father retired to take a seat on the Wizards' Council and she still treated him as if he was recently out of law school. She patted the bun sitting primly on top of her head. Not one strand of her silver hair was ever out of place. It was always pulled back in a French twist, her dark suits never revealed a crease or wrinkle, and she ruled his office with an iron fist. The narrow red-rimmed glasses that sat on her aquiline nose were unnecessary, but suited her take-charge manner. He had to pay his paralegals a small fortune because otherwise they wouldn't last more than fifty years with General Mae in charge.

Trev was tempted to remind her that she had made the appointment in the first place, but what was the point? Mae never made a mistake—and was the first to say so.

"Ms. Romanov called." Mae slapped a stack of pink message slips on his hand.

"Who's her lawyer?"

"She doesn't have one." Mae turned back to her computer monitor, which glowed with characters in an ancient language. "It would be better if you drove up there to see her personally." She gave him a pointed look over her glasses.

He rubbed his jaw with his hand thoughtfully. "It would be better to wait until she retained counsel."

"Our law doesn't follow the same rules as mortals," she reminded him. "You can see the defendant without her counsel present. It didn't seem that Ms. Romanov was too eager to hire anyone to represent her. My Russian is a bit rusty, but I'd say she is not happy about this lawsuit. But I'm certain your charm can persuade her to settle this case amicably and as soon as possible."

"That would be nice," Trevor thought. But his client certainly wasn't in that frame of mind.

Trev thought of the workload on his desk. The cases he needed to review. Others that had to be filed. The meetings that filled his calendar.

But when Mae told him he had to be somewhere, he damn well better go there.

Mae was never wrong.

Chapter 2

"WOOEE! LOOK AT THAT ONE," HORACE MUTTERED OUT of the corner of his mouth. "You think they're real? Boy, I'd love to get my claws on those babies."

Stasi put the stack of La Perla bras and thongs she'd just priced to one side. The eight-inch grayish-stone gargoyle sat on the counter by her elbow. He had an elongated snout that resembled a monkey's, long arms and short legs, along with pointy horns and leathery-looking wings. More than once customers had commented on Stasi's choice of décor, and she had recently had a few complaints about the sudden appearance of the gargoyle in one of the dressing rooms when a customer—always a shapely one—was trying on lingerie. She glared at Horace.

"You're gross."

"You're repressed."

"You're a pervert in stone," she told the snarky gargoyle, who slowly turned his head to grin at her.

Horace raised a stone eyebrow. "You be cursed in this rock for the last thousand years, then we'll talk. Of course, if Jazz would do her thing, I'd be back to my normal self. What good is having a curse eliminator for a friend if she doesn't help you out?"

"First of all, you were never normal. Second, she wouldn't be helping *me* out, just you. Besides, yours wasn't a typical curse. You never should have fooled around with that troll's girlfriend once you found out he knew a really powerful sorcerer. You need more than a curse eliminator to get out of this one."

Horace's gray stone head swiveled enough to look toward the display windows. His narrow mouth widened in a grin.

"Maybe that's what I need. Come to think of it, maybe that's what *you* need."

"What do you...?" Stasi didn't need to finish her question as a man—a tall, very handsome man— entered her shop. Nor did she need anyone to tell her that this apparition was not just a man, but a wizard. And since a wizard had never entered her shop before, she just *knew* which wizard he must be. She touched her creamy pearl ring for reassurance, looking at the soft glow the bead exuded.

Wowza!

Her enemy should have looked uncomfortable standing in the middle of a shop that was designed purely for a woman's sensual nature. But he didn't. In fact, if she wasn't mistaken, he was the type of man who would purchase expensive lingerie for his women. She gauged he usually spent a few hundred dollars, and if he wanted to shop here, she would happily take his Black AmEx. If he wanted to discuss the lawsuit, she'd be only too happy to zap him right out of her shop, even if "wowza" did keep floating through her head.

But life was playing a horrific joke on her. It was bad enough having a wizard in her shop, especially this wizard, but the sight that almost blinded her had her biting her lip to keep her scream contained. As it was, a tiny squeak escaped her mouth.

All because a half circle of dainty red hearts glowed and pulsed over his head.

No, no, no, no, NO!

Stasi felt her entire system go into major overload and she almost had to sit down. She refused to believe what was shining before her eyes. She blinked, then blinked again, hoping that what she was saw a figment of her imagination. It wasn't. The hearts were still there in living color and looked as if they'd even increased in their scarlet brilliance.

Cupid has a very warped sense of humor.

"Is there something I can help you with?" She finally managed to unglue her tongue from the roof of her mouth. She felt as if her raspberry pink sweater and the pink, brown, and cream print skirt that swirled around her calves were suddenly made transparent as the man fixed her with an unnerving gaze. It wasn't easy for her to look him in the eye when he had those damn hearts over his head.

"This is very nice," he commented, walking around. "Interesting fragrance, too. It makes me think of fresh snow."

She said nothing, because frankly, she couldn't think of anything to say. It was enough of an effort to keep her gaze off the damn hearts.

He continued walking around, stopping at small round tables covered with rich cream colored silk and lace cloths, chosen to complement the colorful lingerie on display. Several armoires set against the walls displayed hanging camis and chemises, and baskets set here and there were filled with decorative sachets.

He fingered a black silk bustier and matching thong that had two books beside it.

"*Night Huntress* and *Dragon Wytch*. Do they have something to do with the lingerie?"

"I choose the books to go with the items, yes. Call it a theme package. Now is there something I can help you with?" *Such as show you the door before I contact Cupid and have more than a few words with him.*

He crossed the shop in a matter of steps and held out his hand. "You must be Ms. Romanov. I'm Trevor Barnes."

Stasi ignored his outstretched hand, something that would normally be anathema to her polite nature, and deliberately crossed her arms in front of her. There was nothing like body language to let someone know they weren't welcome.

"I know who you are. I just don't know *why* you're here." Her ice-cold voice could have come from her diva witch friend Thea's lips. With just one word, Thea could freeze a man at ten paces.

"Interesting accessories." A gravely voice sounded from the counter.

Stasi froze. The last thing she wanted was for the wizard to realize just what floated over his head.

Trev raised an eyebrow and looked down at the gargoyle, who eyed him with similar suspicion.

"Pissed off a troll, did we?"

"What was your first clue?" Horace didn't have to make a face. His own was horrible enough.

"The horns. You must have had a lousy lawyer. How many more centuries do you have to go before you've served your sentence?"

Horace perked up. A faint light like a glowing fire gleamed in his eyes. "Do you mean I could get out of this rock?"

"Are you so desperate for clients that you have to go soliciting, Wizard Barnes?" Stasi asked, holding a tight rein on her emotions before she could start to hiccup a mega bubble fest.

"I'm just curious, Ms. Romanov." He flashed his pearly whites. "And I go by Trev."

"I might have to be polite to you, *Wizard Barnes*, but I don't have to be friendly." Her normally soft golden brown eyes were hard and narrowed, and if Trev had been looking at her ankles, he would have noticed an unearthly sheen coming from the creamy pearl dotting the handle of the tiny gold broom that hung from her anklet. She could feel the metal heating her skin. A deep breath calmed that down. She tried to cover by retreating behind the counter.

"I thought we could discuss the case and try to arrive at an amicable settlement that I can present to my client. Maybe we can avoid the trouble of having to deal with this in court. Also, I haven't heard from your counsel." Trev turned up the charm factor, but Stasi was immune.

"Probably because I haven't retained one yet." Her jaw tightened so much she feared her teeth would shatter in her mouth.

"Oh, this is great!" Three twenty-something women dressed in ski pants and parkas that would probably never get near the ski slopes walked in and scattered in different directions. "I'm so glad Claire told us about this boutique."

"And it smells so good in here, too," a blonde with highlights gushed. "It's like this rich vanilla cream with cinnamon."

"You must have a cold," the brunette said as she inhaled deeply and picked up a tiny hanger holding an equally tiny thong. "I smell berries with something almost spicy. Like those spice drops Kevin loves to eat all the time."

"Chocolate. I smell milk chocolate." The slender redhead made a beeline for a filmy chemise displayed next to a copy of *Sex and the Single Witch*.

"Interesting. Each customer who comes in detects an individualized scent," Trev murmured.

"It makes them buy more."

"Especially the one smelling chocolate?" He watched the redhead pick up a chemise in every color along with an armload of books.

"She's PMSing. Anyone PMSing tends to smell their favorite form of chocolate." Stasi planted her hands on the counter and stared at Trev. "I normally don't ask people to leave my shop, but I have customers here and a business to run."

He nodded. "We need to talk. Or at least retain counsel and have him or her contact me."

"I'll see you in court, Wizard Barnes." She made sure to keep her voice low so the women wouldn't overhear her.

"I have an idea it will be sooner than that, Ms. Romanov." He smiled and left the shop; the damning red hearts still arced over his head.

Stasi was relieved that mortals couldn't see the hearts, and more than grateful she had customers to deal with. Otherwise, she would have been tempted to indulge in a hissy fit that would make Thea's tantrums look like a Zen moment. By the time the three women left, her breathing had returned to normal. Sort of.

Wizard—she refused to even think of him as "Trev"—Barnes was gorgeous with a capital G. Dark blond hair with a hint of bronze highlighting the thick strands, kept short because he was the type, skin tanned from the sun, eyes so blue they rivaled a cobalt stone, and his designer suit was cut to make his lean body look fabulous. The man might work in an office, but it had to be more than good genes that gave him a body like that. She guessed he enjoyed a morning swim every day, and not just a leisurely dog paddle, either. As she stared at the spot where he had been standing, her vision momentarily blurred until objects appeared to dance in front of her eyes. *Valentine red heart-shaped objects.*

She suddenly felt as if a bomb had been set off inside her.

"Uh." She blindly fumbled for the stool she kept behind the counter. "Uh." Her forehead connected with the counter in a nasty thump.

"Was that who I think it was? Oh, no." Blair slipped inside the shop, closed the door behind her, and waved her hand to activate the lock. "Oh honey, that's going to leave a mark." She hurried over to the counter.

"Uh," was all Stasi could utter.

"Yep, hot boy is the wizard," Horace offered up. "I've got to say, if I wasn't into women I'd do him in a second."

"Uh!" Stasi's mumble now had a gurgling sound.

"What was he doing here? What did he want? Is Carrie dropping the case or shall I whip up an eternal yeast infection for her? I will do it, you know," Blair promised, leaning over Stasi, rubbing her back in soothing circles. She leaned closer in hopes she'd hear the slight sounds coming from Stasi's mouth. "What did you say?"

"Ha—" she took a deep breath. "Hearts. He wore hearts."

Blair straightened up as the meaning clicked in. "No way!"

She nodded. "Big dancing red hearts way." A loud hiccup echoed in the shop with an ethereal bubble floating in the air. Horace exhaled a deep breath, sending the bubble dancing higher.

Blair shook her head. "It has to be a sick joke on Cupid's part. Even he wouldn't be this nasty."

"Yes, he would. *Hic!*"

"Hold your breath."

"They have to stop on their own." Stasi accepted the glass of water Blair brought her.

"Why did he come?"

"To discuss an amicable settlement."

"As in you give in to whatever she demands?"

She nodded. "I told him I'd see him in court."

"The way Wizards' Court runs, the case might not be heard for a thousand years."

"Human plaintiff, remember? Any case involving a mortal is fast-tracked. It said so in the paperwork." She buried her face in her hands. "All I wanted was a beautiful Samhain this year." Her words were muffled by her hands.

"And it will be. Nothing is going to ruin it." Blair hoisted herself up on the counter and swung her legs back and forth. Her hair had been pulled up into a perky ponytail. Dressed in a navy and green plaid skirt that skimmed her knees, a crisp white blouse with a Peter

Pan collar, and a cream-colored long-sleeved sweater, along with navy knee socks and loafers, she looked like the consummate schoolgirl. Since she owned and ran a shop featuring vintage and retro merchandise, she liked to dress the part.

Stasi happened to look up and see a familiar figure cross in front of the display window before reaching for the shop door. A wave of Blair's fingers released the lock in the nick of time. She hopped off the counter to stand beside Stasi.

"Good morning, Stasi," the visitor chirped, stepping inside the shop.

"Poppy," the two witches greeted the woman whose personality was perfectly paired with her voice. Both were chirpy with a hint of squeak, and she never seemed to remain still for more than five seconds. Blair liked to compare Poppy to an evil Tweety bird. Her thin body was attired in a bright blue tunic-length sweater and matching leggings paired with impossibly high heels. Even her candy pink lip gloss seemed to add to her bird-like appearance.

Stasi found the woman irritating, but managed to keep her feelings masked.

"Such a chilly morning, isn't it?" Poppy offered a sunny smile as she walked toward them carrying a large plate. "I tried out a new muffin recipe this morning and thought I would bring by some samples. Perhaps if you offer them to your customers they'll like them well enough to come down our way." She set the plate on the counter and drew off the cellophane covering with a dramatic flourish. "They have cinnamon and other spices in them, plus a few secrets of my own. I thought if everyone liked them I'd bring them out for Halloween. Reed and I keep hearing how the town goes all out in October, so I thought I'd try some Halloween theme recipes."

"Well." Blair winced when Stasi's shoe made contact with her ankle as a less-than-subtle reminder to be polite.

"Thank you, Poppy, it's very nice of you to bring us some treats," Stasi said with a smile that only a close friend would know was false.

The woman waved off Stasi's thanks. "It's a good excuse to be out and about and also announce some wonderful news. Our sister, Amaretto, will be visiting us for the festivities. Rhetta is Reed's twin, and hasn't been up here yet, so we're looking forward to her visit."

"That will be nice for you," Blair said in a monotone.

"Oh yes, it's wonderful," she chirped.

The blonde woman glanced around the shop. For a moment, a hint of distaste crossed her features before it was replaced by her usual bright smile. Stasi stared at her, wondering if she'd imagined the expression. She had a sudden hankering to get a peek at Poppy's lingerie drawer. She believed a woman's lingerie revealed her true personality and so far, she hadn't been able to get a handle on what Poppy was really like. But to be honest, she didn't want to be Poppy's friend, no matter what. There was something about the woman she just plain didn't like.

"It's amazing you can manage to sell such expensive lingerie up here," she commented.

"As you noticed last summer when you opened Fresh Baked Goods, we get a lot of tourists from the resorts,"

Stasi replied. "The women love to stop by for lingerie and reading material."

Poppy fingered an erotic novel displayed next to a bright red satin bustier. "Yes, I imagine so." She looked up, smiling again. "Well, I must get back to the bakery. I have several batches of muffins in the oven. I hope you enjoy them. Ta ta." She waggled her fingers and almost skipped out the door.

"Ta ta." Blair's farewell held a hint of mockery in it, but Poppy was already gone.

"Don't do that." Stasi picked up the plate and dumped the contents in the waste bin under the counter.

"Hey! Did you ever stop to think I might be hungry?" Horace slid across the counter and looked down. "I bet they taste as good as they smell."

"It's the principle of the thing," Stasi said.

"I figured it was because Reed has a crush on you," Horace pointed out.

Stasi shuddered at the thought of the co-owner of the bakery, Reed Palmer. The man was charming, good looking, and he was one of the reasons why Fresh Baked Goods was so popular. It wasn't just Poppy's muffins, cakes, and breads along with espresso and cappuccinos that kept it filled with customers. The men went in for the baked goods; the women went in for a chance to flirt with Reed, who Stasi admitted was good looking even if he didn't ring her chimes. Stasi and Blair were among the few of the small town's holdouts.

But that didn't stop Poppy or Reed from dropping off cookies and muffins every so often. And each time the offerings were dropped in the trash the moment Reed or Poppy left.

"What if we went to Carrie?" Blair said. She hesitated. "You could offer to work up a spell to get what's-his-name back if she'll drop the suit."

Stasi straightened up to her full five-foot-four-inch height. Resolve shone in her golden brown eyes, turning them to deep topaz, and faint sparks, like glitter, seemed to coat her skin.

"Anastasia," Blair's tone held a warning.

"Carrie is a vicious, hateful woman who treats men as if they're a piece of gum stuck to the bottom of her shoe. She doesn't have a speck of romance in her selfish, mercenary soul. There is no way in Hades that I will bargain with *that woman!*" Stasi spun on her heel and headed for the rear of the shop.

"Don't even think about it. You've been served by the Wizards' Court. If you retaliate against Carrie, they can also take you before the Witches' Council," Blair warned, fast on her heels. She took in her best friend's dark expression. "Anastasia?"

Stasi headed for a rack filled with plastic covered hangers. She carefully stripped the plastic coverings off the first few hangers and inspected the colorful chemises. One chocolate brown silk chemise with mocha-colored lace had Blair reaching out with a moan of pleasure on her lips.

"I really want this." Blair held the chemise up against her body.

"It's yours." Stasi smiled.

Blair paused. "Wait a minute, you're distracting me on purpose. Stasi, what did you do?"

"Nothing." Stasi pulled the plastic wrapping away from another chemise, this one a shimmering sapphire blue with silver lace.

The delectable lingerie briefly diverted Blair's attention as she mentally tagged it *mine,* but she quickly brought herself back to the subject at hand. Foreboding settled in her stomach like a heavy lump as she saw something flicker across her friend's face.

"Oh my… you did something, didn't you? *Stasi!*"

"Hey! You two trying on bras and panties?" Horace appeared in the stockroom entry.

They turned as one. "*Get out, Horace!*"

He reared back a little, his leathery wings rustling stiffly in the air. "Geez, I'm heading out if both of you are on the rag at the same time."

Stasi stepped in his direction, her hand up, palm out. "Out of here *now!*" A burst of power sent the gargoyle tumbling backward through the filmy curtains that separated the shop from the stockroom.

"Fine! All you had to do was ask me to leave!" he shouted back. "*Ow!*"

Stasi blew on her finger as if it was a smoking gun barrel then turned back to Blair.

"I did nothing she didn't deserve." She swept her hand in front of her. "If I had done what I truly wanted to, the Witches' Council would have called me in."

"Only if they thought you did something…" The truth hit her like a huge rusty cauldron. "You didn't. You *did! Stasi!* You made sure Carrie's husband wouldn't return to her!"

Stasi refused to look at her friend as she continued to strip plastic coverings off the newly arrived clothing. "Carrie thinks every man she meets is perfect for her and will love her until the end of time. Except once she snares her prey, she treats him like something she'd scrape off her shoe. Perhaps she needs to learn that not every man will bow to her vicious behavior."

Blair advanced on her with the subtlety of a Sherman tank. "I don't even want to think how many years this could add to your banishment if they find out. For someone who's basically flown under the radar for decades, this has got to be the absolute craziest thing you've ever done." She stepped forward, still trying to wrap her mind around the idea of her gentle friend doing something that… well… something that she'd do!

Stasi was the best of the best among their class at the Witches' Academy. She had embraced academic life, loved her classes and all their teachers, including old Grizelda, who smelled like musty clothing and actually cackled. Sweet-natured Stasi had stood strong with her classmates when she could easily have remained at the academy and realized her full potential, possibly even attaining status on the Witches' Council. It had meant so much to the others and had even inspired guilt in some, because they all knew Stasi was destined to be great among their community. Instead, Stasi had refused to betray her sister witches all those years ago and was banished to the outside world with the rest of them. So far, not one of the witches had behaved well enough to end their banishment. During the past centuries they had more or less adapted to the mortal world and many enjoyed the lives they now had.

"That sachet didn't inspire romance, did it? You slipped a rejection spell in it, didn't you?" Blair advanced on Stasi, who now had no place to retreat. "You made sure Carrie's husband wouldn't return to her."

"She didn't want him anyway." Stasi hated that her voice sounded suspiciously like a whine. "She just didn't want anyone else to have him. She was the one who drove him away. I just made it permanent." She set her chin in a determined manner.

"You can't do that! You believe in true love. If there wasn't Cupid, there would be you."

Stasi heard the pain in her friend's voice, but she refused to succumb to it. Blair knew what Carrie was like.

"She deserved what she got, and Kevin is safe from her manipulations," she said finally.

"And if the Wizards' Court figures this out, you will be in so much trouble it will never end. As it is, they make Witches' Court look like a playground!"

"Then it's my trouble, and no one else's." Stasi turned her back on Blair.

"It's on your head then." Blair threw up her hands and stalked out of the boutique.

"Nice thong, Blair!" Horace shouted after her from his favorite vantage point on the floor. "Love the naughty schoolgirl look you've got going there."

Trev revved the engine and listened to the discreet growl emitted by his midnight blue Jaguar XK convertible. He had always admired the sound of a quality machine, and his Jag offered that up big-time. The winding mountain road was a breeze for the low-slung vehicle as he drove upward to a nearby resort where he'd spend the night before returning to Los Angeles. He only wished the weather was warmer so he could have the top down.

For now his mind was centered on Anastasia "Stasi" Romanov. He rarely dealt with witches. All his business associates were wizards, sorcerers, and sorceresses. To be frank, he considered witches to be rather déclassé, although he had the good sense never to say that aloud. He had heard that Eurydice, head of the Witches' Council, was a major force to be reckoned with if she felt any of the witches under her protection were threatened.

He'd walked into the shop in the tiny mountain town expecting to meet a timid witch who would be properly intimidated by his wizard status and immediately agree to anything Carrie wanted, so that the matter wouldn't go to court and he could usher his newest client out with a huge sigh of relief.

Instead, he found a lovely woman with snapping golden brown eyes—and a pervert of a gargoyle, who he could see was protective of the young witch. For a moment he'd even been tempted to ask her to meet him for dinner at the resort's dining room, but after the way she looked at him as if he was the vilest creature on earth, he wouldn't have been surprised if she would have added a little something disagreeable to his meal.

And what was with the red hearts dancing over her head like some insane Valentine TV commercial? He made a mental note to ask Mae to research it. He figured it had something to do with the romantic nature of the boutique, but the sight was more than a little disconcerting.

He pressed a button on his steering wheel. "Office."

"Mr. Barnes' office." Mae answered on the first ring.

"Ms. Romanov has no counsel," Trev said.

"How nice that you arrived safely, Trevor," Mae smoothly overrode his comment. "We're doing fine here, thank you for asking. Nothing important has happened since you left, although your father did stop by hoping you could have lunch with him."

He mentally uttered a few choice words. After all these years he should know better. Mae stood on ceremony and any time he forgot that, she was quick to remind him. But he had a small arsenal up his sleeve.

"I hope you enjoyed lunch with Father." He grinned. Mae hadn't said a word, but he easily sensed she hadn't expected that. There was no doubt in his mind that Mae and his father had been having an extremely discreet affair for the past few decades. The idea of his prim and proper assistant and pompous sire getting hot and heavy between the sheets was a vision he preferred to be burned out of his brain.

He noticed the sign for the resort where he had a reservation for the night and made a quick turn. "Would you do me a favor and have someone do a little research on something that might have to do with witches?"

"Does this have to do with the Anderson/Romanov case?"

"Not directly, but since Anderson is pretty much suing for alienation of affection, it might be related. See if there's a reason why a witch would have glittery red hearts dancing over her head. And I'd like Anastasia Romanov's history."

The silence on the other side of the line was charged. "Did you say glittery red hearts over her head?" Mae said finally in a voice that didn't sound like her normal self-contained self.

"Yes, why?"

"No reason. You'll be in tomorrow?"

"Not until the afternoon, since I'm staying up here tonight,"

"Fine." Mae disconnected before Trev could say anything else.

And if he had thought about it he would have sworn there was a very un-Mae-like hint of mirth in her voice.

Chapter 3

"DON'T FORGET WE HAVE A TOWN MEETING TONIGHT," Blair reminded Stasi as they started fixing dinner. Her earlier snit with Stasi was over. She could never remain angry at her best friend for long, even if she privately thought Stasi had lost her mind for what she'd done to Carrie Anderson. But she was also impressed with her friend for coming up with such an innovative way of dealing with the overbearing woman.

"I thought the Haunted Moonstone Lake festivities were already agreed upon. It's almost the end of September and there's no time to start setting up something new." Stasi added a dusting of paprika to the scalloped potatoes she had pulled from the oven. "I swear, every year, they discuss the matter to death then go on and do the same thing they've done in the past. Orange flickering bulbs will be set in the streetlamps so they'll look like flames, Arnie will portray Old Miner Caleb roaming the town looking for the fiend who stole his gold." She spooned the potatoes on to their plates next to the pork chops Blair had cooked up. "And Miss Priscilla, our ghostly schoolteacher, will tell stories at the old schoolhouse on the edge of town."

"And we'll all wear costumes." Blair wrinkled her nose. "At least they agreed we all don't have to wear period clothing the way we have in the past. Although, I bet Agnes Pierce will bring it up again tonight."

Stasi nodded. "From the way she acts you'd think that Agnes was Moonstone Lake's mayor, instead of her husband." She unconsciously rubbed her butt. Floyd Pierce was well known for his habit of sneaking in a discreet pinch to the posterior. He left Stasi alone after he received a shock equivalent to sticking his finger in a light socket when he pinched her butt at last summer's Fourth of July picnic. She smiled at the memory of the heavyset man falling into a mud puddle that just happened to be nearby. Oh yes, that was a fun day.

"Even if I do choose to wear a period costume for a day, I am *not* wearing a corset," Blair declared. "Those things hurt. It took years for the dents to go away after they finally weren't necessary anymore."

"I hated the constriction, but I loved how feminine we looked." Stasi looked down at her size Bs and recalled how very well uplifted they had been when she wore a body cinching corset. She just loved lingerie—it was an art form for her.

"Just as long as Agnes doesn't suggest that we dress up as the Wicked Witch of the West and Glinda, the good witch." Blair playfully stuck her finger in her mouth, miming a gagging motion.

Witches and the various other preternatural creatures that inhabited the world had slowly become known among the human population, but they still pretty much kept to themselves. There were human factions that didn't like the idea of supernatural beings living among them, while others embraced them. Stasi and Blair had lived off and on in Moonstone Lake since the late 1840s, when the community sprang up almost overnight as a mining camp. At first they'd hidden their identities by going away for a while and then returning in the guise of a daughter, niece, or granddaughter. Many of the long-time residents had known them from childhood. Once they had found out exactly what Stasi and Blair were, they were still inclined to accept them—especially since the two witches did what they could to protect the small mountain town from developers who wanted to raze the area and turn it into just another resort. It helped that Stasi and Blair didn't overtly display their powers and made sure their monthly trips to the lake at full moon went unobserved. They also discouraged anyone from seeking spells from them. Stasi might add a hint of a love charm to the sachets she tucked into her customer's bags, and Blair enjoyed her skill with revenge spells, but she kept everything low-key; nothing more dangerous than a nasty itch or a bad smell or an ingeniously designed run of allergic reactions or minor pratfalls.

They loved their town and their lives, and even if men under the age of fifty weren't too plentiful—except for tourists—that was fine with the witches, since they weren't looking for permanent entanglements anyway. If they had ever cared to be honest about their actual ages, they were far older than Abel Ransome, spry at ninety-four, even with eyeglasses thicker than the bottom of old-fashioned Coke bottles.

The two sat down at the table with their plates while Bogie floated upside down underneath with his mouth open in hopes something might drop his way.

"Too bad someone won't come up with an idea other than haunted Moonstone Lake," Stasi said.

"The town is a 160-year-old mining town, originally famous for its brothel and gambling hall. What do you think?" Blair nibbled on her dinner. "And Agnes so loves playing the *grande dame* with her library talks, afternoon teas—by reservation only, of course—and the midnight ghost walk and Halloween Dance."

Stasi sighed. "Maybe she'll come up with something new this year."

"We can wish."

Stasi tugged her wool cap down over her ears against the early evening chill as she hurried down the sidewalk.

"I don't know why Blair couldn't have waited five minutes for me," she muttered, hurrying down the sidewalk in the direction of the town hall.

With her head down, she didn't see the large obstacle until it was too late.

"Oof!" She looked up and stared into Trev's blue eyes and damning red hearts over his head. He instinctively gripped her arms so she wouldn't fall, but she quickly stepped back, forcing him to drop his hands.

"Are you all right?" he asked.

"Fine." She was positive she'd just swallowed a load of bubbles.

"Look, I'm not trying to make life difficult for you," he began.

"You are and that's fine. It's your job." She tried not to get swallowed up in those deep blue eyes, which were looking at her with an expression she couldn't identify. "Just as my being the defendant means I'm not going to make it easy for you."

Perfect. A few residents who were also hurrying to the town meeting had slowed down and were eying them curiously. Stasi hoped she could blame her blushes on the cold night air instead of Trev's close proximity.

"I—uh—I have to go," she muttered, yet she didn't move an inch.

He cocked an eyebrow, not caring that they were the center of attention. "Would you have time for a cup of coffee? I was just going to get some," he asked.

Stasi was suddenly conscious of the ends of her hair sticking out every which way from under the knit cap she'd jammed on her head, and her nose was probably a lovely shade of red from the cold. Not to mention her cheeks were burning. "Town meeting. Very important we all be there on time," she added, deliberately raising her voice so their small audience would get the message. Luckily, they did and continued on down the street. She pushed past him, aware down to her toes of his solid build, the breadth of his shoulders, the intent expression on his handsome face.

Trev wanted to persuade her to stay, but he could see this wasn't the time. She looked so damn cute in that dark pink knit cap with tendrils of hair drifting in the cold air, her face glowing. He walked to his car, but not without a quick backwards glance at Stasi that showed she looked just as good going as she did coming. She was practically running toward the large building at the end of the street, with those shimmering red hearts dancing above her head.

Wizards and witches don't mix.

"Old wives' tale," he muttered to himself. "Especially when the witch is cute, and charming even when she sees me as the enemy, and there's something more than magickal about her. I'm definitely going to have to find out more, and without Mae's help or interference."

"Good going, Stasi," she mumbled to herself as she climbed the steps to the town hall. "You could at least have sounded more coherent. He must think you're an idiot." *No, he doesn't. He was very interested in you. Just like you're interested in him. Wizard or not, the man is hot stuff! Go for it!* She resisted the urge to clap her hands over her ears. It wouldn't have helped, since the voice was inside her head.

"And how wonderful that Halloween falls on Saturday this year, so that we can make our annual dance even more spectacular!" Agnes Pierce, a short woman in her sixties who resembled a plump partridge in a fuchsia wool suit with black piping, stood at the podium while her husband, the honorable mayor, snoozed—and snored—in a chair in the rear. "The members of the decorations committee have been busy little bees coming up with new ideas, and the festival committee has thought up a wonderful legend for this year. It's a truly frightening story about the death of a miner who now haunts the town looking for his murderer. I believe Wilson Carruthers will be playing the part of the dead miner." She indicated a white-haired man with a bushy beard who stood up and dipped his head. "Marva, would you like to come up and tell us the committee's ideas?" She looked out at the small group scattered throughout the room that made up the town hall/community center.

Stasi had always privately viewed the red velvet curtains on the stage as more than a tad tacky, and right now they clashed terribly with Agnes's suit. She would have loved to coax the plump woman into both a suitable foundation garment and an outfit that wasn't straight out of the 1960s. At the moment all she needed was a pillbox hat to finish the look.

The large two-story building was touted as the town's historic Gold Rush saloon and brothel. Only Stasi and Blair remembered the origins of the structure's notorious history—a high-flying madam named Grubstake Lil who held a double-barrel shotgun in one hand, had her other palm out for the money, and made sure her bartenders were serving only watered-down whiskey. Gambling was the second favorite pastime, and there were no second chances for a cheater. Merely a spot with a view on Boot Hill. No miner in his right mind went up against the ironed-willed woman or he risked losing his favorite body part. It was no surprise that Lil died a very wealthy woman.

"Floyd's the lucky one," Blair muttered, as she and Stasi shifted in their chairs, growing more uncomfortable with each passing moment as they listened to Agnes drone on about *her* plans for the upcoming holiday. Blair had snagged them two chairs in the back row. Unfortunately, the first few speakers had been more long-winded than usual. "At least Marva's reports are generally short and sweet. Color me happy on that."

Stasi looked at her friend, whose attention was focused on a man seated near the front, directly in their line of sight. His faded blue plaid flannel shirt was open over a khaki T-shirt tucked into jeans that looked molded to his body. His black hair was thick and had a slight wave to it as he impatiently pushed it out of his face.

"Blair, you're drooling," she murmured.

"Not even close," she replied in a voice too soft for anyone to overhear. "More like imagining him wearing his tool belt and nothing else."

Stasi looked down at her lap to hide her grin. Blair had set her sights on the town's hunky handyman more than a year ago and so far, she had failed in her attempts to wangle even a coffee date. Jake was willing to come in and build new shelves for her and he'd even fixed their building's outside stairs, but alas, that wasn't enough for Blair. She was presently plotting—uh—planning what she could next hire him to do for her. Stasi's money was on Blair, since when the witch was on a mission she never failed. Just like the Canadian Mounted Police, she always got her man.

Stasi looked for Mrs. Benedict. The gray-haired widow sat near the front pointedly ignoring Stan Chalmers, who sat next to her. Every time he leaned over to whisper something in her ear, she turned away. Stasi hid a smile. Mrs. Benedict wasn't going to make it easy for her suitor to get back in her good graces after his defection to the bakery.

"And lastly, we anticipate our haunted town will generate more tourism this year than we have in the past. We do hope *all* the business owners will participate by wearing period costumes as in the mid-eighteen hundreds." Marva directed her arrow-like gaze straight at Stasi and Blair, bringing both witches back to what was going on.

"We always wear costumes during October, Marva," Blair piped up. "It's just with my shop offering retro merchandise from all time periods, I like to cover *all* the decades instead of just the Gold Rush period."

Marva smiled thinly. "Which you can do all the other months of the year, can't you, dear?" Problem summarily dismissed, she turned to the rest of the group. "Now, we'd also like some volunteers to help us with the refreshments for the dance."

"Why is so much of this coming up this late?" Blair muttered. "We're usually discussing this *ad nauseam* in August."

"Marva had her gallbladder surgery then," Stasi whispered. "She refused to hand over her duties to anyone else while she recovered and insisted this could be done in the one meeting."

"They want a costume? Fine, I'll give them just what they want," Blair muttered. "I'll wear those pajamas with the trap door in the back and borrow Fluff and Puff."

Stasi covered her mouth in an unsuccessful attempt to hold back her giggle. The magickal bunny slippers hadn't been too welcome in Moonstone Lake since the day they'd slipped into Floyd's precious Escalade and left bunny droppings everywhere.

A silver-haired woman seated in front of them, whom they knew to be a good friend of Agnes,' turned around to direct a frown at them. Blair mouthed *sorry!* while Stasi offered an apologetic smile.

"Poppy and I are only too happy to help out with refreshments." Reed Palmer stood up. More than one woman smiled at his tall figure. He was nattily attired in dark slacks, a white shirt with faint green stripes, and a dark green v-necked sweater, and his dark auburn hair gleamed under the lights. He may have appeared to be every woman's dream, but there were a couple of witches who didn't see him that way. "We can make up all sorts of holiday themed treats for the dance."

Marva beamed her thanks and went on to other matters.

Fully aware that Reed's gaze had turned to her before he sat down, Stasi kept her eyes straight ahead. Almost from the moment of his arrival in the small town, the bakery owner had let it be known to Stasi he was more than a little interested and had tried more than once to get her to go out with him. She never liked hurting anyone's feelings, but she was ready to flat out tell him to leave her the hell alone.

She didn't know why she disliked the man. There was nothing she could point to, there was just something about him that bothered her. She knew Blair would have no problem letting him know she wasn't interested, but Stasi was always afraid of hurting someone's feelings. She hadn't dated in some time, mostly because no man had attracted her interest.

But that didn't stop Reed from heading straight for Stasi at the snack table after the meeting.

"Must be nice to have a persistent admirer," Blair murmured with a wicked grin as she made a quick turn of her own in the direction of Jake Harrison.

"Some friend you are." Stasi's dour mutter quickly turned into a smile as she spun around when her name was called. She grabbed her coffee cup with both hands to keep the hot liquid from sloshing over her hands.

"It's good to see you, Stasi." Reed's smile tended to trip the ladies' hearts, but Stasi was happy to be immune to the man's charm. "You look lovely tonight."

I'm wearing a sweater that's more than ten years old, my jeans are ripped in the knees, and I have on hiking boots that should have been tossed in the trash years ago. Not to mention I'm wearing a ponytail that makes me look like I'm still in high school and I left off all makeup but lip balm. "Thank you, Reed; words every woman loves to hear."

He bent his head down toward hers. "I was able to obtain tickets to the Bon Jovi concert playing down at the casino next weekend, and I hoped you might like to go with me." His teeth flashed white.

She rubbed her nose to stop the tickling sensation she always felt when Reed got too close to her. She wasn't sure what cologne he wore, but she always felt the need to sneeze anytime Reed moved into her personal space.

"I'm so sorry, Reed, but Blair and I have plans for this weekend," she lied without one ounce of guilt. "We have company coming soon and we need all our free time to prepare for them."

If she hadn't been looking at him directly she would have missed the flash of what she swore was fury in his forest-green eyes.

What's he so mad about? I hate lies and I'm having to give him a whopper. If anything, I should be mad at him for making me lie! she rationalized.

"If I'd had more notice I could have rearranged things, but I can't leave Blair to do all the work herself." She started feeling a nasty pinch under her arm. If Reed hadn't been quick enough to grab her coffee, it would have spilled on both of them. He moved it to the table where it sat out of danger. She mentally zapped a stinging pinch back to Blair.

"Since my sister would feel the same way, I can understand."

"Reed." A woman with auburn hair that positively shimmered under the lights stepped up and placed her hand on his arm. The look she flashed Stasi felt like a challenge, although Stasi wasn't sure why.

"Rhetta, this is Stasi Romanov. She's one of our local shop owners, along with her friend Blair. Stasi, this is my twin sister, Amaretto. Rhetta for short."

"Yes, I've heard of you." Rhetta's smile was borderline glacial.

And I'm sure not one word was good and I just bet you're not too happy that your brother is pursuing me, either. Stasi's smile gave away nothing of her thoughts. "I'm very pleased to meet you. I know Poppy was happy you would be visiting."

Rhetta turned to her brother. "Agnes wants to talk to you."

Reed nodded. He paused before he moved away with his twin. "I don't give up easily." His smile was supposed to make it a tease, but Stasi felt as if she was being stalked.

She breathed a sigh of relief once she was alone.

"These cookies are so good. I don't know what Reed and his sister put in them, but I swear I have more energy after I have a few of these." Marva bustled up and set several oatmeal chocolate chip cookies on her plate. She arched a questioning eyebrow at Stasi.

Stasi shook her head. "I already had a couple." She wondered how many more lies she'd be telling before the evening was over.

"Then you have much better willpower than I do," Marva chuckled. "I don't know how you can stop."

She paused long enough to pick up a cinnamon muffin. "Roger! We need to talk about the play!" she called out, hurrying after her prey.

Stasi picked up her coffee and sipped the hot brew while she watched the byplay between Blair and Jake. Blair moved forward and Jake moved back.

"Why do I feel as if I'm looking at me and Reed?" she murmured. "It's not just Reed, I don't want anyone."

As if her words triggered the sight, dancing red hearts seemed to flash before her eyes. And if that wasn't bad enough, she could clearly see Trevor Barnes standing beneath the hearts in all his glorious splendor. She closed her eyes tightly, but the image only became more intense. Stasi swallowed the squeak that threatened to erupt even as the coffee turned to acid in her throat.

I should have sicced Cupid on Carrie. He never likes anyone screwing up their love lives, and I bet he could have done a real number on her.

Trev didn't like the unsettling feeling that was churning his stomach as he drove back to LA the next day. He preferred his life sane and orderly, and right now it didn't feel like that. He soon reached the parking garage below the high-rise building in Century City that housed the law offices of Grimm, Barnes, Conover, and Fisteen. While the centuries-old business didn't openly advertise themselves as wizards—after all, wizards weren't actively trolling for business—it wasn't a state secret, either. Anyone making an appointment knew the senior partners only appeared in Wizards' Court, while a few of the associates dealt with mortal cases, and any dealings between supernaturals and mortals.

He drove into the garage, pulled the Jag into his reserved parking space, and headed for the express elevator that served the penthouse offices. He'd had a leisurely dinner at the resort the night before, followed by a couple of hours flirting with a sexy brunette in the bar. He'd been sorely tempted to ask her to spend the night with him, but found he couldn't voice the words. Instead, he slept alone.

No surprise that Mae greeted him in the reception area. He never questioned the fact that his assistant always knew when he was in the building. He called it part of her charm. She held out a large, steaming cup of coffee to him. He accepted the coffee while she took his briefcase.

"What was Ms. Romanov like?" she asked, following him down the hallway.

"Stubborn, determined to fight the case, and she has no clue what she's in for." He walked into his office and set his coffee cup down on his desk. "Do you have the information I requested?"

"Oh yes."

Something in Mae's voice had him turn around. The look on her face bothered him. Her expression held a shade of smug along with a hint of smirk and, if he wasn't mistaken, downright amusement.

Namely, she knew something that she enjoyed and she knew he wouldn't like.

"Ms. Romanov's history has been downloaded to your computer. I'm sure you'll have many enjoyable hours of reading, since she has been in the mortal world since the year 1313 when she was expelled from the

Witches' Academy along with her classmates," Mae said briskly.

"Did you find out what those damn hearts mean?" He watched with horrified fascination as her smile just grew bigger and bigger and her eyes twinkled with merriment. The feeling grew that it wasn't news he wanted to hear.

"Honestly, Trevor, have you forgotten the bedtime stories you heard as a boy? No, I guess this one was aimed more for witchlings and young sorceresses." Mae moved to a nearby chair and sat down. She peered over her narrow rimmed eyeglasses. "But you are a clever man with a very intelligent brain. Tell me something, when do we see red hearts everywhere?"

"Valentine's Day, when Cupid has his say and you remind me I need to buy chocolates for the female staff," he grumbled. "So because the witch plays with romance, she's in league with that romance radical?"

Mae chuckled. "Oh no, Cupid has always worked alone, but I'd say that he has other ideas."

Trev rubbed his forehead with his fingers. A headache was rapidly blooming. "Just spit it out, Mae," he snapped, picking up his cup and sipping his coffee, which suddenly tasted bitter.

"Cupid's way of letting someone know they've met their true love is to arrange red hearts over their heads. And if you saw red hearts over her head, she must have seen the same over yours."

Luckily, Mae had made sure she was seated far enough back that the spray of coffee from Trevor's mouth didn't hit her. She waited serenely as Trev stared at her as if she'd well and truly lost her mind.

"Bloody hell!"

"Excuse me. Ma'am. Ma'am."

Stasi felt as if she needed a crowbar to lift her heavy lids. Why had she eaten those cookies? She knew that the cookies from the bakery never set well in her stomach. But Reed had tracked her down and offered them to her personally. She'd had no polite way to refuse them. At least she'd only eaten two, but she'd still gotten an upset stomach that even her favorite ginger tea didn't help.

"Ma'am?"

She opened one eye a slit and stared at the transparent figure standing at the bottom of her bed. Bogie stirred from his curled up position by her hip and growled. Stasi stroked his back, soothing his distrust of the uninvited visitor.

"Fergus?" Her voice was raspy. "It's too early."

The man—a boy really, no more than seventeen years of age—was dressed in dirt-stained trousers and faded red flannel shirt. His battered hat sat on wispy blond hair, and there was no mistaking the freckles sprinkled across his cheeks and the smallpox scars dotting his forehead. He was so young only peach fuzz dotted his cheeks.

"I'm sorry to come in here to your bedroom, ma'am, but somethin's wrong." He blushed hotly as he pulled off his hat and held it between his hands. His hair stuck up in unruly spikes that had nothing to do with fashion, since that style wasn't in vogue in 1854. "We're all feelin' it." He blushed again as Stasi pushed her hair away from her face and sat up.

She knew his mentioning all of them had nothing to do with the living residents of the mountain town. "And you came to me because?"

"You and Blair are the only ones who can see us."

She exhaled a deep breath, forcing her sleep-heavy brain awake. "I don't need a boy who's been dead for 140-odd years in my bedroom before I've had coffee. Why didn't you wake up Blair?"

He shifted from one foot to the other. "She's—uh—she's—"

Stasi waved a hand, fully understanding his discomfort. Blair had been so tired the previous night, Stasi figured Blair had pretty much shed her clothes on the floor and flopped naked into bed. The sight of a nude female was obviously more than boyish—and virginal—Fergus could handle.

Stasi glanced at the clock and was happy to realize that the coffeemaker would already have a pot of coffee brewed. "Okay, I'll meet you in the kitchen in a few minutes. She released a sigh as the ghost didn't move but continued to stare at her lace-covered breasts. She wished she hadn't opted to wear her favorite creamy yellow silk nightgown. "*Now, Fergus!*" He was gone in the blink of an eye.

"Why can't someone else deal with the spirits this time of year?" Stasi mumbled, pushing aside her pastel pink and blue duvet and stumbling out of bed with the bathroom in mind. In record time she brushed her teeth and hair, pulled on her mint green fleece robe, and found her slippers. Once that was done she headed down the hallway and stopped at the open doorway to Blair's room. All she saw was a lump under the covers and a lace-edged pillow pulled over Blair's head. How Fergus knew she was naked was a mystery to Stasi. But ghosts seemed to know things, and she wasn't sure she wanted to know how. "Why don't you wake up, Auntie Blair, sweetie," she suggested, watching Bogie glide through the room and hop up first onto Blair's bed and then onto Blair's back. The dog's barking was high-pitched enough to shatter glass as he jumped up and down on a now awake and cranky Blair, while a softly laughing Stasi headed toward the kitchen.

"This is so mean, Stasi!" Blair shouted.

"So was you sending Fergus to me!" Stasi called back. "Once you've got some clothes on, come out to the kitchen."

She found Fergus seated on a chair at the table. He hopped up and pulled his hat off the minute she entered the room. Except, when he hopped up, his body slid through the kitchen table and the crystal bowl set in the center. The display of silk fall leaves and pussy willows didn't even move.

Stasi shook her head and headed straight for the coffee. "Sit down, Fergus." She poured herself a cup of cinnamon-flavored coffee and took a chair. "And don't call me ma'am again."

"Yes, ma'—. Yes, Miss Stasi."

She sighed. She figured that would be the best the young man could do and it didn't make her sound as if she was sitting in a rocking chair knitting a shawl. "Fine, we'll go with that. Now, what's going on?"

Blair walked in wearing a hot pink silk robe worthy of a 1930s film star and matching high-heeled marabou trimmed mules. The glamorous effect was ruined by her serious case of bed head as she dug her fingertips into her scalp and rubbed vigorously.

"What are you doing here so early, Fergus?" Like Stasi, she didn't hesitate in pouring her caffeine fix. She waved the ghost down when he started to stand up again. "I swear you were the only male back then who had manners. October is next month and you all usually don't show up until then." She plopped into the chair across from Stasi and yawned widely. "At least bump up the heat." She wiggled her forefinger at the thermostat, which obligingly moved upward, and warm air wafted out of the vents.

"There are things goin' on, ma'am." He shot a quick look at Stasi. "Sorry. Anyway, there's somethin' goin' on in our realm. It ain't the same as it's been before and we all feel real unsettled like."

"We have a lunar eclipse coming up along with Mercury retrograde. That might be why you're feeling uneasy." Stasi conjured up a rawhide chew and handed it to Bogie, who happily moved off to a corner with his treat.

"Sounds like a disturbance in the force." Blair grinned.

"You and Darth Vader."

"Just the voice. Otherwise, it's still Han Solo in those tight breeches that revs my engines."

"It is disturbin'," Fergus admitted. "We all don't feel right—it's like we're bein' pulled in different directions." He held up one hand, rough and calloused from working his claim until he was killed by a greedy fellow miner who wanted to add Fergus' claim to his own. The murderer was immediately lynched, and ghostly Fergus showed up every October, as did many of the former residents of Moonstone Lake. The two witches were just grateful that not all of the spirits showed up every year, or the corporeal residents would be heavily outnumbered. They had no idea how the ghosts decided each year who would appear and who wouldn't, and they were certain they were better off not knowing the logistics. The only constant was Fergus, who showed up every year without fail. Blair was convinced the young ghost had a crush on Stasi, but Stasi was positive his interest was centered on Blair, even if she tended to shock his boyish sensibilities.

"Disturbing how?" Blair settled back in her chair and crossed her legs. When she crossed her legs, her robe opened to reveal her thighs as she bobbed her foot in her marabou mule up and down to a tune only she could hear. She sipped her coffee, sighing with relief as the caffeine coursed through her system.

All the witches might not agree on everything, but they did agree that coffee was essential to get going in the morning.

Stasi tapped her nails against the tabletop in thought. "We have a lunar eclipse coming up along with Mercury retrograde, but there's something else in the air that doesn't feel right and I haven't been able to pin down the source. I couldn't sleep and I looked out the window at the woods last night and…"

"And?" Blair waggled her free hand asking for more.

Stasi shook her head. "And, I have no clue what, but something out there didn't feel right." She turned back to Fergus, who was perched uneasily on the chair. "What do the others say? Do they sense anything more specific, or just have the feeling that something isn't right?"

"You know how they can be. Lot of them don't talk much. Clyde just mutters a lot about his claim, and ole Bill says there's evil here and he ain't comin' out this year," he admitted. "We were all hopin' you'd know what's goin' on. You all bein' witches and all." He looked longingly at the coffee they drank. "That sure looks good."

Stasi felt sorry for the spirit, but knew offering him food and drink would only mean she'd have a mess to clean up, since it would go right through him. And he couldn't taste it, anyway.

"All I can do is some research to see what's going on," she said. "But with the lunar eclipse and Mercury retrograde happening at the same time, the energy might be interfering with your realm. We're feeling upsets here, too."

Fergus's head bobbed up and down, but his worry hadn't gone away. "It's just that… some of us are fadin.'"

"We told you long ago that you needed to move on," Blair said gently. "That you couldn't stay chained to earth forever. I know some of you moved on, but this could mean it's some of the others' turn to leave the realm."

"I don't want to go anywhere else. I got nothin' but you two," Fergus admitted. "My ma took off when I was three and my pa died when I was ten."

Stasi remembered when the young man used to come into the café for an occasional dinner. He had been shy and polite and blushed if any woman even smiled at her. That hadn't changed just because he was long dead.

"Why don't you go back and talk to the others, see what they feel, and have them give you some sort of idea," Stasi suggested. "Then come back and tell us. But please don't come early in the morning or the middle of the night. While you don't need sleep any longer, we do."

He nodded. "All right. Ladies." He bobbed his head and disappeared.

"Jazz has Irma in her car, we have long dead miners that pop in and out." Blair yawned. "Why can't we have pets like other people?"

Since it was Stasi's week to cook breakfast, she headed to the refrigerator for eggs and some smoked ham cut into small cubes.

"I still think we need to go out to the lake," she decided, pulling out a whisk. "We have to make sure nothing's happening there."

Blair refilled their coffee cups and pulled a carton of orange juice out of the refrigerator. She cocked her head to one side.

"Hm, silence on the other side of the door. I guess we won't be having company for breakfast."

Stasi scrambled eggs and managed to stay upright as Bogie wove a floating pattern around her legs.

She chuckled as a scratching on the back door sounded.

"You spoke too soon."

Blair heaved a deep sigh as she walked over to the back door and opened it. The Border collie sat on the mat, looking up with a hopeful expression.

"Don't you have a home to go to?" she demanded. "You're not scrawny, so someone feeds you other than us." She stood back as the dog swept past her.

Bogie looked over, and gave a pained sigh at the larger dog's arrival. Stasi smiled and reached down with a piece of cooked egg for him.

"You have to admit he's well-trained and very

well-behaved," Stasi said, watching the dog sit down next to the table—not surprisingly by the chair where Blair usually sat. For all Blair's muttering and complaining, she never failed to share food off her plate.

The collie raised a paw and whined.

Blair shook her head as she poured juice and popped bread in the toaster, while Stasi finished up the scrambled eggs.

"I have to say that for two hot looking chicks, we must be having a miserable life when we share our breakfast with a lovesick ghost and two dogs," Blair said, returning to the table with plates of toast.

"It could be worse," Stasi reminded her.

"As in?" Blair pinched off a piece of buttered toast and tossed it to the dog, who caught it with a quick snap of his jaws. He pricked his ears alertly and cocked his head, watching her intently.

"Smiley Joe could have shown up with Fergus."

Blair groaned at the mention of the long dead miner. Smiley Joe was missing most of his teeth, and what few he had left were stained from years of chewing tobacco. Not to mention he sported a glass eye that didn't match his other eye color, and had an alarming way of staring at their cleavage with his one good eye as he uttered a low laugh as if he found something amusing. Neither of them had the nerve to ask him what he found so funny. They didn't think they'd like the answer.

"There must be wards we can put up to keep out ghosts," Blair muttered, sitting down to her breakfast and furry fellow diner. She leaned over and pinched something off the top of the dog's head, then returned to finger comb through his fur.

"What are you doing?" Stasi asked.

"I think I found a flea."

The dog looked up and curled his lip, uttering a low growl.

Stasi giggled. "I think he's telling you he's flea free."

"Yeah, well, he needs to have a closer look at the top of his head."

Chapter 4

STASI SHIVERED FROM THE MORNING CHILL AND wrapped her sapphire pashmina shawl more closely about her as she walked down the sidewalk. She felt the need for a short walk to clear her head before she opened the shop.

"All I wanted was a lovely peaceful Samhain," she grumbled to herself.

"Having a good conversation with yourself, Stasi?" Ginny Chao teased. She was a descendant of one of the men who'd originally come to the United States to work on the railroad, then tried his luck in the mines. He proved to be a better cook than a miner, and was successful enough that he was able to bring his wife over from China and open a small café. Over the years, the restaurant was handed down within the family. Ginny had inherited it from her grandmother. She greeted Stasi with a smile as she swept the wooden sidewalk in front of her restaurant. Ginny's Sit 'N Eat café never lacked for customers, thanks to her down-home cooking and homemade cakes and pies. The town council, consisting of four elders, usually took up a rear table as they debated town business over coffee and pie. Floyd, his honor the mayor, once suggested that it was good for business for them to be there and it wouldn't hurt Ginny to comp their food. She tartly informed them she lost business by them taking over her best table, and they'd not only pay for their food but leave a decent tip, or they could go elsewhere. They grumbled and threatened to move down to the bakery, which offered an eating area, but all knew the small round bistro-style tables wouldn't easily handle four oversized men. So they stayed and paid the bill, along with leaving a tip for their waitress.

Like all the longtime residents, Ginny knew that Stasi and Blair were witches and had lived in the town several times under similar names. Now that the supernatural community was better known and an open secret among the mortals, the two women were comfortable with the residents understanding what they were, even if they didn't know the witches' entire history. Luckily, no one had given them grief. At least, not until Carrie decided that Stasi had used witchcraft to ruin her marriage.

At twenty-seven, Ginny looked the same age as Stasi and the women had become close friends.

"You might want to stay away from Fresh Baked Goods," Ginny advised. "Carrie's in there holding court telling anyone who'll listen to her that she found the perfect way to sue you for ruining her marriage and that by the time she's finished with you you'll have nothing. She's even hinting you did it because you wanted him for yourself. I'd say she has you rated up there with the Wicked Witch of the West."

Stasi sighed. "At least I don't have the green skin. Carrie did this to herself, and I'd be more than happy to tell her so. I should probably just settle the lawsuit, but it's the principle of the thing." She ignored the tiny whisper inside her head reminding her that she did add a little negativity to Carrie's sachet. Even if the hateful woman deserved it, it wasn't something Stasi should have done.

Ginny shook her head. "Don't do it, hon. Carrie's always had a nasty streak and now it's coming out full bore."

"Maybe she should have picked up a few romance books for inspiration instead of relying on lingerie," Stasi groused. "That or shop at Fredericks of Hollywood."

Ginny playfully covered her eyes. "Oh please, the vision of Carrie in crotchless undies and a bra with cutouts is much too painful!" She touched Stasi's arm. "Do you have time for a cup of coffee?"

"For you, yes."

The two women walked inside, and Stasi settled in a booth by the door while Ginny fetched their coffee. She noticed that Floyd and his cronies were already ensconced at their table. She was surprised when Floyd frowned at her before turning back to his friends.

"Agnes is Carrie's aunt," Ginny reminded her, noticing Floyd's expression. She set down a tray with two coffee cups and two cinnamon streusel muffins. "Not from the bakery," she whispered with a conspirator's grin.

"You must cut into their business." Stasi pinched off a corner of the still-warm muffin.

"Their main business seems to be all the varieties of breads they bake." Ginny took the bench across from her. "My mother swears by their cinnamon raisin bread. She has a slice every morning for breakfast and even snacks on it during the day. Dad loves one of the rye breads they offer. Everyone seems to have a different favorite."

"I wasn't surprised everyone was in there when they first opened. We didn't have a bakery, and it was nice to pick up treats on a moment's notice." Stasi nibbled her muffin. "But now it's as if people can't exist without them."

"Reed and Poppy have talked to me about selling their baked goods here, but I love making my pies and cakes." She looked around the small café that had been a town staple for more than 150 years. Stasi remembered when Ginny's great-great-grandparents had cooked under a canvas tent and dished out beef stew and biscuits to hungry miners back in the mid-1800s. It was the beginning of the small café where Stasi and Blair had worked as waitresses when the couple was able to erect a building. They later moved their café down the street to its current, more visible location. Ginny made improvements to keep the equipment up-to-date, but otherwise the interior retained its down-home charm, and Ginny still served up the beef stew and homemade biscuits her great-great-grandmother had been known for.

Ginny sipped her coffee while keeping her eye on the tables and booths, which were mostly empty at this hour. Stasi knew within an hour the place would be filled with the lunch crowd and Ginny's two waitresses would be kept running.

"You know the problem with a small town?" Ginny said, finishing up her muffin. "Everyone knows everyone's secrets. I couldn't stay out one minute past curfew without someone calling my parents. Everyone knew when Rena Madison was having an affair with Adam Baxter before their sheets had a chance to cool down, and it's a known fact you don't go near Mrs. Grover's house on the tenth of the month because she's positive that's when the aliens will touch down and take her up to the mother ship."

"And pretty much everyone who lives here knows two witches live in their town, even if they take off for a while and return under other names every few decades," Stasi murmured.

Ginny nodded. "It's because of you two that our town hasn't been gobbled up by developers." She smiled at Stasi's shake of the head. "How many other towns around here have been taken over by resorts and spas and city folk who want to build expensive vacation homes they use maybe a couple times a year? I remember when that one developer stopped here last spring. He sat in the next booth with a map, sheets showing costs, and pages of notes. He stayed overnight in Lisa's B&B and was gone the next day."

"Maybe the town wasn't what he was looking for."

"He was interested in the lake," Ginny said softly.

That got Stasi's attention. "The lake?"

The other woman nodded. "He asked a lot of questions about the lake, namely the legends behind it."

Stasi feigned a laugh. "The only legend about the lake is the monster that's supposed to live out there."

"Some say witches are legends, but they're not. And kids have seen odd things out there late at night."

Stasi thought of the many nights of the full moon when she and Blair, and sometimes other witch sisters, walked out to the lake for a ceremony they'd begun the first full moon after the town was officially named Moonstone Lake. The word moonstone meant sanctuary, and that was what the lake represented for the witches.

The full moon ceremony was one secret Stasi and Blair kept to themselves. They considered it enough they'd come out of the witchy closet to the townspeople, who were willing to consider it a town secret that need go no further, even if Floyd and Agnes thought it had huge tourism potential.

"Hey chicks." Blair walked in, looking very 1950s in a white cotton blouse with a Peter Pan collar, a bright pink chiffon scarf tied around her neck, a pink circle skirt with a black fuzzy poodle appliquéd on it, white socks, and black-and-white saddle shoes. She'd pulled her dark auburn hair up into a perky ponytail adorned with a matching scarf and pink lipstick on her lips.

"Wow, we need Elvis playing in the background." Ginny chuckled. "How cute!"

Blair grinned and dipped a short curtsey. "I feel very Sandra Dee today," she replied, sliding in next to Stasi. "What's up?"

One of the waitresses brought over a cup and filled it with coffee.

"Just the usual," Ginny replied. "Carrie's working on a smear job."

Blair's expression darkened. "The bitch needs a major attitude adjustment."

"Please, don't," Stasi begged, fully aware of what Blair could whip up at a second's notice. Her revenge spells were one hundred percent effective, and some were long lasting. Stasi had no doubt that Blair would conjure up a revenge spell that Carrie wouldn't forget for a very long time. And in the process, she'd be in so much trouble with the Witches' Council her banishment would never end. And Stasi wasn't about to allow that to happen.

"Carrie's a bitter woman and I really should pity her." Stasi stared into her coffee cup as if the contents would give her the answers she was looking for. "She'll never be happy because she won't allow herself to be. She looks for a man who follows her lead without looking for a man who truly loves her."

"Says the woman with dancing hearts over her head," Blair muttered.

Ginny's head snapped up. "What?"

"Nothing." Stasi issued a stealthy pinch to Blair's thigh. She glanced at her watch. "We need to open the shops." She reached for her purse, but Ginny waved it away.

"My treat. And don't worry about Carrie. Some idiot will show up and she'll latch on to him and forget all about making your life miserable," she assured Stasi.

Stasi manufactured a smile for her, but it wasn't easy. She knew deep down that Carrie was determined to do what she could to make life difficult. And she sensed it wasn't just because her cheating husband didn't return.

"Any reason why you felt like a 1950s teenager today?" she asked, as she and Blair walked up the side-walk to their shops.

"Just showing Agnes I have team spirit about wearing non-western clothing the rest of the year. October is coming up fast, so I have a limited amount of time." Blair made her full skirt swish with its stiff crinoline petticoats. "I wore this when I wanted to try high school life, remember? I was even homecoming queen."

"And flunked geometry."

Blair waved her hand in the air, but made sure no multi-colored sparkles accompanied her gesture. "Ah yes, Mr. Henderson. Pretty darn cute for back then."

She grinned. "But alas, I was nothing more than a naïve seventeen-year-old girl in his eyes. I should have gone back ten years later to see if he was still single."

"Why didn't you?"

"I was afraid if I did I'd find him fat and balding, which would ruin my teenage fantasies. And I had some pretty hot fantasies about that guy."

They stopped at their respective front doors. Blair turned to say something else to Stasi, and suddenly what felt like a blast of cold wind assaulted the witches, and disaster struck. Just as a stately, shiny navy Lincoln Continental rolled down the street, a ginger colored cat strolled down the sidewalk, the woolly felt poodle on Blair's skirt shifted its head to bark at the cat, the feline took off running, and the poodle peeled itself off Blair's skirt in hot pursuit.

"Oh no!" both witches shouted in unison, running after the fuzzy poodle and the cat.

"No harm to any, if you please!" Stasi wailed, throwing out enough of a burst of power to push the cat and poodle out of the way of the oncoming car. The sound of brakes squealing mingled with the poodle's barks, yowls from the cat, and a woman's scream.

"Oh for Fates sake, it's Agnes," Stasi groaned, as the car jerked to a stop, literally plowing through the dog and missing the cat that had been pushed to safety, thanks to Stasi's magick.

"I hit a dog! I hit a dog!" Agnes leaped out of the car, her face white. She tottered back and forth on high heels that were more than a little dangerous for her plump figure. She ran around to the front of the Lincoln and stared at the empty road. "Where is it?" She looked up at Stasi and Blair, who now sported a poodle on her skirt again. "Where did it go?"

"Agnes, are you all right?" Stasi ran over and helped the woman to the door of her shop. She pushed open the door and led Agnes to a silk cushioned chair.

"I'll park the car for you." Blair ran over to the vehicle.

"But—"

"Let me get you a glass of water." Stasi ran to the back and returned with a paper cup.

"What happened? Did the old hag finally lose what little sense she had?" Horace muttered as she scurried past.

"Quiet, you," she ordered.

"Where did the dog go?" Agnes waved her handkerchief in front of her face and accepted the cup. "I didn't hit it, did I?"

"He probably ran off," Stasi replied, noting the older woman's still pale features. "Dogs are very quick."

"You're sure it got away?"

"He was still running after the cat." Blair walked in. "Your car is parked out front."

Agnes turned then stared at Blair's skirt where the dog had returned to his spot. "How odd. It looks just like…" She shook her head. "Never mind."

Stasi shot Blair a *get out while you can* look. Blair took the hint and beat feet while muttering she had to get her shop open.

Agnes downed her water as if it was whiskey, took a deep breath, and stood up.

"I realize you girls aren't like the rest of us," she said stiffly, now having regained her composure, "but tricks like that could affect tourists. Although,

I'm sure there are some who would appreciate such magickal stunts."

"It wasn't a stunt, Agnes," Stasi corrected her. "Just a shift in energy. It can happen this time of year."

Agnes's narrow features grew even more pinched. "We have honored your wishes by not advertising that witches live here, which could greatly build up our tourism. But it could do even more good at this time of year."

"We have plenty of tourists that stop here without resorting to gimmicks," Stasi reminded her, leaning back against a small table displaying white and pastel cotton bikini pants and bras along with Vicki Lewis Thompson Nerd romance novels. "Moonstone Lake has the look of a haunted mining town during the month of October only. We're not Salem Village, Agnes." A sick feeling settled in the pit of her stomach as she spoke of the famous New England village best known for its witch trials in 1692. Not one victim executed during that time was a witch, and Stasi had lived in abject fear that she would be discovered while she lived there. Afterwards, she fostered guilt that she had survived when those who had not one speck of magick in their blood didn't.

Agnes sniffed loudly and stood up. "True, we aren't, and at least we have a rich history from the Gold Rush." She dropped her handkerchief inside her handbag and snapped it shut. "You and your friend may make light of what Floyd and I do, but we take our duties seriously and this time of year does bring in more tourists than even the summer season. Reed and Poppy may be new to the community, but they are more than doing their part. I hope you and Blair will keep that in mind."

For a second, Stasi seriously thought about darkening the moustache above Agnes's upper lip.

"I plan to start decorating the front windows this week for the month-long event," she replied, following the woman to the door. "Blair and I've always done our part."

Agnes stopped just short of the door. She looked around as if she feared the shop was filled with eavesdroppers. Stasi had to lean over to catch her words.

"I know my niece comes in here a lot," she murmured. "Missy is very fragile, and I would like to ask you not to do anything odd for her."

Stasi swallowed her cough of astonishment. "Odd? What kind of *odd* things are you talking about, Agnes?"

The older woman refused to look at her. "You know very well what I'm speaking of. As I said, Missy is fragile. I don't like her coming in here thinking her world will be all the better because you offer it."

Stasi could feel her blood start to boil. "Missy is a very sweet seventeen-year-old girl who comes in here to buy sport bras because I carry some with lace. She doesn't need anything *odd* and I don't offer anything *odd*." She bit off each word. "If I did it would be nothing more than self-confidence, a sense of sensuality within a woman. It's a state of mind, Agnes, not of the body. Perhaps you should try it sometime."

The older woman straightened up. "After what Carrie has said, people are wondering just what you *do* give your customers. I'm sure you know that if you do something that isn't proper, we have the right to shut down your business."

"Do not threaten me, Agnes." Stasi was steaming mad. "Trust me, you won't win." Agnes backed up a few steps and hurried out of the store before Stasi could say anything more.

"Amazing, little Stasi has balls. I'm proud of you, kid," Horace spoke up from his perch on the counter by the register.

"The old biddy," Stasi muttered, watching Bogie appear in his bed just behind the counter. She placed a Snausage in reach. "Maybe if she'd buy some decent lingerie she'd develop a personality that was actually likable."

"You're better off to be mad at her than consider her coming in as a customer. The idea of His and Her Honor doing the horizontal tango is downright scary," Horace said.

"That's nothing I'd like to think about either. But her daring to threaten me was beyond the pale. I should at least have ruined her manicure."

"Ooh, tough talk from scary witch," the gargoyle taunted. "You lost your balls, Stasi. You need to stand up to that old harridan more. You did pretty good this time, but you could do better."

"I'm not Jazz who can throw a fireball with more accuracy than a Major League pitcher. And I'm not Blair who can come up with the nastiest, grossest revenge spell. I don't *like* being angry and fighting with people. I just want to make people feel better about themselves, their sexuality."

"Yeah, but you took a stand against Carrie and that was a great first step."

"Oh sure, and it got me sued." Stasi went into her office and pulled a small moneybag out of the safe she kept there. She had no need to worry about thieves.

Anyone stupid enough to break into the safe would think a diamondback rattlesnake guarded her money. And while the bite would feel very real and the sense of venom racing through their bloodstream equally valid, they'd merely have the scare of their lives. To date, she and Blair hadn't had one break-in. Plus, she knew Horace could emit a scream that would shred eardrums. He hated anyone interrupting his fourteen-hour sleep cycle.

No one needed a security system if they had the right magick on their side.

"You forgot to set up the coffee maker," Horace grumbled, making his way to the end of the counter.

"Having a distorted gargoyle is bad enough, but one with a caffeine addiction is too much." Stasi had the coffee dripping into the pot in no time.

"No thanks to this curse, I have few pleasures in this world. After seeing old Agnes, who I'm positive wears old lady panties and one of those girdles made back in the 1950s, no way I want to look up her dress." He covered his eyes with his paws while his horns seemed to swivel in opposite directions.

Stasi poured coffee into a small cup and inserted a straw. She carried it back to the counter and set it in front of the gargoyle, who uttered sounds of joy before latching onto the straw.

"You know that wizard will be back," he said once he'd had enough caffeine to be a bit more personable.

Stasi closed her eyes against the vision of dancing red hearts over her head that she could see in the floor-length mirror near the counter.

"There's no reason for him to come back unless he's here to see Carrie. Maybe someone needs to dump red paint on her head," she muttered, restocking scented sachets that resembled silk or velvet bustiers, wedding gowns, or evening gowns. These she didn't imbue with any form of magick and allowed the scents of vanilla and lavender to do their work instead. The sachets she tucked into each package looked like silken pink or coral roses and gave the buyer a sense of well-being and heightened sensuality. Nothing made her happier than seeing smiles on her customers' faces. A smile that was now on her face as she thought of tourists who would stop by to find lingerie to perk up their day. A smile that disappeared the minute she walked back to the counter and found a sheet of papyrus lying near the register.

"*No!*" She slapped the counter near the papyrus, but didn't touch it.

Unfortunately, her presence was enough to trigger it. The document rolled upward and actually bowed to her.

"Greetings, Witch Romanov, ye have been served with additional papers regarding the case *Anderson vs. Romanov*. Please read and respond immediately." The papyrus returned to its resting place.

Stasi's snarl was worthy of a pissed off Were as she read the words detailed in elegant calligraphy.

Her fingers flexed, sparks flying around her as she paced the shop.

Horace made his way over to the document and leaned over it. "Wow, she's really mad at you. She wants your powers stripped from you, monetary damages, and even your property. I can't believe the wizard would allow this."

"Well, he would," she said grimly, picking up the box of bustier sachets she had left near the display and shoving them under the counter where they'd be handy when she needed to restock. "He's a lawyer and a wizard. Both are nasty."

"I don't know. Your Eurydice is about as scary as they come."

Stasi's heart skipped a few beats at the name of the head of the Witches' Council and headmistress of the Witches' Academy. The witch was formidable, and not one witchling attending the academy dared go against her. Not until one of Stasi's class cast that illegal spell.

Stasi never admitted it to anyone, but she had been scared witless when she stood with her fellow witchlings and was banished to the outside world. She was grateful she didn't know who'd cast the spell. And she knew she wouldn't have survived long if she hadn't been with Blair, who'd been her best friend all through the academy.

Through the centuries, she'd had adventures she couldn't have dreamed of, kept her heart whole—since she knew she would outlive any man she met—and discovered that she enjoyed making women feel good about themselves.

And now she felt as if her life was falling down around her. She bit her lower lip to keep the tears from falling.

"Hey." Horace waddled over to her and hesitantly patted her arm. His leathery wings shifted back and forth sending a faint breeze into the air. Concern wasn't something the gargoyle did well, but he was trying. "It's okay, Stasi. You're going to win. You'll see. That skank is trying to make you miserable and you can't let her know she's upset you. Hell, if you want, set me outside her house some night and I'll give her the most miserable night of her life."

Stasi looked down at the stone creature. "Stop looking at my breasts!"

He shrugged. "A goyle's got to do what he can."

She uttered an incomprehensible word, stalked out of the shop, and headed next door. Blair was dancing to the sounds of Bill Haley and the Comets' classic hit "Rock Around the Clock" as she arranged a selection of Madame Alexander Wendy and Ginny dolls from the 1950s.

Blair spun around and caught sight of Stasi's expression.

"What happened?"

"Horace was comforting me."

She froze. "Excuse me?"

Stasi nodded. "He was patting my arm and saying nice things. Well, except for calling Carrie a skank."

"Horace is never nice. He's a Peeping Tom and a pervert. He's happiest when he gets a flash of breast or thigh."

"He did stare at my breasts for a second, but I think he *was* trying to make me feel better. I received another papyrus from the Wizards' Court." Stasi ran her fingertips over the edge of a Red Flyer wagon that sported a hefty price tag.

Blair's crinoline petticoats made a dry rustling sound as she crossed the shop and hugged her friend.

"She wants me stripped of my powers." Stasi's words stuttered around the lump in her throat. "She wants what makes me *me* gone."

Chapter 5

THANKS TO THE WEEKEND COMING UP, TRAFFIC THROUGH Moonstone Lake was fairly heavy as people stopped off either to visit the shops or for a bite to eat.

Stasi was grateful to be kept busy as she assisted customers with lingerie choices. She was pleased to see that her new stock of silk and lace chemises in bold colors went fast.

"I always spend a fortune when I come in here," one woman told her as she added five leopard print bustier sachets and two in black velvet to her selections. "And your shop always smells so good." She inhaled deeply, her breasts rising up and attracting Horace's avid attention. "I wish you sold it in potpourri, although I don't know if my boyfriend would like our house smelling like my favorite mochaccino."

Stasi did an internal happy dance as she mentally added up more than $1000 in purchases. The mental reminder that she'd need the money if Carrie won her lawsuit tried to intrude, but she hip-bumped it out of her mind. She'd had her self-pity party that morning and she refused to let thoughts of the woman ruin the rest of her day.

"Perhaps I'll start stocking various potpourris," Stasi said.

"I think that's why I buy so much when I come in," the woman chuckled. "It's like walking into my favorite coffee house." She glanced outside where a man stood in front of a dark blue BMW, a cell phone to his ear while he stared impatiently at the shop window. "I guess his patience is wearing thin, but once he gets a load of what I bought he'll change his mind. I'm sure I'll be back when we come up in a month. You'll have your Halloween ghost town going on then, won't you?"

Stasi nodded. "A lot goes on then."

The woman picked up her bag and left.

"Those definitely aren't real," Horace announced, once the door closed. "Think her boyfriend paid for them? Along with that ass implant that's easy enough to see she had. It sure looked like Botox and a chin implant had their way with her, too. She's got more plastic in her than Barbie. Maybe you should take her suggestion and stock potpourri."

Stasi shook her head. "That's Emma's specialty with her body and bath line. Besides, then the individual scents wouldn't be as unique." As if her name had been uttered, she was called to the front window. Her fall-themed display included a burnt orange chemise and chocolate colored camis and boy shorts hung on padded silk hangers, and autumn toned leaves were scattered along the shelf, along with twinkling orange lights strung along the back of the display. This was her favorite time of year and Stasi tended to go all out.

She looked out the window and stared at Carrie Anderson, who stood across the street in front of Sam's Dry Cleaners. She carried plastic-wrapped clothing in one hand, a coffee to-go cup with the bakery's name imprinted on the side in the other, and a dark scowl on her face. Stasi knew if looks could kill she would have been molecules scattered to the wind by now.

"Why do you hate me so much, Carrie?" she whispered. "What started all this?"

Horace peeked through the linen half drapes at the back of the window. "Is she saying witch or bitch?" He studied the shape of Carrie's mouth as she spoke.

Stasi turned away. "To her it means the same thing."

"Too bad you can't zap her back a few centuries. Let her try to survive with no indoor plumbing, no grocery stores, and having to take care of all her kids without the benefits of television and DVDs. Wouldn't it be nice to see her grubbing away in a garden? Or working as a scullery maid? Come on, Stasi, can't you just imagine her emptying chamber pots?"

"Don't tempt me."

"When do you think the wizard will show up again? He's going to hear about her ranting and raving, unless she's ranted and raved to him, and you know he'll come up if that's happened."

It was bad enough that Stasi saw the man in her mind's eye with his bronzed blond hair and brilliant blue eyes, but the thought of those damned red hearts over his head was enough to send her screaming out into the street. Not only was he a wizard, but he was representing her worst enemy—and all Stasi could think about was the way his lean and muscular body filled out his perfectly fitting suit.

"Who filed this paperwork?" Trev's searing gaze moved from one frozen face to another seated along one side of the conference table. Each face held the deer in the headlights look because they all knew one of them was about to be mowed down. Trevor didn't believe in taking prisoners when he was on a rampage. And right now, he was ready to inflict serious damage on the one who had created what he called an unholy mess.

"She-she said you were amending the lawsuit and wanted it done immediately," stammered Crisdean, a mere two hundred years old. His ordinarily pale skin was even lighter with terror. "You were out of contact range."

Trev turned on his assistant, but Mae was impervious to his temper. "And you allowed this?" Danger rode every word.

"As if a young wizard with law degrees from three different universities would listen to a mere *clerk*." The young man blanched at hearing the words he'd arrogantly thrown at Mae.

Trev didn't even think about reining in his annoyance. "Mae is in charge when I am not here. She knows more about magickal law than any of you will ever know. And I don't care what any of my clients say. When I am not here, you will inform them I will take care of their problems when I return." He advanced on Crisdean with the stride of a predator. "How large is your caseload right now?"

"I-ah-I've only been here a few months, sir."

Trev nodded. "Then I would say you need to understand just how this office works. And the best way to do that is to start at the bottom. Starting today you will be working in the archives. I understand files from the years 1400 to 1623 are in disorder. I suggest you put them in proper order. Mae will oversee your duties." Pronouncement made, he strode out of the room leaving behind one stunned young lawyer and others heaving sighs of relief that it wasn't them.

"You were harsh on him," Mae said, closing the door behind her as she entered Trev's office.

"Just as my father was rough with me when I did the same thing," he replied, staring at the paperwork strewn across his desk.

"Mrs. Anderson was trouble the moment she stepped into this office. If I didn't know better, I'd say other forces were at work here." She poured coffee from the waiting carafe and set the cup in front of Trev.

His head snapped up. "Why would you say that?"

"Because a colleague of Anastasia Romanov's has had trouble in the past. One Jasmine 'Jazz' Tremaine, originally Griet of Ardglass, destroyed one Clive Reeves, who used dark magick to prey on vampires to gain immortality, and she once broke into Dyfynnog's castle to steal a pair of bunny slippers he had created. She later vanquished him and earned the wrath of Angelica, the director of the Protectorate. All of the witches in her class at the Witches' Academy have been in trouble at some time or another. Considering they were expelled from there in the year 1313, it's only natural they'd misbehave from time to time. But no one expected them to still be in the mortal world 700 years later." Mae allowed herself a tiny smile. A clear sign of approval on her part, which totally floored Trev. He'd always thought his assistant was more than a bit tightly wrapped and frowned on any form of misbehavior. He wondered if there was more to the woman than he could even imagine. He also doubted there was a way for him to find out. Mae was better than the CIA when it came to keeping secrets—whether they were hers or someone else's.

He shook his head. Since he rarely bothered with witch matters, except in a legal context, he hadn't heard the tales of the wayward class of witchlings.

Mae waved a hand and a stack of paper appeared in front of Trev. He skimmed through the pages.

"It seems these witches like to irritate people."

"I'm sure they consider it a gift." She settled more comfortably in her chair. Her burgundy knit suit complemented her silver hair. "The thirteen witches may be scattered across the world, but they can also act as one. If a call goes out, the others will be there to help."

"According to this report, Jazz Tremaine only used the help of her vampire lover and a ghost to level the mansion and release the vampire wraiths."

"Some do prefer to work on their own. Anastasia is well loved by the others. They won't allow Carrie Anderson to win this case."

His ego was pricked. "Then they don't know me."

He didn't miss Mae's smile. "What?"

"Some things happen for a reason." She stood up. "I am off to show young Crisdean the archives." She walked to the door.

"Mae?"

She stopped and looked over her shoulder.

"Was I ever that arrogant?"

Mae smiled. "Much worse, but you changed your mind about the importance of the office help after your father set you to do my work for two weeks."

"That was the longest two weeks of my life," he agreed. He stared at the pile of paper. "I may have to make another trip up to Moonstone Lake and stay a few days. I can always keep up with my other work from there. See if I can get a room at the resort where I stayed before." He went on to issue further instructions.

Mae nodded, not bothering to write down a word. She never forgot a thing. Trev knew that for a fact.

"And while you're up there you should have an excellent chance to get a better handle on Carrie Anderson," she said. "Something tells me there's more than meets the eye with her."

Trev looked up sharply. "You didn't say that before."

"Yes, I did, but you didn't listen." With this she opened the door and left, carefully closing it behind her.

Trev leafed through the stack of papers and picked up the most recent report on Anastasia Romanov. The first thing to catch his attention was an arc of shiny red dancing hearts at the top of the paper.

"Oh hell."

"I'm going down to Grady's to pick up a sandwich. You want one?" Blair stuck her head in the door.

Stasi glanced at the clock, surprised to see time had passed so quickly. "Definitely. One of their mesquite tri-tip and a Diet Coke."

"Done." Blair studied her face. "Are you okay?"

"If you mean do I still want to turn Carrie into something disgusting, yes, I do, but I think I can restrain myself."

"Good. Be back in a few. I put a Closed for Lunch sign out. We can use the table at my shop."

"Don't I get a sandwich?" Horace called out from his vantage point in the dressing room. The resorts had covered their slopes with artificial snow, and a group of cheerleaders from UCLA had stopped in a little while ago on their way up the mountain for some skiing. Thanks to them, Horace hadn't left his corner by the dressing room mirror. One of the young women had joked she felt as if she had a voyeur in the room and it was a good thing the gargoyle was made of stone.

Stasi didn't bother to tell her the truth. One, she wouldn't have believed her, and two, Horace really didn't have that much enjoyment in his life. He'd gotten more than his share that morning and was still on Peeping Tom overload.

"You're not eating anything in there," Stasi told him. "We're eating at Blair's."

The gargoyle appeared between the silk curtains and hopped over to the counter. A few words and he was perched on it.

"Do you think Wizard Barnes would take my case?"

"Your case as in what? Lifting the curse?"

Horace nodded. He reached up and touched one of his horns. "It's really an excessive sentence for such a minor crime."

"Head of the largest troll community in the world, then you insulted the wizard who cast the spell along with his family two hundred generations back. That could have something to do with it. You have more than your share of bad habits, Horace. What about the time when you racked up a $1,000 phone bill with all those 900 number calls? This is why people get annoyed with you."

"Ah yes, Tiffany." He heaved a deep sigh. "She had a voice that brought all sorts of images to mind and worth every penny."

"Except you weren't the one paying." She locked the register and picked him up, tucking him in her leather tote bag.

Stasi didn't need a key to open Blair's shop door since the doors were attuned to both witches. She set Horace on the red and chrome 1950s table and wandered around the shop.

She paused at one shelf that held several dolls, one of them blonde and blue-eyed. Stasi reached around and pulled the string at the back of the doll's neck.

"Tell me a story," the doll said in a slightly tinny voice.

"If none of you had kids, why so many dolls?" Horace asked.

"Some of us collected them," she explained. "Perhaps because we didn't have a normal childhood. And I think deep down we knew that some items could become collector's items. Thea has original Barbie dolls and designer wardrobes you wouldn't believe for them." She moved on to several Hummel figurines. "Plus having a collection gives us a little depth in whatever life we're living at the time. Except for Maggie, who prefers her gun and knife collection."

"That's one scary witch."

"Not really." She thought of the Nordic-looking blonde who was happiest when she was kicking ass—and working in private security allowed her to do just that.

"She should work as an enforcer."

"They'd like that, but she refuses to become a vampire. Not that it would be an easy turn, since a vampire can't drink our blood."

Horace shuddered. "Gross."

"Says the one who eats bugs."

"Hey! They're full of protein. Plus, tell me the last time you've seen a spider around here," he pointed out.

"At least you're good for something," Blair teased, walking in with a bag that smelled of rich barbecue spices and balancing two large drink cups. She carried her booty over to the table and set it all out including a half sandwich cut up in gargoyle-sized bites.

"You didn't forget the seasoned fries, did you?" Stasi asked. She loved the fries with tangy seasonings on them as much as the barbecued sandwiches.

"Of course not, and it's a large order." Blair arranged napkins and wet wipes—absolutely necessary with sandwiches that were as messy as they were delicious.

"What about me?" Felix, the Kit-Kat clock, asked from his hanging position on the wall.

"You can't eat our food," Blair pointed out.

"I bet I could if you'd let me try." His tail twitched in a very un-clocklike manner, while his large eyes ticked back and forth.

"There are days when I'm convinced dogs would be less trouble." Blair sat down and picked up her drink. "But then I remember how they shed and drool and some have nasty gas and the feeling goes away."

"Bogie's not like that!" Stasi argued.

"You forget about the night he got into the salsa." Blair made a gagging sound. "Don't worry, I love your furry buddy; he's sweet." She chuckled. "Not like Fluff and Puff, whose to-do list details every insidious idea known to witch. Although there are times they come in handy when someone pisses us off," she muttered. "Maybe Jazz should rent them out. She could make a fortune."

Stasi studied her friend, whom she felt she knew as well as she knew herself.

"Did anything happen at Grady's?" she asked, half-afraid to inquire. She'd noticed more than one town resident hurrying past her shop as if even that was tainted. "Did someone say something?"

Blair looked up and smiled, recognizing her friend's worry. "Nothing more than the usual customers arguing politics and others discussing the upcoming Halloween festivities. And Grady feels that Carrie is nothing more than an empty-headed idiot and wouldn't even make a good statue. His words. He admitted he hoped we'd turn Carrie into a cockroach."

Stasi unwrapped her sandwich, allowing the rich aroma of mesquite-grilled meat and grilled onions to invade her senses. She picked up one of the cups that held Grady's homestyle hickory sauce and drizzled it over the meat. The sounds she uttered as she bit into her sandwich were not unlike those of a woman in the throes of passion.

"If Grady wasn't seventy-two I'd marry him for his cooking alone," she murmured.

"Considering we're both much older than he is, we'd be the ones robbing the cradle." Blair set the large paper dish of seasoned fries between them and squirted out a liberal pool of ketchup.

"Sometimes I wish we hadn't told them what we are." Stasi looked off into the distance, her sandwich momentarily forgotten.

"People are more sophisticated now. We would eventually have had to use glamours to change our appearance. How many more times could we have come back here as our nieces or granddaughters or even split up as we've done?" Blair brought up. "And then basically sneaking out here every month to the lake because we know there's power there, even if we don't know what it is."

"I wish whatever it is would give up its secrets. We did ours. Only fair to reciprocate." Blair dipped her fries in the ketchup.

Stasi pinched off some meat and allowed her hand to drop. Tiny teeth nibbled away with amazing delicacy— Bogie couldn't resist the barbecued meat either.

"You need to talk to Trevor Barnes," Blair announced.

"He's not my lawyer." Stasi concentrated on her food.

"As if a little thing like that's stopped us in the past. Maybe he can reason with Carrie."

"Nothing's happened yet and there's no court date set, so I'm not worried." Of course she was, but she wasn't about to admit it. Plus, she didn't really want to see him again. Not as long as he had those red hearts over his head.

"Pull the other leg," Blair scoffed.

Stasi sighed. She should have known she couldn't fool her.

"I know what. Let's see if Jazz can come up early. She might have some ideas for us."

Stasi looked toward the window and watched a gust of wind pick up a piece of paper from the sidewalk and send it flying. Ed Ramsey, who owned the video store, pulled his jacket up around his ears and trudged down the sidewalk.

"We'll have snow soon," she said, without thinking.

Blair looked up. "We're not due to have any snow for at least another month. It still isn't cold enough."

She shook her head. "No, we'll be having an early snowfall, and it could be a heavy one." It wasn't a gift, but Stasi was almost always accurate when it came to reading the weather. If she said they'd have an early snowfall, they would. "Maybe it's due to the retrograde, but the air feels heavier and out of balance."

"We can't make the world perfect, Stasi," Blair said gently. "It's not our job and I'm very grateful it's not."

"But something's going to happen," she insisted. "I can feel it deep within me."

"That's the lawsuit and nothing more," Blair argued, then relented. "All right, Mercury retrograde isn't helping, but let's not read something into it that isn't there. We can't be paranoid, Stasi." She sighed. "I'll close early and fix dinner."

Stasi nodded. She finished her sandwich and her share of the fries. Once they cleaned up the table, she returned to her shop.

But for once her heart wasn't in it.

"The air smells heavy," Horace announced, watching Stasi finish emptying the cash drawer.

"Air can't smell heavy."

He drew in a deep breath, his chest expanding until it looked as if it would burst then he blew it out with one fast exhalation.

"Heavy air. Not good."

She shook her head. "Have you been sneaking upstairs and watching horror movies again?"

He rolled his eyes. "Oh puleeze! Those filmmakers don't know what true horror is. No, this is our world, not the humans'."

Stasi felt a faint skittering over her flesh as if spiders crawled up her arms. She quickly put away the moneybag and headed for the door.

When she opened it, something lying against the door fell backwards onto the floor.

Stasi felt a chill chase across her skin as she bent down and picked up the object.

"Put it down!" Horace's order rang out so loud she dropped it.

"How can you see what it is?" she asked.

"I don't need to." Within seconds, he was beside her. His face was scrunched up as if he smelled something incredibly bad.

"Destroy it," he ordered, backing away. "Don't hold it again, don't study it. Just get rid of it. It's not good."

Stasi didn't question Horace's command. She was aware he knew more about magick than he generally let on.

"Pretty dolly oh so sad. Pretty dolly oh so bad. Pretty dolly I say nay. Pretty dolly go away if you please." She waved her hand over the object and it sizzled and sparked before turning into a pile of dark ash. "It should be white," she murmured, knowing any time she turned an object to ash it was grayish-white, not the dark gray she was staring at.

Horace looked on from a distance. "Not with this kind of magick."

She looked at him. "What kind is it?"

He shook his head. "I'm not sure, but I do know it's not something you should be around."

As Stasi stood up, a chilling blast of wind blew past her and she shivered.

Once upstairs, Stasi thought she'd never been so happy to be in the warm, brightly lit kitchen with Blair. She said nothing about the incident to her friend.

She knew this was something she had to deal with herself. Because she was positive Carrie was somehow behind this. Anyone who could hire a wizard lawyer could also hire someone to cast dangerous spells.

Chapter 6

"MA'AM? MISS STASI? PLEASE WAKE UP!"

Stasi groaned and rolled over. "Oh Fergus, please don't!" She opened one eye a slit and saw darkness out her window. "It's not even dawn."

"Please, ma'am, somethin's real wrong and we need your help."

Stasi opened both eyes and stared at the wavering figure standing at the foot of her bed. While she could always see through the ghost, this time he was nothing more than a vague shadow. She sat up, shivering at the chill in the air.

"What's wrong?"

"We don't know," he replied, twisting his hat between his hands. "'Member Cyrus? We were talkin' and he just up and disappeared."

She pushed her hair back and struggled to think, but sleep was pulling her back. She mentally zapped herself awake and reached for her soft fleece robe lying across the end of the bed, accidentally upending Bogie who had snuggled inside it. He uttered a soft growl of protest and moved over to curl up in a pile of warm blankets.

"Perhaps he was tired of barely existing here and moved into the next realm." She wrapped the robe around her and stood up, teetering back and forth a bit as her bleary brain tried to wake up.

Fergus shook his head. "No, he wouldn't move on, not if he could help it. Cyrus always said there was no reason to go elsewhere. That all he knew was here. And Rena's gone, too. And some of the others look like I do now. There but not there."

Stasi searched her memory banks, then recalled the woman who had once worked upstairs at Lil's. Rena liked crossing the veil during October because she enjoyed the company of men. More than one man during the Halloween season revealed that he'd felt the icy chill of a small hand on his private parts. Others woke up convinced someone was having sex with them and it wasn't the most pleasant of experiences, either. Stasi couldn't believe that Rena would move on. She enjoyed her trips here too much.

"I suppose you couldn't wake up Blair." She knew how much her friend adored sleeping. Waking Blair up was a major project.

"She sorta woke up and threw a book at me. I guess she forgot it'd only go through me." He grinned. "She's not going to be too happy when she sees she broke a vase."

"Serves her right." She looked at Bogie and nudged him back awake. "You know the drill, baby. Go wake up Auntie Blair while Mommy makes coffee."

Bogie yapped once and took off like a streak of light… literally.

Stasi muttered a few choice words when she saw that the clock blinked two a.m.

"Why can't anything happen in the middle of the day, or even early evening?"

By the time Blair's curses and mutterings died down and she showed up in the kitchen, Stasi was sitting at the table drinking coffee and warming a coffee cake in the microwave oven.

"Honestly, Fergus, maybe you don't need sleep on your realm, but we still do," Blair grumbled. "Damn, it's cold! Heater, turn on. Make it so!" She waggled her fingers in the direction of the thermostat. A moment later the furnace kicked on. She poured herself coffee and plopped down in a chair. "What's going on now?"

"Cyrus, Rena, and some others have left their realm," Stasi said quietly.

"Like a vacation left?"

Stasi shook her head.

"You mean they're gone gone?" Blair chugged her coffee in an attempt to wake up.

The microwave timer dinged and Stasi got up to collect the coffee cake, which she set on the table along with a knife and forks.

"Fergus!" She spoke sharply when the ghost started to dim. "You need to concentrate on remaining here."

He bobbed his head. "Yes, Miss Stasi, but it's not easy. It's as if I have this feelin' I'm goin' away too."

"Why would this be happening?" Blair forked up a bite of coffee cake.

"I don't know." That was what worried Stasi. She was presented with a problem she couldn't solve. She enjoyed problem solving, especially with romance, but this was much more important. She considered the ghosts friends. For them to lose what little existence they had was frightening.

"Ma'am." Fergus's eyes were wide with fright, which wasn't normal for a ghost, who shouldn't experience the emotion. But Stasi knew when realms grew unstable anything was possible. And that was what she feared was happening now. She sipped her coffee, hoping the caffeine infusion would push her brain into some sort of alert mode.

"I don't know why this is happening to some of you," Stasi said, glancing at Blair, who yawned widely and nodded her agreement.

"You said there was all this stuff goin' on. Retro something," he said.

"Mercury retrograde, and the upcoming lunar eclipse." Stasi rubbed her forehead, wishing she could easily conjure up answers, but she knew it was never that simple.

Fergus opened his mouth to say something, but a plaintive howl from outside stopped him.

"That damn dog," Blair muttered. "There's not that much of a moon out there to howl at."

Stasi cocked her head and listened. "No, that's not a howling at the moon sound." She stood up and moved to the window over the sink that gave them a prime view of the woods. She frowned at an odd light that flickered in the distance. "There's something out there." She rushed to the back door and pulled it open, running out onto the small deck. She looked back inside. "There's odd lights over the lake."

Blair shot to her feet and followed Stasi as she practically flew down the stairs.

"There's nothing magickal in the woods," Blair said, running to keep up, grateful she'd slipped on her favorite fuzzy duck slippers and not her stiletto mules.

"Nothing that we sensed." Stasi dodged low-hanging branches and bushes as she continued running toward the lake.

What was usually a peaceful ten-minute walk was a four-minute dash as the two witches ran along the path they'd taken many times before. As they broke past the stand of trees to reach the open area surrounding the lake, they found the Border collie barking and howling as he ran along the bare dirt.

"Okay, boy, we got your message, what's up?" Blair called out.

The dog stopped and ran back to them, continuing to bark.

"Sheesh, you'd think he was Lassie warning us Timmy fell into a well." Blair tried to grab for his collar, but he danced out of their reach and ran closer to the lake, then stopped short.

The lights they had seen from the house appeared brighter and danced over the surface of the lake.

"What is this?" Stasi moved forward toward the rock outcropping they walked upon each month when offering up to the moon. Blair was fast on her heels.

"*Oomph!*" Both witches suddenly bounced off an invisible barrier and fell backwards onto their butts.

"What was that?" Stasi slowly got to her feet, rubbing her rump, which had struck a sharp rock when she fell.

"I don't know." Blair stood up and this time walked a great deal slower until again, she hit the barrier. Stasi followed her and both raised their hands, feeling what they couldn't see. They jumped back when dark green sparks flew off the barrier and burned their palms.

"Barrier we can't see. Barrier we refuse to flee. Barrier reveal thyself, make it so!" Blair shouted, throwing her hands out.

The barrier shimmered with her power, then threw it back at her with enough muscle to send her flying backwards a good ten feet to land on her back.

"Damn it!" Blair lifted her head and glared at the barrier as the dog ran over and licked her face. "Ick! Dog germs! For Fates sake! You're licking my face after you probably spent most of the evening licking your balls." She tried to push away the dog, but he kept coming back to lick her face again.

"Are you all right?" Stasi asked, helping her up.

"Nothing's broken." She brushed leaves and dirt off her robe. She stared at the barrier and the green light orbs hovering over the water, sometimes moving closer to them, then dancing away. "Where did this come from? There was no sign of it two days ago when I was out here."

"I don't know." Stasi approached the barrier with tentative steps. After what happened to Blair she wasn't about to take any chances. She kept her power under control, not allowing even one spark to appear. If it could throw Blair that far, she didn't want to think what it might do to her if whatever fueled it got really angry.

"Let's see if it goes all the way around the lake."

"Then can we go back and put on warm clothes? It's freezing out here!"

Stasi nodded. "Good idea. Whatever this is, I don't think it's going anywhere."

They didn't run back to the house, but they did hurry and changed into warm clothing in no time.

Stasi pulled her jacket hood up over her hair as they returned to the lake. Even with her fleece pants, wool gloves, and heavy jacket she could feel the hint of snow in the air.

"We've never had odd lights float over the water before," Blair commented.

"That we've known of," she replied. "We only knew about it tonight because the dog was howling and we were already up."

"Maybe that's why Fergus was feeling odd." Blair kept a respectful distance from the barrier as they walked the circumference of the lake. The dog kept pace next to her, his tongue lolling, as if they were out for a middle of the night stroll.

As they walked, Stasi cast periodic glances toward the woods. She sensed something unsettling among the trees, but she couldn't quite put her finger on what it was. Since she didn't feel any malevolence, she didn't mention anything to Blair.

"The lunar eclipse didn't cause this," she said. "This was created by magick."

"Yeah, but whose?"

"I didn't exactly finish the course on all the alternate magicks."

"Whoa, snappish much?"

Stasi winced. "Just feeling unsettled."

"Aren't we all." Blair stared at the rock as they finished the walk and ended up where they began.

Stasi walked slowly toward the barrier again, but this time licks of fire appeared along the bottom edge, slowly sliding upward until a wall of flame covered the barrier. She couldn't feel any heat coming from it, but she knew it could hurt her as easily as real fire could and probably even worse, since it was created by magick.

"That's not good." Blair tugged on her arm, pulling her backwards.

"No kidding." Stasi gulped. "I think we need some help with this."

"What in hell is that?"

Both spun around as the dog lowered his head and growled.

Trev stood at the edge of the trees, dressed warmly even if his hair was unruly. He looked as though he had thrown on his clothes, not caring that pillow creases marred his cheek, his face was slightly puffy from sleep, and his hair was going in all directions. He stood there staring at the flame-covered wall.

"What do you see?" Stasi asked, not bothering to wonder why he was there.

He didn't reply right away, but looked intently at the barrier. "A barrier created by magick to keep certain types of magick out. Namely you. The flames are a warning. Normally you can't see anything."

"Which is why we literally ran into it," Blair said. "So, Counselor, any reason why you're out here in the middle of the night on *our* property?"

He grinned at her. "You know the drill. Magick calls to magick. Any idea what it is?"

"None," Stasi replied, determined to ignore the red hearts over his head even as she noted with dismay they seemed to have grown larger and bolder in color since the last time she saw him. "What about you? Do you have any thoughts on it?"

Trev walked forward, his hands held up high, palms out. He ignored the Border collie, who appeared to consider him an interloper and was staying on the wizard's heels as if to keep a close eye on him.

"Don't get too close," Stasi warned him. "Blair tried finding out what it was and it practically threw her against a tree."

"Someone put a lot of power into this," he murmured, studying it as if it was a complicated problem. "First to erect the obstacle, then to protect it from intruders. It's nothing I'm familiar with, but there are many forms of magick out there that I've never had to deal with before. A spell this strong could only have been done with blood to bind it."

The witches shivered in fear. Spells requiring blood were dangerous and powerful. Ones they wouldn't even consider.

"You never answered Blair's question. Why are you out here?" Stasi asked, noting that his eyes seemed to have a glow of their own in the dark, along with the hearts' glimmer.

"I woke up and felt something odd floating through the air. I felt drawn to here, and when I saw strange lights over this way I thought I'd investigate."

"Why don't you run along, Counselor," Blair suggested with a bite in her voice. "I'm sure you wouldn't want Carrie to see you with us. Don't worry. We witches are used to cleaning up messes and we'll do just fine here." She looked down at the dog, who'd grabbed hold of her sleeve with his teeth and was gently pulling on it. "Hey! I'm talking here."

The dog whined and pulled again.

"What's his name?" Trev asked, grinning at the dog's persistence and silently thanking him for his aid. He was hoping to have a chance to be alone with Stasi.

"Pain in the ass," Blair snapped.

The dog snorted on her sleeve.

"He doesn't have a name?" He realized she was joking… sort of.

"He's not my dog."

"He's been a lucky stray in that he looks well groomed and well fed and…" Trev looked downward, "hasn't been neutered."

This time the dog's growls were more canine snarky.

"It seems that's a medical procedure he intends to avoid," Blair said, trying to get the dog to release her sleeve, but he only tightened his hold.

"I think he wants you to go with him," Stasi said, wanting the same. She was curious about why Trev was here, and she didn't want an audience when she got her answers.

Blair looked from the dog to Stasi to Trev. "Okay, but if he tries anything, zap him a good one," she told Stasi before she allowed the dog to lead her back through the trees toward home. "Fine, I'm coming! If you tear this jacket, I'll use your fur to make myself a new one."

Trev chuckled. "You'd think she doesn't like him."

"He isn't hers," Stasi said. "He shows up on our doorstep every so often for food. I think Blair considers him occasional entertainment."

"You mean she doesn't—?"

"Doesn't what?"

Trev chuckled. "Nothing. I'm sure it will all work out."

Stasi studied him, liking this more vulnerable side of him. She could see his shirt half tucked into his jeans under his jacket and buttons in the wrong order. "Why do I think you know something we don't?"

"I think the two of you do know, but for some reason you prefer to keep it tucked away." He glanced back at the barrier. The flames were gone with no sign they'd ever been there. With the barrier invisible, no one could tell the lake was protected. The question was, why did someone or something feel that need? And who or what was that someone? The lights over the water flickered in and out until one by one they winked out of sight.

"I can tell you that no wizard created this."

"And no witch had his or her hand in it either," Stasi said. "This couldn't be caused by Mercury retrograde or the lunar eclipse. This is all pure magick. We just don't know what kind."

Trev took her arm to steer her back to the house. "It has to be someone who lives locally. They'd have to be able to return to feed the power on a regular basis."

Stasi pulled back. "There's no sense of an avoidance spell here. We can't allow just anyone to stumble out here. We can provide some sort of protection for ourselves, but a mortal could be in danger." She stared at the lake, racking her brain for just the right spell.

"I think I have something that would work," Trev offered. "If you don't mind?"

"You'd help?"

"Of course." He rubbed his palms together. "I'm a little out of practice, but this should do it."

Stasi stood back and watched as Trev drew closer to the unseen barrier, but remained far enough back to be out of harm's way in case the barrier fought back. Multi-colored sparks of light danced off the wall as he held his hands up and chanted under his breath. The wind picked up, sending the few remaining leaves scattering, and the air grew so cold, Stasi saw her breath frost the air. She widened her stance as the wind grew even stronger, almost pushing her off her feet. The air grew so heavy and dense with power it felt like a living thing wrapped around her. If she hadn't been watching closely, she would have missed the flare of intense cobalt blue that whooshed from Trev's eyes like a serpent winding its way around the lake's boundary until it met back where they stood, the serpent's mouth grabbing hold of its tail as it froze into a ring that she could tell held a lot of magickal muscle. She looked out over the water, again seeing the strange green lights dancing off the water's edge, but floating further away from them than before.

"I sensed you had a great gift, but I had no idea it was this strong," she whispered, awed by the immense control she felt still coming from Trev. She stared at the ring circling the bottom of the barrier. She knew it would deter a mortal from coming out this way, but not harm any human or animal that might come close.

Trev blew out a breath and a sharp laugh. "I haven't done anything like this in a long time. I guess they're right. It *is* like riding a bicycle. You never lose your touch, but it sure takes a lot out of you." He blew on the tip of his forefinger as if it was a gun barrel. He turned back and grinned at Stasi, looking more like a boy proud of his accomplishments than a powerful wizard.

Stasi fell in step with him as they retraced the path back to the house.

"Thank you."

"You and Blair have a big job here." He nodded when she looked at him with surprise. "It wasn't difficult to figure out, Stasi. The two of you have done your best to protect the town from developers without interfering so much you'd end up in trouble with the Witches' Council. You walked a fine line and succeeded."

Stasi stopped when they reached the back stairs. She could hear Bogie's frantic barking inside, then the Border collie's echoing barks and Blair ordering them both to be quiet. She guessed they realized they were on Blair's last nerve, because they quieted down immediately.

She stopped on the bottom step, which allowed her to be closer to eye level with Trev.

"We've lived here on and off since the town first sprang up during the Gold Rush," she said. "Something about the lake gave us this sense of completion, and we vowed we'd never allow anyone to harm this area. We set up wards throughout the woods to protect the wildlife and to keep the town safe. They're nothing major, just a bit of a safety zone."

Trev reached out, tentatively at first, and then stroked her hair, threading strands between his fingers. Her first thought was to step out of his reach; the second was to stay where she was. She opted for Door Number Two. And didn't move a muscle when Trev moved that all-important extra step that brought him right up to her.

"Few work so hard to protect an entire town," he murmured, keeping his gaze centered on her face.

"It's our town," she whispered, as if speaking too loudly would break the spell that sprang up between them. A spell that had nothing to do with magick, but with what arced between the opposite sexes. She tipped her face up, silently inviting what she knew would happen. She was curious whether this was a good idea.

She reminded herself that she was determined to do what she normally wouldn't, and that thought kept her still on the step.

Trev lowered his head until his mouth rested a breath above hers.

"You're a tempting woman, Anastasia Romanov," he whispered.

She smiled.

"You found what I said funny?"

She shook her head. "You didn't call me a witch."

"Magick may in your blood, but it's your femininity that calls to me." His mouth covered hers in a kiss that sent pure fire racing through her veins. She was amazed the steps didn't go up in flames as she first rested her hands on his shoulders then slid them up around his neck. His mouth slid across hers, stroking and seeking until she opened her mouth. He was a man kissing a woman, showing her his attraction, and she couldn't help but respond with all she had.

Trev quickly unzipped his jacket and Stasi's, pulling both open before bringing her fully against him. The warmth of his body kept the night's chill at bay as they stood there, tasting each other and feeling the urgency build. She tasted pure male and the power that was in his blood. For a moment, Stasi was tempted to climb up on him and have her way with him. In all her years, she hadn't felt the intensity she felt now with Trev, or wanted a man as badly as she wanted him.

"Stasi," he murmured, cupping her face with his hands, turning his head to another angle as he feasted on her mouth.

"Trevor," she whispered back, feeling joy deep within. The sensation was so strong she felt overwhelmed.

"So beautiful. So caring. Why would you do what you did to Carrie?" he muttered, lost in the moment and not realizing he had just said the absolutely worst thing he could say. Stasi broke away from him so fast he rocked back on his heels, almost falling backwards.

"What's wrong?" His eyes were still a filmy, unfocused blue.

She blinked back her tears. "You bastard." To make matters worse, she hiccupped and an iridescent bubble escaped her lips. A second quickly followed. She wanted to conjure up one of Jazz's fireballs to throw at him for making her hiccup. "You son of a bitch!"

Before Trev could backpedal to figure out what went wrong, Stasi pulled back her hand and punched him in the gut. He exhaled a painful whoosh of air and covered his stomach with his arms.

"What was that for?" he wheezed.

"You think about it. You think good and hard about it!" she spat at him as she lifted her hands. "Snowman, come to me. Snowman let me see. Snowman do your job, if you please!" She spun on her heel and stomped upstairs.

"Stasi!" Trev's advance toward her was halted by what felt like a ton of snow falling on top of him. He cursed and sputtered as he tried to brush the snow away from his head and body. "Damn it, Stasi!" Her reply was the back door slamming and the light by the door winking off. Trev muttered as he walked off, replaying the moment in his mind. He uttered a variety of curses as his last line echoed inside his head. He headed for his

car, planning how he was going to get himself out of this
mess without Stasi deciding to do some serious damage
to him. Because at the moment he wouldn't have blamed
her for wanting to turn him into a warthog. "Carrie, I'd
love to throttle you for getting me into this mess." He
scuffed the ground with his boots as he walked. "But if
you hadn't come into my office and made my life miserable I wouldn't have met Stasi—who seems to be determined to make my life another kind of miserable."

Chapter 7

"HE'S HORRIBLE! HIC!" STASI BATTED AWAY THE bubble and zapped the one that followed. She told Blair about Trev's spell to keep people from harming themselves at the barrier and then his kiss, along with how he had ruined it. "He deserves warts!"

The dog whined and nosed his way into her lap while Bogie floated up around her shoulders like a furry neck roll.

"Drink this," Blair urged, pushing a cup of tea into her hands. "And don't stop until it's all gone."

"Thanks—*hic!*" She did as ordered then waited. She smiled then groaned as another hiccup ballooned in her chest and bubbles filled the air.

Blair shook her head. "This is more than nerves." She took the cup from Stasi's fingers before she could drop it and refilled it. "Drink again."

"I'm drowning in tea!" Stasi wailed after the third cup. "*Hic!*" By then, the kitchen was rapidly filling up with the bubbles. Bogie reached out and batted at them, while the Border collie was happy bumping them with his nose and snapping at them.

Blair dropped into one of the chairs and took Stasi's hands. "It's the hearts. They're going to mess you up big time."

"I'm going to smack Cupid back to his creator... *hic!*" She covered her face with her hands. "I'm going to borrow Fluff and Puff and tell them to eat all his enchanted arrows. That'll fix him! He'll be out of business, that lowlife matchmaker who thinks he has the market on romance."

"Uh, ladies." Fergus stood uncertainly among all the bubbles that floated through him. "Did you figure out what's going wrong?"

"Not exactly, Fergus," Blair said. "But we're working on it. Just be careful when any of you come over here, okay, and let us know if anyone else disappears?"

"Okay." He nodded and vanished.

Blair turned to the dog next. "Don't you have a home to go to?" He sat back on his haunches and lifted a paw, bobbing it up and down while he cocked his head to one side. "Oh no, you can't stay here." But the dog had already taken off down the hall. She ran after him. "Bad dog! You cannot sleep in my bed!"

"She'll lose the battle and let him stay and he'll take all the covers as he has before," Stasi said, pulling Bogie around to sit in her lap. She stroked the dog behind his ears. He looked so blissful, if he'd been a cat he would have purred. "Closest she's had to a man in her bed for some time."

She tidied up the kitchen and returned to bed, noting that by now it was well after four. She felt so tired she was ready to drop where she stood. But once she was undressed and under the covers, with Bogie curled up on the pillow by her head, she lay wide-awake.

"He does a nice thing at the lake, then he kisses me," she murmured. "How am I supposed to face him in Wizards' Court after this? Forget that, how am I supposed to face him in this town?"

To make matters worse, when she fell asleep she wasn't counting sheep but hearts dancing in a conga line.

"That dog hogs the bed," Blair grumbled as she and Stasi ate breakfast. Both dogs had their heads in bowls of kibble. "And he snores."

"I don't know. I would think it would be like sleeping with a huge stuffed animal." Stasi looked out the window and frowned. "There wasn't any sign of snow when we were out there a few hours ago."

Blair joined her at the window and peered out. "Wow, there are several inches out there now." When the collie barked, she headed for the back door and opened it for him. "Typical guy. First they charm you into bed, then they eat and run without one word about calling you."

Stasi continued staring at the trees collecting falling snowflakes on their branches. "We need to check the lake again."

"What's wrong?"

She shook her head. "I don't know, but something feels very troubling out there." She ran to the coat rack and grabbed her jacket along with Blair's and threw it to her.

"But you said Trev cast a spell of protection," Blair said.

"He did, but something still feels off. We really need to go back out there and we need to go now."

"Boots this time," Blair reminded her. "The path will be slippery with the snow."

Her warning proved true as they slipped and slid along the path.

"The air smells odd," Stasi commented, as they grew closer to the end of the stand of trees.

Blair wrinkled her nose. "Yeah, it smells almost like dead fish."

They stopped short at the sight before them.

"Yowza." Blair whistled softly.

"This is really not good." Stasi felt her stomach sink all the way down to her toes.

They stared at a barrier that was no longer invisible to the naked eye. Now it stood crisscrossed with lines of dark green and gray, while the blue ring Trev had conjured was cracked, broken in places, and covered with splashes of black as if a strong fire had burned it. The normally placid surface of the lake was showing whitecaps, even though there was very little wind. Stasi and Blair kept their distance as they walked around the lake and found the blue ring in the same condition all the way around.

"That was the most powerful spell I'd ever seen and it was destroyed as if a first year student cast it," Stasi whispered, as they walked back to the house. The minute they stepped into the kitchen they grabbed more coffee to warm up. "Something's very wrong and I think we need help."

"Agreed."

Stasi glanced at the coffee-pot-shaped clock and noticed the time. Her first thought was not to open the store, but she knew she had to keep on as if nothing was wrong. "I'll call Jazz today. I'll also try Maggie. Her gift is protection spells."

Blair nodded. "I'll do some research on the retrograde and lunar eclipse and see if it does have anything to do with this."

"It's October first, town decoration day, remember?"

Blair groaned, then brightened up. "That's right. Jake said he'd help us set up the heavy stuff."

"Yes, Blair, think of the important things," Stasi said dryly before heading to her bedroom to get ready.

When the women went downstairs and around to the front of the building they found a lot of activity going on. While the town's main street wasn't long, it featured shops geared for tourist trade and always decorated for holiday occasions. Men stood on ladders arranging orange twinkle lights over store windows and doors, while men and women wearing western clothing busied themselves decorating windows and setting out carved pumpkins, scarecrows, and hay bales. The few empty stores were draped in black and decreed to be the sites of a famous gunfight or a gruesome death. Wilson Carruthers, now in a battered hat, wore wool pants and a flannel shirt sporting a blood-spattered front where he'd been "shot." With his matted beard and dirty face, he looked menacing and perfect for a haunted town.

Stasi had chosen a simple soft pink and blue plaid skirt and pink cotton blouse under a matching plaid fichu with a delicate cameo pin attached to her collar. Her felt spoon bonnet matched the blue in the plaid. With the snow on the ground, she opted for thermal tights to keep her legs warm and wore ballet flats. She had pulled her hair up in a simple knot with a black lace snood covering the bun. She had kept her makeup to a minimum, using only a hint of blush and a lightly tinted lip balm.

"I always liked that outfit on you," Blair said, going for the dramatic with a midnight blue velvet riding habit and flat brimmed hat with a matching veil. A few stray curls teased her cheeks. The full skirt was looped up over her wrist, she held a riding crop in her left hand, and wore black riding boots. She looked down at Stasi's full skirt. "But you took the hoops out."

"I did it as a matter of self-defense. I hated hoops even back then. It seemed every time I sat down they'd fly up and smack me in the chin. I added a little 'extra,'" she held up her fingers to form quotes, "to make it look like I'm wearing hoops."

Blair rolled her eyes. "Yeah, we don't want Agnes's Fashion Police coming after you. Although, I bet she won't be wearing a steel-boned corset or hoops."

"I don't know how we functioned back then."

"I don't know how I managed to ride sidesaddle for so many years and not fall off." Blair grinned. "At least we're not in the era where we'd be wearing a bustle. They were almost as bad as wearing hoops."

"Ladies." Jake sauntered up dressed in his usual jeans and flannel shirt topped by a denim sheepskin lined jacket. A worn cream-colored Stetson and battered cowboy boots finished his look.

"Morning, cowboy," Blair purred, batting her lashes. "All you need is a horse."

He doffed his hat. "Thank ya kindly, ma'am. Looks like you could use one too."

"Shows what you know. Riding sidesaddle isn't as easy as it looks."

"You've ridden sidesaddle?"

"Just once on a dare," she said, in hopes of covering up her gaffe. "Last time I visited one of those horse farms in England."

"I wouldn't have thought you'd be the type to ride."

Blair's smile grew larger. "Depends on what I'm riding."

"Could we keep this conversation G-rated, please?" Stasi begged, not sure whether to laugh at her friend's less-than-subtle flirtation or punch Blair in the arm.

"Maybe I better get to moving the heavier decorations out of your storerooms," Jake suggested.

"Good idea," Stasi agreed. She turned when two women wearing what had been called camp dresses from the Civil War era walked in their direction, carrying bags from Fresh Baked Goods. "Ladies." She inclined her head.

"Martha, Jeanine." Stasi's smile dimmed as the women abruptly crossed the street and didn't bother to acknowledge them. She turned to Blair. "What's going on?"

She frowned. "I don't know, but it doesn't feel right."

"Miss Romanov, do you want me to help you put your lights up?" a boy asked, also dressed as if he'd lived during the town's beginnings.

"Thank you, Tyler, we appreciate your offer." She smiled back.

"Tyler Madison, you get back over here!"

He snapped to attention. "Mom? I was just helping—"

His mother ran over, grabbed his hand, and glared at Stasi as she pulled her son away.

"You stay away from my son," she hissed, dragging the protesting boy off.

Stasi was stunned. Blair swore under her breath.

"Ladies." Trev walked up, looking twenty-first century in jeans and a rust colored sweater topped with a dark brown leather jacket. "Don't you two look as if you'd stepped out of a history book."

"You've been to the lake again," Stasi said, noting his grim features.

"What? No, I saw the two of you being snubbed." He turned to Stasi. "What about the lake?"

"Whatever kind of magick powers you may think you have, the barrier shattered the spell you cast." She went on to explain what she and Blair had found earlier that morning.

Trev's features darkened even more. "No one and nothing should have been able to interfere with that spell."

"Maybe not everyone reads your rule books," Stasi snapped.

"Good one," Blair muttered.

Trev held up his hands. "Truce. Tell you what, let me string those lights for you, then I'll go take a look at the lake."

Stasi was tempted to refuse his offer. She knew Jake would be only too happy to help them put up the lights. Or they could even use magick and have them up in a wink, but they tended not to use their power too obviously.

"It's for both shops," Stasi said. "And we accept your offer." She noticed someone else she had considered a friend crossing the street rather than approach them. The snub hurt a great deal, but she wasn't about to show it.

While Trev busied himself checking the orange and white twinkle lights before stringing them up, Stasi set out period underwear in the display window, showing a corset, crinolines, and bloomers along with a few lace-edged chemises popular in the late 1800s. She draped a string of pearls along the bottom shelf and arranged a silk fan and two tiny embroidered silk purses there also.

Blair put out toys from that same time period, including two porcelain dolls with ringlet curls and silk dresses, a set of soldiers dressed in blue and gray, and various pull toys. The center of the display was an old-fashioned rocking horse. A discreetly placed sign in a corner explained that the items on display weren't for sale.

Trev studied her window. "Serious collectors would kill for those."

"They can try, but it won't do them any good. I have a few people who come up here every now and then hoping to buy some of the antiques I refuse to give up."

"Such as Felix," Stasi said. "Her Kit-Kat clock. It's just as well, since few would understand why their clock would talk to them. Most of this we only bring out for special occasions."

Trev looked around, seeing tourists stroll down the sidewalk, stopping at some windows to look in at the shop owners in their period dress. It looked like any other day in the small mountain town, but the three could feel the shifts of unnatural energy in the air and the awareness that something was very wrong and needed to be corrected before something truly bad happened.

"I don't like this." Stasi rubbed her hands along her arms.

"Did you call Jazz and tell her what's been going on?" Blair asked.

"I left her a voice mail and asked if she'd come up early." Stasi felt a strange prickling sensation along the back of her neck. "Excuse me." She held a handkerchief to her lips as she hurried into her shop.

"Oh no." Blair grimaced.

"What's wrong?" Trev felt torn between following Stasi to see what was wrong and seeing what he could learn from Blair.

She looked around, then leaned in. "Stasi lived in Salem Village from 1691 to 1693. She was a companion to an elderly widow." She nodded at Trev's shocked expression. "It was pure luck she was never accused, because many thought she was too pretty and too sweet and witchcraft must be involved. Alda Gibbons, the woman she worked for, lost her husband to the sea. He was a ship's captain, and his ship went down during a storm on the return trip from England. When the accusations began, Stasi knew it would look worse if she left, so she dampened her powers as much as possible and kept a very low profile. Luckily, the town respected Alda and I believe that helped Stasi. But still, she was there during that terrifying time and she's refused to erase those memories."

Trev ducked his head. "Excuse me." He turned to Stasi's shop.

When he went inside, he found her seated on the high-legged stool behind the counter. She had taken off her bonnet and sat there with her head resting on her arms. Horace squatted next to her, stroking her arm and muttering words in a long dead language. His wings rustled together with a raspy sound. Bogie floated around her, whimpering and moving in to offer comforting kisses. And then there were those red hearts mocking him.

"This isn't Salem, Stasi," he said quietly, leaning across the counter to rest his hand on her head. He inhaled a faint scent he knew to be wholly her own.

She lifted her head a fraction of an inch. "Blair told you."

"She's worried about you."

She groaned. "I will turn her into a pigeon."

"Fearful people do strange things, but mortals are a lot more advanced nowadays."

"Sure, they hire wizards to sue witches. *Hic!*" She glared at the bubble that floated in the air. Bogie nosed it and it disappeared.

Trev chuckled. "You seem to do that a lot when I'm around."

"Go away. *Hic!*" She slipped off the stool and headed for the stockroom.

Trev followed her partway and watched her pull a bottle of water out of a small refrigerator.

"I'm going out to the lake and take another look around," he announced. He ran the back of his fingers down her cheek. "Have dinner with me."

She stiffened. "I thank you for helping us, but don't you think our having dinner out would be wrongly construed if Carrie found out?"

"The only one seeing it that way is you." He took a step forward. "Have pity on me, Stasi. I really do hate eating alone."

"I've seen the looks women around here give you. You wouldn't be alone for long. The Sit 'N Eat is your best bet. I won't say Ginny will protect you, but she'll make sure you have a hint of privacy. But if you feel brave enough, try Grady's. It's more a honky-tonk at night, so you might have to fight for your dignity."

"Then protect me."

She sighed. "You won't stop, will you?"

He grinned, aware he was wearing her down. "No, I won't."

"I close the shop at six."

"I'll pick you up at seven." He left before she had a chance to change her mind.

Trev zipped up his jacket and tucked his hands in the pockets against the frigid air as he took the trail around Stasi and Blair's building. With the snow and patches of ice on the ground, he was grateful he wore hiking boots appropriate for the rough ground.

"Not a good day for a walk."

Trev stopped and looked over to see the town handyman standing near the back steps. His shearling-lined jean jacket was buttoned up against the cold and Trev envied the dark-haired man's flannel-lined jeans. He wouldn't have minded a pair of those right now.

"I have to admit that when I want to kick back I'm more tempted to head to Tahiti or the Caribbean for scuba diving and wind surfing," Trev agreed, echoing the man's relaxed stance. "Blair doesn't know the truth about you, does she?"

Jake grinned. "That woman is so smart and so quick-witted, but I have to say there's times she totally drops the ball."

Trev grinned back. "You ever plan to tell her?"

Jake looked off into the distance. "I'm sure the time will come, and she'll want to kill me on the spot for keeping it from her. Some relationships aren't meant to progress too fast. I know she's interested, and I feel the same, but for now, it's kinda fun this way." He moved forward, walking with Trev. "What about you and Stasi? Even I can see there's something brewing there."

"Wizards and witches don't make a perfect pair," Trev said simply. Even though there was a time-honored edict that wizards and witches don't mate, there were still red hearts floating over Stasi's head, along with a matching set over his, but Trev didn't feel like going into details.

"I'm sorry your spell didn't work out at the lake," Jake said, walking beside him.

Trev shot him a sideways look. "You know about that?"

"Stasi told Blair."

"And?" He wondered if she'd also told her friend about the kiss.

Jake's teeth flashed white. "Some things it's best not to mention."

He froze just as they reached the end of the stand of trees ringing the lake.

"What do you sense?" Trev asked, trusting the other man's perception more than his own.

"Something dirty, cruel," he murmured, walking more slowly now, then stopped. "Whoa, something did a real number on your spell."

Trev walked around Jake and stared at the now visible barrier around the lake, which looked armed to the teeth with the crisscrossed strips of magick and the ruins of the protective ring he had constructed to protect mortals from stumbling onto the barrier and being harmed in the process. Now, it was as if whatever had created the barrier wanted everyone to know about it. And he guessed who would be the first to be blamed.

Jake watched Trev approach the barrier, then stop when flames licked around the bottom edge. He backed up to a safe distance and watched the flames die down, but he sensed that they lingered in the ground waiting for an unwary victim.

"You can't destroy it, can you?" he asked.

Trev shook his head. "Not without some potent help. And with no idea what created this, I wouldn't even know who to ask."

"What kind of magick do you think it is?"

Both men turned at the sound of the feminine voice. Stasi stood at the end of the path. In deference to the cold morning, she wore a brown wool cloak with the hood pulled up over her hair. There was a determination stamped across her delicate features that Trev hadn't seen before.

"You don't know, do you?" She moved forward, not slipping once on the snow even though she still wore the fragile ballet slippers. "Neither of you know what monster is out there frightening people into thinking Blair and I are evil and turning our beautiful lake into this horror."

"Hey, I just ran into Trev and came along for company," Jake explained, looking easygoing and with no evidence of the sharp intelligence he'd shown Trev a few moments ago. "He was trying to explain this to me." He pointed to the lake. "Man, anyone comes out here they'll think aliens have landed or the lake monster finally decided he wanted to be alone."

"The lake monster?"

"A local legend," Stasi said. "Sometimes you can look out and see bubbles or a shadow of something in the middle of the lake, but there's never been a problem with anyone out there fishing. Kids come out here on a dare to find the monster. So far, no one has succeeded and not one child has been eaten."

Trev turned back to the barrier. "It needs to be hidden or at least masked."

"No offense, Trevor, but you weren't very successful the last time," Stasi said sharply.

He ignored her as he moved toward the barrier again. Jake walked with him, his boot heels crunching on the icy ground.

"Is the lake a tourist spot during your festivities?" Trev asked. "Any ghost tours given out here?"

Stasi shook her head. "All the ghost walking tours are in town and at the local cemetery. They feel it's more colorful. The lake monster legend isn't even talked about much except among the kids. I think they'd prefer to keep this place their own secret."

"Can you cover the barrier?" Jake asked.

"I can try. Considering what happened last time, who knows? But this time I'll study the structure more and not just show off," he murmured.

Stasi stepped back. "I must return to the shop." Her speech turned more formal as if she had mentally stepped back in time. She turned around, her cloak flying around her ankles as she walked away with both men watching her.

"You need to come up with some serious mojo to force Caustic Carrie to back down on the lawsuit," Jake said. "If you don't you'll never have a chance with Stasi."

Trev turned away from the enticing sight of Stasi walking away. "I'm not allowed to do that. Besides, as I said, wizards and witches don't mix."

"An old wives' tale," Jake scoffed. "There's another witch that will tell you just because they say one thing doesn't mean it doesn't happen. Especially since she's with a vampire."

"Amazing a vampire would stay with a witch, since blood taking is so important a ritual for them with their lovers," Trev said, surprised. It was well known that a witch's blood was poisonous to a vampire. Any vampire who dared take a witch's blood would suffer a serious case of heartburn at the least and death at the worst.

"Then you don't know Jazz Tremaine and Nick Gregory. They're playing the odds and so far, they're winning. And no way he'd try to take even a taste of her blood. She throws a mean fireball," Jake added, following Trev as he moved closer to the barrier, then started walking around it.

Trev studied the ground, watching how the flames would immediately lick the ground if they moved even an inch closer to the barrier. Even as the blaze increased the air remained cold.

"Fire but no heat," he murmured.

"More damage that way," Jake commented. "If you don't feel the heat you don't realize how badly you're burned until it's too late."

Trev deliberately moved a step closer. The flames shot higher, still not providing heat but something more sinister that Trev could only sense. It took some time for the facts to pop up in his head, but when they did he knew he was facing something more than he had expected.

"Not burned. Melted," he said finally. "You don't feel any heat, so you'll venture too close. Once you've gotten within its range, the fire will lick at your skin and instantly melt it like wax. By the time it's finished, you'll be nothing but a puddle on the ground. It will even melt your bones."

Jake grimaced. "Sounds like something out of a bad sci-fi or horror movie. *The Lake That Ate the Town.*"

"This isn't normal magick." Trev crouched and picked up a small stone. He arched back and threw the stone as hard as he could. The men watched the stone hit the barrier and bounce back so hard and fast it buried itself in a tree trunk. "If the stone had hit one of us we'd probably be cleaved in two."

"That still doesn't tell us what kind of magick it is," Jake said.

"It's got to be some kind of power from the earth, but it's nothing I'm familiar with." Trev glanced at him. "Feel like a hike?"

"Sure."

As the two men, each bearing his own special form of magick, walked along, they found a common denominator. They both were fascinated with a witch, and each had their own reason for keeping their distance. Even if they knew deep down it was a losing battle.

"So, girlfriend, tell all. What are you going to wear on your date with the wizard?" Horace asked as Stasi closed out her register. It had been a slow day, so it wouldn't take her long. "You're not going to wear one of those sack dresses are you?" He cast a derisive look over her period costume. "Now, if you were in Regency clothing, I'd say fine. At least they showed off the bod, but what you're wearing covers too much." He tapped a claw against his chin. "Maybe you could borrow something sexy and sassy from Blair. She's got some outfits that could qualify as pretty good slut wear."

"I have very nice date clothes," she pointed out. "And Blair will make you suffer if she hears you calling her clothes slut wear."

"Honey, you haven't been on a decent date in ages and as for getting laid…" he paused, "well, that's been even longer."

"I am *not* discussing my sex life or lack thereof with you."

He perked up. "Will you tell me if the wizard nails you? Come to think of it, maybe you won't have to tell me. Maybe you'll just float in here wearing that post-coital glow. Oh wait! You'll have your phone with you. Maybe you could take a few pictures for my scrapbook. Hey!" His arms and legs windmilled in the air as Stasi picked him up by his wings and gave him a little shake. "Not nice!" He glared at her.

"Then stop acting gross." She held him a couple of inches above the counter then released his wings.

Horace fell to the counter and rolled over. He stood up in a crouch, rubbing his butt.

"You used to be nice," he muttered.

She picked up the moneybag and noticed Bogie had already disappeared from his bed. "Good night, Horace."

"Just remember, it's okay to give a little tongue with a kiss," he called after her.

"I'm telling Jazz to bring Fluff and Puff with her," she caroled as she left the shop, flipping the sign to *Closed* and locking the door. She smiled as she heard Horace's wails of outrage. The gargoyle and the bunny slippers had major issues.

She met Blair, who was also closing up shop.

"Do you want to go down to the Sit 'N Eat?" Blair asked. "I don't know about you, but I don't feel like cooking or even heating up."

"I—ah—I'm having dinner with Trev." Stasi looked across the street, so she wouldn't have to see her friend's reaction.

Blair's lips widened in a knowing smile. "Really?" she drew out the word. "I wonder how this date will go."

"It's not a date." She rounded the side of the building and headed for the stairs leading to the top floor.

"He asked you to dinner?"

"Yes."

"And I'm sure he'll pick up the check."

"He better."

"Then it's a date. This is worth me nuking something for dinner. What are you going to wear?"

"Considering it's going to be thirty degrees tonight, I'm thinking something warm." She picked up Bogie, who had greeted her at the door. Since he wasn't fond of cold weather he usually transported himself from the shop to the apartments.

"Maybe this time you can convince him to persuade Carrie to drop the lawsuit." Blair followed Stasi into her bedroom and headed for her closet, examining the contents. "I have just the thing." She left the room.

"I prefer to cover my legs, thank you very much!" Stasi twisted and waggled her fingers at her back. The hooks released and she quickly peeled off her clothing. "It's not a date!"

"You know, in mortal court you wouldn't be allowed to have dinner with the opposing attorney. I say you go for it. Enjoy your night out—and this is the perfect way to enjoy it." Blair entered the room carrying a hanger in one hand and a pair of shoes in the other.

Stasi stared at the soft wool pants and jacket in a rich shade of periwinkle. What made the outfit outstanding was an off-the-shoulder lace top in dark lavender. Only the thinnest of nude colored fabric separated her skin from the elegant lace, so it would look as if she wore nothing underneath. Once she took off the jacket, she'd be dressed in a way to tease a man's imagination. Blair held up a pair of *come and get me* stilettos that perfectly matched the outfit.

Stasi's lips broadened in a smile as she imagined adding her favorite pearl pendant and earrings to it.

"Oh yes, this will do nicely."

Chapter 8

TREV HAD THOUGHT STASI WAS BEAUTIFUL THE FIRST time he met her, and each time he saw her reinforced that feeling. Tonight she took his breath away. The hint of lace in the neckline of her jacket had him wondering just what was under that soft wool fabric.

"You look lovely," he murmured in her ear as he helped her on with her cream wool ankle-length coat. Her hair was pulled behind her ears with tiny clips holding back the loose curls. He could smell the scent of spring on her skin and hair.

She lowered her lashes with a demure expression on her face. "Thank you." She picked up her bag, which instantly transformed itself from a black leather tote to a small purse that matched her suit perfectly. She slipped the gold chain over her shoulder.

"You kids be good now," Blair chirped from her sprawled position on the couch with a glass of wine nearby. "And have my baby back by midnight."

"She thinks she's a sitcom mom." Stasi headed for the door. "I worry that the day will come when I'll find her vacuuming and wearing a housedress and pearls."

"You care for each other like sisters," he said, as he helped her into his Jag. In deference to the cold weather he'd left the top up.

"We've been friends for so long we feel more like family than any blood relative," she admitted, settling back against the buttery soft leather. She leaned over and placed her hand on his arm as he pushed the keyless start. "May I ask for one thing this evening? No talk about what really brought you up to Moonstone Lake?"

He cocked an eyebrow, as he couldn't resist teasing her. "Even if you were the reason I came up here?"

She frowned at him, schoolmarm at an unruly student. "You know what I mean, Trev."

He was relieved that she felt the same way he did. The last thing he wanted to discuss tonight was business. "Tonight is for us." He clicked on the ignition and backed the car out.

As they drove down the quiet street, Trev noticed a shadow alongside the building that held the general store, which carried everything from hoes to penny candy. It wasn't until a hint of light caught the wispy features that he realized it was a ghost wearing clothing from the 1800s, and he looked upset. He noticed that Stasi saw the ghost also and sat forward a bit. Before either could make a comment the spirit disappeared. Since Stasi didn't say anything Trev thought it best to remain silent.

The drive up the winding road to the resort was short and didn't give them much time for conversation.

"Do you come up here often?" Trev asked.

She nodded. "They offer lovely spa treatments and it makes for a nice getaway." Her grin flashed in the dashboard lights. "Their restaurant also has some killer desserts."

The warm temperature inside the resort's lobby was a welcome change from the night chill as they crossed the carpeted expanse to the dining room's entrance.

Trev gave his name to the *maitre d'* and helped Stasi off with her coat before shrugging off his leather coat.

They were soon seated near a window at a table placed a little apart, offering privacy from the other diners. True to habit Trev took the side that had his back to the wall and where he had a prime view of the foyer. This was the act of a male in protection mode.

The tiniest of smiles tipped Stasi's lips upward. "Ah, the protective wizard. It makes me feel all warm and fuzzy inside." And then she slid her pantsuit jacket off.

Trev almost swallowed his tongue as he surveyed the all too sexy lace top. She had even added a hint of a pearlized powder to her exposed shoulders and collarbones that left her skin gleaming. He reminded himself he had to say something without sounding like a fool, but so far nothing had come to mind.

"Why did you and Blair choose Moonstone Lake?" Trev asked after the waiter brought them their drinks, Johnny Walker Black Label straight up for him and a glass of Chardonnay for her.

She sipped her wine as if figuring out her reply. "In some ways, because of the lake. At that time, Blair and I had been working in a medicine show." She took a deep breath and spoke softly enough that only Trev heard her words. "Step right up, ladies and gentlemen! Right here in my hand I have the cure for all reasons. The cure for all seasons. All you need is Professor Phinneas Peggins' Soothing Syrup. One teaspoon of this magic elixir every morning and night will have your heart singing the *Hallelujah Chorus,* your lungs open and clear, and your bowels will never work better." She laughed softly at Trev's wince, but she didn't stop her patter. "Ladies, you will never worry again about female trouble or monthly hysteria once you take this medicine of the ages. And a teaspoon once a day to your children will have them happy and healthy with never a day sick. Only ten cents a bottle, ladies and gentlemen. One tenth of a dollar. One thin dime. Nowhere can you buy this kind of protection and it's cheaper than seeing a sawbones who will want to cut off your leg and charge you a dollar for it. Don't wait too long because your health is the most important thing there is. Who will be the first to want to keep their vigor?"

He was stunned. "You actually were out there selling that poison?"

"Back then people didn't consider it harmful, although Blair and I were more familiar with what the ingredients could do," she defended herself. "Since we didn't want to see anyone sick or dying from it the way people did from drinking various other forms of those patent medicines, we managed to tweak the professor's formula—which was originally a non-healthy dose of opium. It might not have cured everyone's ills, but it didn't turn them into addicts, either."

Trev grinned. He had seen his share of medicine shows back when they were popular, so he knew any woman in the show was scantily clad to prompt the men to buy. The idea of Stasi in a bit of fluff was tantalizing his senses.

"So what happened?"

"It was a bitterly cold winter that year and to stay warm the professor drank too much of his own medicine. Instead, he didn't wake up," she explained, remembering. "Blair and I were stranded there, out of work, no money because the professor hadn't paid us in months, and the restaurant in town needed waitresses. Not as glamorous maybe, but it was work. Back then Moonstone Lake was nothing more than a tent city and jobs for women weren't plentiful unless you wanted to work in one of the saloons or gambling halls. We were lucky to get what we did. Ginny Chao's great-grandparents were some of the first mortals to befriend us."

"You could easily have conjured up stagecoach tickets and left town."

She shook her head. "We're not allowed to use our magick for personal gain and our obtaining tickets without using cold hard cash would have been considered that." She traced the snowy white tablecloth with her fingertip, her pink polished nail shimmering in the soft candlelight. "When we were expelled from the academy we were told we were fully on our own. We had to make our way using our wits, not our magick. Over the years we discovered it was fascinating to see what we could do to make a living." She wrinkled her nose as if recalling some of her past jobs. "Eurydice wanted to make sure our banishment wasn't easy for us."

"What prompted you to return to Moonstone Lake so often?" he asked.

"I guess a part of it was how we felt about the lake from the first day we were there. It seemed to call to us."

Trev toyed with his glass. "Called to you as in magick?"

She shook her head. "Not exactly. The town wasn't called Moonstone Lake back then. Rain and mud was an everyday occurrence during the spring, and our first spring here had more rain than usual. The lake overflowed its banks. Blair and I were afraid it would flood the town, so we went out there one night to set up protection. What we saw was a lake surface the color of a moonstone. Moonstone means sanctuary. We felt it was a sign for us and we decided to stay as long as we could."

"How long did you stay that first time?"

"Almost ten years. We used some glamour for subtle aging purposes. We found a way to buy the building we have now and we've kept it going all these years. In between times we were here, we rented out the building."

"And now that everyone knows what you are? Will you stay past the time you'd normally leave?" He finished his drink and shook his head when the waiter came by to see if he wanted a second one.

"No, we won't stay. Even with them knowing about us we wouldn't feel right seeing them grow older while they see us stay the same, and even if we used a glamour to appear older for a while, they would know it wasn't so. It would be… hard." She set the menu down.

"How would you feel about *Chateaubriand* for two?" Trev asked when the waiter approached them.

"It sounds wonderful."

A nod of Trev's head had the waiter returning and he placed their orders. "And something tells me the lady would love to indulge in the chocolate soufflé for dessert," he said.

Stasi's mouth watered at the thought of the dessert that the resort's dining room was famous for. And for a second the image of a chocolate-covered Trev entered her mind.

Bad Stasi! Bad!

She quickly brought herself under control. She recalled her resolution to be Ms. Tough Witch and settled back in her chair with a small smile.

"So why did you go into law?"

"Family tradition. Every son has gone into some form of the law."

"Is going into law a tradition you enjoy or one you've felt compelled to follow because it was expected of you? You just don't seem like a lawyer to me," she commented, wrapping her fingers around the stem of her wine glass.

"A tradition I very much enjoy. I like the intricacies of the legal profession and I even practiced a few times among the humans for a while, so I could better understand their law," he replied. "You might not believe it, but law has many challenges and I like nothing better than a challenge."

She studied the expression in his cobalt eyes and was positive he was looking at her as another challenge. The room suddenly felt warm, but even warmer was the heat that simmered deep within her body.

She wanted to fight the attraction she felt for Trev, but no matter how hard she tried to see him as the enemy, she feared she was in the midst of a losing battle. She knew she was in a conflict that would leave behind at least one casualty since there was no chance anything could ever come of this. The supernatural communities were very tightly knit, and veering out of expected protocol wasn't easy. That Jazz and Nick managed to do so was something Stasi envied.

But she couldn't see that happening with Trev and hearts over their heads notwithstanding, she didn't want to think about romance with him. She reminded herself that she was a witch and he was a wizard. She was the defendant in a lawsuit, and when the day came that the case would be heard in Wizards' Court, he would sit at the opposite table and do his best to destroy her life. So why couldn't she just stay away from this man before he took her heart, too?

She enjoyed her simple life, and judging by the cost of the Egyptian cotton button-down shirt and well-tailored wool slacks he wore, she knew he lived a vastly different lifestyle. One she had no desire to share.

So why did the idea that the day would come when he would walk away with her heart bother her so much?

To distract herself, Stasi looked around the dining room, only half filled since it was the middle of the week and skiing season wasn't in full gear yet. Her gaze was arrested by one set of eyes that looked at her as if they wanted to slice her in half.

Stasi didn't know Connie Benton well, other than that the woman occasionally shopped in her boutique around the holiday season for gifts for her nieces. But she did know that the woman was a close friend of Carrie's. There was no missing Connie reaching into her purse and pulling out her cell phone. The woman was faster than the Internet in getting the news out. Stasi had a bad feeling that if Carrie was home, she could end up here and wouldn't be averse to creating a big scene. She mentally urged the chef to cook fast.

Trev noticed her distraction and looked around.

"Someone you know?"

She shook her head. "She's from town and one of Carrie's closest friends. This isn't good."

"There's no crime in our having dinner together. For all the woman knows we're discussing the case. It's nothing new in our world." He dismissed her worries.

"It's a big problem in their eyes. Don't forget that Carrie's idea of the court system is what she sees on television and that has nothing to do with our world at all. The plaintiff's attorney wouldn't be having dinner with the defendant."

Trev leaned back when the waiter set their salad plates before them and the sommelier brought a bottle of *Chateau Latour Pauillac* that Stasi feared cost more than the entire meal.

"If you allow her to bother you, she wins," he said softly. "Is that what you want?"

"Not at all. Especially since I intend to win." She picked up her wine glass and tasted the Bordeaux. "This is very nice."

Stasi did her best to ignore Connie's venomous gaze and enjoyed her dinner. It turned out to be remarkably easy, since Trev kept the conversation going, discussing his travels over the years. They were both surprised to learn they had sometimes been in the same cities at the same time.

"Really? I know that hotel very well!" Stasi exclaimed when he mentioned his frequent stays in Lisbon.

"You stayed there also?"

She laughed and shook her head. "I worked as a maid there for several months. Who knows, I may have made up your bed for you," she teased.

His eyes darkened. "A pity you made it up and not the opposite."

That all too familiar sexual heat flickered to life again as she thought of Trev tumbling her into his bed. She reached for her water glass since she was positive the wine started a major wildfire in her stomach. Judging by the cerulean glow in his eyes, the feeling was definitely mutual.

Trev held up his wine glass. "To a lovely evening and getting to know you better."

Stasi stared at him, convinced the red hearts that plagued her every time she saw him were pulsing to a seductive beat. Coupled with this, she had a wild vision of a naked Trev and herself equally nude lying among tumbled covers. For a moment she couldn't breathe. She was amazed her hand wasn't trembling as she picked up her wine glass and softly clinked it against his, but she didn't say a word. She feared if she did speak it would be closer to the kind of remark Horace would make than the sort of polite words she would ordinarily come up with. If she didn't know any better, she'd swear she was bespelled by the man.

It's Cupid's hearts doing this. It's creating an attraction that wouldn't ordinarily be there.

"*Hic!*" She wasn't sure what was more horrifying—that she had hiccupped or that the bubble floated from her lips to Trev, suspended momentarily in front of his mouth before it winked out of sight. If he had said one word she would have gladly crawled under the table and made herself disappear. Luckily, he settled for a smile and changed the conversation.

Dinner was perfect and by the time the rich chocolate soufflé and coffee arrived, Stasi had forgotten that anyone else existed in the semi-private world their table provided them.

"After the main course I didn't think I could eat another bite," she lamented, staring at her now empty plate. "I'm just glad you helped eat the soufflé so I didn't feel like a glutton."

"I'm a sucker for chocolate too."

She eyed his lean frame. "No one would know it."

"I only indulge on special occasions."

"The great thing about chocolate is that it doesn't need a special occasion." Stasi smiled. "This was very nice, thank you." She noticed a change in his expression. "What is it? Please don't tell me I have something between my teeth."

Trev pulled in a deep breath and blew it out. "Please don't take this the wrong way, but I'd like the chance for us to have more time to talk."

"I thought that's what we were doing now."

"I mean privately." He pulled a plastic card out of his jacket pocket and placed it on the table. "I thought we could go upstairs to my suite where we'd have more privacy."

Stasi stared at the gold plastic key card positive it was pulsing with a life of its own and mouthing the words *say yes*. She found she couldn't ignore the room key card any more than the red hearts over Trev's head or the knowledge she had her own share of the damn images courtesy of Cupid.

"Anastasia?" he whispered her name, his expression showing he was unsure about her response. "Nothing has to happen. I just want to talk to you in a place where we don't have to worry about anyone overhearing our conversation. I'm sure if we went back to your place Blair would be all ears." He flashed a brief grin. "My room is large enough to make you feel comfortable. I want to know more about you and I'm not talking about the case. Please," he added in a whisper that said more than all the words before it.

His plea made her decision easier to make, but that didn't mean she wanted to make it easy for him.

She remained silent for so long, she could tell that Trev thought she was going to reject him.

"One thing I could never get enough of here is their chocolate soufflé," she murmured. "Why don't you see if they'll have one sent up to the room?"

She was surprised to see more relief in his eyes than triumph. That told her she'd made the right decision. He pushed the key card across the table toward her. "It's room 422." He drew his black AmEx out of his wallet. "If you care to go up first, I'll follow after I ask for a soufflé to be sent up to the room."

Stasi picked up the card and left the restaurant, veering left to the elevators. She pushed the button for the fourth floor and walked into the waiting car.

I've lost my mind.

She was blind to her reflection echoing in the mirrors all around her.

How can we be alone in a hotel room and just talk?

She worried the elevator would stop at one of the lower floors and she would lose her nerve, but luckily, it continued upward.

I can't tell Blair about any of this.

Blair will know everything the minute I get back.

She'll probably conjure up a brass band and fire-works to celebrate.

I can't breathe!

The elevator dinged for the fourth floor and then the door slowly slid to one side. Blair stepped out carefully, and walked down the thickly carpeted hallway until she reached the correct room.

"Oh my," she whispered, walking into a luxurious mini-suite. Her gaze swept from a sofa that looked so comfortable she wanted to sink down into it to the open arch that revealed a king-size bed covered in a creamy spread and mounds of pillows in cream, gold, olive green, and dark brown. Proof of occupation was a laptop sitting on a desk near the French doors and a blue sweater tossed on a chair in the bedroom. She had a sudden urge to poke through the drawers and see whether he was a boxers or briefs man. Luckily, she squelched that idea before her thoughts caused the drawers to fly open and reveal their contents. The last thing she wanted was to be caught with her hands in his underwear.

Stasi felt a quick flash of heat as that thought took on a whole new meaning.

She walked over to the French doors leading onto the balcony. The early snowfall—very early, Stasi thought idly—covered the deck floor and standing outside to watch the skiers enjoying the slopes by torchlight after dark would have been comfortable only for a few minutes, before a serious chill set in.

She looked over her shoulder when the door opened and Trev walked in, carrying her coat over his arm.

"You don't stint, do you?" she asked, gesturing to her surroundings.

"I like my comfort." He walked over to the mini-bar and pulled out a bottle of champagne.

Stasi's eyebrows lifted at the label. She wasn't particularly conversant with wines and champagnes, but she knew expensive when she saw it.

I told you this was a bad idea!

Proof positive Blair wasn't in her head. If she had been, she'd be urging Stasi on and requesting she take notes. Not to mention Horace would beg for video.

She laughed at the distinctive pop of the cork and watched Trev pour champagne into two crystal flutes.

"The soufflé will be up in about twenty minutes." He handed one of the flutes to her and held his up for a toast. "To an evening of relaxation and conversation."

She hesitated before tapping her flute against his. "As long as the name Carrie Anderson isn't brought up."

His cobalt eyes lit up with suppressed laughter. "Who?"

Stasi sat on the couch, toeing off her heels before she curled her legs up under her. Her pant leg shifted upward revealing her ankle bracelet.

"I noticed Blair wears one also." Trev indicated the delicate gold chain with its gold broom charm topped by a creamy pearl that matched the ones in her ring and pendant.

"We all wear one because it's a part of us. Each witch has a different stone. Blair's is blue topaz, Jazz's is amethyst, Thea wears a red diamond."

Trev settled on the couch beside her, half turning so he could see her face. He rested his glass on the top of the couch. "I have friends from my days in the Wizards' University, but I don't think I have the closeness with any of them that you have with your friends."

"We were close in school and even more so when we were expelled from the Witches' Academy," she replied, lifting the flute and sipping the bubbly liquid. She took a second sip because the first tasted so good. "After a while, we drifted to different parts of the world, but we always managed to find each other when we needed to." She hid her smile when Trev switched his glass to his other hand and his arm managed to stretch along the back of the couch, his fingertips just touching her shoulder.

"Do you think you need them now?"

She laid her head back against the couch and closed her eyes. "No."

She felt her glass taken from her fingertips and heard the soft clink as it was set on the coffee table in front of them. The cool air was displaced with the warmth of his body as he moved closer and his mouth hovered over hers while his hands cupped her face.

"I thought we were here to talk, Wizard Barnes," she murmured with the tiniest of smiles.

"There are so many ways to speak, Witch Romanov. I've always found this one to be the most effective." He moved his hands up, spearing his fingers through her hair, dislodging the loose knot on top of her head. Her golden brown tresses fell down in careless disarray.

She could taste the champagne he'd drunk, but she also caught a hint of his energy in the unique flavor of the tongue that was gently seeking out hers. All that made him what he was. She found it more intoxicating than the champagne she'd drunk, and she felt the world tilt around her. She gripped his arms with her fingertips; afraid she'd slide off the couch if she didn't hold on to something. Right now, Trev looked like her best bet.

"Anastasia," he murmured, before he deepened the kiss and pulled her into his arms. "From the first moment I walked into your shop I felt as if I was looking at someone not only exquisite, but so beautiful, warm and caring you made me feel I was well and truly alive."

She released a startled laugh. "Obviously, you have a different memory of that moment than I do. I recall that I acted like a virago because I wanted to blast you into another realm. I wanted to turn you into a spiny red-bottomed worm."

Trev's smile was warm against her lips. "You really like to punish a guy, don't you? Is that what you want to do to me now?"

Stasi traced the angle of his jaw with her fingertips. "Well, maybe not at this moment. We'd have to send you to the bottom of the sea to live. Plus you wouldn't look like surfer wizard dude, would you?"

"Ah, but then I would have to retaliate and turn *you* into a spiny red-bottomed worm, so I would have company living at the bottom of the sea." His lips coasted across her forehead and down along the curve of her cheek until they returned to her mouth.

The dizzying sensation returned while Stasi saw Trev's red hearts doing the salsa behind her closed eyelids.

"Stop thinking about them," Trev murmured.

Her eyes popped open. "How did you—?"

"If you saw the expression on your face you'd know." He exhaled a soft breath in her ear, causing her to shiver. "It's just us here. Stasi and Trev. Wizard and witch."

"Wizards and witches get along like cats and dogs. They're oil and water." She smiled under his feather-light touch, and inhaled the faint essence that was a combination of his after-shave and the musky scent of his skin. She knew the former was expensive, but when coupled with the latter she was convinced the scent was priceless.

"Then it's time we throw that old wives' tale out the window and prove them wrong. I can't get enough of your taste." He proved it by trailing his tongue down her neck. He unbuttoned her jacket and opened it to reveal the dark lavender lace camisole she wore with a matching bra underneath. His fingers brushed against her skin as he touched the pearl that rested in her shadowy cleavage. The orb took on a warm glow from his touch. "Between this pearl and the bit of lace that teased me all evening I could have eaten cardboard and not cared." He rested his hand against her chest just under her left breast then moved upward to cup the plump flesh, his thumb teasing her nipple to a point. She hissed in response and closed her eyes to better savor his magickal touch.

By no means was Stasi a virgin, but she had never before felt what she felt merely from Trev's light touch setting her skin on fire.

She felt his mouth skim over her smile.

"Open your eyes, Anastasia."

She lifted her heavy lids and looked into a never-ending sea of blue.

A mere thought had his shirt buttons flying through the air.

Trev barked a laugh as the buttons formed a circle and spun merrily around the room.

"Vixen," he teased, leaning in to kiss her deeply.

Stasi's mouth parted under his and she felt the whirlpool of emotions escalate as he swept her up in an embrace full of passion and desire.

Chapter 9

THE KNOCK AT THE DOOR SEEMED TO BOOM THROUGHOUT the room.

"Damn, damn, damn, damn," Trev muttered, lifting his head. "Someone's timing is very very wrong."

Stasi stifled her giggle—he didn't seem to appreciate the humor in the situation. "I think our soufflé is here."

He stood up, looking down at his buttonless shirt that gaped open even though it was still neatly tucked into his slacks. He pointed his finger at her. "Don't go away."

She held up her hands and this time couldn't hold back her laughter. "I'm not moving a muscle."

Stasi watched Trev do what he did best as he ushered the server in and out with remarkable velocity. The man was sent on his way in no time with a sizable tip.

Stasi looked slowly from Trev, for whom she had a strong desire, to the soufflé, for which she now didn't. She'd never hear the end of it if her friends knew she was willing to pass up chocolate, even if it was for a very sexy man.

She enjoyed looking at Trev, especially with his shirt open showing his bare chest. He was muscular and didn't look like a man who sat behind a desk all day. She swore he glowed like the sun.

"What a shame," she murmured with a tilt of the lips.

Trev tensed, looking like a man who was ready to hear bad news, as in, she'd changed her mind and wanted to go home.

"What's a shame?"

She stood up and reached down to pull her lace camisole up and off. A lace and silk bra of the palest lavender highlighted her pale skin. "That the soufflé will have to grow cold." She walked into the bedroom and began carefully folding down the comforter. "I don't think the hotel would be happy with me if I dabbed it here and there on you."

Trev was floored, but for once he refused to be cautious. He looked at the woman who'd bewitched him, and wondered if it wasn't more than a pun. He wasted no time following her scantily clad form.

Stasi had not quite finished folding the comforter down to the end of the bed before Trev gripped her arms, spun her around, and lowered them both to the sheets.

He knelt on one knee as his mouth started in the hollow of her throat and continued down to the lace edge of her bra.

"Warm, scented sweet and spicy at the same time," he murmured, tonguing a path along the lace.

"Calvin Klein's Euphoria," she said automatically, finding her senses more than a little muddled.

In a twinkling Stasi found her bra gone and cool air bathed her breasts before Trev lowered his head and his mouth warmed them. But she wanted more.

"You're wearing too many clothes." She pulled at his shirttails, tugging them out of his trousers, and then pushed his shirt off his shoulders and reached for his belt. Soon she'd edged his slacks down enough that he was able to kick them off. She got a nice glimpse of the tanned long limbs of a swimmer before Trev moved in.

"Now *you* are." He returned the favor and whisked her pants off, murmuring his approval of the matching lace bikini panties with tiny bows on each hip. "I approve your choice in lingerie."

"La Perla never goes wrong." Her laughter was cut short as he began trailing kisses down the center of her breastbone, making sure to veer off to drop a kiss on each of her nipples, which immediately peaked under his attention.

"You take my breath away," Trev muttered, leaving a kiss in her navel before moving further down.

"Oh my—!" Stasi was positive all the air was pushed out of her lungs as Trev gazed on her pink plump inner lips sparkling with moisture, and she gasped when he placed his mouth there and suckled gently.

"*Hic!*" Stasi was caught up in the sexual cyclone, and her hiccups were coming fast and furious as Trev created a suction that she was convinced turned her body into a firecracker.

She tore at the covers and scrambled to reach his shoulders as he continued the pleasurable kiss that sent her spiraling.

"Trev!" she moaned, feeling the tightness in her body increase until she thought she would fly apart. "*Hic!*" Another iridescent bubble joined its friends floating through the air above them. Pretty soon the ceiling was covered with them.

He drew back just enough that she felt his absence before he leaned in and kissed her again.

"I can't—!"

"You can." And then he hummed against her clit and sent her spinning over like a top. At the same moment he felt her muscles pulse and clench in orgasm, he drew up and buried himself deeply within her.

Stasi immediately linked her legs around his hips and arched up, inviting more. Trev was only too happy to give her all he had.

When she looked up into his face at the moment her second orgasm came, she saw in those blue eyes a look she knew she would never forget. And if she didn't know better she'd have sworn the red hearts winked at her.

"*Stasi!*" Trev's cry was drawn out as he arched upward then down.

Stasi watched the play of emotions cross his face and wondered how she'd ever lived without him.

But she hadn't known him very long and although she thought she should remind herself that witches and wizards don't mix, she only knew that they seemed to be mixing very well right now.

And now she saw her downfall in one man's face. If she thought she was in trouble before, now she knew she was, because it would be much too easy to fall in love with the wizard who had shown up with the intention of destroying the life she'd worked so hard to create. But she knew she had it within her to fight back and she would do just that.

How did my life get this complicated? she mused, just before all other thoughts were swallowed up by the passion that flared between them once again.

Stasi couldn't stop smiling. She started to lift her hand but allowed it to drop back down onto the sheet.

"I can't move." She closed her eyes, content to let the lethargy roll over her. She hadn't just had sex, she'd had *awesome sex*. The kind she read about in romance novels.

"I agree." Trev rolled over and pulled her into his arms. He somehow managed to pull the covers up over them as he moved them up to the head of the bed. He half sat up with his back against the headboard and gently cradled her in his arms.

She draped her arms over his, enjoying the embrace that, to her, meant more than sex. Most men didn't like to cuddle and cuddling was something she liked.

She kept her eyes closed because she feared if she opened them she'd discover it was all nothing more than an erotic dream and she'd be in her own bed... alone.

When Stasi did open her eyes, they widened to the size of saucers as she looked up at the ceiling—it was filled with iridescent bubbles like many delightful tiny balloons that bobbed throughout the room.

"Oh no! *Hic!*" Another bubble floated upward and joined the rest. "Don't laugh!" She twisted around and pounded on his chest, but it only caused Trev to laugh harder.

"I've never seen anyone hiccup bubbles before." He barely managed to contain his mirth. "This is very cute."

"It's horrible." She deliberately plopped back against him as dead weight. She was satisfied to hear a groan.

Trev wrapped his arms around her to prevent her from doing it again.

"The lady needs her treat. Bring it warm. Bring it neat, I so beseech," he called out, snapping his fingers. Another snap of his fingers had *Vivaldi* playing softly in the background.

Stasi purred as the scent of warm chocolate reached her nostrils and a dish appeared in front of her.

"Milady." Trev reached around her, dipped a spoon into the warm chocolate soufflé, and brought it to Stasi's lips. She moaned with delight then took the spoon from his fingers and fed him the next bite.

They shared the dessert along with more champagne.

But the soufflé paled in contrast to the more than magickal night Trev gave Stasi. By the time they left his room, the bedroom was filled with bubbles. Stasi's lips were swollen and her face a bright pink as she thought of all they'd done.

"I have never hiccupped that much in my life," Stasi groused, as Trev helped her into his car. "You should have allowed me to get rid of them."

"No way. I'd rather see the maid's reaction when she comes in tomorrow morning." He picked up her hand and kissed her fingertips

Once they reached Moonstone Lake, Stasi felt an odd shyness overtake her. She looked out and noticed Fergus standing by a building. She'd noticed him there when she and Trev drove out of town. For the ghost to still be there, something had to have happened. When he saw her, she gave him a bare nod and mouthed the word *later*.

"Thank you for dinner," she whispered as he helped her out of his car. She smiled. "And dessert."

He followed the line of her cheek with his fingertips. "I want you again. I don't want to let you go. I want to tuck you back into my car and drive us back to the hotel. I'll order up another chocolate soufflé."

She looked down at the ground. "Part of me feels as if we've been too hasty in making love. That we should have waited. Especially with all that's going on. Part of me is happy we didn't wait."

"Then listen to the latter. That's where the truth lies." His kiss followed his fingers' path.

Stasi went up the stairs, aware of Trev's heated gaze on her back. She touched the doorknob and whispered a word that allowed the lock to disengage. She knew their wards kept them safer than any dead bolt.

"I knew it!" Blair was wrapped in fleece pajamas and fuzzy slippers, lounging in a chair at the table, coffee in one hand and the local newspaper in the other. The Border collie was stretched out on the floor beside her. She huffed out a breath. "It's so unfair! You had sex and all I had in my bed was that dog."

Stasi looked at the dog who appeared to roll his eyes then utter a low snarl at Blair.

"How is sex with a wizard?" Blair asked. "Tell all. I'll hate you later because it was obviously great, but I still want to hear all the details."

Stasi's smile only grew broader. That way she didn't need to say a word. Her facial expression and blush was more than enough.

Blair threw up her hands. "I really hate you."

Chapter 10

"YOU COULD HAVE LIED AND TOLD ME HE WAS LOUSY, so I'd feel better," Blair grumbled.

"I didn't tell you a thing." Stasi concentrated on brewing herself a cup of tea and bringing it to the table. The dog got up long enough for her to pat him on the head, then he returned to his spot by Blair's feet.

"I know you didn't, but you didn't have to. The look on your face when you came in was enough, and the red hearts are positively glowing." She made gagging sounds. "I hate you. I'm stuck with my dolphin vibrator while you're getting the real thing."

The dog suddenly sat up on his haunches and barked.

"Quiet you, besides, you're not my type," Blair told him. "I like my guys with a lot less fur. Trust me, I've known guys who could double as a dog. No thanks."

"Then do something about it," Stasi urged her. "Walk up to Jake and jump his bones. You've wanted to do that anyway, for how long? So just plain do it. Give the man a thrill. You said you want him to add some shelves to that one corner in the shop, so when he's there drag him into the back and have your way with him." She stirred her tea, the spoon continued swirling through the ginger-scented liquid even after she lifted her hand. She toyed with the creamy pearl ring on her right ring finger. The gold warmed under her touch, and the pearl shone with an unearthly glow.

"He always backs off," Blair grumbled. "I'm positive he's interested, but anytime I start to act on what I feel he practically heads for the hills. Besides," she leaned forward across the table, "I'd rather hear about your evening."

"Expensive wine, *Chateaubriand* for two, and we had their chocolate soufflé for dessert." She smiled at the memory of how that second soufflé was consumed. Especially the spoonfuls Trev had placed on her breasts then licked off. Naturally, she had returned the favor.

"Hello!" Blair snapped her fingers in front of her. "Fine, you're going to sit there and glow and let your hearts dance in a conga line." She stood up and whisked her coffee cup and plate to the sink. "I'm going to bed... alone," she stressed to the dog, who'd risen to his feet when she got up. "You snore and shed. We won't even talk about those nasty farts you let loose every so often. At least Bogie doesn't do that."

Stasi couldn't help it. The laughter spilled out of her lips before she could stop it.

Blair glared at her as if she wanted to zap her but good. Instead, she muttered a few words about "friends who won't share" and "wait until I have out-of-this-world, screaming-my-lungs-out sex and I won't give you all the details." The dog promptly dropped flat and covered his eyes with his paws.

Blair didn't quite slam her bedroom door, but it was closed with a finality that stated she was miffed with her best friend. Stasi smiled—she knew Blair would be over it by morning.

She slipped off her jacket and mentally reheated her tea, deciding she'd sit there for a while and enjoy the quiet.

But it wasn't to be.

The faint sound of wind chimes alerted her first. Transparent faces in the kitchen window were her second warning.

"What the Fates?" She sprang out of her chair and ran to the door, pulling it open. Fergus and a young woman dressed in a simple faded calico dress, a white shawl and bonnet with brown hair pulled back in a simple knot, floated inside. What alarmed her the most was the layer of frost on the young woman. She wondered how that could happen to a ghost. The cold weather normally didn't affect them. "Why didn't you just come in?"

"Irene wasn't sure she'd be welcome, Miss Stasi," Fergus explained. "I saw you and that man leavin' town, so I hoped I'd see you when you got back."

Stasi looked at the two, especially Irene. Something was obviously chilling the young spirit.

"What happened, Irene?" she asked softly, not wanting to frighten her.

"I was out by the lake. Fergus told us it didn't look right and I wanted to see what he meant. While I was out there something pulled at me, but I couldn't see what it was." She kept her eyes downcast. "It was like it wanted me to go somewhere. I got scared and managed to get away. I went right back to our realm, because I felt safe there. When I told Fergus what happened he said I should come tell you about it."

A faint tinkling sound brought Stasi to her feet. She walked over to the sink and looked out the window. The two sets of wind chimes that hung over the deck danced in a breeze that she could see didn't affect the trees beyond. That told her the breeze wasn't from the Four Winds.

"Something's out there," she whispered. "Protect us four. Seal the doors. Let no harm come to us, if you please." She waved her hand and immediately felt secure power glide over the building. She knew the moment the spell was complete and felt safer.

Until two glowing green balls bounced off the kitchen window so hard cracks appeared in the glass.

"Godalmighty!" Fergus shouted as Irene screamed and Stasi jumped backwards. "What was that?"

"I have no idea." Stasi watched the balls glide backwards then remain motionless. She felt as if whatever powered the globes was watching them. "Windows, repair and cover if you please!" She was positive the spheres were still out there even with a heavy veil dropped over all the windows. The chill in the air disappeared as the cracks repaired themselves.

She took a deep calming breath and turned around to face the spirits.

Fergus looked as shocked as Stasi felt and Irene cried soundlessly.

"That's what pulled at me, wasn't it?" Irene sobbed. "What do they want? They didn't show themselves before, but I know that's what they were."

Stasi jumped when the phone rang. She placed her hand over her chest to keep her galloping heart where it belonged.

"What now." She glanced at Caller ID, which said wireless caller. "Hello?"

"Stasi? I didn't wake you, did I?"

She breathed a sigh of relief to hear Trev's voice. "No, not in the least."

Trev's voice sharpened. "What's wrong? And don't tell me it's nothing because I can hear it in your voice."

"There are a couple of strange orbs outside the kitchen window. The oddest thing is they bumped against the glass." Stasi lowered her voice even if she doubted the balls had the ability to hear her. Although the way things were going lately, she wouldn't be surprised if the orbs suddenly announced, "We come in peace!"

He muttered a low curse. "What do they look like?"

"I'd say they're the same as what's been hanging over the lake. For some reason they've come into the town, and I don't think their showing up outside our window is a coincidence." An icy chill traveled down her spine. "I warded the doors and the building because I was afraid they would find a way to get in. What if they're all over the town?"

"I'll be there in twenty minutes. Adjust your wards to allow me inside."

"No—!" But he'd already hung up. "Damn him!" She shook her phone, because it was the only thing in close range.

"What's going to happen?" Irene asked finally over her tears.

"There goes Blair's good night's sleep," she muttered, leaving the kitchen. "Even though you're spirits, you can't leave the building, so stay there. I'll be back." She paused long enough to pound loudly on Blair's door. "Wake up! We have company!"

The door opened a crack and a heavy-eyed Blair looked out. "As in what? Notice I said *what* and not *who?*"

"Get dressed. Trev will be here soon." Stasi ran into her room, throwing off her fancy clothing and exchanging it for jeans and a heavy sweater. She dug her fingers into her hair and fingercombed it back and up into a loose knot secured with a few hairpins.

"Since I know neither of us are the threesome types, might I ask why he's coming in the middle of the night and if it's for more sex with you, then just puncture my eardrums now," Blair hollered from her room. She was in the midst of pulling a sweatshirt over her head as she walked into the room. "Are you going to tell me what's going on?" She dropped onto Stasi's bed and pulled on her boots.

"Remember those strange lights over the lake? Two of them are outside the kitchen window." Stasi couldn't resist a quick swipe of lip-gloss. She silently dared her friend to say one word. Blair wisely remained quiet as she twisted her hair up into a ponytail.

"Miss Stasi, that man is here!"

"Fergus too? My cup runneth over," Blair muttered, getting up. "I'll get the door. You might want to add some perfume and a bit of mascara before you meet Wizard Charming." She ducked as a brush sailed over her head.

"I put extra wards on the door!" Stasi called after her.

"Piece of cake." Blair waved her hand over the door and opened it. She looked past his shoulder. "Out of here you two!" she shouted at the glowing balls of light, pushing power at them.

"Don't bother," Trev pushed the door shut behind him. "I tried banishing them, but they merely sucked in the spell. They did nothing to bar me from coming up the stairs, so I'd say they're just watching you and not meaning any harm."

"Sucked in the spell? Are you saying they're not magick?" Stasi ran into the kitchen.

"Nothing that I'm familiar with and I don't think they're the same as the lights over the lake. I think those orbs are able to absorb whatever is thrown at them."

"Can they absorb us?" Fergus asked, crushing his hat between his fingers.

Trev did a double take when he noticed the two ghosts in the kitchen. "I don't know." He glanced at Stasi. "Who are they?"

"Irene and Fergus. They once lived here in town." Stasi was surprised she wasn't blushing when she looked at Trev. Especially after what they'd shared not all that long ago. Amazing what fear did to a witch.

She guessed he'd been in bed since his hair was unruly and the jeans and shirt he'd pulled on were wrinkled. There was no sign of the high-powered wizard attorney now.

"They want us," Irene announced, her voice wobbly with tears. "They want something we have."

"Nothing, no matter what magick is involved, can take you unless it's of your own free will," Blair told her.

Irene shook her head. "No, those lights and what's out at the lake want something we have. They pulled at me and it wasn't gentle-like."

The witches and wizard exchanged looks of concern. Trev shook his head, silently admitting he had no idea and Stasi and Blair were just as stumped.

"Is there a place you can go where you feel safe?" he asked Fergus and Irene.

"We have our own realm. A place where I guess you'd say we rest when we can't come into town," Fergus replied. "But the veils between us and here is thin this time of year, and while most of us don't like comin' here 'cause of the mortals, some of us still like to. But nothin' comes there from here, so I guess we'd be safe there."

Trev shook his head.

"It might not be a good idea to come this year, Fergus," Stasi said, sensing the sorrow already welling up inside him. She knew even ghosts had feelings and tried to make sure never to hurt them. "We don't know what's going on and we need to find out the cause before this can hurt any of you."

"There's others that want us to come here, Miss Stasi," Irene murmured. "My great-great-granddaughter is here and she can see me. She loves to hear my stories about when I was her age."

She closed her eyes. "I know."

Fergus kept shaking his head, and Irene used her sleeve to dab at her eyes.

"We can leave the building?" he asked. The minute Blair nodded he took Irene's hand and they winked out of sight.

"I'm sorry. I guess I brought you out here for nothing."

Trev pulled Stasi close to his side. "I wouldn't say it's nothing if those orbs were somehow fueled by what's going on at the lake."

"If you two will excuse me I'm going back to bed. I'm sure that lazy dog's taken all the covers by now. Good night." She waved over her head as she walked to her room.

The minute they were alone, Trev folded Stasi into his arms. She slid her arms around his waist and rested her cheek against his chest, hearing the comforting thump of his heartbeat.

"They did unnerve me," she admitted in a tiny voice.

"Little Peeping Toms." He used his fingertips to lift her chin. "I'm going to take advantage of the moment, Anastasia." His lips slanted over hers, his tongue wrapping itself around hers and teasing it back into his mouth to play.

Trev's scent was as addictive as the man himself. She closed her eyes, remembering them lying in his bed. Trev trailing kisses up and down her body, teasing her until she alternately cried for mercy and threatened dire curses on him if he didn't give her release. She felt the heat from his skin against her cheek and recalled his mouth doing things to her that would have been illegal in some realms. As if she cared when he was doing such wonderful things to her.

"I'm not an empath, but you're projecting so loud I'm surprised even Blair isn't feeling this," he whispered against the curve of her ear.

Stasi could feel the heat of her blush race across her cheeks. She parted her lips when his forefinger traced the seam, then she fastened her teeth on the digit. She felt so comfortable in his embrace.

He's the enemy! her head reminded her.

He has red hearts over his head! her nether regions argued. *Remember how he made us feel not all that long ago. Oooh baby!*

He'll only hurt you. He's got a reputation as a ladies' man. Oh honey, how many orgasms did he give you?

She should have known her nether regions had slutty aspirations.

Listening to her lower half, she edged her fingers between his shirt buttons and encountered warm skin.

When that wasn't enough, she released two buttons, giving her enough room to slide her palm inside. She noticed his breathing grew more ragged as her fingers splayed wide across his chest.

He slipped his hand under her sweater and cupped her breast with his palm, gently kneading her softness. Her nipple peaked under his touch.

"One good silence spell and we could be in your room in seconds."

"I don't think that would be a good idea," she replied, mentally kicking her nether regions' saucy ideas out of her head.

He nodded and rested his chin on the top of her head. "I know you're right even if I want to disagree." He dropped a kiss against her hair and walked back into the kitchen. He looked out the window and Stasi, standing behind him, could see the spheres were gone.

"It wouldn't hurt to ward the doors again after I leave," he told her, kissing her until she was senseless, then he hurried out before he gave in and tried to change her mind to allow him to stay.

As he walked down the stairs Trev sensed the power of the wards Stasi set. He left, knowing she would be safe behind the protection spells.

But it did nothing for the way Trev felt in leaving her. He cursed the hard-on of all hard-ons as he climbed into his car and put it into gear. He would have preferred spending the rest of the night with a warm and willing woman. Especially one he already knew was as generous in bed as she was in every aspect of her life. Instead, it looked like he'd be spending it under a cold shower. He made the return trip to the resort in record time.

Trev shed his clothes on the way to his bathroom and stepped into a shower that dropped water so icy it was amazing he didn't turn into an icicle.

As it was, the cold shower did nothing, as his erection didn't droop a speck.

In the end, he took things in hand, so to speak. With Stasi's delicate face firmly planted in his mind it only took a few pumps of his hand to bring him to orgasm.

He only wished it had been her hand or her lips on him.

"Are you going to smile or cry?"

Stasi looked up from her slumped position on the bed. Blair, now in her robe, stood in the doorway. "Maybe a little of both."

Blair's eyes widened. "The hearts are working."

Stasi flopped back onto the bed. "I hate those hearts! I wish they'd just disappear! Do you know how hard it is to look at him and not see them? To ignore them if we're around humans who can't see them?" Stasi slid up the bed until she sat against the headboard. Bogie materialized from his bed and curled up on the pillow beside her.

Blair dropped on the end of the bed and sat cross-legged.

"Jazz just called. She said she had a sense something was wrong up here."

"That's an understatement," Stasi said dryly. "Did you tell her what happened so far?"

"I told all." Blair's smile grew wider.

"You didn't!" Stasi grabbed her pillow and threw it at her friend. "How could you tell her that Trev and I—!" She faltered.

"Danced the horizontal tango? Bumped pretties, because no way I can say bumping uglies. Hit the mattress. Augh!" She ducked as a trickle of ice-cold water dripped from a small glass floating over her head. "No, I didn't tell her about Trev, but it shows where your mind went. She'll figure it out on her own anyway. She asked why you left a message only saying we had some problems as if it's nothing major when it's a lot more than that. I told her it's best she see it for herself. She said she and Nick will be up tomorrow night."

"The more help the better," Stasi said, meaning it. She knew if there was a major problem, they'd need all the help they could get.

And if anyone was good at solving problems, it was Jazz Tremaine.

Chapter 11

STASI RAN DOWN THE BACK STAIRS AS A LARGE BLACK Lincoln Navigator slowed to a stop by the bottom. She shaded her eyes with her hand until the bright headlights were switched off. The sounds of bickering could be heard through the closed windows and grew more heated as doors opened and the six occupants climbed out into the cold night air.

"All I said was that there was no reason why we couldn't make one more teensy weensy stop," Jazz pointed out, following Nick to the back of the SUV. "Do you know how hard it is to find sno-balls nowadays? It's not like I can walk into any grocery store and find them. That mini-mart carries them all the time, both the pink and the white ones. I always stop to stock up on my way up here! It wouldn't have taken me longer than a couple minutes to run in and grab up whatever they had."

The tall vampire's jaw was locked so tight Stasi was amazed it didn't snap. She was positive he'd be flashing some fang next. Clearly Jazz was now working on his last nerve, and it was rapidly shredding. "We were already running late, Jazz. Don't worry, we'll stop there on the way back and you can stock up on your precious sno-balls so you can go on a coconut marshmallow covered cake binge to the point where you'll be moaning and groaning with the stomachache of all stomachaches. But we'd already made enough stops. There was no reason to keep Stasi and Blair up any later than we had to." He stepped over to hug Stasi and drop a quick kiss on her forehead before he moved to the back of the SUV and opened the rear cargo hatch, hauling out suitcases and tote bags.

"As entertaining as the two of you are, next time let's have a movie playing for the rest of the inmates. There is a DVD player and screens in there, you know?" Krebs, Jazz's mortal roommate, helped Nick sort out the luggage. He groaned as he pulled out one obviously heavy bag. "What is it with you women and tons of luggage? We're only going to be here several days."

"You men are handsome all the time. We women need more work." Letiticia touched the back of his neck with her slender porcelain-pale fingers. He instantly smiled back at the lovely vampire who had captured his heart.

"At least, now I can go inside and not be out here freezing to death," Irma grumbled as Sirius hopped out of the vehicle after her. The ghostie mastiff immediately zoomed in on a nearby tree to mark it as his.

"What is it about you always claiming you're going to freeze to death during the winter or roast to death during the summer when, hello? you're dead!" Jazz picked up a tote bag.

"Blair, the kids are here!" Stasi laughingly called upstairs.

"Very funny." Jazz ran over and hugged her tightly. "Just because Nick doesn't need to make stops doesn't mean there aren't others that have to," she whispered in her ear.

"No one can have to make that many bathroom stops unless they have a bladder the size of a pea." Nick's preternatural hearing meant he didn't even have to eavesdrop.

"We had to make a total of three stops and he acts like it was thirty." Jazz directed a stern look at the two bunny slippers, who slid out of the vehicle wearing hungry eager expressions on their furry faces and looked around for their next opportunity for mischief. "You'd better keep your promise to behave or you won't be taking any road trips for centuries."

Fluff chattered away, bending one ear then straightening it in an *aye aye sir!* gesture while Puff sighed, rolled his dark eyes, and bobbed a reluctant yes.

"Don't give me the Boy Scout routine because neither of you would have been allowed in," Jazz reminded Fluff. "And luckily, you never ate one, either. That I know of."

The slippers chattered away as they raced up the stairs.

"So you're all right with Krebs and Letiticia dating?" Stasi whispered. She knew Jazz hadn't been happy when Krebs started seeing a vampire. Letiticia was a client of Krebs'; he designed and maintained social websites meant for the supernatural communities and they'd met online.

Jazz grimaced. "Not completely, but we have an understanding. She doesn't lay a fang on Krebs and I don't push her outside on a bright sunny day."

Stasi chuckled. "That will work."

Frenzied barking sounded from the top of the stairs and intensified as Bogie floated downward. The small dog snarled and snapped at the slippers, who had stopped halfway up the stairs but didn't look the least bit intimidated by his canine warnings. He showed more restraint at the sight of Sirius.

"You behave, too," Stasi chided the dog, who quieted down but still displayed a curled lip to show he wasn't taking any guff from reprobate bunny slippers.

"You have no idea what this trip has been like. Not only did Jazz say I couldn't smoke during the trip, the others backed her up. If you want to get technical, the only one who might be bothered by the smoke is Jonathon, and he's such a gentleman, he wouldn't have minded." Irma started to hug Stasi then backed off as she remembered that as a ghost she'd only go through the witch, leaving a nasty cold sensation behind. "And don't you look pretty tonight! What a shame you had to stay up for us. Nicky was late picking us up," she confided.

"And you look ready for the cold weather. It's not all that late now that the days are already growing shorter." Stasi smiled as she admired Irma decked out in gray wool pants, a soft blue, green, and pink print sweater, and a pink fur-lined parka. Once Jazz had found the right spell to allow the ghost to update her wardrobe, Irma had tossed out her 1956 navy floral dress and gone wild for modern clothing. Even her gray perm was gone now, and she sported soft waves in a becoming shade of ash brown. The only habit from the 1950s she hadn't given up was her love for Lucky Strikes, even though Jazz had loudly decreed the car and the carriage house were no smoking zones.

"She wanted to wear ski pants, but I told her no way." Jazz stamped her Ugg-shod feet on the ground and tucked her hands inside her jacket. "I love Samhain, but I do wish it happened during a warmer time of year. Has Thea shown up yet?"

Stasi shook her head. "She retreated to Paris for some *haute couture* therapy. She's in mourning."

"What happened?"

She leaned over to murmur, "Her latest book didn't make the *New York Times* bestseller list."

Jazz reared back. "But she at least made the extended list, right?"

Stasi shook her head. "Not even *USA Today*."

Jazz's coral-glossed lips formed an O. "Whoa. She must be having a major meltdown. Ever since book lists were invented, her books under any of her pseudonyms have always been in the top ten for weeks."

"It didn't happen this time and saying she's not happy is an understatement," Stasi whispered as if afraid of being overheard.

"Then it's a good thing she's not coming. If she's having a witchy hissy fit it's better she destroy her own belongings and not yours."

"Very true," Blair agreed, running down the stairs and hugging each in turn. "We have wine waiting along with a pot of coffee on. We know Nick can partake and I assume you can, too?" she asked Letiticia.

"I can, thank you." She smiled. "I've never been up this way, so I'm looking forward to celebrating Samhain with you."

"We have plenty of guest rooms upstairs, but there's also special rooms fixed up in the basement," Stasi said.

"I want to make snow angels." Jazz hopped onto Nick's back and wrapped her legs around his waist and arms around his neck, dropping a quick kiss on his cheek. "Can't you see this big bad vampire as an angel?" She grinned.

"How many espressos have you had?" Stasi asked, guessing the source of Jazz's energy.

"Five, six triple shots, who's counting?"

"Hence all the bathroom stops," Nick muttered, but there was still a devilish light in his dark brown eyes, as he walked Jazz over to a fresh pile of snow and arched backward, dumping her. She shrieked as the snow slid down her collar. With a speed that almost rivaled his, she grabbed his arm and pulled him down next to her.

Stasi laughed. She knew if Nick hadn't wanted to be pulled down into the snow, he wouldn't have allowed Jazz to get the better of him. She envied their banter and play as lovers who'd known each other for centuries. And she knew the trouble they'd had in the past. She was pleased to see they were beyond that.

"Honestly, get a room, you two!" Blair called out on a note of laughter. "It's going to be a blast having you all here." She ushered them upstairs. "We haven't had anything close to a full house for some time. This feels very right."

"Tell us what's going on with the lake and what happened last night," Jazz said, once they were settled in the family room with glasses of wine.

Stasi began with the night she and Blair had discovered the barrier and odd lights over the water then told about Trev's spell and how it was destroyed, and ended with the previous night's orbs outside the window.

"When we woke up this morning there was a heavy snowfall and no sign of the orbs," she finished. "But there was the sensation that something had tested the wards on the building. I think if they hadn't been strong enough, whatever those orbs were would have gotten in."

Jazz was curled up in an oversized linen-colored chair with brick red and moss green pillows behind her. Nick sat on the floor beside the chair, leaning against Jazz's leg, and the bunny slippers snoozed on top of her Ugg boots that lay on the floor.

"I wonder why it wouldn't allow you to get too close or even figure out what it is?" Jazz mused out loud. She leaned over and picked up her boots, dislodging Fluff and Puff, who grumbled at being ousted from their soft bed. "I want to see the lake." She pulled on her Uggs and stood up.

Krebs looked over from his prone position on the moss green couch, with his head resting on a linen-colored pillow set on Letiticia's lap as she stroked his hair away from his forehead. "Now? It's one o'clock in the morning!"

"You don't have to go, Krebs." Jazz looked down at Nick with an expectant air. He sighed and stood up with fluid grace. "You don't need to go with us," she told Stasi and Blair, who likewise stood up.

"It might be a good idea to keep the power base strong in case there's something else out there," Stasi said.

"Then we may as well make it a group field trip." Krebs glanced at Letiticia, who nodded.

Irma continued to rest in an easy chair with Sirius lying at her feet. "I hope you all don't mind that I stay behind."

"Works for me." Jazz grinned, pulling her coat back on.

"More snow," Stasi groaned, when they walked outside and found the heavy white flakes falling in silence. Their boots crunched on the cold ground.

"You usually don't have snow this early." Jazz looked around.

"Considering everything else, it's not surprising." Blair adjusted her rust wool cap down around her ears and pulled on matching mittens. Stasi wore a matching set in teal blue.

"Does the lake ever completely freeze?" Krebs asked, dodging a low-hanging tree branch.

"No, and that has surprised us because we've had cold enough winters for it to happen," Stasi replied. She stopped and looked down the path. "You can see the lights even from back here." She pointed straight ahead.

They all stood quietly and watched the dance of green lights perform a ballet in the air.

"Nothing like this has happened in all the years we've come here. Why now?" Jazz voiced the question Stasi and Blair had been asking themselves.

Jazz slowed down when they moved past the trees. The three witches stood side by side, staring in horror at the lake that had centered them for so many years. Instead of the usual serene silver blue surface, the water was frothing dark blue with black waves, as if a volcano boiled deep within it.

The barrier was still crisscrossed with green and black stripes, and the cobalt ring around the edge that Trev had laid down in a powerful spell lay in pieces.

"Yikes!" Jazz shook her head. She cocked her head to one side as she studied it. "This doesn't make any sense. The only way an obstacle like this could happen is with the use of mega-watt magick. Yet, I can't even feel any form of power coming from the barricade. Maybe the wizard's spell did enough harm that now it just needs a little help coming the rest of the way down." She held up her hand revealing a roiling orange-red flame that was triple the size of what she normally conjured up.

"*No!*" Stasi and Blair shouted at the same time Jazz threw the fireball at the barrier.

"Fuck!" Nick grabbed Krebs by the collar and threw him to the ground then hit the dirt as Letiticia also dropped flat.

The moment the fireball hit the barrier, a roaring sound assaulted their ears as a wall of flame swiftly covered the surface and flared back at them. Stasi, Blair, and Jazz were thrown backwards, pushed forcefully among the trees.

"Ow!" Stasi winced as her back connected with a tree trunk. She glared at her friend. "The barrier has its own protection. I told you what happened when Blair first tried to get it to reveal itself when it was totally invisible to us. Did you honestly think a fireball would make a difference?"

Jazz picked pine needles out of her hair. "Anyone can make a mistake," she muttered in self-defense.

"Not when you almost turned us all into torches." Nick glared at her as he stood up.

"Damn, woman." Krebs got to his feet and helped Letiticia up. "I should have known better. You had to go all big bad witch, didn't you? What's your next plan? Blowing up the whole town?"

"Okay, sometimes I get carried away. And this turned out to be a bad idea." Jazz groaned as she slowly rose to her feet and approached the barrier with belated caution. She winced as flames licked along the ground. She looked over her shoulder. "I thought you said the fire held no heat?"

"It doesn't."

"It does now." Jazz backed up until the flames died down. She used the tip of her boot to draw a line in the dirt then stepped over the line, watched the flames flicker upward then disappear when she stepped back. "And no protection spell seems to work?"

"The one Trev cast was destroyed within a few hours," Stasi said, gesturing to the broken ring.

Nick was even more cautious as he moved closer to the line Jazz drew in the dirt.

"This feels very old," he murmured and glanced back at Letiticia who nodded her agreement. "A type of magick not used very often."

"It's as if the barrier was formed from the water itself," she said. "Definitely an old magick."

"But if it was formed from water how did the flames survive?" Stasi asked, intrigued by the female vampire's observation.

"With some forms of water magick cold fire can exist even around water." She appeared deep in thought as she moved forward in her graceful glide and stood next to Nick. "I've felt something like this before, but I can't recall where or even who created it. It was many years ago. Possibly the 1600s." She turned to Nick. "You also could sense it was old. Does it seem familiar to you?"

He shook his head. "As an enforcer, I didn't deal much with the magick community. We were more concerned with rogue vampires, not so much with what witches, wizards, and sorcerers did."

Stasi moved forward to stand at the line in the dirt. She licked her lips, afraid to say the word that had finally slipped into her brain and stayed there like a dark stain.

"What if this is the work of a warlock who works water magick?" she whispered.

Sharp indrawn breaths from Blair and Jazz echoed the fear in Stasi's voice.

"Don't say that." Blair stepped forward and gripped her shoulders. "Don't even think it."

"What if it is? It's nothing any of us has ever seen. The lake is virtually a prisoner inside this barrier. It must be either very old or something so dark we weren't taught how to fight it."

"I may not know exactly what it is, but I do know it's not the work of a warlock."

Stasi turned at the sound of a familiar voice. She wasn't surprised to see Trev standing there, nor did she even wonder how he came to be out here in the middle of the night. Magick calls. But she was a bit startled to see Jake standing next to him.

"Am I seeing what I think I'm seeing?" Jazz stared slightly above Trev's head then slightly above Stasi's, who winced.

"Yep, it's exactly what you think you're seeing," Blair said under her breath. "Scary, isn't it?"

"And I thought it was bad when Mother Nature got even with me for accidentally calling down thunder."

"Problem at hand, please!" Stasi snapped before turning to Trev. "You're that sure?"

He nodded, unfazed by her challenge. "A warlock wouldn't have been able to destroy my spell."

"Sure of yourself, much?" Jazz taunted.

Trev walked toward them. "Jasmine Tremaine, curse eliminator and driver for All Creatures Car Service. You own a 1956 T-Bird convertible haunted by one

Irma Carmichael formerly of Jasper, Nebraska, who killed herself in the car leaving her cursed to haunt it. You've only recently been able to release her from the vehicle that's been in your possession since 1957. You live in Santa Monica with a mortal, Jonathon Shaw III." He nodded toward Krebs. "You've made a name for yourself by finding a way to destroy a man who had dealt in the black arts to further his life span by draining vampires of their life force. Then, not to be outdone, you went toe-to-toe with an Elven noble, killed a powerful wizard who had broken his share of wizard laws, and made an enemy of the director of the Vampire Council. All of which has frustrated the Witches' Council and added to your years of banishment. You don't choose to make life easy for yourself, do you?"

"Wow, I had no idea I was so well known. But what can I say? I don't always play well with others," Jazz shot back. "You must be the wizard ambulance chaser who thinks he's going to best Stasi in court. Guess again. We've given the Witches' Council the mother of all migraines. Do you honestly think the Wizards' Court can put the fear into us? Because if you mess with one of us, you get all of us. We're a package deal."

Nick covered his face with his hand. "Subtlety, love," he murmured. "Try it."

Stasi hid her smile. "She doesn't know the meaning of the word. Besides, this could be fun."

"Your client is a nutcase," Jazz spoke as if she was talking about nothing more serious than the weather. "She's a vicious human being who isn't happy unless everyone else around her is unhappy. You might not admit it, but I just bet she's making you miserable, too.

Carrie likes to play the victim, but she's not even close to being one."

"For someone who doesn't live here, you seem to know her pretty well," Trev commented.

"I've been up here often enough to meet her, and what I've seen isn't pretty. I'm not a lawyer, thank the Fates, but I'd say Carrie won't give the impression of a pathetic victim when you go to court." Jazz's smile was more feral than pleasant. "By the time she's finished, the judge will be only too happy to throw her in the deepest, darkest dungeon around and throw away the key."

Trev kept his hands in his pockets and studied her face. "I'm glad you're on Stasi's side. Do you think you can persuade her to find herself an attorney to represent her?"

She waved her hand. "Already taken care of."

Stasi straightened up. "What? Jazz, I don't—"

"Later."

Trev looked from Jazz's set features to Blair to Nick, Krebs, and Letiticia. "Contrary to what you all believe, I have no intention of hurting Stasi. I want her protected just as much as you do, but I also have my client's interests to protect."

"Then tell her, her best bet is to back off," Blair snapped.

"I'm not the enemy here." He looked at Stasi. "Or am I?"

She feared she was blushing and that everyone could sense the heat coming off her skin or see the hearts were doing more than pulsing with dazzling color. She kept few secrets from Blair, but she hadn't confessed her feelings about Trev, because they were still jumbled up and she needed time to sort them out.

"We're opponents," she said quietly. "The lake is our problem, Trev. I thank you for your help before, but we can take it from here." She forced herself to look coolly into his eyes, seeing the cobalt blaze flicker to life as he read the truth in her eyes.

She was rejecting him.

"You know I can help you," he spoke in a voice so low only she could hear him. "There is nothing Carrie can do about it, either."

She stilled the war going on in her stomach and her heart. "When it all comes down to it, you are the enemy, Trev. You're right. You need to protect your client's interests. And I need to protect mine."

"We all need to work together," Jake said.

"What's this 'we,' handyman?" Blair taunted. "What do you expect to do? Hammer good sense into Carrie's hard head?"

He grinned. "You'd be surprised what I can do, witchy woman. Come on, Trev." He moved off. "Remember what I said about Jazz and her accuracy with fireballs?"

"It's not over," Trev murmured to Stasi.

"You're right, it's not, but that's only because we haven't gone to court yet." She swallowed the lump in her throat as she watched the two men walk away.

"When did they do the male bonding thing?" Blair asked.

"I don't know, and it worries me." Stasi looked back at the barrier. "I'm cold. Let's go back to the house."

"I can make a few calls and see if anyone has heard of this," Letiticia offered during their return.

"That would be great, thank you." Stasi's reply sounded distracted as she thought of Trev and his reaction to her rejection. She knew it had to be done. She needed to put some distance between them. So why did it feel so wrong?

Chapter 12

Stasi was positive the ear-splitting screech that filled the air shredded every nerve ending and shattered glass from here to Alaska. She jumped out of bed and threw on the jeans and sweater she'd discarded only a few hours earlier.

"That's Horace!" Blair ran out of her room while Jazz emerged from one of the guest rooms.

"He'd only do that if someone broke into the shop," Stasi said.

"We need to protect the others." Jazz's coppery red hair flew around her head in snarls as she muttered a few words, sealing the room Krebs and Letiticia slept in along with her own room where Nick rested. The fact that her heavy forest-green wool sweater was inside out showed that she was still half asleep. She waved a hand to close her jeans while Fluff and Puff protested being awakened so early by her jamming her feet into them the minute she jumped out of bed.

"Nick will have your head for keeping him out of this," Blair told her as she watched the spell cover the door.

"I'd rather he not be out there until we know what's up," she said grimly. "He was in morning rest, but if Horace keeps it up he'll be awakened and fear the worst."

"What is that unearthly sound?" Irma demanded, popping up with the dog standing by her side.

"Go back to bed, Irma," Jazz ordered.

Stasi tasted the metallic flavor of fear in her mouth and heard a roaring in her head that had nothing to do with the intensity of Horace's screeches. "Someone's broken into the store." She ran for the back door and threw it open, practically flying down the stairs and running around to the front of the building. She would normally have gone through the rear door of the shop, but she knew she needed to see the front. She slid on the icy surface of the sidewalk, almost falling as she skidded to a stop and saw revealed in the early morning light what her intuition already knew.

She blinked back tears that froze to her eyelashes as she stared at the catastrophe that had once been her and Blair's shops. Frosty air blew through the broken windows covering the front of the building. Black paint had been splattered everywhere, showing flecks of ice as it froze to the wood. She could see obscene words spray painted on the walls inside and nothing of value had been left untouched. Even the weathered pine building showed deep gouges and slashes as if someone had gone after it with an axe.

"Oh no." For once Jazz was shocked enough only to whisper the two words, but without missing a beat she started to chant under her breath.

"No." Stasi's voice was a bare breath of air as she placed her hand on Jazz's arm, effectively stopping her before Jazz finished the spell that would pull the wrongdoers back to the scene of the crime. She knew Jazz and Blair would make mincemeat out of whoever had vandalized the two businesses, and right now she didn't want to see them. She started to teeter-totter back and forth, aware of a strange roaring in her head that left her feeling as if all the oxygen had been sucked out of her brain. Her blood had turned to ice and she feared no amount of heat could warm her. "Please." The word came out as a strangled sob.

"Honey, don't." Blair grabbed hold of her before she fell to the ground while Jazz caught her on the other side. She stared at the disaster in front of them with disbelieving eyes that also held a glimmer of tears. "I don't understand this. Why didn't our wards work? They've never failed us before. What had enough power to bypass them?"

"Having a problem?"

Stasi spun around to find Carrie standing on the other side of the street with a coffee to-go cup in one hand and a large bag from the bakery in the other. The woman's smirk was more than Stasi could take.

"Looks like I'm not the only one who sees you for what you are," she called out. Stasi started to step off the sidewalk.

"Don't, Stasi," Trev's voice rang out from nearby. He walked quickly toward her, standing in front of her before her second foot left the curb. "You'll only bring the wrath of the Wizards' Court down on you. It's not worth it."

"The Wizards' Court has nothing to do with me. You vindictive little—" Jazz stalked across the street. Blair was swift on her heels with equal fury blazing in her eyes.

Carrie held her stance even as she watched the two furious witches coming toward her. The air was thick with anger and their magick, their hair waving around their heads in the icy air, and multi-colored sparks flying about looking for a target, which just happened to be standing across the street from them. She realized she was their objective and almost lost her balance as she backed up a step, but she managed to save her footing in time.

"Are you proud of yourself, Carrie?" Blair gritted out, gesturing backwards toward the destroyed storefronts. Dark blue sparks shot from her fingertips and settled to the ground. "This isn't just vandalism, this is pure hatred and even if you didn't do this yourself, you know who did because you had to have been behind it!"

The woman lifted her chin, her lips narrow and colorless under a thin application of lipstick. "Why would I bother myself with your ugly little shops? I tell people not to buy there. That your merchandise is inferior."

Blair ignored this and closed in on Carrie, who took another step backward, avoiding the sparks. "But you seemed to have forgotten something. Stasi's the nice one. She's the one who dreams of romance and she doesn't believe in retaliation. I'm the one who's extremely gifted in the art of revenge. Or did you happen to forget what happened to Gina Carson's husband last year after he cheated on her and she wanted him to pay for that?"

Jazz stepped closer. "You've never been cursed, have you, Carrie? Never seen what can happen to someone who's been well and truly hexed." Her purr was soft and insidious as her moss-green eyes gleamed and her lips broadened in a daunting smile. "And the range of curses out there is truly amazing, if I do say so myself. Some curses are fairly mild, a nasty case of hives or projectile vomiting for a few days, or weeks, but then there are the unforgettable ones. I've seen curses where nasty-smelling pus oozes out of every pore in your body and there's no way to cure it. Or maggots cover every inch of your body and no matter what you do, they don't fall off. Or your skin literally peels itself away." The bunny slippers looked up and gnashed razor-sharp teeth that were rumored to have consumed their share of mortals.

"If you use a spell it will reflect on *her*," Carrie sneered, holding her ground.

Jazz took another step forward. "There's nothing that says I can't bitch slap you back to the Paleolithic period."

"Stop it, Jazz!" Stasi's voice snapped like a whip. Her power flew across the street ahead of her like a sheet of ice as she walked toward the three women. She didn't take her eyes off Carrie the entire time. "Leave us."

Blair arched an eyebrow and opened her mouth, ready to argue that she wasn't leaving her friend. Jazz merely smiled and pulled on Blair's arm. Amid Blair's muttered protests, the two women returned across the street to where Trev stood still, his face unreadable.

Stasi didn't say a word as she kept her eyes on Carrie.

"You can't touch me." Carrie's voice was full of false bravado. "Did you think I wouldn't find out you had a cozy dinner with *my* lawyer?"

"Be careful, Carrie, you're sounding like a jealous lover."

Carrie's face turned bright purple. "Everyone thinks you're this sweet little thing, but it's all fake, isn't it? You didn't think someone would stand up to you, did you? Did you fuck him in hopes he would convince me to drop the suit? No way that will happen. You ruined my marriage, and I want you to pay for it. And if you do anything to me, I'll make sure he brings you up on charges. You don't think I'm very smart, but I know enough about your kind of law that punishment would be a hundred times worse than anything my courts would do to you."

"I don't have to touch you, Carrie," Stasi said softly, but each word was steel coated and her eyes burned with an icy fury. "You're not worth any pain the Wizards' Court would hand out."

"You deserve to be ruined." Spittle flew out of Carrie's mouth. "And don't threaten me with your black spells. If anything happens to me or if Trevor says he's dropping me as a client, I'll find a lawyer who will make sure you're punished."

"I don't use baneful magick and I don't threaten. I only make promises and in all my years I have never broken a promise." Her stone-cold gaze bored into the woman. "Besides, you're not worth the effort. You're a shallow, cold-hearted woman who hates the world because you feel it's wronged you. You were that way as a child and you still are." Her smile held no warmth as she noted the flicker in Carrie's eyes. "I have a long memory, Carrie. As a child, you were cruel to other children, and some of them still carry the scars. You and I both know your husband didn't leave you because I cast a spell. He left you because he saw you for what you are and he found a woman who loves him and doesn't want to control him." She shook her head. "You're not angry because he left you. You're angry because deep down you know you're incapable of making any man happy."

Carrie's face mottled with rage. "*Witch! Witch!*" She made it sound like the vilest of curses.

For a moment Stasi's stomach filled with acid as old memories of that shrieked accusation assaulted her mind. By sheer force of will she managed to hold on to her composure and walked away from Carrie and her vehemence.

Trev's expression gave her no hint of his thoughts as he passed by Stasi and walked toward Carrie. Once he reached her, he lowered his head until his lips almost touched her ear, speaking for several moments. She calmed visibly, and he led her away down the street. Not once did he look back. Stasi reminded herself she didn't expect him to, but it still hurt.

She covered up her pain with the reminder she had told him to leave her alone, that Carrie was his client and she knew the woman was his priority.

Just as right now, her main concern was cleaning up her and Blair's shops as best she could. As it was, their shops wouldn't be re-opening for a couple days.

"Why do they always have to use the cheap black paint?" Jazz grumbled, zapping open Stasi's door and stepping inside. "This is just gross! Oh yeah, real original, assholes. At least learn how to spell correctly and come up with something more innovative than the old standbys!" She stared at a rear wall scrawled with obscenities. She took one look at Stasi's shocked expression and smiled reassuringly. "Don't worry, we can take it all away."

"*Damn* it! That was the last original Scrabble game I had!" Blair could be heard wailing as she moved through her shop. "I'm putting out some search spells and when I find out who did this, I'm kicking some serious ass into the next century."

"You took your time getting in here! Someone almost put an axe through me!" Felix wailed from his spot on the wall. "Half of my tail is gone," he moaned, as his newly bobbed tail swung back and forth in perfect time.

"Be grateful. You're about the only thing not destroyed," Blair growled, picking her way through the debris that littered the floor. "They snapped the heads off all the Madame Alexander dolls! And they were mint condition, too!"

Stasi felt as if she was moving through molasses as she walked into her shop. She stood in the doorway and looked at a chaos that punched holes in her heart. The books had been torn to pieces and thrown all over, while the lingerie had been shredded and some pieces were wet with a sticky substance that she didn't even want to think about.

"I guess we should call the sheriff," she muttered in a monotone.

"But you won't call him, will you?" Jazz didn't bother to wait for an answer as she zapped what had once been an exquisite camisole lying on the destroyed carpet. The fabric went up in smoke, leaving behind white ash.

"It wouldn't matter. The sheriff's Carrie's uncle on her mother's side." Stasi stepped carefully through the mess. "Boyd thinks she's a sweet little thing, just a bit high strung. His words. But we will need to take videos of the exterior of both shops for insurance purposes and inside to show damage to our stock."

Suddenly Stasi realized that what had originally woken her up was now silent. "Horace? Where are you? Horace!" She ran behind the counter then through the stock room. She breathed a soft sigh of relief to see that whoever had trashed her shop hadn't had time to go into the back. The stock hanging on racks in the back hadn't been touched. She finally found the gargoyle hiding under her desk. She was sorry the vandals hadn't been greedy enough to try to take the bewitched moneybag. She would have felt a bit cheerier if they'd suffered for their crimes. The moneybag had its own ways of dealing with thieves and it wasn't pretty. "Their turn is coming," she muttered, firmly believing in karma.

"It's a miracle I wasn't killed!" The gargoyle tried to scramble up her arms the minute she started to pick him up. "All this shouting woke me up then something broke the windows and they swarmed in like gors beetles." He mentioned a beetle used in transformation spells; the beetles were the size of lizards and their skin had an odd purple cast. They were also meaner than black mambas when caught. "We can move now, can't we? What about Palm Springs? Wait a minute, no, not there. A lot of old people there and no way I want to see all that wrinkled skin tanned to the consistency of old leather. LA? There're lots of hotties down there. Or Hawaii. Maybe Australia," he babbled. "Florida. No, they have lots of old people there too. And if the old ladies still wear those muumuus I'll see way too much cellulite and fat along with their Depends. I'd have to wash my eyes out with acid. But after what happened we can't stay here!" He grabbed her arms and shook her, which wasn't an easy feat for an eight-inch gargoyle, but he had his strength behind him. His wings swept back and forth, increasing in intensity.

"Horace, calm yourself! And we're not going anywhere." She winced as his claws dug into her arms, snagging her sweater. She wasn't used to seeing the gargoyle hysterical. His gray skin was mottled red and bright pink with agitation and his wings flapped so fast they created a strong breeze. She stroked his horns, usually guaranteed to soothe his frazzled nerves, but it didn't seem to be doing the trick this time.

"I'm proud of you, lovey." Jazz walked in and sat on the extra chair. "Oh for Fates sake!" She grimaced when she realized that her sweater was inside out with the tag hanging under her chin. She quickly pulled it over her head and set it to rights. Once that was done, she finger combed her hair, piling it on top of her head in a loose knot that she secured with a pair of dark jade chopsticks she pulled out of thin air. "You did the right thing by standing up to that harridan and putting the fear into her. I always knew you had it in you. There was no reason for you to take her shit."

"I felt like a shrew." Stasi busied herself carefully peeling each of Horace's claws out of the knit of her sweater, and then set him gently on her desk. He immediately scuttled back to rest against her sleeve, rubbing his face against her arm as if he was a cat seeking reassurance. She had never seen her sharp-tongued gargoyle rattled, and this upset her as much as seeing her beautiful shop destroyed. Horace could be a pain in the neck, but he didn't deserve to feel like this. She was only grateful he'd had the sense to hide, since Horace was too proud to admit he was a coward and would run from danger if he felt the least bit threatened. She didn't think anything could happen to him, but that didn't mean someone might not have tried.

"Did you deck Carrie? Tell me you rearranged her ugly face," Horace begged, wiping his nose against Stasi's sleeve. "I didn't hear her voice when they broke into the stores, but we know the shrew had to have been behind it, right? How about warts? Did you at least give her warts or some disgusting skin disease that no dermatologist in the world can cure?"

"I didn't touch her, but I did let her know there's nothing she can do to scare me." Stasi reached into the small refrigerator and pulled out two bottles of lime-flavored sparkling water. She handed one to Jazz, who unscrewed the cap and drank deeply.

"What I saw out there was a woman so filled with hate that no other emotion could have found its way inside her." Jazz set her bottle on the desk. "When you said things were upset around here and told me what happened to the lake, I thought it was nothing more than someone messing up a spell and that Carrie was nothing more than an empty-headed twit who wanted this lawsuit because she has a grudge against you. She's a twit, all right, but she's not empty-headed. She's beyond that. She's making serious trouble for you, Stasi. That's why I found a wizard lawyer for you. He's not afraid to go up against Trevor Barnes, either."

Stasi idly ran her finger along the length of the cold plastic bottle. "I saw that kind of hate in Salem Village in 1692," she murmured. "It was a dark time back then. Once the accusations and trials started, people grew afraid they would be targeted next, so they would accuse someone else, even if it was a family member or close friend, to divert suspicion. As a result, so many were hurt and tortured, others died, and they all carried one sort of pain or another. I don't think one person was unaffected by the time it was over. It was bad in Europe with the witch finders, too. Look what Witch Finder

Matthew Hopkins did in 1644. People now think he was nothing more than a character in a movie, when we all know he was so much more and many innocent people were killed because of him. The problem with Salem Village was that it was such a small area that it took no time at all for fear to spread like a plague."

"I wish you had contacted one of us back then," Jazz whispered, easily feeling the hurt within Stasi's heart. "We had no idea what was going on there until it was over. For Fates sake, Stasi, we could have lost you to that mob!" Her eyes sparkled with unshed tears.

"But you didn't lose me. I dampened my magick and did my best to seem harmless. As long as I was in Salem Village I had to be so careful that I didn't do anything that would draw attention. I'm sure they would have seen my leaving there as a sign of guilt." Her eyes grew dark with past terror. "I didn't feel safe for the next hundred years. Sleep wasn't easy to come by and the nightmares took even longer to leave me."

Jazz's expression of horror echoed Stasi's. Not that long ago she'd had her own bad dreams to deal with. She had been able to destroy a part of her enemy and had to grudgingly deal with the other part, but she'd had Nick and others to help her. Stasi had been alone then with only her dread of being targeted for company.

"Don't let anyone rob you of your power," she advised. "Believe me, if anybody knows what feeling powerless is like, it's me."

Stasi couldn't help but smile. "As I well know. That forty-eight hours of you without your magick was not a pleasant time."

"And you think it was fun for me? I was never so glad as when I got up that morning and found that face-covering zit gone." Jazz drank some more of her water. "What do you want, Stasi? Do you want the attorney I found for you, so you can trounce Carrie in court? Because I can't see her lawsuit going anywhere but down the toilet. Do you want all of us to go out there and band together to bring the lake back to life and find out the source of those lights and who, or what, caused that barrier? Do you want to walk away from here and never look back? What feels right to you?"

Stasi used the time to drink more water. She would have killed for a cup of coffee, but the vandals had smashed the coffeemaker to bits and she was too tired to conjure up a cup.

"I want the town to go back to the way it was," she said finally. "I want people to smile and say hello to each other like they used to. I don't want fear to settle in here and I don't want anger to rule their lives."

"They're human, Stasi. They're ruled by their emotions."

"So are we." She looked at Horace who had finally sidled over to the edge of the desk and curled up in a ball, fast asleep. His snores were loud enough to wake the dead. She hadn't seen Bogie down here and gathered that the dog had been smart and stayed upstairs. "Magick doesn't rule our lives. It enriches us."

"Tell that to humans who are only interested in a good hex to take out an enemy or at least make them miserable. Don't forget that I've met more than my share."

Stasi reached across the desk and took Jazz's hands in hers. "All humans aren't like that. Thank you for being here, Jazz. Blair tends to let her temper loose and while she doesn't mean to, things usually only get worse."

Jazz had to laugh at that, since her Irish temper was legendary. "And I don't?"

She smiled. "Yes, but you stepped back and let me handle Carrie on my own, even though I'm sure you wanted to take a bite out of her. That meant a lot."

Jazz waved away her thanks. "I only did what was right. She's your fight and you need to be the one to battle her. I know why Blair feels she needs to step in. She wants to protect you. We all do. You're our sweetheart witch. Until Carrie got under your skin, you would never say anything bad against anyone. You see the good in someone no matter how deep it might lie. Because of your soft-hearted nature we always felt you couldn't fight your own battles, but now you're showing that you can, and you're displaying an impressive amount of teeth when you're doing it. You don't need our protection anymore. You do just fine on your own, and I'm so proud of you. Now that we've gotten that out of the way, let's go on to a more pleasurable subject." Her eyes twinkled with wicked laughter. "Tell all about the hot wizard. Does he kiss as good as he looks?" She laughed when she saw her friend's blush start along her forehead and travel down her face to her throat. "You didn't? You did!" Fluff and Puff chortled along with her. "You had your way with the man."

"It was sort of mutual," she admitted.

"Hello? Stasi?"

"Ginny!" Stasi was never so glad for an interruption. She jumped to her feet and ran out of the office with Jazz following her.

The lovely Asian woman stepped carefully through the mess holding a drink carrier with coffee cups and a bag. She smiled at Nick, who was busy using the video camera to record the extent of the damage.

"Oh Stasi," she moaned softly, shock widening her eyes. "Hello, Jazz." She held up the carrier and bag. "I thought you might need caffeine and sustenance. I baked them fresh this morning." She looked around the trashed shop. "I think I should have brought a bulldozer instead. How could someone do this?"

Jazz immediately latched onto the coffee and oohed and ahhed over the pastries in the bag before grabbing one. "This is perfect, thank you."

"Carrie is out of control," Ginny said flatly, turning back to Stasi.

"There's no proof she was behind this," Stasi murmured, sipping the hot coffee with a sigh of relief and allowing the caffeine to flood her system.

"I bet we could find proof if we did a little searching." Jazz had a lemon Danish in her mouth and coffee in one hand while she busied herself piling the shredded books in one corner.

"No. This isn't all her doing." Stasi paused to stare at the basket of delicate sachets that were soaking wet. She didn't even want to think how they got that way.

Both women stared at her.

"You don't just mean she had help from someone, do you?" Jazz said.

Ginny looked from one to the other. "Um, no offense but you two are scaring me."

"Don't be scared," Stasi told her then muttered, "*Not now!*" when she spied two visitors coming to the shop.

"Oh my." Poppy stood in the open doorway, her hands covering her mouth while her eyes went wide with shock. "Oh Stasi, this is terrible. Your beautiful shop is destroyed." She tiptoed inside with her sister, Rhetta, walking more slowly behind her. Poppy was dressed in pink wool leggings and a pink, blue, and yellow print sweater. Her blond hair was pulled up in a frizzy ponytail secured with a pink velvet ribbon. Rhetta was more sedately attired in olive jeans and a cream turtleneck sweater. Her leaf-green gaze slid sideways to Ginny and centered on the bag that Ginny still held.

"Is there any way we can help?" Rhetta asked.

"No, but thank you for asking."

Jazz studied the two newcomers as she hoisted herself up to sit on the counter.

"Hello, I'm Poppy Palmer." Poppy directed a bright smile to Jazz. "And this is my sister, Amaretto, but we all call her Rhetta. I own the bakery, Fresh Baked Goods, with our brother, Reed."

"Jazz Tremaine. I'm a good friend of Stasi's," she said. "A group of us came up for the Halloween fun. It's nice to meet you."

Stasi almost smiled at Jazz using the human term instead of Samhain, which they celebrated every October. But the way things were going, she feared this year their celebration wasn't to be.

Poppy stared at Jazz's face and subtly backed off even though Jazz wasn't displaying any aggression.

"Well, you must come down to our bakery for coffee and some of our wonderful pastries. Our brother Reed whipped up some marvelous pumpkin spice muffins today that will be coming out of the oven any time now." She waggled her fingers at Stasi. "Honey, if you need any help at all, you call us, okay? I know Carrie is trying to make things difficult for you, but not all of us believe you're that way. I mean, if you were, we'd all be in danger, wouldn't we?" She looked around at the disaster that had once been Stasi's pride and joy. "Some people just don't understand."

"Thank you." Stasi deliberately didn't say she'd call because she deplored lies and that would have been a whopper. She had no plans to call on anyone. And she especially wouldn't call on anyone who lived in this town, not even Ginny, because she didn't know if her friend would eventually turn against her, too. Stasi had seen it happen before. Right now, she didn't know who she could trust other than the ones she felt closest to.

"You're supposed to be working for me," Carrie spat out as Trev marched her up the sidewalk. "So why did you have dinner with that bitch? You better not have tried to persuade her to settle, because I want her in court. And there's no way I'll drop this case. She's playing with peoples' lives and I don't want to see it happening any longer."

"Watch it, Carrie," he warned. Feeling his anger building up, he stopped and jerked her around to face him. "You have treaded a very fine line before, but if you had anything to do with the destruction of those shops, you have gone beyond the pale."

"I've done nothing wrong. She probably trashed her own store, so she could blame it on me."

If Carrie had looked at Trev at that moment, his expression would have struck real fear into her heart.

Instead, she felt a sense of suffocation surround her. It was only momentary, but it gave her pause. She breathed easier when the sensation was removed. She immediately knew he had caused it.

"I should have gone to Wizard Fitzroy," she muttered. "He would have seen the truth about Stasi and done something about it. She wouldn't have been able to seduce him."

Trev felt the air in his lungs turn to ice. The idea that she was accusing him of impropriety was bad enough, although he knew he was likewise walking a fine line where Stasi was concerned. But the wizard attorney she referred to was infamous for fighting dirty in the courtroom and managing to get away with it. He was also well known for hating witches with a passion and had declared more than once the world would be a better place without them. He also enjoyed dealing with humans. Trev figured it was because humans were in awe of Fitzroy, and there was nothing the pompous ass liked more than feeling as if he was a god.

Trev considered him a bully of the first degree. He hated going up against him in court and partied hearty when he won, but each court battle was hard won due to the wizard's trickery.

"Consider yourself lucky you didn't retain him, Carrie," he said in a dangerously soft voice. "You would have learned the price was too high."

Her smile was just as deadly. "Maybe you should have fucked her and gotten it out of your system. Otherwise, you're no good to me." She jerked her arm out of his punishing grip and walked away. "*Ow!*" She jumped and spun around, facing him with hatred in her eyes.

"Who knew mosquitoes would show up this time of year. Remember what I've said, Carrie. I fight fair and win. I wouldn't have taken this case if I didn't believe in the merits of it. But don't push me and don't try to take matters into your own hands."

Carrie didn't say a word. She turned back around and stalked off, finally turning into Fresh Baked Goods.

Trev blew out a cleansing breath but didn't feel any calmer. It wasn't like him to be at odds with a client, no matter what his personal opinion of them might be, but Carrie was as vindictive as he'd ever seen. He knew what she was doing in the bakery and hated her for not allowing him to keep control of the matter. He was tempted to walk right past the business, but he also wanted to know what was going on.

He drew a deep breath and walked inside, inhaling the scent of yeast, sugar, spices, chocolate, and various fruits, but he also sensed fury there and a strong taint of fear. Ordinarily, he would have found the bakery part of the fragrance tempting his taste buds, but his anger with Carrie had killed any semblance of an appetite and the fury and fear filled his stomach with acid. The counter was busy with customers buying breads and pastries while the separate counter for coffee was equally busy. He stopped there for a cup of French roast and found an empty table in the corner.

"She and her friends will take over the town. Take *us* over," Carrie groused from another table where she sat with a large muffin and coffee in front of her. "Sometimes I think they had the right idea in Europe by burning witches." Trevor was shocked to hear this sentiment was met with cheering. "Have any of you been out to the lake? There's something wrong there. I don't know what, but I'm sure they have something to do with it and we've got to stop them!"

Trev straightened up at that. It took all of his will-power to keep his spell around him, but something must have leaked out because Carrie noticed him in his corner. He made an effort to offer her a bland smile. She nodded back warily as if wondering at the change in his demeanor.

"More coffee?" The woman who'd been manning the coffee counter approached. "We offer free refills."

He looked into her leaf green eyes and saw interest there along with something else he couldn't figure out.

"Thanks." He hadn't realized he'd already drunk half the cup until then.

"I'm Amaretto Palmer. Rhetta for short." She filled his cup. "You look like an almond Danish man." She gestured toward the pastry counter.

"I'm not much for sweets," he lied. He knew from then on the only sweets he'd care for was chocolate soufflé shared with Stasi.

"You should give it a try. I think you'd enjoy it." She paused. "So tell me, how does a wizard lawyer deal with a human woman?" She nodded toward Carrie.

Why did he feel as if that wasn't the question she really wanted to ask?

"We're no different than any everyday attorney. We handle a lot of the same type of cases. A few different ones, of course." He quickly finished his coffee. When Rhetta lifted the pot, he gave her a charming smile and shook his head. "I have some work to do. Excellent coffee, by the way. I'll have to stop in again." He knew she would think he'd be stopping in for more than the coffee, but that was fine if he ever needed her as a source of information. He was going to need all his resources to discover what was going on among the townspeople. It appeared the bakery was a good place for that.

"Please do," she murmured, moving on.

Trev sucked in more cleansing breaths as he headed for his car. He pulled his cell phone out of his pocket and hit the speed dial.

"It's the weekend," Mae announced without any form of greeting.

"And I want this in play first thing on Monday," he told her. "No more cases with humans, plaintiffs or defendants, and I don't give a damn what part of the magickal community is involved. Refer any of them to Fitzroy."

"Give me something new to do. I've been doing that since the first day that woman walked into the office." She hung up without another word.

Trev stared at his phone as if it was a creature he'd never encountered before.

"Damn that woman. She never lets me have the last word."

Chapter 13

"YOU DIDN'T THINK TO GET ME UP WHEN YOU WERE first alerted? Damn it, Jazz!" Nick growled as he picked up loose boards as easily as if they were tooth-picks and put them in a neat pile. Vampire strength came in handy. Even in his annoyance, he paused long enough to slide his arm around Jazz's waist and press a kiss against her temple. She looked up and smiled at him, her delicate features alight with love. He shook his head. "What were you all thinking? How do you know the bastards still wouldn't have been here and ready to do damage to you? Yes, you all have power, but that doesn't mean you can go up against everyone. Look what they did here! That alone gives you an idea what they could have done to you. Mob mentality is a dangerous and unpredictable factor." His expression turned dark with memories—all preternatural creatures had been persecuted at some time.

"What, do you think we can't take care of ourselves against some crazy mortals? Trust me, after what I've put up with in just the past six months, this is a cakewalk," Jazz argued, then she muttered a few words and waved her hands in front of the rear wall of Stasi's shop. In moments, purple mist covered the black-painted graffiti, dissipating the filthy words that had been scrawled on the surface. The wall was back to its pristine condition. Once that was finished, she began picking up piles of shredded books and dropping them into a bucket. "There was no one here by the time we got here, so it had to be quite a crowd that ran in, did as much damage as they could, and got out," Jazz reasoned. "Horace's warning shrieks are too high pitched for anyone mortal to hear— except dogs, and I'm sure there are some major canine earaches this morning, along with cracked and broken glass here and there. As for Carrie, yes, it got a little charged, but nothing risky, and if you had been down here you might have gotten fangy and that wouldn't have been a good idea. It was bad enough Fluff and Puff did their thing." The bunny slippers squeaked their self-congratulations.

Nick flashed said fangs at her and returned to his task.

Letiticia walked through the shop picking things up. She muttered words in an ancient language under her breath as she dropped bits of lace and silk into a trash can.

"Animals," she spat out the word. "All of them."

"It's like a disease that begins with one and pretty soon more are infected." Stasi started to pick up a trash can, but Krebs took it out of her hands. She smiled her thanks and apology all in one. "I'm sorry your getaway began with such drama."

He grinned. "You forget I share a house with Jazz. Drama is her middle name."

"Actually, I don't have a middle name," Jazz called out on her way to the other shop to help Blair.

Stasi walked over to Letiticia and Krebs. "I feel guilty. I wish you two would enjoy today instead of helping us clean up here."

"We truly don't mind," Letiticia protested. "The more hands, the faster the work will be finished."

"But I do." She smiled gently. "There's more than skiing offered at the resort, and there are other small towns to explore. We even have an authentic ghost town about ten miles away. Please?" She begged with her eyes as eloquently as she did with her voice.

Letiticia slowly nodded. "But we will be back later and help then."

"Here." Nick tossed Krebs the keys to the Navigator. "The windows are specially tinted, so Letiticia will be safe if the sun gets too bright."

"My dear, I'm almost as old as you are." Letiticia laughed, pulling on Krebs's hands. "We'll be back later." They left through the rear door.

Stasi picked up a delicately scrolled stool with a velvet covering that had been hideously slashed, and set it upright, then realized one of the legs had been broken. She carried it to the pile of trash and set it on top. She refused to admit she kept looking outside in hopes she would see Trev. His absence gnawed at her.

It's those red hearts that're doing this. If I hadn't seen them, I could easily have handled Trev as nothing more than the attorney for the plaintiff.

Sure, Anastasia, you keep telling yourself that. You're such a fickle witch. First you send him away, now you want him back. Make up your mind! And don't even think about how he looked naked. How he made you feel. What the man could do to you.

Stasi glared at a pair of what used to be apricot lace boy shorts so hard a trickle of smoke curled up into the air. It was easier than dismissing the thoughts streaming through her head.

"Ah ah ah," Jazz chided, walking back into the shop.

Stasi made a face and eased off.

"You know, maybe in a way this is a sick blessing in disguise," Blair said, walking in behind Jazz.

"Explain the blessing part, because as I look around at the landfill that used to be my beloved boutique, I don't see anything to be thankful for."

"We've talked about putting an archway in this side wall to connect the two shops, so what better time to do it than now? There's already holes in the wall, so why don't we just go ahead and finish the job?"

"And I suppose you have someone in mind to do that for us?" Stasi asked.

Blair didn't even blush. "I called Jake and he said he'd be right over to give us an estimate."

"We can't do it until the insurance claims adjustor comes in."

"So we factor this in."

"She's right," Nick agreed. "It is a good time and you'd have additional protection with Jake."

"And his hammer," Blair joked. "He'll be here in about ten minutes. He's chopping wood for Mrs. Benedict." She looked at her reflection in the shards of the mirror that was barely managing to stay hung on a wall. "At least we know someone will have seven years bad luck. Hm, I need a bit of glamour." She disappeared back to her shop.

Nick watched her go. "She has no idea, does she?"

"Idea about what?" Stasi asked, puzzled by his question.

He turned and looked at her and Jazz. "Jake."

"What about Jake?" Stasi looked blank.

Jazz shrugged her shoulders, indicating she didn't know what he meant. "Please don't use riddles. It's been a long day. Just tell us straight out."

He considered her request then shook his head. "No, no, this is way more fun. Especially since you don't seem to know, either." He ducked as Jazz threw a battered hot pink and cream woven basket at him.

The rocking sounds of *The Monster Mash* sounded from the other side of the wall.

"As you can tell, she recovers quickly," Stasi murmured.

"Where did you put the video you took of the shops before we started?" Jazz asked.

"It's safely upstairs."

"Am I going upstairs too?" Horace asked from his spot on a shelf behind the counter.

"I guess so."

The gargoyle brightened up as much as an ashy gray gargoyle can. "Can I sleep in Blair's room?"

"Not a chance, perv!" Blair shouted through a gap in the wall. "I haven't forgotten that night I woke up and found you under the covers."

Stasi shook her finger at the gargoyle. "For that, you're sleeping in the kitchen."

"Hey." Jake walked in and looked around. His jeans and flannel shirt were covered with wood chips. He wore his baseball cap visor down low, although the day was cloudy. He nodded at Nick and introduced himself before approaching Stasi. "At a glance I'd say I'll need to replace some drywall, but cutting an archway between the two stores shouldn't be a problem."

"Maybe this wouldn't be a good idea," Stasi said.

"Putting in the archway?"

"You working for us. I don't want you losing work from anyone else in town because of us."

Jake took a deep breath, his hands on his narrow hips as he looked around. "Have I *ever* gone along with what anyone else said?"

"No."

"Did I ever infer you and Blair were the spawn of the devil?"

"Oh no! Is that what they're saying?" She pressed her hand against her stomach, feeling acid building up to volcano level.

"I don't listen to gossip, Stasi, and people around here are smart enough not to gossip around me because I'm known to shut them down fast," he assured her. "But you do have a guy who likes you a lot and is really worried about you."

"He's working for the other side."

"And if he hadn't been retained by her you wouldn't have met him."

"We're still opposites that aren't meant to be." She looked around for something to make her look busy, but everything had been cleaned up and Nick and Jazz were occupied carrying the trash out back to the Dumpster.

"Stop checking out the stock room," Nick could be heard grumbling. "You have enough clothes for ten closets."

"Ha! You haven't seen Thea's closet then. It's practically a house in itself. Ooh! This is so cute! And it's in my size!"

Stasi smiled at their wordplay as she heard the steel rear door open and sounds of the trash falling into the Dumpster.

"You need to smile more and worry less," Jake advised softly.

She threw out her arms to encompass the vandalized shop. "I shouldn't worry about this?"

Jake walked around the store, his knowledgeable hands stroking the damage. Once-elegant armoires were now nothing more than shards of wood, shredded wires hung out of the walls where light fixtures had been pulled off, the carpet was so covered with a variety of stains that it would have to be pulled up and thrown out, and all the mirrors, from the ones in the shop to the full-length ones in the dressing rooms, had been shattered. "Some more clean-up, new paint, new carpet, and whatever you need for your displays, and you'll be ready to go again. I can put off the low priority jobs and get right to this if you want me to."

"I do, but even once it's redone, it won't be the same." Stasi settled on her stool. When she felt a nudge at her ankle she looked down to find a worried looking Bogie staring up at her. The small dog floated up and perched himself on the counter with his head resting on her arm, nuzzling it with his nose for reassurance.

"Do you notice that very few people have come by to see what happened?" Blair walked in pulling a Red Flyer wagon loaded with a cooler. The sides were badly scratched and the wagon wobbled because the wheels had been bent. "Cowards," she muttered, allowing Jake to hoist the cooler onto the counter. "Jerks. Last time I donate to the town center rebuilding fund. Or the volunteer fire department or any other cause that pops up during the year." She reached down and patted the dented wagon before she looked up. "Don't we carry paper on the mayor's house?"

"Don't even think it," Stasi warned.

"So what do you think, cowboy?" Blair asked Jake. "Is there a problem in punching more holes in the wall dividing our stores?"

"I checked to make sure it's a load bearing wall and it can be done," he replied, pulling a can of Cherry Coke out of the cooler. "You can either have an open archway, a curtain to divide it or even swinging half doors. For now, I want to board up the windows and the front door. You can come and go through the rear door until I finish with the front." He glanced toward where the windows used to be.

Stasi and Blair followed his gaze and noted several people standing across the street. What caught Stasi's attention were the blank looks on their faces as if they were looking at nothing more innocuous than an empty wall. They remained there even as the snow began to fall in a soft white curtain.

"Pod people," Blair murmured.

"Don't blame all for what a few think." Jake leaned against the counter, his elbows resting on the wooden surface.

"They don't just think," Stasi said dryly. "They also act. And right now, we're the targets. Longtime residents have known what we are for quite some time, but now something is making them change. It's very unsettling."

"It all started with Carrie," Blair pointed out. "She's the catalyst. She's always loved to stir up trouble and now she's been able to stir up a shitload just because she thinks she has the right." Her gaze bored into Stasi's.

Stasi returned it with defiance. She ignored the mental reminder that she *had* added a little extra to the sachet she'd tucked into Carrie's bag. She wished she could ignore Blair's telling look. Guilt weighed heavy on her that Carrie's anger had been cast against Blair, too, when she had done nothing to deserve it.

Collateral damage.

"I can smell disaster a mile away," Jazz announced, walking in from the stockroom with Nick on her heels. "And she reeks of it." She glanced at Stasi who quickly ducked her head. "Stasi?"

Blair quickly busied herself with rearranging the contents of the cooler. "Jake, sweetie, do you want to come over and see what needs to be done to my place?" she asked, pulling his sleeve.

He picked up his Cherry Coke can. "Sure thing."

Blair deliberately waited until Jake started walking. *Is that a world-class ass or what?* she mouthed with a grin as she followed him outside.

"Why do I feel there's more to this than Carrie acting like a bitch?" Jazz asked softly as she perched herself up on the counter. Her jeans-clad legs swung back and forth.

Nick immediately backed up and even Stasi looked wary. Jazz's absolute least favorite word was bitch, so for her to use it meant her anger level was rising.

Jazz spun around on the counter and sat there cross-legged. "You *did* do something, didn't you?" Her whisper was so low mortal ears wouldn't have heard her words. "That's why Blair looked at you the way she did and why you're not as traumatized as you should be. You expected something like this to happen. You expected some sort of punishment."

"Blair shouldn't have been a target." Stasi forced herself to face Jazz. "Just because Carrie is furious with me, there's no reason for Blair to suffer too."

"I'm the one with a temper. Blair's the one who believes in exacting revenge. Thea's happiest when her fans tell her how much they love her books. Lili is the absolute best healer in the universe. Maggie's happiest when she kicks ass. And then there's you, Stasi. You have the largest, kindest heart in this universe, and you give Cupid a run for his money because you believe everyone has a perfect match. How many times have you been called before the Witches' Council since we were expelled from the academy? Four, five? Compared to the countless times we others have been called? And your time was only increased because you did what you felt was right. But this time you interfered with a human's well-being. You messed with her love life in a way even Cupid wouldn't have done."

Stasi's expression turned to stone. "You know what? I'm tired of explaining myself and defending myself. Perhaps Carrie should do some soul searching and not worry about what might or might not have been in the sachet I put in her bag."

"Do you mean this sachet?"

"Oh shit," Jazz muttered, looking over her shoulder at the dark-visaged man standing in the doorway. There was no look of the clean-cut wizard lawyer now. This was a man who was furious and wanted everyone to know it, judging by the energy that blasted around him like a nuclear explosion. Even Jazz knew enough to stay quiet.

Stasi didn't move from her spot as Trev walked inside holding a familiar pink silk heart-shaped sachet edged with cream lace. To anyone else, it smelled like lavender. The expression on Jazz's face and the fury on

Trev's told her that both could smell the slight difference in it.

"Carrie sent this over to me a little while ago," Trev said, bearing down on Stasi, who, to her credit, didn't budge an inch. "She was afraid it was hexed and hoped I could tell if it was safe. She had decided to cut up all the sachets you'd put in her bags, but for some reason she couldn't cut up this one." He slammed the silk bag down on the counter. "Guess why? I'm amazed you didn't arrange for this one to somehow end up missing or destroyed."

"Out," Nick snapped.

"Good idea. Leave, wizard, until she has her lawyer with her," Jazz agreed, then muttered, "Those red hearts can be totally irritating, can't they?"

Nick walked over and grabbed Jazz's arm. "I meant us."

"But—!" she sputtered as he dragged her out of the shop.

Trev took several deep breaths, but his anger wasn't easily handled. "What were you thinking, Stasi? This is all the proof she needs to show you interfered with her marriage. All I had to do was pick this up and I could feel what you had put into it—and it wasn't a simple feel-good-about-yourself spell like the other sachets have."

"Obviously you didn't go beyond the external layer," she said, amazed her voice could remain even. She had seen Trev smile, seen him laugh, seen his face taut with desire. But she had never seen him furious the way he was now. "There is nothing there that would harm her. Only reveal what she truly is."

Inside, she was a quivering mass and wanted nothing more than to curl up somewhere and burst into tears. She refused to show any of that to him or even hint that her emotions were on overload.

Trev's jaw could have doubled as granite as he pushed his face into hers. "It is still *wrong*." She didn't blink. He muttered a few choice curses under his breath as he leaned back. "Do you realize what can happen to you in Wizards' Court? How this transgression alone can warrant having your powers stripped from you?"

"Do you realize what it's like to see a man who used to smile all the time, who truly loved life, turn sad and despondent? A man who after eight months of marriage looked as if he'd aged ten years?" she said softly. "Kevin Anderson is a good man. A genuinely nice man. All he wanted was a loving home and family, and Carrie took all his dreams away from him."

"He's an adult. He had to have known what he was getting into when he married her," he argued.

She shook her head. "Kevin is the kind of guy who looks for the good in everyone, and he wanted to be a father in the worst way. Carrie can be very sweet and persuasive when she chooses to be. Most men aren't looking for a readymade family and steer away from women with children. Kevin was the perfect victim. He wanted a family and she had one. He didn't listen to anything anyone said because he was positive he was what Carrie needed."

"He didn't need to marry a woman with children to have a family."

"Unfortunately, he did. He had the mumps when he was in college. He became sterile as a result," Stasi murmured.

Trev looked down at the sachet on the counter. "I need to take this to the court."

She licked her lips, which felt dry. No wonder, with the icy cold air still coming into the shop.

"I understand. Jazz said she has a lawyer for me. Ask her for his name and anything else can be handled through him, just as you wished in the beginning."

When he looked up his eyes flared with energy and desire so strong, it rocked Stasi back on her heels. She had no warning when he reached out and gripped the back of her head with his hand and brought her toward him.

She already knew the man could kiss and did it very well, but until then she'd never experienced a kiss that literally took her breath away.

His tongue swept through her mouth, leaving behind the taste of his anger. His hold was firm, but she knew if she stepped back he would release her. He was furious with her, but he wouldn't hurt her. She allowed her fingertips to touch his arms and feel the warmth of his body through his jacket. She tipped her head back, allowing his tongue to slide down the curve of her neck and nip her skin.

"You are the most exasperating woman I've ever met," he muttered against her throat.

She smiled. "I'm a witch."

"In more ways than one." He looked up and drew back a space. He kept his hand cradling her neck while his thumb stroked the corner of her mouth. "I want to help you."

"You're the opposition, Trev. Jazz found an attorney to help me. You told me in the beginning I needed an attorney to protect my interests. You're right. I do." She kept her voice gentle. Not that there was any reason to be angry with him. She realized sadly that she was even getting used to the red hearts that refused to leave either of them. She could see their reflections in the remains of a mirror still hanging on a nearby wall. Trev was showered, well-groomed, and smelled very nice indeed, while she looked like something left out on trash day. She hadn't given much thought to her appearance that morning. Her sun-kissed locks still hung in a tangle and her coral pink sweater bore stains from her morning's work. She didn't need to look down at her jeans to see they were in the same disreputable condition. And yet, the reflections in the mirror, dancing red hearts and all, were of two people who looked right together.

"I'm going to find a way."

His words surprised her. "I know you have to use what Carrie gave you and I understand. I can't hate you for doing your job."

He pushed away from the counter. "Good thing, because the last thing I feel for you is hate." He walked out without looking back.

Once Stasi recovered, she noticed the sachet still lay on the counter, but this time the fabric was burned black and the spell was eradicated. She tentatively touched it with her fingertips, afraid the charred silk would flare up.

And then she cried.

Chapter 14

"I NEED TO GET MORE BOARDS, THEN I'LL FINISH COVERING the windows," Jake told Stasi, tactfully not commenting on her tear-stained face or red eyes.

She nodded, thankful for his discretion. "Thanks. Once that's done, I'll get out of here." Jake went out and she looked around the empty shop, her mind in turmoil.

She set Horace near her bank bag, which lay on the counter along with a box of her bookkeeping records. After today she wasn't leaving anything irreplaceable in the shop. She assumed her laptop had been spared damage only because she and her friends had come downstairs so fast.

Even with her office unharmed, she couldn't go back there, especially when she was alone. She had shooed Blair out of the store after her place was boarded up. She wanted a little time alone. She wanted to figure out why this was happening. What the trigger was.

Besides Carrie's out-of control hatred and lust for revenge.

Instead of perching on her stool, Stasi hiked herself up on the counter and sat cross-legged, facing the broken windows. She noticed people were only walking on the sidewalk across the street, and they barely glanced over, then hurried on.

She sighed. "It's as if we have the cross for plague painted on the front."

"You're not going to cry again, are you?" Horace asked. "No offense, but I don't do well with tears."

Stasi smiled and hiccupped. Then she almost did cry when she saw that the bubble wasn't its usual iridescent color, but held hints of red and black.

"Oh stars, you're in bad shape," Horace groaned.

"You're not being helpful." She sniffed, digging through her pockets for a handkerchief and coming up with zip. Out of habit, she looked around, but there wasn't anything that would help, so she did the unthinkable and rubbed her nose with her sleeve.

"I still say we move."

"And I say no. We won't run away." She knew she could speak for Blair because the sharp-tongued witch wasn't one to run from a fight either.

"And here we thought the lawsuit was the worst of it." Horace picked his fangs with his claws.

Stasi had no warning until she felt a sharp sting across her cheek and forehead. She fell off the counter to the floor and lay there stunned as pain radiated throughout her face.

"What the hell?" The next thing Stasi knew, Trev was there, kneeling beside her. She moaned as he carefully eased her up into a sitting position. He pulled a white handkerchief out of his pocket and dabbed at her face.

"What happened?" Blair and Jazz were there within seconds and both crouched beside her.

"Something hit her," Trev said grimly.

"I'll go upstairs and get a healing poultice." Blair stood up.

Trev frowned as he lifted the handkerchief, now splotched with red. "Don't you heal instantly?"

"Part of our banishment is that we heal like humans." Stasi closed her eyes against the sharp pain crossing her forehead. She lifted her hand to touch it, but Trev gently pushed it back down. "We have healing poultices and our broken bones might knit faster than others, but it's not made easy for us." She suddenly covered her mouth with her hand as a wave of nausea swept over her.

Jazz swiftly found a bucket and set it within reach.

"That blow was hard enough to cause a concussion." Jazz went in the back and brought out a bottle of water so Stasi could rinse out her mouth.

"Please, I'm embarrassed enough as it is! *Hic!*" As before, the bubble was a tainted color.

"What the hell?" Jake walked in carrying a load of boards.

"Did you see anyone nearby?" Trev asked.

He shook his head. "I came around from the back." He stooped down and picked up one of the stones that had struck Stasi. He held it up, one of the edges red with blood. Stasi felt her stomach start to heave again. "Someone took the time to sharpen this stone. This has gone too far," he rumbled. A low growl traveled up his throat.

"Wow, I am so impressed," Blair said. "My growls usually sound like a sick cat. How do you do that?"

He continued to study the stone and left the store with it in his hand. They could see him stop on the sidewalk and lift his face as if searching for a scent in the air before he moved on.

Trev still dabbed gently at the wounds. "Those cuts are deep. You need stitches."

"I need my bed," she said, feeling that woozy sensation come on again. When Trev helped her to her feet, she immediately started to wobble. He muttered under his breath and swept her up into his arms.

"You need to see a healer," he corrected. "No matter what, the local doctor should treat you."

She closed her eyes to stop the world from whirling around her. "No. Just my bed and one of Blair's healing poultices. Lili, our healer, can tell her what to do." She swallowed. "Please."

Her soft plea was Trev's undoing. He carried her out of the store and walked around the corner to the stairs, taking them so smoothly Stasi wasn't jostled even a hint.

He headed unerringly to her bedroom and gently placed her on the bed.

Blair placed Horace and the moneybag on Stasi's dresser.

"You could dress this place up some with mirrors on the ceiling," Horace commented, craning his neck. "Hey!" He fought the cloth that Jazz dropped over him along with a gargoyle-sized freeze spell. "Unfair!"

"I'll make some tea." Blair headed for the kitchen.

"Out." Jazz stared at Trev.

He opened his mouth to protest but before he could say anything he was magickally pushed out of the room and the door closed after him.

"I'd laugh, but I think it would hurt too much," Stasi whimpered.

"Then don't." Jazz was as gentle as possible as she extracted Stasi from her clothing and put her in a nightgown, carefully arranging the covers around her.

"Your wizard is sitting in the kitchen with a cup of tea, Bogie's chewing on his boot laces, and Fluff and Puff each have a licorice root to keep them occupied," Blair announced a moment later, coming in holding a mug and two small herb-scented cloths. "I was able to get Lili on wallmail and she suggested this. She said if the cuts on your forehead and cheek aren't too deep and wide, we could use a butterfly bandage to close them up." She gently affixed one warm cloth on Stasi's forehead and used something to attach the other to her cheek.

"Didn't we do something similar for Jazz not all that long ago?" Stasi inhaled the soothing fumes from the mug and carefully sipped the hot liquid.

"At least you still have your power." Jazz sat on the end of the bed, leaning against the footboard.

"Yeah, yeah, forty-eight hours of hell, you eating your weight in See's chocolates, moaning and groaning your life was over," Blair teased.

"If I didn't know any better I'd say this town was cursed." Jazz pulled the chopsticks out of her hair, allowing the copper-red waves to tumble down. She twisted them back up and stuck the chopsticks back in. "How many years have you two lived here without any trouble? Even after the longtime residents knew the truth, they left you alone; in fact, you've made friends with them. I don't think Carrie's current angst should have been enough to infect the town to this extent. So what has happened to cause the problems and who's really behind it?"

Blair sat up. "A curse I can understand, but *why?*"

Stasi yawned. "I'm sorry. I love you both, but between the early wake-up call and everything going on today, I'd like nothing more than to take a nap."

"Good idea." The two witches got up and left, closing the door after them and ignoring Horace's plaintive "I don't get uncovered?"

Jazz headed for the freshly made coffee the minute she entered the kitchen. "You do know that your *client*," she made the word sound like the vilest of curses, "has been out to make as much trouble as she can for Stasi and Blair and it looks like she's having unprecedented success."

Trev sat sprawled in the chair, a half-filled cup in front of him. Jazz took pity on him and topped it off before she dropped into the chair across from him. Irma drifted in with Sirius close by. She leaned against the counter. The cigarette between her fingers disappeared the moment Jazz shot her a look of warning.

"I went down and took a peek at the stores. It looks like a war zone down there. Who would do such a terrible thing?" Irma asked.

"That's what we'd like to know." Blair sighed.

"The lawsuit hasn't turned out to be what I thought it was," Trev admitted with a weary sigh. "Maybe she had provocation, but I'm sure Carrie has been lying."

"Ya think?" Blair snorted. "Drop the bitch. I'd say hand her over to the Wizards' Court, but since she's human they won't do anything to her. I still say she started all this and it's a crime in our community. She needs to pay."

"It's not that easy. Due to our Code I can't drop a client."

"I'd say vandalism, taking the law into your own hands, and inciting the public to riot are excellent reasons no matter what your Code says." Jazz drummed her fingernails on the table.

"But none of that is proven."

They looked up when the door opened and Nick and Jake walked in.

"I ran into Nick and asked him to help me track whoever threw the stones, but we couldn't find anything," Jake announced. "We've got all the windows and doors boarded up and he made sure no one can get in the back doors.

"I can't believe you lost them. You're an excellent tracker," Jazz said.

"Something was masking the trail." Nick growled, pouring coffee for himself and for Jake. "How is Stasi?"

"I wallmailed Lili and she told me what to use," Blair replied. The witches had their own system of communicating by means of magickal letters that could show up on a wall anywhere in the world, no computer required. Very convenient. "Stasi's sleeping now and I'll check on her in a little while."

Trev silently stared at his cup, idly rubbing his finger around the rim.

"Those red hearts over both your heads aren't just one of Cupid's pranks, are they?" Blair said softly. "You have feelings for Stasi."

"She told me that witches and wizards don't mix," he murmured. "And it was easy for me to believe her. Something isn't right in this town. The taint needs to be found and eradicated."

"I don't know what you learned in wizard's law school, but you can't destroy any kind of taint without knowing the source."

"There is a place that can help us." Stasi stood in the doorway.

Trev jumped up and ran over to support her. He took her mug of tea out of her hand and helped her to his chair.

"I couldn't sleep after all," she admitted. "Trev's right. Perhaps we don't know who's behind this, but that doesn't mean we can't do some research on how to end it."

Jazz had a sick look on her face. "Please don't tell me you're saying what I think you're saying, because research means…"

Stasi nodded. "The Library."

Jazz dropped her head to the table. "No. No, no, no, no."

"You don't have to go."

"The town doesn't have a library," Jake put in.

Stasi shook her head. "The Library—and you have to capitalize it—is magickal. It holds every magick reference known to our kind and even more that we don't know about."

"It's a terrible place filled with bats, monster spiders, big snakes, and beetles and Fates know what else." Jazz made a face. "Along with a horrible wizard in charge."

"The Librarian doesn't like Jazz," Blair explained.

"That's an understatement," Jazz mumbled. "But then, I'm not too fond of him either."

"Perhaps he'd be nicer to you if you returned your books on time and you weren't so rude to him," Nick suggested.

She uttered a low snarl. "Get staked."

"So you think this library can tell you what's going on around here?" Jake asked.

"Capital L no matter what," Stasi reminded him.

He laughed. "You can tell I didn't think of it as a capital L?"

"We can tell," Jazz said, getting up and beginning to forage for food. "And so can the prissy man who runs the place. If we don't show him proper respect we're banned for two or twenty or two hundred years." She gazed into a near empty kitchen cabinet and looked over her shoulder.

"We haven't had time to shop lately. I'll go to Grady's and pick up barbecue for us." Blair pushed back her chair and retrieved her coat from the coat rack.

"I'll go with you," Jake offered, pulling his heavy coat back on. "I don't think any of you should be out alone until this is settled."

For once Blair didn't disagree. She left with Jake in tow.

Nick straightened up. "Letiticia sent me a message. She said the roads are blocked due to heavy snowfall and she and Krebs can't get back. They're going to stay at the resort."

"The roads are never blocked for long, although they may not get plowed until morning," Stasi said.

He shook his head. "Letiticia senses something unnatural at work there also. As if they're being kept away from here." He got up and walked over to the window, pulling aside the café curtains. All they could see was a veil of white. "It looks like a record snowfall."

"And early in the season, too." Stasi looked worried. "We haven't had so much snow this early for at least fifteen years. Poor Blair will freeze out there."

Jazz picked up Stasi's mug and warmed it up in the microwave.

"We need to check the lake."

"Not until after you eat," Nick said. "In fact, it would be better if I went than you. Even Irma would be better."

"If you think I'm going out in that blizzard, guess again, Nicky," the ghost argued. "My arthritis has never liked cold weather."

"You're dead!" Jazz groaned. "You haven't suffered from arthritis since 1956!"

"I still feel it," she stiffly informed the witch.

"Perhaps you don't feel the cold the way we do, but it can still affect you," Jazz reminded the vampire.

"It's not far, so I'll be fine." He sipped his coffee. Even if his diet was iron-rich, he was able to enjoy most liquids with beer, wine, and coffee being his drinks of choice.

"Then I'm going with you."

"I don't think so."

Jazz opened her mouth to argue her point when she caught Stasi's pained expression. She mouthed *I'm sorry* and returned to her coffee.

"I'm going to visit The Library tomorrow," Stasi said in a tone that brooked no argument.

"I'll go with you," Trev told Stasi.

"I can do this on my own. You have a client to consider."

Trev listened to her words—she wasn't leaving him with any options. But that didn't mean he wasn't going to accompany her.

Stasi closed her eyes. She wanted nothing more than to forget the past two weeks. The town she loved, her retreat, had been severely damaged. She feared it would never return to the way it used to be.

"Whew! I thought we'd never get back!" Blair laughed, stumbling into the kitchen with Jake behind her. Both carried bags that exuded the welcome scents of rich spices and beef. Jake pushed the door against the snowy onslaught. "Jake has a great sense of direction. I was ready to use a ball of light to guide us, but he had no problem."

"I'm sure he didn't." Trev exchanged a knowing look with the carpenter.

Blair dropped the bags on the table. "Grady's gone over to the dark side," she informed them.

Jake shifted uncomfortably. "He saw us approaching and told us to go to the back door. He's afraid he'll lose business if he serves you."

"I wasn't going to take the food, but Jake disagreed. I never thought Grady was a coward," Blair muttered. "I think the only reason he even gave us the food was because Jake was with me."

"You can't blame him. He doesn't want his business to end up like ours." Stasi picked at her sandwich.

Suddenly no one had much of an appetite, but they ate because they knew they needed to.

"I'm going to take a turn around the town. See if I can hear anything." Jake pulled on his heavy jacket.

"With this snow I can't imagine anyone will be out," Blair said.

"You'd be surprised."

"I'll check the lake now." Nick helped clean up and balled the bags into a trash bag.

"I'll go with you." Trev grabbed his jacket.

"Be careful," Stasi urged, more worried than ever.

Trev walked over and leaned down, dropping a tender kiss on her forehead where the skin was raw and scabbing from the cut. "I'm always careful," he whispered.

Stasi had no idea she had a dreamy look on her face as she watched the wizard and vampire leave.

"What?" She noticed the expressions on Blair, Jazz, and Jake's faces.

"It's your face, honey," Irma said. "Go look at it."

"She's right. Take a look."

"What? Do I have some kind of rash now?" she laughed, heading down the hall for her bathroom. She always felt soothed when she walked into the room that she had fixed up as a sanctuary with dark rose and cream towels and a tub that invited relaxation. It wasn't until she stood at the pedestal sink and looked into the mirror that she understood her friends' surprise.

While the cut on her cheek was still reddened and scabbing, the one on her forehead was almost completely healed and showed no sign of scarring. She was positive within an hour there would be no sign she had even been injured.

"How?"

"When he kissed you." Blair leaned against the doorjamb. "You didn't need a healing poultice. All you needed was a kiss from Wizard Charming."

"When he comes back, you should have him kiss your cheek," Jazz suggested. "He acted as if he has no healing powers, but this is proof he does."

Blair shook her head. "I bet it has something to do with Cupid's decree that they're right for each other."

"Love is a crazy thing," Jazz intoned.

"Shut up, both of you!" Stasi threw up her hands then was stunned by the sparks that jumped from her fingertips. Both Blair and Jazz hopped backwards. Stasi pushed past them and walked into her bedroom, slamming the door behind her.

Blair and Jazz looked as if a sweet puppy had leaped up and gnawed their fingers off.

"I think it might be a good idea to leave her alone," Blair muttered, retreating to the family room. "She's had a hard day."

"I agree." Jazz followed her.

Irma sat in an easy chair with Sirius lying at her feet and Fluff and Puff now curled up in a corner of the couch.

"You girls don't seem to have good luck with men or with what's going on with your lives," Irma commented.

"Says the woman whose husband cheated on her with the town skank and she took it so hard she killed herself in her husband's beloved car just to get back at him." Jazz dropped onto the couch near the slippers, who promptly slid down and complained until she pulled off her Uggs so they could cover her feet.

"A great car you wouldn't be driving today if I hadn't."

"She's right, you know." Blair took a spot on the other end of the couch and curled her legs up under her.

"No reason to remind her," Jazz muttered.

The bitter cold assaulted the two men as they stood in snow that was rapidly covering their boots.

The barrier Stasi and Blair had first encountered had lost the crisscrossing lines and now sported a silvery-black sheen that reflected the water, where waves had frozen into place, making the scene before them look like a surrealist painting.

"Why is this happening now?" Nick asked again, not expecting an answer. "There've been Mercury retrogrades and lunar eclipses at the same time before, but there hasn't been a problem like this."

"It really does feel personal. Someone's targeting Stasi and Blair," Trev said, walking toward the trees. He placed his hand against a few different tree trunks then walked further down. Nick noticed his direction and followed.

"Other than your client, you mean. Tell me something, wizard, why did you take on the case? Couldn't you sense this Carrie didn't have all her marbles and was on the warpath?"

"Have you taken on cases involving humans and vampires?" Trev asked him.

Nick nodded. "Only if I feel the human needs protection or would be in danger if they tried it on their own."

Trev noticed his expression. "But it hasn't always gone well," he guessed.

"A mortal woman wanted to see her son who'd been turned. I set up a meeting with him in a Were coffee shop that doubles as neutral territory," Nick said quietly.

"But she didn't just want to see him, did she?"

"No, she felt she was saving him by staking him. Luckily, his sire, who was present, didn't demand retribution." Nick idly kicked a stone away. "So once again, why did you deal with a mortal who obviously is missing more than a few gears and has issues with Stasi?"

"At first glance, the case appeared credible and during her first visit Carrie put on a good face as the wronged one. She laid out a good story that I believed. It wasn't until I started a deeper investigation into the case that I learned there was more vengeance in her mind than lawful retribution. It was all my fault. I'd just come off a case that required a lot of work and emotional energy. I was exhausted and all I saw was a woman whose marriage was ruined by a spell." Trev shook his head.

"You really fucked up there." Nick suddenly laughed. "Of course, if you hadn't taken the case, you wouldn't have met Stasi."

Trev's grin grew wider. "Yeah."

"And if you ever hurt her, I will take you apart and scatter you to the Four Winds." Nick's tone was so affable he could have been talking about the weather, but there was no denying he'd just made a vow he would keep.

Trev knew the truth when he heard it. "If I hurt her, I will let you do that and more." He looked back at the frozen lake and noticed an area in the very center that seemed to bubble up like a lava pool. "Why would someone target the lake? What does it have to do with what's going on in town?"

"The lake means a lot to the witches. They come here every month on the first night of the full moon and hold a small ceremony. Jazz says it centers them. Moonstone means sanctuary and they want to keep it that way."

"Except this month is giving them a lunar eclipse the first night of the full moon and Mercury retrograde is adding to the insanity." Trev sighed, turning to walk back toward the building and the stairs that led to what he was quickly considering a piece of his heart.

"We're in here!" Jazz shouted from the family room when the kitchen door opened and closed.

"What did you find?" Blair asked, barely lifting her head from the back of her chair.

"It's not getting better. Where's Stasi?" Trev knew she wasn't in the room even before he entered.

"In her room."

He nodded and walked away. He tapped lightly on her bedroom door and walked in.

Stasi was still in her robe and curled up on her bed with a paperback romance novel in her hands. One lamp was on in the corner, lending a soft light to the room.

Trev stayed in his spot studying her. Her mint green fleece robe wasn't the least bit sexy, but he reacted as if she wore nothing at all. He mentally cursed his hard-on since he didn't think this was an appropriate moment to strip her out of the robe and make love to her until they were both breathless. Instead, he stood there enjoying how the color accented her delicate rosy skin and the blond highlights in her hair. She wore it tucked behind her ears, a hint of curl in the ends. For once he didn't feel as if the red hearts above her head were mocking him. He was seeing them as a sign of what was to be.

The idea of being with this witch who had a soul for love and romance no longer seemed foreign to him. In fact, he longed to move forward with Stasi, to find out everything he could about her.

He straightened up when she looked up and stared at him, expressionless. There was no sign of the wound on her forehead. Then he recalled he had kissed her on the forehead, on the damaged site, before he left. He'd used no magick in the kiss, yet somehow it had healed her. For a wizard who had no talent for healing so much as a paper cut, this was something he hadn't expected. He wondered if that was another sign that they were meant to be together.

The longer he looked at her, the stronger the emotion washed over him—he wanted nothing more than to have the chance to heal all of her.

Chapter 15

"STOP LOOKING AT ME," SHE SPOKE SO SOFTLY HE ALMOST didn't hear the words.

"I can't help it."

She grimaced as she ducked her head. She slipped off her bed and walked over to the bathroom door.

"Tell the others I'll be right out. It's time we took some action." She closed the door in his face.

Trev remained in the same spot, grinning when he heard Horace's plaintive plea.

"Could someone please take this cover off me?"

"No."

"I promise not to watch you get dressed. You spoil all my fun!"

His grin widened. "I know the feeling, gargoyle," he whispered, returning to the family room, where he heard the others talking fast and furious. Nick stood in a corner, his head bent as he spoke into his cell phone.

"Krebs and Letiticia are still up at the resort. They can't get anywhere near the town," Nick announced, closing up his cell phone. "Letiticia said they could only drive so far on the road and the car just stops. They even tried walking and all of a sudden they couldn't take another step. She said whatever is doing it is targeting mortals and the supernatural alike. People up at the resort are agitated because they can't get down the road. She said she sensed that same disturbance that she and Krebs had."

"Even more spells," Jazz groaned.

"Stasi has a plan," Trev declared.

Jazz eyed Trev as he settled in a chair. "Tell me something, wizard, why are you helping us? Your client has developed a nasty dislike for Stasi and it's pretty much spilled over onto the rest of us. She wouldn't like it if she knew you were here."

His usually easygoing nature was gone and something cold and hard replaced it. "I don't like bullies."

"Then we agree on two things."

"Two?"

Jazz nodded. "Stasi and disliking bullies."

Trev stilled. He knew his feelings had been growing more jumbled where Stasi was concerned. He was already aware he could no longer blame it on Cupid. Not after the night they'd shared. A night he was hoping to repeat very soon.

"Why don't we figure out what's happening here first, then we can decide what to do with Caustic Carrie," Blair suggested.

"We might be able to do something about the situation here once we do some research. The problem is we don't know what we're dealing with." Stasi walked in wearing a pair of navy yoga pants that rested on her hips and a pink t-shirt that stopped short of her navel. Her feet were bare and her broom anklet sparkled when she walked.

She chose to sit on the arm of Trev's chair. He rested his hand just above the waistband of her pants, savoring the warmth of her bare skin.

Jazz buried her face in her hands. "There must be another way."

"There's no better place to look for answers," Stasi pointed out. "Who's with me?"

"Correction, there's no better place to be humiliated and receive more questions than answers," the red-haired witch argued. "The last time I had to go there I was directed to the middle of the La Brea Tar Pits. That damn realm was literally in the middle of the pits! Even magick couldn't easily peel that nasty gunk off my skin. The time before that he sent me to a swamp."

"There aren't any swamps in LA," Blair said.

"He found one." Her lip curled up in a snarl.

"Maybe if you returned your books on time you wouldn't be in so much trouble there," Stasi pointed out.

"Fine, then don't go with us."

"Oh, I'm going. Maybe with you asking for the entrance, I'll see something nicer."

"Are you talking about The Library?" Trev asked.

Stasi nodded. "Jazz and The Librarian," she pronounced "the" with a long e, "don't get along." She ignored Jazz's mutterings about a smarmy pompous egotistical ass disguised as a lowly librarian.

Trev grinned. He looked up, missing the warmth of Stasi's skin when she rose to her feet.

Jazz and Blair stood up while Nick remained seated. Since vampires weren't welcome at The Library, he was content to stay behind.

"I'm going too." Trev stood up, remaining standing behind Stasi. "Wizards are allowed there," he reminded her. "I can help you. With more of us there, we could find answers faster."

"I could go," Irma volunteered.

"The Librarian doesn't like ghosts any more than he likes vampires," Nick spoke up. "We'll sit here and watch the snowfall."

"Maybe we can find something good on cable."

Stasi looked down at her clothing. "I'd better put on some warmer clothes. I'll be right back." True to her word, she returned in less than five minutes now dressed in jeans, a sky-blue wool sweater, and hiking boots. She turned to Nick. "We'll set the wards to protect the building from intruders, but they'll allow you and Irma to come and go if you need to."

He nodded. "Safe journey. If anyone does try anything I know what to do." His eyes abruptly glowed a dark reddish black and his fangs extended.

"This is why I love my bad boy." Jazz wound a dark red wool scarf around her neck and reached for her coat.

Stasi, Trev, Blair, and Jazz bundled up and walked out to the corner of the yard behind the building where they couldn't be seen by anyone on the street. Just to be safe, the witches set up a ward that screened them from view. Stasi knew watching them perform magick would endear them even less to the residents.

"Your idea. Your request," Jazz said. "If I ask, we could end up in the middle of a volcano. Although right now, that might not be such a bad idea." She stamped her feet against the cold ground.

Stasi closed her eyes and centered herself. She opened them and held her palm up. "I humbly request entrance to the realm that will offer me guidance that I can find nowhere else. We wish to visit The Library."

Within seconds a tiny golden glowing ball of light hovered in front of her face.

"Hello." She smiled. "Will you take us to the door, please?"

The ball pulsed twice then floated around the side of the building.

"At least it's late, so there shouldn't be too many people out." Stasi stuck her hands in her pockets and trudged down the wooden sidewalk. "So you use The Library too?" she asked Trev who walked beside her.

He nodded. "There's an excellent legal archive there."

"Wow, quick trip and nothing disgusting around," Jazz commented when the ball stopped in front of a shop halfway down the street. "The candy shop? From now on you can ask for The Library realm every time."

Stasi stood before the shop, the other three behind her. "I seek The Library," she spoke in a clear voice. The windows divided in half and slid backwards, revealing a massive, ornately carved wooden door. Stasi stepped forward, gently palmed the large bronze griffin-shaped doorknocker, and rapped it three times against the door.

The griffin opened its citrine colored eyes and peered closely at Stasi and the others. For a moment, his gaze centered on the red hearts floating over Stasi and Trev's heads. "What is your purpose here, wizard and witchlings?"

"I require counsel I can find only here. May we be allowed to enter?" Stasi waited, knowing it was up to the guardian of The Library's door whether they would be admitted or not.

The griffin smiled. "You may all enter." The door slowly swung open with nary a creak or groan.

"No password? You always make me give you a damn password," Jazz grumbled.

The griffin cocked his head to one side. "When it's just you, you require one, as does the other witchling."

"Don't provoke him," Stasi said under her breath as she practically pushed the others inside.

After the winter cold outside, the warmth inside The Library caused them to slip off their jackets.

Stasi closed her eyes and inhaled the scent of ages—old dust, paper, and materials that fairly screamed the magick embedded in them. At one time, she had thought of applying to be a Library Matron—she loved the history the realm held. But her banishment cancelled that dream. After all these centuries, she suddenly felt it didn't matter, because she had found something even more worthwhile. She glanced at Trev, who smiled back at her. Oh yes, very worthwhile.

As they walked through the dim vestibule, torches adorning the wall burst into flame, lighting their way until they reached the end of a passage that expanded into a room that seemed to go on for miles. Rows of intricately carved shelves held ancient grimoires, books, scrolls, and parchments. Stasi recalled a rumor that a portion of Alexander's library was back among the stacks, but in all her visits here she hadn't discovered them and her questions about the scrolls was only met with silence.

Stasi stopped at the front counter and smiled at the man seated on a stool behind it. In all the times she'd been here over the decades, she had never seen him wear anything other than bottle green, old-fashioned knee britches with off-white stockings, a faded green brocade waistcoat over a linen shirt the color of old parchment, and a bottle green, long-tailed coat. Just as he always had stacks of ancient scrolls, leather bound books, and even a few stone tablets carefully arranged on the counter near his spot of power.

Narrowed black eyes peered at her over the rim of ancient half-spectacles perched on his beak-like nose. His thinning brown hair was pulled back into a queue neatly tied with a black grosgrain ribbon, and he appeared ageless even though she had seen him from time to time over the last seven hundred years. Stasi didn't mind his constant lectures on the "do's" and "don'ts" that he made sound like law.

His lips pursed tightly as his gaze swept over them. Like the griffin, he stared at the red hearts but said nothing about them, to Stasi's great relief. "You did not consider dressing appropriately?"

Stasi inwardly winced. The (pronounced with a long e, thank you very much) Librarian had rules that were unbreakable. His idea of proper decorum and dress headed the list.

"This was an emergency, sir," she said respectfully. "I hope you will understand."

He inclined his head in barely a nod before he turned to Trev. "And you, young wizard, what are you doing in the company of these witches?" A faint curl of the lip appeared when he gazed at Jazz, who merely smiled back and, for once, kept her mouth shut.

Trev smiled and bowed. "I am helping them solve a mystery in their town, Uncle Peredur."

Uncle Peredur? The two words rang in Stasi's head and, judging by the shocked expressions on Blair and Jazz's faces, they felt the same.

"He's your *uncle?*" Jazz may as well have asked if the wizard Librarian was Hades, Lord of the Underworld.

"On my mother's side."

"Unfortunately, the upstart took after his father." The Librarian swung back to Stasi. "What do you wish?"

"We believe there is a type of water magick harming our town and we hoped to find materials that would help us discover a way to combat it," Stasi replied.

He peered at her over his spectacles. "And why do you believe that, witchling, when you left the Witches' Academy before you even finished your advanced classes on other magicks?"

"It's all up to you," Blair whispered.

Stasi took a deep breath and began to tell the story of the barrier around the lake, the shifts in energy in the town, and the sense of unease that had been moving through the area.

"One of my human clients is suing Stasi, and I am beginning to think that the lawsuit is also part of this," Trev spoke up.

"The barrier around the lake is able to defend itself, so that we can't take it down," Jazz chimed in.

The Librarian's bony shoulders rose and fell in a deep sigh. "I would suppose you used witchflame." His attention swung to Blair. "And you?"

"I was ready to take down the human who has made Stasi's life a living hell," she freely admitted.

He turned away and consulted a stone tablet, then a scroll. "I do not believe this is merely water magick, but Fae. Try section 8,000,038."

The Librarian snapped his fingers, and a two-foot-high green marble hourglass appeared on the counter. He turned it over, the white sand flowing downward.

"Stennert will guide you." He flicked his fingers to the right.

The nine-foot-tall creature standing at the head of the passage could have doubled as Sasquatch's brother.

"I can't believe he's your uncle," Stasi muttered when Trev stepped up the pace to walk beside her.

"Could he have been adopted?" Jazz asked. "I see absolutely no family resemblance. I mean, he's so… and you're so…"

"*Quiet.*" Stennert's voice rumbled in the passage like rolling thunder. His monster-size feet created mini-earthquakes on the floor every time he took a step, and they grabbed hold of each other to remain upright.

Stasi was positive they'd walked miles, but she knew the various realms The Library resided in were deceptive since they spanned time and space in a way she doubted she would ever understand.

Any time she visited The Library she was used to seeing visitors from various time periods using the facility, and this occasion was no different. She noticed a wizard dressed in the form fitting pants, elegant black coat, and elaborately knotted cravat made famous by Beau Brummel.

She was so engrossed in looking through the portals to see who was there that if Trev hadn't taken hold of her arm she would have slammed into the furry Stennert when he halted.

"In here," he growled, throwing out a long arm ending in dark talons. "I will return."

Jazz turned to Blair. "Didn't Arnie say that?"

Blair shook her head. "'I'll be back' was his."

The four stepped through the portal, feeling a tremendous shift of power as they crossed through.

Stasi smelled herbs used to keep the fragile contents of the library from crumbling into dust. While they didn't smell bad, she could still feel her nose tickling. The sheer size of the cavernous room caused her hopes to plummet.

"I guess our best bet is to each take a section," she said as they looked around.

"This is definitely better than some of the sections I've been sent to," Jazz said. "No having to wear special gloves, no disgusting smells. I told you The Librarian doesn't like me."

"I don't recognize this language," Blair said, perusing a scroll.

Trev moved to her side and glanced over her shoulder. "It's a healing spell for rashes," he said.

"Really? I wonder if Lili knows about this one." Their fellow witch had always been a healer and now worked as a doctor.

"According to the scroll that particular rash was prevalent back in the fifth century." Trev moved on. "And if you're not careful in handling those kinds of scrolls, the rash can transfer itself to you."

Blair dropped the scroll as if it was on fire and wiped her hands on the back of her pants as she moved on. "Note to self. Don't touch anything unless it's been translated first."

"I'll second that motion. Since The Librarian feels it's Fae, we need to check that out first." Stasi headed for shelves carved in the stone walls and gingerly fingered a book. She stared at the fine leather binding for a moment before she carefully pulled it out. She staggered under the weight and would have fallen backwards if Trev hadn't taken the book out of her hands and carried it over to a table. "It didn't look all that heavy," she said, following him. She perched on a stool that waddled up to her and edged its way under her bottom.

Trev was breathing hard by the time he set the book down. "I think it gained twenty or thirty pounds just from the shelf to here."

"It's probably one of those books that will provide what you need once you speak your needs," Jazz told them. "You gave a general subject, so it added more to its memory."

An "eek!" escaped Stasi's lips as she watched the book nearly triple in size. "I'll never get through all of this!" She carefully lifted the cover. "Maybe it has a search feature." She lifted the first few pages.

"Ask."

They all jumped as a voice with an upper crust British accent reverberated around them.

"I wish to know about Fae magick," Stasi said, crossing her fingers.

"What country?"

"United States." Blair gestured for a stool and sat down across from them.

"California forests," Jazz added, hopping up onto the table.

"No sitting on the table." The edge of the table dipped down, dropping Jazz onto her feet. She sighed and nabbed another stool.

"And water and magickal barriers," Stasi said. "Human behavior out of the ordinary. Fear. Mercury retrograde and a lunar eclipse."

"Do you prefer to study forest Fae or water Fae?" the book asked, ignoring the last part of her request, as the pages drifted back and forth.

"We need both," Stasi explained.

"There is no both. There is one or the other."

Stasi looked at the others. "Could both be involved?"

"I know my uncle said Fae, but we still don't know if they are behind what's going on in the town," Trev said.

"And early snowstorms," Jazz said.

"One subject at a time, please," the tome pleaded as the pages fanned back and forth. "I'm only one book."

"Would you have an idea where we could start?" Stasi asked.

"Not without more information. But you are in a large section and I may not have what you're looking for."

"I'll look around and see if there's anything more." Blair got up and headed back to the shelves while Jazz did the same.

"What if we narrow it down to forest Fae that have the power to control water?" Trev suggested.

"Forest Fae have no power over water unless water sprites allow them to," the hardbound book stated in its stiff upper lip accent.

Stasi shook her head. "I've never heard of water sprites in the area. They would have made themselves known to us."

"Then you are in a sticky situation, aren't you?" intoned the book.

"Fine, then what about water Fae?"

The book's pages began to turn. Trev narrowed his cobalt eyes. "No," he said slowly, "I've worked on cases involving water Fae. It's been a couple hundred years, and I don't remember all the details, but even if they were at the lake, I don't think they could have the kind of influence on the townspeople that we're seeing."

"Please, book, can't you even point us in the right direction?" she pleaded.

"Not without a place to start." The pages started flipping back at light speed then the cover slammed shut.

Stasi sighed and looked around the room, recalling the many times she'd come to The Library seeking answers and finding them here. This time wasn't proving as easy as in the past. She mentally ran through the list that seemed to be growing every second. "Forest Fae," she said firmly.

"Righto." The cover opened again, the pages fanning until it reached about a third of the way through.

Trev patted her shoulder and moved off to examine a section of shelves.

Stasi stumbled her way through the archaic writing and wished she could ask the book to update the language, but she knew it wasn't possible. It wasn't the first time she'd read the works of someone from ages ago. Except now time was short, and she needed fast answers. But she couldn't find anything to indicate that forest Fae were capable of creating all the phenomenon they had been witnessing.

Trev walked up waving a scroll. "Okay, here's something on water Fae. The good news is that they are definitely capable of wreaking havoc on a given body of water." He sighed. "The bad news is that from what I just read, the only thing less likely than finding water Fae on a mountaintop in California is to find water Fae and forest Fae working together.

Stasi sneezed from the dust. A headache from the herbs was starting to pound its way through her head. It seemed everything they read could answer one question but never connect it to the whole scenario. It wasn't just the lake that was disturbed; it was the town, the people, even the weather.

"We know water sprites don't inhabit the lake, but what if it's something else?" Jazz brought up. "There's always been the rumor that a monster lives in the lake. What if it's true?"

"Then it has to be a monster that can also exist on land," Blair reminded her.

"The Librarian said Fae and that feels right," Stasi insisted.

Trev stood behind Stasi and began massaging her shoulders. She felt the warmth of his hands ease the tension that had been building up. She reached up and covered one of his hands with hers. The contact gave her hope, along with a good dose of warm fuzzies.

He bent down and whispered in her ear, punctuated with a soft kiss. "We'll find an answer."

"I hope so." She scooted back and stood up. "The Librarian must feel the answer is here, or he wouldn't send us here," she murmured.

"The Librarian also has a twisted sense of humor," Jazz said. "I know you're related to him, Trevor, but please, the wizard doesn't even like us witches."

"Uncle Peredur is happiest working here alone and doesn't like interruptions," Trev explained, grunting as he pulled out a heavy stone tablet, frowned as he read the contents, then pushed it back in.

"Uncle Peredur. Who knew The Librarian had relatives. He's not married, is he?" Blair asked. "No offense, but I can't see him having little Librarians running underfoot."

"There's no room for a wife in his life."

"Understandable, when he didn't make room for a personality." Jazz whistled under her breath as she scanned her section of shelves.

"You two are so mean about him," Stasi chided them as she watched Trev struggle with the large and heavy hardbound book and return it to its spot.

"I have something!" Blair ran back to the table with a tiny book that fit in the palm of her hand. "Forest Fae who worked with water spells."

Stasi grabbed the book and used her fingertips to carefully turn the fragile pages. "So it has happened in the past. But those Fae were punished for uniting forces with water sprites and banished from the world—where does that leave us? How were they stopped?"

"You must go." Stennert's thunderous voice startled them so much Stasi dropped a book and Jazz almost fell backwards.

"Sheesh, give us some warning, will you?" the red-haired witch snapped.

Stasi looked at the book in her hands. "We need more time."

The furry monster shook its head. "You must go." It flexed its talons as if it was ready to step inside and carry them out.

Stasi knew that was an option she didn't want to consider. "Then we have some materials here we need to check out."

The monster shook its head. "You must go. They must remain."

"He's your uncle. Won't he let Stasi take what she needs?" Jazz asked Trev.

"Most of the older materials can't be checked out, and Uncle Peredur never breaks a rule he personally set up," he said.

They trudged out of the section, again feeling the power of the portal they passed through. Behind them, the portal shimmered briefly, then winked out of existence.

Stasi felt the chill of the stone walls as they walked up the passageway. Trev moved up and slid his arm around her shoulders. She was upset and frustrated and it was tempting to shrug off his touch. But she wasn't a fool and his embrace felt comforting.

The Librarian eyed the hourglass as the last grains of sand trickled downward. When the final grain fell, the hourglass disappeared in a wink of light.

"You barely made it back in time."

"Don't ask what would have happened if we were late," Jazz whispered.

The wizard frowned at her then turned to Stasi. "You did not find the answers you sought."

She nodded, not bothering to ask how he knew. It was common knowledge he knew everything because he was quick to remind everyone of that fact.

"It appears what we seek is a combination of things that shouldn't be connected."

The Librarian set down his plumed pen next to the inkstand. "You must think from all sides, witchling. Look at what is within and what is beyond. And you would do well to learn to respect time, young witch," he added, glancing at Jazz. "Good day." He picked up his pen, dipped it into the inkpot, and began writing.

"Good-bye, thank you for coming, and don't let the door hit you on the ass on your way out," Blair muttered.

"Thank you, The Librarian," Stasi said politely, even though she didn't feel he deserved any thanks, because she was more confused than ever.

The wizard glanced at Trev. "Give your mother my regards."

"I will, Uncle Peredur." Trev bowed again before following the three witches to the door.

"Good-bye," the griffin called after them before the door disappeared and the store's windows slid back into place.

"Wait a minute." Blair reached out to clutch Stasi's arm as they stood huddled together on the sidewalk. "How could all of this snow have fallen in the time we were gone?"

As they looked around, one by one the streetlamps along the street dimmed, then winked out, leaving them in complete darkness. The same happened with the pumpkin-shaped twinkling lights ringing every shop window.

"It's as if someone is individually turning off each light," Stasi whispered. She held up her hand. "Listen."

"To what?" Trev asked, turning in a tight circle.

"That's the thing. Usually you can faintly hear Grady's jukebox this far up the street. Or someone's TV from one of the cabins nearby. There's always an electrical hum, but now it's gone," she whispered in keeping with the silence around them. She felt the cold seep through her jacket and settle in her bones. She began to hear the faint sound of voices in the distance and see bobbing lights that she assumed were flashlights, but she had no idea why they were out there.

The pristine snow was so deep it covered the road and piled up onto the sidewalks. It was falling heavily around them, and the air was so cold their noses and cheeks rapidly turned red from the icy wind that assaulted them.

Stasi felt her breath freeze in her lungs, and she labored to breathe, but it started to hurt. She noticed the others had the same problem. She opened her mouth to suggest they use some witchflame to warm their hands, when she noticed a heavily bundled figure struggling toward them through the snow.

"Ginny?"

The café owner stopped, keeping her distance from the group. Stasi felt that the distance was more than physical and the knowledge hurt.

"I looked out and saw you out here. Why are you doing this to us?" Ginny asked, her voice breaking. "We know you and Carrie are quarreling."

"Talk about an understatement!" Stasi cried out. "That's not even close to what Carrie wants to do to me."

"But you're hurting all of us." Frost punctuated her words.

"I'm not doing this! I don't know what's going on," Stasi said, anguished because she knew her friend was upset. But she had no idea why Ginny was blaming her now when she had been her biggest ally since the beginning of her troubles with Carrie. She felt the reassuring pressure of Trev's hand slipped into hers and she took strength from his touch.

"What do you mean you don't know? Look around!" She threw her arms out. "The power went out yesterday morning. The highway is blocked by the snowstorm, and even our men can't go down the road far enough to clear it. And now Carrie's youngest is missing. Everyone is out looking for him, and they think you had something to do with it." She started to back up. "I don't know you anymore, Stasi." She continued to back up. "Please don't come to the café anymore. You're not welcome. Just please go away."

"Wait! Why are you saying this? This isn't you, Ginny!" Stasi cried.

But Ginny didn't answer her.

"I haven't changed! I didn't do this," Stasi protested, starting after her then halting when Ginny's face flashed with fear.

The woman shook her head. "This is all wrong. We all loved you two, and now you do this." She wiped her eyes with her gloved fingers. She turned around and returned the way she had come.

Stasi wanted to cry, but she knew her tears would only freeze on her face.

"Come on, Stasi, we need to get inside and get warm." Trev took her hand and led her around the back of their building.

The foursome was quiet as they climbed the rear stairs and stepped inside the kitchen. They were surprised to find the room dark and as cold as the outdoors.

"It's about time you got back," Nick greeted them in a voice taut with worry. "All hell's been breaking loose around here." He hugged Jazz tightly.

"It must have started snowing this hard right after we left in order for it to pile up this much," Stasi said, pausing to allow a frenzied Bogie to float into her arms. The dog whined as he licked her face and brushed his paws against her shoulders. "Did the snowstorm cause a blackout? We were outside and watched the streetlamps go out one at a time, but the power had to have been out for some time to get this cold inside. We have a generator for emergencies."

Nick's expression was grim as he surveyed the small group. "You've been gone for two days."

Chapter 16

"TWO DAYS?" STASI'S MIND REELED. SHE KNEW THAT time moved differently in The Library, but any of the other times she visited the realm she returned home to learn it was only a few hours later. Never two days.

Nick continued to hold Jazz tightly, as if afraid to let her go. She buried her face against his shirtfront, then moved her face to the side.

"Nick, love, I know you don't need to breathe, but I do, and I think you're cracking a rib," she wheezed, struggling in his embrace.

"I was afraid something had happened to all of you," he admitted, releasing her, but touching her hair as if he needed to assure himself she wasn't a figment of his imagination. "The snow started falling hard and fast a few hours after you left and it was easy to sense the emotions going on out there."

"It's been a nightmare," Irma agreed, walking into the room wearing a flannel bathrobe and fuzzy slippers and with her hair up in curlers. Sirius and Fluff and Puff were on her heels. The slippers immediately raced over to Jazz, chattering away as they tried to slide up her legs. "I went with Nick when he went outside to see what happened when the lights went out. It was so cold out there I swear I thought my bones would turn to icicles."

"Says the dead woman," Jazz muttered.

"At least my nose doesn't look as if it belongs on a reindeer," Irma sniped back.

Jazz immediately held up her hands in surrender. "Sorry. What was happening?"

"The power started going out in the homes one by one. Even their generators won't fire up." No one bothered to ask Nick how he knew this, since his hearing was more sensitive than anyone's. Not to mention Irma could enter any building without anyone being aware of her presence. Since the ghost had gained her freedom from Jazz's T-Bird she liked to "visit." Jazz never asked whom she visited or what she saw. She figured she was safer not knowing.

Irma's hand was shaky as she lifted her hand with a cigarette glowing in the darkness. No one said a word as she puffed on it several times.

"None of this is good," Irma pronounced.

Stasi looked around her at their grim faces. "Raise your hand if you're not spooked by all this."

No one moved a muscle. The silence was deafening.

She couldn't stop the whimper that escaped her lips. If Trev hadn't been holding her, she knew her knees would have given out on her and she would have been on the floor.

"Okay, let's get a grip. I'll make some coffee." Blair headed for the counter.

"No power," Stasi reminded her. "And the back-up generator is dead, too."

Blair wiggled her fingers. Sparks be-bopped around the digits. "Then it's a good thing we have an additional backup, because right now I would kill for some high-test caffeine," she said as she went to work.

"What did you find out?" Nick asked. "Nothing useful," Jazz replied. "Except that The Librarian has relatives. Who knew? It seems Trev's his nephew. Which is further proof you can't choose your relatives."

"Oh honey, everything will be fine." Irma patted Stasi on the shoulder. Stasi tried not to flinch as a frigid sensation swept through her body from the ghostly touch. "These things happen to Jazz all the time, and somehow she always manages to get out of them. She usually leaves a mess behind, and that head witch is never happy with her, but Jazz always manages to come out of that dung heap smelling like a rose."

"Although I still have you in my life," Jazz muttered, rummaging in the freezer. "Oooh! Cinnamon rolls." She placed them on a paper plate and zapped them with a bit of her power. Pretty soon the kitchen smelled of cinnamon, vanilla, and sugar.

The coffee was ready, and Blair handed out filled mugs.

"Let's go into the family room so we can be comfortable and see if we can re-group," Stasi suggested and they filed into the other room. She walked around the room lighting candles. She wasn't surprised that Nick hadn't bothered with them, since he could see just as easily in the darkest night as anyone could see in the bright light of day.

At that moment, she wanted to curl up in her favorite easy chair with the plump pillows. Trev wasn't about to let her go too far from him, so she shared the chair with him and luckily, it was large enough for two. She discovered sharing the space wasn't so bad, especially when she felt so cold inside.

Blair dropped into her favorite chair and stretched her legs out on the matching ottoman, while Jazz and Nick settled on the couch.

"Okay, so we don't know any more than we did before?" Nick asked, stealing some of Jazz's coffee. She took her cup back and took a big swallow. A flick of her fingers refilled the cup without her having to get up. A second cup appeared in Nick's hand, and she grinned at him.

Stasi laid her head back against Trev's shoulder. "The Librarian said we should look up Fae, even if some of the spells don't seem to be Fae inspired. The book said you could only ask about one type of magick at a time, except what we have here is inter-connected. But who says that there aren't Fae working with someone else to create all this?"

"Fae don't play well with others," Jazz brought up. "They have their areas and they don't leave them. They always want to be the big fish in the little pond."

"And this is a small town," Stasi murmured. Her brow furrowed in thought. "Not that many new people have moved here in the last couple of years."

"The Palmer siblings, Mr. and Mrs. Lucas, that wood sculptor who bought the Frederick's vacation cabin," Blair thought out loud. "That's it."

"And the only ones who have basically constant interaction with everyone in town are Reed and Poppy Palmer," Stasi said. "And now Reed's sister is here."

"I've never liked them. They're always bringing over cookies and muffins."

"Which we do our best not to eat except those couple times we weren't able to refuse." Thoughts came fast and furious, suppositions that Stasi refused to voice until she knew she was correct.

Blair jumped to her feet when they heard a knock at the back door.

Nick waved her down. "I'll get it."

Stasi closed her eyes and pinched her nose. She felt the need of a good headache spell but was too weary to chant the words to make the pain disappear.

"You need to relax," Trev whispered, gliding his fingers across her forehead as he chanted a few words under his breath.

She looked up and smiled as her headache disappeared. "First my forehead. Now you cure my headache. You should have been a healer."

"No way. I've been known to faint at the sight of blood." He brushed a kiss across her temple. "I'm a lawyer, I'm not exactly hero material."

She kissed him back. "You're *my* hero."

"This is cozy." Jake followed Nick into the family room. He had shed his coat, but snowflakes still lingered in his dark hair. He grinned at Blair as he picked her up and sat down, then settled her down next to him. She growled at his highhanded manner but didn't move out of the chair.

Jazz got up and went back into the kitchen, returning with a coffee mug that she handed to Jake.

"We heard the power's out everywhere," Stasi said.

Jake practically inhaled the hot liquid. "Thanks, this really helps. Yeah, like you, everyone's using candles and lanterns. Generators won't kick in, and that makes no sense. But considering what's going on around here, I guess it does make some kind of crazy sense. Cell phones aren't working either. Word has it the cell towers are inactive, but no one knows why or why not one generator in this town works."

"I used telepathy to connect with Letiticia," Nick said. "It's the same situation at the resort. The guests are in a total panic, since they can't get down the hill. Even the snowmobiles up there aren't working. Some of the people want to hike down the mountain, but like before they only get so far and can't seem to go any farther."

"So we're trapped up here."

Jake nodded. "That's pretty much it." He finished his coffee and glanced at Blair. "Is there any more?"

"Do I look like a waitress?" But she got up and came back with a coffee carafe, walking around to refill everyone's cups, leaving Jake's cup for last.

"I'm sorry, everyone, but my witch here looks like she's ready to fall over from exhaustion." Nick got up and pulled Jazz to her feet. With his arm around her shoulders, he guided her toward the guest bedroom. "Good night."

A chorus of good nights followed them.

"I guess I'll be next." Blair pushed Jake to one side so she could climb out of the chair. "Go home, Jake."

"You're throwing me out into the cold? There's no power, remember?"

"If I remember correctly, your cabin has a fireplace. You won't freeze."

"You can sleep on the couch, Jake," Stasi said, not wanting to send anyone back out into the icy air. "There are blankets and spare pillows in the linen closet."

"Sounds good to me." But he kept his eyes on Blair, who ignored the question in his dark eyes and headed for her bedroom, while Irma headed for the room she used and Bogie followed her.

Stasi was grateful when Jake went into the hallway in search of the linen closet, giving her and Trev a bit of privacy.

"With the roads blocked, you won't be able to return to the resort," she said softly.

He kept his attention on her eyes. "Maybe Jake will let me share the couch, or I can make up a pallet on the floor."

She stood up and held out her hand. "Or perhaps you'll receive a better offer."

Trev took her hand and got up, standing close to her. "Are you sure?"

She nodded without a hint of hesitation.

Jake returned with an armload of blankets and a couple of pillows. He didn't look surprised to see Trev follow Stasi into her bedroom and murmured a good night. She closed the door and ran her hands along the door seam. Magickal energy flashed along the door, effectively sealing them in.

"Privacy spell," Trev guessed.

She nodded. "No sound will leave the room and no one can enter without my consent."

He grinned, sincerely hoping her intent was what he was imagining it would be. He stood there waiting to see. "Or leave."

She couldn't help but grin back. "Or leave." She paused long enough to pick up Horace and tuck him in a drawer, not only closing the drawer but also sealing it with a spell.

"No fair!" The gargoyle's muffled protest reached them from the drawer. "I never have any fun!" His grumbling finally settled down.

"He can't hear, or peek out either," she assured Trev.

"Good idea. We wouldn't want Horace taking notes, would we?" he grinned.

Stasi went around the room lighting candles until the room glowed warmly. She walked forward with delicate grace and curled her fingers along his sweater's hem, then pulled it up over his head, dropping it to the carpet.

"No just zapping the clothes off?" he teased.

Stasi shook her head. "Let's try it slow and easy this time." She stood up on her tip-toes and bent her head to the side, inhaling the musky scent of his skin mixed with the dry musty whiff of old books, and magick. She lapped the rough skin the way a cat did, tasting what she smelled. Feeling his strength in his flavor. She smiled when Trev shifted from one foot to the other under her touch. "Don't move," she whispered, peeling off his T-shirt and dropping it to the floor to lie beside his sweater.

"You're already killing me here," he groaned.

"I haven't even started yet." She fingered the cold metal of his belt buckle and took her time unfastening it.

Trev closed his eyes and took a deep breath only to discover it put him in closer proximity to Stasi. He inhaled the spring-like fragrance of her skin; something that reminded him of bright flowers and green grass. "I was afraid you'd say that."

She turned her attention to the other side of his neck. "Just be glad I'm not a vampire." She breathed against his skin as she worked on his jeans' fastenings.

She slowly lowered the zipper, mindful of his erection thrusting its way forward. She laid her palm against the full flesh straining against black cotton.

Trev felt his breath leave his body. "Depends on where you bite."

"By the time I finish you won't care." She knelt down and dispensed with his boots and socks, slowly sliding his jeans off past his hips.

Trev didn't miss that Stasi was eye level with his cock, which had a mind of its own and was ready to burst through his briefs. The fact that she was taking it slow wasn't helping, but the look of her fully dressed and kneeling in front of him while he was naked was sexy as hell. He only hoped he wouldn't die of heart failure before she took pity on him and touched him.

"Poor baby," she crooned, tucking her fingers in the sides of his briefs and pushing them down. "Looking for attention, are we?" She curled her fingers around the base of his cock and slowly slid them upward to the head. Trev hissed a curse then a second one when she just as slowly brought her fingers back down to the root. He started to bend down to grab her when her hold tightened. "Don't move," she ordered with a flash of gold in her eyes.

He breathed heavily through his nose and closed his eyes to better appreciate the sensation Stasi was creating with her touch that maddened him as much as it aroused him. But she wasn't about to stop there.

Because his eyes were closed, he had no warning when she covered him with the silken wet heat of her mouth. What almost had him shooting through the roof was the tingling that spread from her lips all the way down.

"Fates save me," he breathed. He speared his fingers through her hair. He needed that anchor, so he wouldn't fall to his knees. She took him deeply, using the suction of her mouth to create a seal that refused to release him while the tingling seemed to increase in intensity. Trev felt as if his lungs would burst as his balls tightened with each up and down motion of her mouth. Words in a long forgotten language spilled from his mouth. He praised her beauty, gloried in her passion, and was convinced he would die a happy man.

He was even more certain he'd die when she lifted her head.

"You're trying to kill me, aren't you?"

She smiled and shook her head. She stood up in one fluid motion and slowly took off her clothes until she stood in a copper colored silk and lace bra and matching thong.

"You are so beautiful." Trev wanted to say much more, say everything that was deep within him, but the simple phrase was all he could come up with. The look of light and delight on her face told him it was enough because he meant it.

"And you are my sex slave for the night." She planted her hands against his chest and pushed him backwards until he fell on the bed. He obliged her by scooting backwards until he lay on the covers. "You will do everything I say." She peeled off her bra and thong with the teasing style of a stripper and tossed them onto a nearby chair. She pressed one knee on the bed between his spread legs and crawled forward. Her eyes glowed with her power that started sparking around the room.

Trev couldn't take his gaze off her face. He even forgot about the red hearts that turned into a heart-shaped wreath as she settled on his upper thighs while blithely ignoring his bobbing cock.

"Someone's looking for some more serious attention," he said.

She leaned over, her belly brushing against his erection as she reached up for a deep kiss. When she drew back, Trev tasted himself on her mouth. He swore his lips tingled and said so.

"Cinnamon lip gloss," she murmured, feathering light kisses around his jaw. "With a little extra punch, so to speak. Like it?"

"Love it. Buy more of the stuff. A few hundred cases might do it." He slid his hands over her sides, enjoying the feel of her smooth flesh. He hadn't remembered seeing the faint tan lines the last time they made love, but he had been pretty much caught up in lust at the time. He reveled in the rose-pink color of her nipples and the way they deepened in color as she grew more aroused, and the spicy scent that wafted off her skin.

Not that he could keep his attention focused when she was rubbing up against him in such a way that he was positive he'd be a puddle of ooze soon. But then wizards had a few tricks up their sleeves, too.

"Lady of night. Lady my love. Lady hold tight." With a quick flip of his hips, he had her pinned to the bed and he settled in between her thighs.

Before Stasi could voice a protest, Trev was kissing her deeply and had thrust forward until he was fully buried inside her silken heat. He reached down and found her clit, pinching it lightly between his fingertips. She bucked upward, almost unseating him as she screamed inside his mouth, but she still held back that tiny part of her.

"Let go, love," he whispered. "Show me what that witchy body of yours has. Show me what you truly feel." He retreated, then thrust in even deeper and pinched her clit again, this time harder, and had her gasping and pulsing around his cock. "Give me everything you have."

At that moment, Stasi came apart in his arms as a shower of red lights rained down around them. If the couple had bothered to look, they would have realized the lights were heart-shaped, and even the candle flames leaped up in the shape of glowing hearts. But they were too involved in what their bodies shared.

Stasi had barely recovered when Trev started moving his hips in a steady motion that shot her upward again, and this time, he flew with her until the room was lit up with the red hearts that ringed the bed.

Stasi stared at the hearts in amazement. "*Hic!*"

Trev laughed as the iridescent bubble drifted upward. "Again?"

"*Hic!*" She clapped her hands over her mouth, but not soon enough, as another bubble joined the first one. "Look around us," she said in a hoarse voice.

Trev looked at the headboard that now displayed another set of red gleaming hearts, then over his shoulder, where more hearts danced on the footboard.

"Cupid can be pushy, can't he?" He idly stroked her from her shoulder along her sides to her hips, then back up again. Her skin was damp, as was his. He wondered if her bathroom had a shower that could hold two.

"Cupid doesn't like it that I do my part in the line of romance." She gave him a gentle push then rolled over onto her side. He did the same so he could face her. Even then he couldn't keep his hands off her and enjoyed the feel of her skin under his hands. Considering the look on her face, she felt the same way.

"And only two hiccups," he teased.

Stasi scrunched up her nose as she noted the bubbles floating near the ceiling. "Nervous habit. I've done it since I was a child."

"A cute habit."

"Says the wizard who *doesn't* hiccup at odd times." She did some touching of her own.

Trev groaned as pleasure-pain rippled through him. "I'm not so sure I'm all that ready to go again."

"Then I guess we'll just have to find something else to do." She moved in closer. "I like my guests to feel comfortable."

He didn't want to think she had made other men as "comfortable" as he was feeling. But then, they both had been around for centuries. And what was important was that he was the one in her bed now, and he intended to be the last man who knew her bedroom, and her, on an intimate basis.

Trev reached down and pulled a baby blue knit throw over them, wrapped his arms around her, and settled back against the pillows with Stasi's head resting on his shoulder and her arm draped across his chest.

He couldn't remember the last time he'd felt such contentment. It also helped that the red hearts surrounding them were fading.

"This is nice. You like to cuddle." Her voice was drowsy.

"With you, I do." He kissed the top of her head. "You feel very right in my arms." He could feel her smile against his skin.

"Hey!" Pounding sounded from the other side of the room. "When do I get out of here? Hello! I'm suffocating here! Do you really want my death on your head?" The pounding stopped for a second then intensified. "This is gargoyle abuse! I'll report you to the SPCG, the Society for the Prevention of Cruelty to Gargoyles!"

Stasi looked at Trev. Trev looked at Stasi.

"He can't hear or see a thing?" he asked.

Her lips curved upward as she nodded her confirmation.

"Silence for me. Silence for she. Give us peace and quiet until morn by allowing noisy gargoyles to sleep." He threw out his hand and covered her dresser with his power. Silence fell the second the wave hit the wood.

"Ooh, you're good."

Trev chuckled as he realized he wasn't as tired as he thought he was. He wasted no time rolling her over underneath him.

"Let me show you just what good is all about."

Chapter 17

STASI LOOKED OUT THE KITCHEN WINDOW BUT SHE SAW only darkness. "October 31st. Samhain," she murmured. "Somehow this isn't what I expected for this day."

"None of us expected a morning like this. So, anyone have ideas on what to do next?" Blair asked as she stacked pancakes on a serving platter and set them in the middle of the table while Stasi forked up bacon. "Other than what everyone around here except me seems to have been doing lately," she grumbled. She gave Stasi a bump with her hip. "Stop grinning like an idiot." She pivoted and pointed her spatula at Trev. "You too."

Stasi cocked her head to one side, listening to the shower running in the guest bathroom. She was grateful they had a gas stove and water heater. Because the day was weirdly as dark as night, they had lit candles scattered throughout the kitchen. The warmth of the stove had taken the chill out of the air, and the kitchen felt cozy, a haven from the threatening forces that were gathering outside in the gloom. Bogie was occupied with a bowl of kibble, while Fluff and Puff had been appeased with a pancake each. At the moment, she felt happy—a light-as-air sensation that she couldn't remember feeling for a long time, and she knew it was due to the wizard seated at her table. They'd barely slept, but it hadn't mattered because they were too lost in each other.

"Don't complain. You had your chance. All you had to do was drag him into your bedroom and have your way with him. For once he even looked willing." She carried the plate of bacon over to the table, pausing long enough to thrust enough energy into a pitcher of pancake syrup to warm it up, then drop a kiss on Trev's mouth. She felt so happy that she didn't care who knew how she felt about him.

"Um, cinnamon." His blue eyes danced with delight as he licked his lips. "Very tasty."

"Cinnamon syrup's one of my favorites," she murmured.

"Same here." His gaze centered on her mouth that glistened with lip gloss.

"Good morning." A freshly showered Jake walked in. His black hair was still damp and he was barefoot. Blair looked at him as if he was the main course. He took a chair across from Trev and spun it around to rest his arms on the back. "Any coffee?" He looked hopefully at Blair.

"Over there." She gestured toward the pot on the counter. "If you want table service, head to Ginny's."

Jake got up and snagged a coffee cup, filling it to the brim.

"Wow, everyone's up." Jazz stumbled in, wearing flannel pajamas decorated with chocolate bonbons. She got coffee and sat at the table. Her sleepy gaze perked up when she saw the food. "Oooh, Blair's pancakes." Once she had a plate filled and sat down, she looked at the others. "So what's the plan, Scoobies?"

"We are starting to be like them, aren't we?" Stasi replied. "But are we Scoobies as in Velma and Shaggy, or Buffy's Scoobies?"

"I vote for Buffy's Scoobies. That would make all of us Willow," Blair pointed out.

"Krebs isn't here, but I name him Xander. Although, I can't see Letiticia as Darla. I'll be Oz," Jake suggested.

"I don't know." Blair eyed him closely. "Well, I guess so."

"Then it's a given I'm Angel." Nick walked in and retrieved coffee, then leaned against the counter. "Now that we have that settled, what do we do next?"

Stasi rested her face on her crossed arms on the table. "The Library didn't give us one hint other than we're screwed." Her words were muffled along with a hint of a whine. "I'm whining, aren't I?"

"Maybe a little bit." Jazz leaned over and rubbed her back. "You and Blair put up with me whining when I was mortal for those two days. And you're not even close to the shape I'd been in."

"Why don't we eat while the food's hot?" Blair suggested. "Maybe things will seem clearer then."

Stasi lifted her head and looked at the window. The glass had a crackled look from the frost and nothing could be seen but darkness.

"Everything looks pretty shitty right now," she mumbled, but she picked up her fork and started in on her pancakes. After a few bites she put her fork down.

"Eat," Trev urged.

"I will." She looked lost in thought. "I think you need to leave here, Trev. You need to find a way to either leave town or at least stay at the B&B. Once Carrie finds out you're here—and she will find out because Ginny saw you last night—she will make matters worse for you. She knew enough to find you to file the lawsuit."

"All because of that damn sachet," Blair mumbled.

Stasi's cheeks turned a dark pink. "Her boys were with her and pawing the displays with their grubby hands. She was moaning about what a jerk her husband was to leave her and yet there she was in my shop picking up over $500 worth of lingerie in hopes of luring him back, at the same time she's bitching the child support checks are late. Her priorities were so screwed up it wasn't funny. She's a disgrace to the very idea of romance. And I thought of her husband, who's a very nice man who got caught up by the idea of having the perfect family life, when instead he got Carrie and her kids, who act like nasty little gremlins more often than not. What if she had really succeeded in luring him back? He'd finally gotten away from her. I just wanted to make sure he didn't go back to that living hell."

"Kevin is a nice guy," Jake agreed. "Some of us tried to tell him he wouldn't be happy with her. Carrie's previous marriages were proof of that, but he wouldn't listen."

"When Carrie wants to, she can come across as Mother of the Year," Blair said, munching on bacon. "But if life doesn't go her way, she turns into Bitch of the Year." She cast an apologetic look at Jazz since it was known the B word wasn't one of Jazz's favorites.

Jazz waved it off. "Sometimes you have to use what fits. Although I know there are more explicit words out there that would also work, I am a lady." She glared at Nick who had snorted in his coffee. He murmured a quick "sorry."

Stasi's gaze returned to the window. She idly ate as she studied the frosted glass. She dreaded to think what the lake looked like now.

"So much is shifting. It's as if someone's manipulating the forces around us," she mused.

"We have it narrowed down to forest Fae," Jazz said. "But it doesn't explain everything, and it's still not specific enough."

"It will be." Knowing she would need all her strength, Stasi soon finished her hearty breakfast.

Once everyone had polished off their breakfasts, Blair picked up the dishes and coerced Jake into helping her clean up.

"Be useful for once," she told him.

He grinned. "If you only knew."

Stasi left the kitchen for a few moments and returned with her hiking boots on. She walked over to the coat rack and pulled off her coat and scarf. "I'm going to take a walk."

"Not without me." Trev was by her side in seconds.

She opened her mouth to argue with him, but she knew it would only delay her plans. She nodded and waited while he got his jacket.

Even in her warm clothing, Stasi shivered when they stepped outside. Trev quickly pulled the door closed behind them. The yellowish glow of candlelight was a bare glimmer through the window over the sink and the window in the door.

"It's even colder than last night." She pulled her cream-colored fleece cap on and tucked her hair up under it, so it could cover her ears, then slipped on matching gloves. Trev did the same with a navy wool cap and sheepskin-lined leather gloves he pulled out of his jacket pocket.

Stasi looked up, noticing the charcoal colored sky with ash-colored clouds dotted here and there. While the snow had stopped falling sometime during the night, the warning of more snow was in the air.

"I want to see the lake before we do anything else." She started to step down then halted when she noticed the ice on the treads. "Ice to water. Water to steam. Release to air and not be seen, if you please." The coating of ice on the wooden steps immediately melted then rose up in spirals of steam. In seconds the stairs were completely dry.

"I have to admit, I haven't spent a lot of time around witches, but you three are showing me what I've missed," Trev said, following her down the stairs. "And you have some nifty spells."

"They come in handy." She walked carefully across the frozen ground, hearing the crunch beneath her hiking boots. Trev moved up beside her and took her hand in his, tugging her behind him so she could walk in his footsteps. She smiled at his back, feeling warmed by his thoughtfulness, and while she knew either of them could have used their gifts to warm the ground, because she chose not to Trev did likewise.

"Why do you feel the need to see the lake? Do you think something else has happened?" He held back low hanging tree branches that would have smacked them both in the face.

"It's just a sense I have." She touched his jacket, stopping him. "While Blair and I aren't water witches, we've always felt a connection to the lake. When we had to leave the area, we always made sure that the lake was protected," she explained. "Especially when a ski resort was built up here in 1930. Blair and I were afraid that someone would buy the land and the lake would be available for guest use only. We already owned the building, and we purchased the land around the lake. This way we knew the land wouldn't ever be sold."

Trev assessed his surroundings. "You two would be very wealthy."

She shook her head. "Money isn't important to us. Yes, we're typical females. We love nice things and we have our splurges, but it doesn't cost much to live up here and our shops give us a very nice living."

"You are one in a million," he said softly, stepping forward to take her in his arms. He lowered his head to kiss her, but she ducked away.

"In air this cold we'd be frozen together," she warned him.

"I can't think of a nicer way to go. Cinnamon ice, yum!"

She laughed and stepped back. "Come on, Wizard Barnes, we have things to do." She turned him around and gave him a little push.

Stasi felt the odd shifts the moment she stepped into the open area surrounding the lake. The barrier was once again invisible, but she could still sense its presence. On the other side of the lake, a series of green glowing balls floated in the air. The lake's surface was now unruffled, the surface serene and a silvery color.

"It's calmed down, but it's completely frozen over." She bent down and picked up a small stone, tossing it toward the lake. The minute it hit something unseen it disintegrated into dust that fell to the ground.

Trev pursed his lips in a low whistle. "Nothing like adding a little extra oomph to its protection. I don't know about you, but I'd like to keep our bodies in one piece."

Stasi stood up and dusted off her hands. "I agree."

. "You said it normally doesn't freeze?"

"Only a few times, and it's cold enough now for it to happen. If someone came out here and saw the frozen surface, they might think it was good for ice-skating. Luckily, with all the trees and rocky surface, snowboarding or even sledding isn't advised." She frowned as something colorful appeared on the other side of the lake. "There's something over there." She pulled on Trev's sleeve and hurried around the worn path circling the lake.

By the time they reached about halfway to the other side, Stasi could hear the faint whimpering of a child.

"Carrie's son," she whispered, picking up the pace.

"Stasi, wait!"

But she ignored Trev and ran, skidding a few times on frozen ground but managing to keep her balance. By the time she reached the other side she was out of breath as the cold air squeezed her lungs.

A small boy dressed in a red down jacket and heavy pants sat on the snowy ground. His tears had frozen on his cheeks and while he didn't appear to be harmed, he was scared and cold.

"Danny?" Stasi asked, dropping to her knees beside him. She dug through her pockets but found them empty. Before she could conjure up a handkerchief, Trev handed her one.

"I'm Kenny," he whispered, identifying himself as the other twin. "I want my mommy."

She put her arms around him, alarmed at the cold feel of his skin. "Where have you been?"

He shrugged. "I don't know. I went to bed and woke up out here."

Stasi noticed his lips were blue and his skin bright pink and chapped, but didn't see any signs of anything more serious.

"Here, big guy." Trev stripped off his jacket and wrapped it around the boy before he swung him up into his arms. "Let's get you home where you can get some warm food."

"Mommy will be mad, but I didn't run way," he whimpered, hiding his face against his shoulder. "Honest."

"We know that, sweetheart." Stasi rubbed his back. She looked up at the expression on Trev's face. "What's wrong?"

"Maybe it's best that just I take him back," he said. "Tension's high enough as it is and…"

"And Carrie hates my guts," she admitted with a sigh. The realization hurt. She didn't like the woman. Never had. But that didn't stop the pain from rippling through her. She stepped back. "All right. Do you know where her house is?"

He shook his head.

"It's 405 Fremont Lane. It's a winding road behind Grady's BBQ Pit. It's the fourth house on the left."

"I'll be back soon," he promised, kissing her quickly then striding off.

Stasi remained in place and watched them walk. She could hear snatches of their conversation as Kenny lamented how his mom was going to be really mad at him.

Once they were out of sight, she looked back at the lake and the green glimmering globes. She took a deep breath and held up her hand.

"I seek knowledge. I seek information. I seek a way to repair the trouble in my land." She smiled when the tiny gold light hovered over her palm. "Please lead me."

She was surprised when the ball had her turn around and face a large tree. A soft hum from the sphere instructed her to step forward.

"But where are the doors?" she asked, walking until her nose touched the rough bark. "*Ahhhhh!*" Her next step took her literally into the tree, and she found herself falling downward into an abyss.

In what seemed like hours and was probably only minutes, Stasi hit bottom. An "oomph!" escaped her lips as she fell on her rump and rolled to one side.

"Damn it!"

"You're not very graceful, are you?"

Stasi slowly climbed to her feet and rubbed her injured posterior.

If she wasn't mistaken, the griffin doorknocker was grinning.

"That first step is a dilly."

The griffin rolled his eyes. "If I had a bar of gold for every time I heard that. Enter, witchling." The doors slowly swung open.

Stasi wasn't surprised to find The Librarian seated behind the counter with scrolls about him, scratching away with his plumed quill pen.

"You are a stubborn one, young Anastasia," he said in his prim voice as he looked up. His faded eyes were keen as he studied her.

"The answer is here," she insisted.

"And what makes you think that?" He set his quill pen down by the parchment he'd been writing on.

"Because The Library knows everything. It holds knowledge of the ages, whether the past or the future. It knows what is harming our land and frightening the mortals," she told him. Her voice rose. "Maybe you don't like us witches or the mortals, but they're innocents and you're bound by your code to help them. So damn it, we need help!"

The Librarian raised an eyebrow and a corner of his mouth twitched... just a little, but enough to let her know it wasn't a frown. "Now you sound more like Griet."

Stasi wasn't sure what was more frightening. That The Librarian had actually attempted a smile or that he hadn't blasted her out of the realm the moment she shouted at him.

She knew one thing. She wasn't going to back down.

"Will you help me?" She deliberately didn't tack on a please. She'd already yelled at him and she knew he wouldn't easily forget that transgression.

He slipped off his wire-rimmed spectacles and polished them with a snowy handkerchief. "All of you witchlings are the same. You expect your answers to be found in scrolls or books, when they just might be found within yourself. Fear is a strong emotion, young Anastasia. It can only be conquered by an equally strong emotion. Once you realize what that emotion is, you will find a way to save the people of your town. You have already tapped into your inner strength. You just need to use all that is within you." He tucked his handkerchief away and set his spectacles back on his nose.

"That's it? No wonder Jazz says you suck!" She'd already crossed one line, so another wasn't going to make much difference now. *Hic!* She slapped her hands over her mouth, but it was too late. The damning bubble was already floating before her eyes.

His already thin mouth narrowed even more. "Perhaps you need to conquer the past so that you may heal the present."

She opened her mouth, hoping she wouldn't hiccup again, but the elderly wizard had clearly had enough of her questions… and her. He flicked his fingers at her.

"Be gone."

Stasi's eyes widened as she was swept backwards through the doors, which neatly closed after her and *whooshed* her back up the way she came. The sense of going in reverse sent her stomach into overdrive as she was tossed out of the tree and once again landed on her butt.

"I am never defending you again, you pompous ass," she muttered, limping back to the building.

Chapter 18

TREV HAD NO TROUBLE FINDING THE HOUSE, BECAUSE the front yard was filled with people carrying flashlights, the rounded lights bobbing up and down as they moved about. When a man turned and saw him walking up the road, he shouted Carrie's name and waved his arms.

Carrie flew out of the house and almost bowled Trev over as she tried to grab Kenny. The boy broke into tearful howls the minute he saw his mother and reached out with his arms. Trev immediately handed him over.

Others called out to alert the others the search could be called off, that Kenny was home.

"Where was he?" she asked, cradling her son protectively against her breasts.

"He was out by the lake."

"I didn't go out by myself, honest, Mom!" Kenny cried, burying his face against her neck. "I went to bed and when I woke up I was outside."

Carrie's usually faded eyes blazed to brilliance as she stared at her attorney. "*She* did this," she spat out the words. "She took my son to scare the hell out of me. She endangered his life just because she thought she could. Now do you see what a monster she is?"

"Carrie." Reed Palmer walked up and laid a hand on her shoulder. "Be grateful Kenny is back. That's the important thing here. If, indeed, it was Stasi who was behind this kidnapping, then the authorities can deal with it."

Trev studied the man, whose tone and expression seemed full of concern for Carrie, but he caught a hint of something else. He had been around town long enough to hear the gossip that Reed had pursued Stasi, but she had always politely turned him down.

Who says a scorned man can't feel just as much wrath as a scorned woman?

"Stasi had nothing to do with this," he stated.

"She's bewitched you," Carrie sneered. "She's used her black magic to twist your thoughts."

Trev had never before experienced fury like that which rose up in him now, but that didn't stop him from embracing it and using it to his advantage.

He tapped into that internal storm and brought up power that sent the nearby trees swaying, the branches touching the ground even though there was no wind, and the air temperature dropping an additional twenty degrees.

"Why is it no one sees the darkness in *your* heart, Carrie?" he asked in a low voice that throbbed with that same energy. "You're so eager to blame others for your problems without looking inside. If you're that anxious to besmirch a woman's good name, you'll have to do it without me." He turned away, but Reed made a mistake and muttered a curse as he grabbed his shoulder. Trev spun back around and without lifting a finger flung the man onto the ground. "This is none of your affair, Palmer," Trev growled.

Carrie still hung on to her son so tightly he whined he couldn't breathe and struggled to get down. "You can't just drop my case. You have to see it through."

"You're in my playground now, Carrie." Trev pointed his forefinger at her, but he made sure not a lick of power was released, although it would happen if need be. "You know *nothing* about wizard's law. *Nothing* of how we conduct ourselves. No matter how much research you claim to have done about us, you know a bare fraction of how we work. When a client is deliberately harming their opponent, the attorney can make the choice to drop the case and no other attorney will take it on. We do not allow anyone, even our own kind, to harm others. You're out for vengeance, not justice."

"I want her to pay for driving my husband away!" This time she allowed her son to slide down her body. He ran off to the yard, where one of the women caught him up in her arms and carried him into the house. The others stood by watching the drama unfolding before them.

Trev advanced on her. "Do you really want someone to pay for your husband leaving you for another woman?" he asked fiercely. "Then why not the woman he's living with now? The woman he intends to marry once your divorce is final. Why didn't you go after her? Many would consider *her* the reason behind the death of your marriage, not Stasi." He intentionally ignored the fact that Stasi had tampered with the sachet she'd tucked into Carrie's purchase that day. He now knew that Stasi wasn't looking to drive a wedge in Carrie's marriage. She only wanted what was right. And it was right for Kevin Anderson to leave his wife for a woman who truly cared for him.

Carrie kept a wary eye on his pointing finger and remained a safe distance away, as if she thought he might harm her. He laughed and let her think it. Of course he could easily take them all down if necessary.

The temptation was there, but he refused to give in to it. He wouldn't lower himself to their level.

"You saw the sachet she put in my bag. You said it wasn't like the others I had."

Trev stared at her and saw the steely determination on her face, the malice in her eyes that turned her features ugly because of the hate that had built up inside her. She wasn't going to back down. She'd put too much energy into besmirching Stasi's name, and she wouldn't retreat when she felt she was winning.

"You're not telling the whole story, counselor." Reed raised his voice so the others would hear. "Sometimes it isn't just magic that bewitches a man, but the woman herself. You can't deny you've been fucking her, can you?"

This time Trev did release enough power to push the other man back a few steps. "Perhaps you should worry about baking your breads, cakes, muffins, and cookies, baker."

"This is my home. Like the others, I don't want to see chaos here." Reed moved back to stand with Carrie, and others gathered from the yard to make a protective group behind her. "For some reason Stasi and Blair have started creating turmoil. All you have to do is look around. We have no power other than our fireplaces and gas stoves. The roads are blocked so no one can get in or out and the snow keeps on falling. We can't allow this to happen. Even you would have to agree they should pay for their crimes."

"And what crimes are those, Palmer?" Trev shot back. "That they love this town? That they've helped so many of you over the years? Who's been there when you've needed help with a sick child? Or caring for an elderly relative when you needed a break? When the town hit hard times during the Depression, they were up here to do what they could, so the town wouldn't die as so many others did. Did you think I wouldn't discover these things? But it seems many of you choose to forget them."

A few looked away shame-faced, but most were too caught up by the hatred in the air. That was when Trev knew he could talk until his face was literally blue and he wouldn't be able to change their minds. He'd argued landmark cases in Wizards' Court and won. He had persuaded the most skeptical of judges that his client was in the right.

And now, when the case had turned 180 degrees, he couldn't do anything. He shook his head and turned away. He was done with Carrie. Done with them.

"Those wicked witches are leaving this town one way or another," Carrie called after him.

"Your retainer will be returned as soon as possible," he told her. "And papers will be filed in Wizards' Court that the case is dropped."

"You can't do that!" By now Carrie's face was a revolting shade of purple.

He turned back. "But I can. Your case was based on retaliation, not merit. If I don't file the papers, the court will drop it anyway." He looked at the group behind Carrie. "You're all fools." He walked away, intent on getting the bitter taste out of his mouth.

"You're the fool, Barnes," Reed called after him. "You're letting a woman lead you around by your dick."

Trev always prided himself on not allowing someone to push his buttons, but the man's comment was too much for him. He spun around and sent a shot toward Reed's feet. He jumped back before the toes of his boots were singed. The look he gave Trev told him he'd made a mistake. Trev smiled to let him know there was no mistake.

Trev walked away hearing the angry murmurs among the people. In hindsight, he feared he had made more trouble on Stasi's behalf, but as he told Stasi, he didn't like bullies. One bully was bad enough. A town full of them was dangerous.

"Didn't I tell you he was a prissy egotist?" Jazz could be heard saying as Trev let himself in through the back door.

"I told him he sucked," Stasi muttered.

"I'm so proud of you!" Jazz crowed.

"Boy, you'll never get any special treatment from him after that," Blair pointed out.

Trev followed the voices and walked into the family room. Candles burned everywhere, giving the room a homey look. The three witches were sprawled in various chairs, and the Border collie lay on the floor next to Bogie, who kept a suspicious eye on the black and white canine. Irma was settled in a rocking chair with Sirius lying at her feet. Fluff and Puff were off in a corner arguing over a Milk Bone. The collie lifted his head and greeted Trev with a soft *woof!*, his tongue lolling to one side. Trev chuckled and scratched the dog's head before heading straight for Stasi. He was surprised to see she looked rumpled and even out of sorts. But that didn't stop him from pulling her to her feet and hungrily kissing her.

"*I* need someone like that," Blair grumbled.

Her wish was granted as she was pushed backward in her chair and the collie got up and bounded over to her. He kept his paws on her shoulders as he covered her face with kisses. No amount of batting at him deterred him from his task. When he finished, he moved back to sit on his haunches and bark at her.

"The one who wants to be my boyfriend is a dog… literally," Blair moaned, picking up a napkin from the coffee table and wiping her face free of dog slobber.

"Stop complaining about your lack of a sex life and do something about it," Jazz said lazily. "I'd rather hear Stasi's story. It's a lot more satisfying. Of course, now we have to wait until Trev lets her up for air."

And wait they did, until Trev stepped back. His chest rose and fell heavily while Stasi looked starry-eyed. There was no need of hearts now as they looked at each other.

"What was that for?" she asked between swollen lips.

"My retainer, in case Carrie finds another way to pursue her case," he replied. "I took myself off the case. Jazz, let that lawyer you hired know Stasi already has someone fighting for her."

Three witches and one ghost all displayed dropped jaws.

"You did this for me?" Stasi stammered.

"Congratulations, you finally got a brain," Jazz chimed in.

"It's about time," Blair muttered.

"How romantic." Irma looked teary-eyed.

"What have you done, Trev?" Stasi whispered, gripping his arms. "Carrie's already vindictive toward me. Her anger transferred to you too will make matters worse."

"No, she'll learn that she can't use the wizard's legal system for her own twisted ends." He pulled off his jacket and tossed it on the couch. Stasi smiled and picked it up, hanging it on the coat rack.

Blair hopped up and came back with coffee.

"What happened?" Stasi asked, sitting down with him as he drank the hot brew.

Trev began with his arrival at Carrie's house and told everything up to his exit from there. With each word he spoke, Stasi's fingers twisted nervously.

"It's like Old Salem Village," she whispered. "It only took a tiny few to begin the whispers and the paranoia. Now it's here. The return of the past."

"This isn't like that time," he assured her, putting his cup down so he could put his arms around her. He kissed the top of her hair, inhaling the soft scent of lilacs and spring flowers that he knew he would always associate with her. "No matter what, people don't have the old superstitions they suffered back then."

"It doesn't matter. Fear spans time. Even The Librarian said it would come from the past."

Trev looked at her sharply. "You saw him again?"

She nodded. "I fell through a tree."

"Just like *Alice in Wonderland*," Blair said.

"It was a long drop, too." Stasi unconsciously rubbed her bottom as she remembered the shock of falling onto it. "The Librarian said I have to use the past to heal the present. Then I told him that Jazz was right, he sucked. The next thing I knew I was thrown out of there and back up out of the tree."

"You told my uncle he sucked?" Instead of showing shock, Trev threw his head back and laughed. "No one has ever said anything like that to him before. Most visitors show him more awe than scorn—with the exception of Jazz, of course."

"He's mean," she complained. "He likes to give us puzzles instead of answers, or at least a direction in which to search for our own conclusions. Plus I didn't technically say he sucked. I just said that Jazz was right in saying he sucked."

"It's always blamed on me," Jazz said with a long-suffering sigh.

"Something tells me my next family reunion will be interesting." Trev hugged her against him. "My mother will enjoy this story. And you," he whispered in her ear bringing a blush to her cheeks.

The collie got up and wandered to the back door, scratching at the wood. Blair hopped up and let him out and at the same time let Nick in.

"You stirred up quite a hornet's nest out there, wizard," Nick greeted Trev. Snowflakes lingered on the vampire's dark hair as he shrugged off his heavy coat. While he was impervious to extreme temperatures, he preferred to blend in every way he could. His pale skin didn't look out of place on dark winter days, although his skin never got red or chapped from the bitter cold.

"You were out there when it all went down?"

"I not only heard it all, but I played spy for a while after you left. They were too caught up in the moment to even notice me." As a vampire, Nick could move among others without being noticed if he so chose. His additional training as a former Protectorate enforcer enhanced that ability. "For a while it sounded as if Reed was the wronged one, even more than Carrie." He shot Stasi a wry glance.

"I don't know what his problem is. We never even went out," Stasi muttered.

"Which makes his dislike for you even more intense. You kept rejecting him while he was courting you over time, but you paired yourself off with Trev almost immediately," Nick said.

"It's the red hearts." Even as she said it she didn't believe her explanation. She was now convinced the hearts had only made sure she and Trev were thrown together. "The red hearts," she murmured.

"Yes, you said that." Blair flopped back into her chair, lifting her feet to rest on the coffee table. "Red hearts. Cupid's idea of a joke, but it looks like it back-fired on him. They glow, they glimmer, they dance, they conga, I think they've even done the hustle. Wouldn't it be lovely to have a nice quiet night with nothing more exciting than a movie marathon and lots of popcorn? To prepare for Samhain without having to look over your shoulder?" She glanced at a wall that was left blank for a reason. "And why hasn't Maggie wallmailed me back that she's ready to give up those lovely dresses she wore in 1810? And Thea promised me all her jewelry from the Victorian era."

"Thea giving something up? You must have caught her when she was in one of her insane moods." Jazz yawned, snuggling up to Nick. "She never gives up anything, especially jewelry."

"Red hearts." Stasi paced back and forth. She snapped her fingers. "Cupid set this in motion! He wanted to get even with me. He made sure that Carrie found Trev, who would come up here, the hearts would show themselves—and Cupid sat back and enjoyed the show. Yes, I know I'm rambling and none of it makes sense. But look what's happening now. It's gone beyond a joke. I haven't seen any of the ghosts since that last time with Fergus. I know I told him he should stay in his realm, but he's never listened to me before, why would he do it now?"

"Do you think what's between us is some kind of sick joke?"

Stasi turned and her heart sank when she saw the stricken look on Trev's face. She ran over to him and knelt down on the carpet by his knees. "No, I don't," she said earnestly. "But it started out that way. You can't tell me that you came up here expecting all this to happen between us. I saw you as the enemy when you first walked into the shop. Now, I don't." She placed her palm against his cheek. "I don't see Wizard Barnes, attorney. I see Trev, my lover."

He reached down and pulled her up onto his lap. "Good. Now I don't have to convince you we make an excellent match." He cupped her face with his hands and kissed her deeply, tasting the sweetness that was pure Stasi. She smoothed her hands up his chest to his shirt collar and gripped the fabric tightly as she sank into the kiss, her tongue darting into his mouth to twist and twirl around his. It didn't matter the room had no heat at the moment. They were creating more than enough on their own.

"Um, Stasi? Trev? You do know you have an audience here, don't you?" Jazz interrupted with a hint of laughter in her voice.

Stasi immediately drew back and covered her face with her hands. The kiss she shared with Trev before hadn't turned as intimate as this one. Anyone looking at her would have thought she was embarrassed, except her shoulders shook and muffled laughter could be heard.

"I can't believe this." She struggled to contain her laughter but she couldn't. "I don't normally lose control."

"Neither do I." Trev pulled her back against him.

"Maybe Mercury retrograde and the upcoming lunar eclipse seem to have turned our lives upside down, but I'd say something happened for the better where you're concerned," Blair said. There was no doubt in her sincerity. Seeing her best friend happy made her happy.

"Plus, Trev knows if he hurts you he'll have twelve witches to deal with." Jazz playfully bared her teeth at him. It wasn't as effective as if Nick had showed fang, but the intent in her eyes assured Trev he would be in for a world of pain if he ever hurt Stasi.

"I've already thrown myself into the mix," Nick offered. "Stasi's like family."

"Then I'm glad my intentions are absolutely honorable, because Stasi means too much to me to ever let her be hurt."

Stasi's blood warmed at Trev's words and what sounded suspiciously like a vow to her. *Yep, he's a keeper*.

"Witch and vampire. Now witch and wizard. What will happen next? Witch and gnome?" Blair wrinkled her nose at the thought.

"I could fix you up with Dweezil," Jazz suggested with a wicked light in her moss-green eyes.

"*Gross!*" Blair impulsively pulled her sweater up to cover her face and flashed a sight of a silky teal bra.

"Nice bra, Blair!"

Amid applause from Jazz, Blair lowered her sweater and scrunched up her face. "You're not going to embarrass me. Well, now that we've had our warm and fuzzy moment, let's see what we can find for dinner. I've never been so grateful for a gas stove. I haven't cooked anything over an open fire other than s'mores for decades, and I'd like to keep it that way."

Stasi got up to follow her. Trev kept hold of her hand and squeezed it lightly.

"I meant it about my family, Stasi," he murmured. "I want you to meet them, and I want them to get to know you."

She felt the warmth begin at the tips of her toes and move all the way up through her body.

"I wish you could have met my family."

He looked around him. "I think I already have."

She followed his gaze, seeing Jazz and Nick whispering, Blair beyond in the kitchen while Fluff and Puff played a three-way tug-of-war with Bogie. Sirius remained his quiet majestic self by Irma's side.

"You're right. You have." She dropped a kiss on top of his head and went to the kitchen.

"I'll help." Jazz started to get up, but her offer was half-hearted.

Stasi waved her back down. "No thank you. With your lack of cooking skills the whole kitchen could blow up. But you can set the table when dinner's ready."

"That she can do without mishap," Nick agreed.

Stasi walked into the kitchen and watched Blair pull a paper-wrapped package out of the refrigerator and then re-seal it with magick.

"At least the food won't spoil," she said, unwrapping the hamburger and dropping it into a pot to brown. She pulled down cans of diced tomatoes and spices from the shelf. "Chili seems right for tonight."

"We have sourdough bread to serve with it." Stasi brought out a couple of large cans of beans and a box of macaroni. She turned to the back door when she heard a soft knock.

"If it's that damn dog, he's not staying for dinner," Blair growled. "Can you imagine what chili would do to his digestive system and our lungs?"

"Then it's a good thing it's only me," Jake said, coming in and walking over to Blair, shaking himself off, sending snowflakes all over her. She squealed and threatened him with her spoon, but he only laughed and backed off. He pulled off his jacket to reveal a navy thermal shirt under a red and blue plaid flannel shirt. He unbuttoned the cuffs and rolled them back a couple of times to bare his well-shaped forearms.

"You're welcome to stay for dinner. We have plenty," Stasi told him.

"Witches Cauldron Wine and Dine," Blair muttered, retrieving another can of beans from the cabinet.

Jake took the can out of her hands along with the others and rummaged through the drawers until he found a manual can opener.

"I wonder if the snow will ever stop." Stasi looked out the window.

"Fred tried to fire up his snow blower with no success. Same with all the other ones in town. Mine didn't even let out a burp."

"Towns have been buried under water, but I wonder how many have been buried under snowdrifts." Blair suppressed a shiver. "There are children in the town. What will happen to them with all this cold?"

"We'll solve this. We'll find a way."

Jake pushed the opened cans over to Blair. "Why can't you use magick to get rid of the snow?"

"No way we'd try that. Mother Nature would have our hides if we mess with her territory," Jazz said, coming in and pulling out crockery bowls and spoons. "And she has punishment down to a fine art."

"Only because you called up thunder too many times," Blair reminded her.

"Can you twitch your noses or wiggle your fingers or even cross your eyes to get the snow blowers working?" Jake asked.

Stasi paused in setting out the bowls and spoons. "Maybe we could do that. Mother Nature can't be angry if we're tinkering with machinery."

"I don't think it will work," Jazz said. "I'm not being pessimistic. It's just with everything else, why do we think we can make the snow blowers work? I don't know about you two, but the only mechanical device I've used magick on was the car when I ran out of gas on the freeway."

"And that didn't go well," Irma pointed out from her spot in the family room. "The engine almost caught fire."

"Can't happen. It seems the car is safe as long as you're in it." Jazz tapped her chin with her forefinger. "The only good reason to keep you in the T-Bird."

"We need to stop everything," Stasi said. "Fix the lake, the town, the people." She glanced at Jake.

He made a face. "They're... uh... well, they don't see you as their favorite people right now. They all seem to think you're doing this because Carrie filed the lawsuit. That you're on some sort of vendetta and taking it out on everyone. I did some nosing around this afternoon. There's something going on over at the town hall. I saw lots of flashlights and lanterns in there, so I went over to investigate."

"Was that safe, when they know you spend time with us?" Blair asked.

"I wasn't noticed. Trouble is, I could only hear murmurs, and there was some kind of barrier around the town hall like there was around the lake. I slammed right into it." Jake rubbed his nose. "But I hung around nearby and later on they all came out. The barrier must have dissolved when they left."

"They probably want to run Stasi out of town on a rail. Which goes to show they really don't know her," Jazz said. "Blair and I would go after everyone in a heartbeat if we were seriously pissed, but not Stasi. She's the good one. Even if she was targeting Carrie and making her suffer, she wouldn't go after anyone else. Even if they sided with Carrie, the way these idiots are." She shook her head.

"You three are really close," Jake pointed out. He lifted an eyebrow.

Blair shot him a "don't get any ideas" look. "Get your mind out of the gutter, Jake Harrison. You'll never have that particular fantasy fulfilled."

"Nick wouldn't even dare ask such a thing," Jazz told him. "He likes his body parts where they are."

"Trev hasn't gotten that far, but I think he'd be smart enough not to suggest it," Stasi said.

"In fact, why don't you go into the family room and hang out with the guys?" Blair shooed him out of the kitchen. "Let us women do the work."

"Why do I feel as if sarcasm coated those words?" He grinned as he did as she ordered.

"You seriously need to jump his bones," Jazz murmured to Blair.

"I've given him more than enough hints I'm amiable, but he seems to ignore them. I'd swear he was gay, but I've caught him checking out my ass a few times."

"Hence miniskirts and crop tops last summer," Stasi teased.

"Whatever works." Blair looked down at her fleece boot-cut pants and hoody. "And a much better fashion statement. Today, I dress for warmth."

"Don't we all." Stasi filled a bowl with kibble for Bogie, who immediately materialized at his dish, and two matching dishes of kibble for Fluff and Puff, who came chattering in from the family room. "None of you are getting chili," she informed them. "We like to breathe."

"I'm surprised Horace isn't in here whining that he's starving to death," Blair commented.

Stasi shot up. "Horace!" She raced toward her room. "Trev!" She ran in and headed for her dresser.

"I don't even get dinner first?" he joked, walking in.

"We forgot to take Horace out of my dresser. He's still under your spell," she told him, touching the wood and feeling the power still covering it.

"He can't die in there, he's made of stone."

"No, but he can make my life miserable. You have to break the spell."

He sighed. "Peace and quiet be gone, Horace be heard."

"All right, this isn't funny! Let me out! I know you can hear me! I heard that fucking spell break!" The wood drawer almost bowed under the pressure of gargoyle punches.

Stasi slid it open. Horace pulled off the scarf that had covered him, actually shredded it to bits, and hopped up on top.

"You two are in so much trouble," he grumbled, storming the length of the dresser. "I'm reporting you for cruelty. You'll be cited, that's for sure. I won't allow this to be ignored."

Stasi groaned, but allowed the gargoyle to rant and rave. She knew he'd wind down once he got it out of his system—or until he smelled the chili cooking. Horace loved Blair's five alarm chili.

"There's really a Society for the Prevention of Cruelty to Gargoyles?" Trev whispered.

She nodded. "Guess who heads it?" She picked Horace up and tucked him in her sweater's kangaroo pocket. "Come on, Horace. If you want to be useful, you'll brainstorm with us."

"Ooh, nice. Are you wearing a bra?"

A quick zap from Stasi and he settled down nicely.

"When this is all over, I'm taking you to a nice deserted island for a few weeks," Trev said, putting his arm around her shoulders. "Just you and me, no clothes."

"I'll take you up on that vacation." She smiled.

"Can I come too? Ow! You singed my horns!"

Chapter 19

STASI LOOKED AT THE FRIENDS SHE CONSIDERED FAMILY crowded around the table. Nick was the only one without a bowl of chili in front of him—just a glass of wine.

This is what I wanted for Samhain. Friends here, the place filled with warmth, a sense of togetherness and love. Content to forget about her problems even if just for a little while, she ate a spoonful of chili, then reached for a bite of bread to cut the heat in her mouth. As usual, Blair had overdone the chili spices, but no one was complaining. While Irma couldn't eat food, she still sat at the table and joined in.

By silent agreement, all problems were tucked away and conversation was punctuated with laughter.

"I don't see why I have to eat with the animals," Horace groused from his spot on the floor near Bogie, Fluff and Puff, and Sirius. He waved a gargoyle-sized spoon in one claw.

"Just be glad you're even getting some chili," Blair told him before returning to the conversation.

"You actually know how to use a Dust Buster?" Stasi teased Jazz.

"No one at the Full Moon Café would do the clean-up after the lady staked her son," she replied. "Like I wanted to clean up vamp dust either." She sobered. "It was actually a sad moment. She wanted so badly to see her son, even though he had been turned. We just didn't know she intended to end his existence."

"Perils of taking on mortal clients," Nick said. "The only good thing is, his sire didn't retaliate."

"And I was left to clean up the mess," Jazz said. "I'm going to expect a raise the next time I work with you."

"How many Starbucks cards have you worn out?"

"I'm thinking The Body Bakery and Sephora next." She examined her nails, which she had alternately polished orange and black that afternoon. "I'll give you the information."

"Why not give her a salary?" Trev asked.

Jazz shook her head. "Not as much fun. Plus my fee depends on the job he wants me to do."

"Then how come I don't get paid?" Irma piped up. "I saved your scrawny behind at Colin Reeves' mansion, I told you what was going on in that house where the vampire kidnapped her descendant, and I keep the car safe."

"You stink up the car with your cigarettes," Jazz pointed out.

"I was smoking in that car long before you showed up to try to get me out of it," Irma reminded her.

Trev leaned over to whisper in Stasi's ear, "Are they always like this?"

She nodded. "Usually it's worse. After over fifty years together, they're more like demented mother and daughter."

"And Nick?"

"Jazz and Nick have been on and off for the last few hundred years. But there's such a strong connection between them that we think this time might be very long term," she whispered back.

"Even if vampires can't drink a witch's blood."

"I don't think that bothers them."

He sat close enough to her that his hand rested against her back as a warm imprint.

"And Blair and Jake?"

"Even if she seems to fend him off sometimes, she's the one doing the chasing until he gets the message and slows down long enough for her to catch him. Like the dog always chasing a car, except they say a dog wouldn't know what to do if he caught a car, and Blair will know only too well what to do with Jake."

"And you?" He waited until she turned to face him. "What about you? What would you do if you caught *a car?*"

She knew the car he meant had two arms and two legs instead of tires, a mouth she'd never tire of kissing, and a body she'd like to spend eternity exploring. The heat in his eyes told her he was thinking the same.

"The snow is still falling." His voice was pitched for her ears only.

"I know."

"No problem in my staying the night again?"

"Not at all." Her lips barely moved.

"And I don't have to share the couch with Jake?"

She shook her head. "That wouldn't be fair to either of you."

"I wonder what happened to that dog," Jazz spoke up, breaking the spell between the duo. "It's so cold out there he could turn into a dogsicle."

"Dogs are good at taking care of themselves. They look for a warm spot," Jake said, getting up to fill his bowl again. He retrieved Blair's bowl too and looked around to see if anyone else was interested in another helping. As he filled the bowls, he checked the window over the sink and the one set in the back door. "It might not hurt to board up the windows. While they're double paned, there's still a chance they could crack from all the cold. The same for all the other windows up here."

Stasi studied him. "You're afraid someone might decide to venture outside and throw rocks through the upstairs windows, aren't you? That the protection wards won't hold."

"That could be logical," Nick said slowly. "And something we should have thought of sooner. The weather might be keeping them inside, but if it keeps up much longer, frustration is going to settle in and they'll blame you for it."

"We've had bad storms up here before—we've been snowed in for up to a couple of weeks," Blair said.

"But there was no question that the weather was to blame then. No one's blaming the weather this time around." Jake settled back in his chair, deliberately bumping against Blair. She growled a warning he good-naturedly ignored. "I'll go out and get the boards after dinner."

"No, after you help with the dishes," Blair corrected him.

Stasi turned away to hide her grin. For a witch in pursuit of a hunky carpenter, Blair was making it difficult for herself. She couldn't wait to see what happened when the two finally got together. Even with her world falling down around her, Stasi was thinking pretty positively, and she knew it had to do with the sexy wizard cuddling up with her.

And here Dorothy was told to not look behind the curtain. Her smile grew bigger by the second.

"Hold that thought, gorgeous," Trev murmured, kissing her on the cheek. "I'll help Jake with the manly work."

"Mm, something about a guy wearing a tool belt," she purred.

"I'll loan you one, Trev." Jake grinned.

"The man has good ears."

My family. Stasi looked around again. *It's my fault they're part of this disaster, yet you'd think this was nothing more than another get-together.*

The men were generous enough to shoo the witches out of the kitchen with the offer to handle the clean-up.

"Nick washing dishes. I must get pictures of this." Jazz conjured up her cell phone and ran in to snap photos. "It's for my scrapbook! *Nick!*" She returned with soaking wet hair. "He got hold of the sprayer in the sink," she muttered on her way to the bathroom for a towel.

Irma drifted in and settled in the rocking chair she'd sat in earlier.

"I wish I could knit," she sighed. "I used to crochet lovely afghans and knit baby sweaters, blankets, and booties. Every new mother wanted a set from me. Not that anyone here would have a need for them."

"True." Jazz walked in with her hair wrapped up in a towel. "No little witches running around."

Stasi felt a pang around her heart at Jazz's words and if she wasn't wrong, she saw that same hint of sorrow in Jazz and Blair's faces. Part of the punishment Eurydice had laid on them back in 1313 was that they couldn't have children.

Stasi knew it was better they didn't have children. They didn't know what it would be like for a child, considering the lifestyle she and her fellow witches had had over the centuries.

She was tired. Not physically but emotionally. She wanted a chance to pursue what was happening between her and Trev. She wanted to see if there was a chance for them. The L word whispered inside her mind, but she kept tucking it away. She was afraid if it continued it would become real, but what if his feelings weren't as intense as hers?

When Trev later walked into the family room with an armload of boards, he shot her a look that promised some quality private time later on.

Oh yes, she really wanted to pursue this. And she'd know exactly what to do with her prey, too.

"I feel as if we're prisoners," Stasi said, when she and Trev later retreated to her bedroom. He'd taken a shower claiming he was filthy after handling the boards and was now stretched out naked on the bed. Although the view was tempting, she looked at her window with the boards crisscrossed over it. Her linen chest under the window held a couple of leftover boards. Horace was snuggled down in a fleece-lined dresser drawer, snoring loudly, while Bogie was curled up nose to tail in his bed. "I want it to end." She lay next to Trev on the bed, idly pleating the duvet with her fingertips.

Trev caught her hand and brought it to his chest, holding it there and putting his hand over hers.

She slid over closer to him, closed her eyes, and rested her head on his shoulder. She enjoyed the feel of his warm skin and imagined she could feel his heartbeat under her palm. She inhaled the scent of his skin. "Mmm, you smell like chocolate mint." She moved her head just enough to kiss his neck. Out of the corner of her eye she noticed his cock was stirring. She pulled her other hand over and lightly trailed his side. Oh yes, that did very nicely in catching his attention.

"Yeah, I noticed no glacier mountains or ocean waves fragrance body washes in your bathroom," he said wryly. "But I left your creams alone. My masculinity may be secure, but there's only so far I'll go."

"Thank Jazz. She loves her body products."

"And here I have a perfectly good body wash at the hotel that lets me smell like a guy."

"Yes, but now you smell good enough to eat." And she started to move down to prove it.

Trev held her back. "Horace?"

"I put a sleeping potion in that last bowl of chili. He'll be out for a while."

He didn't stop her this time, and pretty soon his eyes rolled back and he muttered something about her killing him.

By the time Stasi finished, Trev was sprawled across the bed looking very happy, indeed. When she crawled back up to him and kissed him deeply, he grinned.

"Woman, you are amazing." His smile dimmed and his eyes turned an even deeper blue. He reached up and tucked her hair behind her ear. "I think I forgot to tell you something."

Stasi had to smile down on him because there was something boyish about him she hadn't seen before. "What did you forget to tell me that has you looking so serious?"

"I forgot to tell you that I'm in love with you."

Stasi was sure her heart had stopped. "You are?"

He nodded. "I know we haven't known each other for long, and our meeting wasn't exactly normal."

"It's the hearts," she blurted out.

"No, it's not. It's all you and me." Trev curled his hand around her neck and brought her face down to his for a kiss that kept on going until they were gasping for breath. His hand trailed a path along her belly and kept going down to the damp slick folds.

"Yes," she gasped, pulling him closer and draping her leg over his calf as she wrapped her hand around his cock and brought him to her.

He buried himself in her, feeling the pulsing of her inner muscles already clutching him in the beginnings of her orgasm.

"I love you so much," she whispered as she rose up to meet him. "I love you." She laughed, feeling joy and freedom in the words.

"Mine. All mine." Trev thrust deeper and faster as his own climax took over.

The red hearts over their heads developed arms and high-fived each other.

Afterwards, Trev pulled the covers over them and they curled up together.

"The lunar eclipse is tonight," Stasi murmured, content to be in Trev's arms. Her heart still sang with the notion he loved her. She realized she'd loved him for the past few days but had been afraid to admit it even to herself. His disclosure freed her to tell the truth. "Not that anyone can tell with the sky already so dark, even though there don't seem to be clouds tonight. It's as if a blanket covered it all. And not a nice blanket, either." Her shoulders rose and fell in a soft sigh.

"Maybe the eclipse will set things to rights." He laced his fingers between hers and brought her knuckles up to his lips for a lingering kiss.

She lifted her head slightly so she could see his face. "Do you think so?"

He was silent for so long she didn't think he was going to answer.

"No, but it sounds good, doesn't it?"

Stasi smiled. She was ready to believe anything if it meant Trev would be in her life. "Yes, it does."

Choking! Can't breathe! Air is heavy. Choking.

Stasi opened her eyes to find the room gray and hazy. She tasted ash on her tongue, and her nose burned from the acrid smell in the air. She sat up in bed, coughing.

"This isn't good, Stasi," Horace choked from the dresser drawer where he'd been sleeping.

Bogie floated up from his bed, licking her face and whimpering his distress.

"Trev. Trev!" She shook him hard. "Wake up!" She covered her mouth and nose with her hand as she slid out of bed, running to her closet and dragging out clothing.

"What the hell?" Trev sat up and started hacking.

A fist pounded on Stasi's door. "Get up!"

"We're up!" she called out, hopping on one foot as she climbed into her jeans.

"Someone set fire to the building!" Jazz called out, fear lining her voice.

"Nick! He has to be the first one out." Stasi tossed Trev's sweater to him as she dug out her own.

He threw it on, not caring it was inside out, and picked up Horace while Stasi grabbed Bogie.

The hallway was filled with smoke that stung their noses and caused their eyes to burn.

"Why didn't the smoke detectors go off?" she asked, but no one was listening as they all made their way to the rear of the building. She feared they'd find the rear stairs in flames and they'd be trapped. Luckily, they were still intact, and they raced down them.

"Who would do this?" Irma asked, following them with her dog on her heels. She and Sirius were the only ones not coughing from the smoke.

"Motherfuckers," Nick spat out, seeing the flames inside his Navigator. But since just one spark could destroy him, he kept a safe distance. He held a wide-eyed Fluff and Puff in one hand and had a tight hold on Jazz's hand with the other.

Still coughing and eyes burning from the smoke, they filed around the side of the building to the front, where the building was engulfed in flames that continued to lick upward.

"Kit-Kat!" Blair screamed, starting to run back to the building, but Jake grabbed her around the waist. She twisted and bucked in his grip, but he refused to release her as he pulled her along with him.

They stopped short at the sight of a crowd standing in the snow-covered street. Carrie and Reed stood at the front of the pack. Most held flashlights or camping lanterns, but what worried Stasi were the ones holding flaming torches.

Trev, Nick, and Jake immediately moved to stand in front of Stasi, Jazz, and Blair.

"Everything will be fine once you're gone," Carrie shrieked, wild-eyed, her face a bright red.

"What in Hades—?" Two men suddenly threw a length of silver chain around Nick, halting his question. He hissed in pain and anger, his fangs fully extended as he pivoted to face his captors. His eyes glowed blood red and he looked ready to fight, but the silver was immediately sapping his strength.

"I told you silver was a vampire's enemy," Reed crowed, raising an arm. His eyes glowed dark with triumph. "Just make sure it doesn't slip off him. We can't afford for him to get loose."

One man got too close and screamed in pain as Nick whipped around and buried his fangs in his arm, tearing brutally at the flesh. Nick howled in agony when another silver chain was looped tight around his throat and he was jerked backward. Fluff and Puff snarled and snapped at the people.

"You bastards!" Jazz started forward with a fireball balanced above her palm.

"Extinguish it now or we will kill your freak lover," Reed warned with a snap in his voice that meant business. He moved forward with a wooden stake in his hand. Someone ran up and slapped a strip of duct tape across Nick's mouth. The vampire's body quivered with the killing fury racing through his body.

Jazz allowed the witchflame to die out, but she remained on guard, turning in a tight circle, watching the mob moving around them.

Stasi sensed the sudden dark shift in the air and knew what it meant. She looked up and watched the last vestiges of the moon swallowed up by the eclipse. Even the stars seemed to wink out, swallowed up by the flat black of the sky. "Darkness is here," she whispered.

"It's all because of you! This isn't the lunar eclipse the news talked about, this is all your doing," Carrie shrilled, stooping to pick up a stone and throwing it at Stasi's head. Trev was quick enough to step in front of her, so the rock struck his shoulder instead.

"You all need to calm down!" he shouted, holding up his hands. His calm manner would normally have settled people down, but this mob was beyond listening.

"You chose your side, wizard," Reed said. "Carrie counted on you, and you abandoned her because you were so eager to spread a witch's legs. You're on their side and there's only one way to deal with traitors."

Suddenly the crowd surged in and the three witches were grabbed from behind. Before they could react their hands were tied in front of them, and they found themselves being led through the town. When Blair stumbled she was almost dragged along until she clambered to her feet. She snarled at her captors, who only pulled harder on her bonds.

Stasi looked over her shoulder and tried to see what had become of Trev and Jake. She watched flames overtake the wooden building she and Blair had so lovingly tended. It was as if all the protective wards they had used to surround their businesses and home were never there. The pain stabbing her heart was so acute she almost fell to her knees and cried. She didn't care about her merchandise, only the memories she had in there. As the roof collapsed and sparks flew upward, men remained close by to ensure the fire didn't spread to the other buildings.

This isn't the time for tears. You can't break down now. Stasi dug down deep for her inner strength and remained on her feet as she was roughly pulled down the street. Memories from 1692 engulfed her. Her ears rang with the accusations from the ignorant pious who had no clue what evil truly was, the tortured pleas from the innocent, and the silence from the guilty. Because even if she didn't deal in the black arts, she still would have been considered evil during that dark time and killed along with those who didn't deserve an early death.

You need to conquer the past to heal the present.

Next time, The Librarian, give us something to work with!

She caught sight of Trev trying to reach them and heard his curses as two men tackled him to the ground. They rained their fists on him until he didn't get up again. His face was covered with blood and his clothing was torn. She was surprised that he didn't use his power to defend himself. She knew he could easily have leveled them all, yet he did nothing. And she knew he held back because of her, even though the result was a beating, because he knew she would not want him to destroy these townspeople who had been her friends. She stumbled and fell onto her knees. The shock and pain raced through her body as the rope around her wrists tightened, but she firmed her lips and refused to react as she made it back onto her feet.

"History said witches don't feel pain." Carrie put her face in hers.

Stasi looked around and was stunned by the look of triumph on the face of Rhetta, Reed's sister, and the bloodlust glazing Poppy's eyes. She saw Ginny with the same anger on her face and even Mrs. Benedict, who

wouldn't step on an ant, raise her arm in fury. She saw
an epidemic of anger. Mob behavior.

"We know what to do with freaks like you!" Poppy
screamed, finding a stone under the snow and throwing
it at her, striking her temple.

Stasi momentarily saw stars, but she refused to wince
at the pain crossing her forehead.

"I only tried your muffins once, Poppy. I had heartburn for days. You use too much baking soda in them,"
Blair sneered. "You know what? I can't see anyone
eating your slop without you using spells to get them
to buy them." She struggled against her captors to fight
back when Poppy ran up and slapped her across the face
so hard her ring cut Blair's lip.

"Don't antagonize them," Stasi ordered. "They love
tormenting us."

"Who's antagonizing anyone? I'm only speaking the
truth. She couldn't bake her way out of a paper bag."
This time when Poppy reacted Blair was ready and bit
her arm, even if it cost her a hard knock to the head.

It wasn't until they were pulled to the town square
where they saw three six-foot high posts erected in
the center with piles of wood around each one that the
enormity of what was about to happen struck them.

Trev stumbled forward, now tied as tightly as the
witches. There was no sign of Jake, and Stasi felt queasy
at what this mob might have done to him. Horror darkened
Trev's blue eyes as he stared at the sight before him.

"You can't do this! This is nothing more than cold-
blooded murder."

"Shut up. Your turn will be coming. Did you think
we'd save you after you betrayed Carrie?" One man

behind him hit him in the back of the head with a board.

"*Trev!*" Without thinking, Stasi started forward, only to be brought up short by the rough rope coiled around her hands. She felt it cut into her wrists, leaving them raw and bleeding, but that didn't matter. People she once thought of as close friends had turned into enemies and were dragging her to her death. What hurt her most was that her friends, who were truly innocent in all of this, would die alongside her.

Chapter 20

"YOU ARE DEFYING YOUR OWN LAWS!" STASI SHOUTED above the rabble. She could see by their wild eyes they wouldn't listen or care, but she still had to try. She didn't bother struggling against the rough hands holding her arms. She knew they welcomed the chance to hurt her further if she fought back. She refused to spill any tears or show fear as she, Blair, and Jazz were tied to the posts.

The tears were even harder to hold back as she saw the fury on Blair and Jazz's faces as they faced their captors. The two witches looked ready to rain down fire on the entire town. The only reason they didn't unleash their fury was because they knew the mortals were under a widespread spell that played with their thoughts and emotions. Even if the townspeople screamed murder, they were still innocents, and Blair and Jazz knew their code wouldn't allow them to harm them with their magick.

Stasi looked over the heads of the mob toward where a bloodied Trev lay motionless on the ground. She felt tears choking her throat, but she found the strength to swallow them before they fell.

I don't know if I can be brave. When it happened before, I hid. I protected myself and did nothing.

The metallic taste of fear flooded her mouth. She took several deep calming breaths in hopes her heart would remain in her body and not pound its way out.

Nick no longer struggled against the silver chains that restrained him. His fangs had fully extended, easily slicing through the duct tape and his eyes glowed a deep blood red. He may have been silenced, but his expression said it all; retribution would be strong and harsh once he found a way to free himself. No one would survive his wrath. Stasi knew the chains had to have been burning his skin with a painful intensity, but his gaze didn't veer from Jazz's face.

"Why can't I stop them?" Irma shrieked, moving through one person after another, pausing to smack a man with her purse, which she'd refused to leave behind when they fled the fire, and even Sirius did his part by barking and snapping at the people. Irma glared at one woman and gave her a vicious pinch on the arm, but no one reacted to the icy chill of her body as she slid through them.

"They're bespelled," Jazz explained, then turned to snarl at the man tightening the ropes around her hands. He blanched and backed up a step, then his expression darkened and he returned to jerk the knots until her fingers turned white. Her eyes sparked green lights. "How you'd like to be zapped back to the prisoner end of the Spanish Inquisition? I'm sure I could arrange the trip." She was furious enough not to react when he maliciously sliced her arm with a small knife before he hurried away.

"We had a good town until you came here," Carrie told Stasi in a harsh voice.

"We were here before your grandmother was born," Stasi shot back, struggling not to give in to panic. "What you all are doing is murder. You're being directed by something that wants *all* of us gone. Once you kill us they can easily encourage you to leave."

"Forget it, Stasi. They don't care," Blair growled. Her face darkened with her temper as she looked out over the people. "You have been angry. You have been bold. What you have wrought here will return to you tenfold," she raised her voice as they shouted at her and even threw stones. She ignored the battle and kept on. "Make it—"

"Don't do it!" a familiar male voice shouted out, stopping her before she finalized her curse. A tall figure moved through the mob. "Don't make it worse for your-self, Blair. As for the rest of you, what you're doing is nothing less than cold-blooded murder."

"Jake, no!" Blair cried out at the handyman, who pushed and shoved his way through the crowd, not caring who fell in his path. The look of dark fury on his face prompted some to quickly move out of his way, but others fought back, only to meet with his fist and boots. That he wasn't overpowered was either pure luck or because it was clear he didn't care who he hurt in the process.

"You're all fools!" he yelled, as he made his way to the front. "Don't do this. They're right. Someone's behind what's happened here, and it's not Stasi, Blair, and Jazz!"

"Burn the witch!" Carrie screamed, running up from the side holding a lit torch in her upraised hand.

Stasi felt the horror of hundreds of years ago as she stared at the flames hovering so close to the wood piled around her. Felt again the fear and anger that had swept the town, just as she and her friends and the mortals of

Moonstone Lake had been gripped by the fear and anger of the past weeks. For a moment, she heard the screams, cries, and prayers of hundreds of years ago when the accused were hanged. And then the abrupt silence that followed and the smell of death before they were cut down and dumped in unmarked shallow graves. The burning of witches was performed in Europe, but Salem courts preferred hanging.

She didn't want to die, but even more she didn't want these people to have their deaths on their consciences, poisoning their souls. She stared at Reed, who watched her with a look that could only be described as triumphant. A baker, who appeared to be just as much behind the hysteria as Carrie was.

Her brain started to click into place. *Baker. Popular with almost everyone in town who constantly bought his goods. The more they ate the more… Poppy and Rhetta who have that look. The look of…*

She mentally slapped herself upside the head. *Good going, Anastasia, you couldn't have figured this out sooner! The Librarian did everything but spell it out for you.* Now it all made a lot of sense.

"You need to listen to me! You're all good people. If you do this you'll regret it all the days of your lives. You're under a spell!" she shouted, feeling a rawness in her voice. "Reed and his sisters aren't who you think they are. They're forest Fae! They have powers and they bespelled their baked goods. They put something in the food that had you going there almost every day for more, and it made you act this way. They started it out gradually then increased it because they wanted it to happen this time of year. The more you ate, the more you became sensitive to whatever they whispered in your ears."

"The past and present!" Blair laughed. "Of course! There were rumors that members of their kind did the same in Salem, because they wanted the seaport to themselves and hoped to drive everyone out."

"My *kind*, Stasi? You've been reading too many fairy tales. Everyone knows now that the witch hysteria in Salem was due to ergot poisoning from contaminated rye flour that caused the hallucinations among the townspeople. My ancestors hadn't even touched ground in this country until after the Civil War." Reed stepped forward. His dark green eyes snapped with cruelty. "We aren't the witches here. Everyone knows you created some sort of spell to ruin Carrie's marriage then managed to bewitch her lawyer so he would side with you." He cast a derisive glance over his shoulder in the injured Trev's direction. "He's no longer innocent in this matter and will also be dealt with after we've finished with you. You've done something to the lake, tampered with the weather so the snow is almost burying the town, and we have no electricity. You've become mad with power and endangered our town. You and your fellow witches have created too much havoc. We can't allow that."

She stared deep into his eyes. *You would do well to learn to respect time, young witch.* She realized with a jolt that timing was crucial to the forest Fae's plans. She needed to stay calm, and keep him talking. "The only one truly mad here is you, if you're using the term to indicate insanity. If you're talking anger, then oh yes, I'm not just mad, I'm furious. Because all of this is your fault!" She deliberately ignored Carrie, who was standing with eyes glazed over, the torch she still held so close to the wood surrounding the stakes. So far, the woman hadn't dropped it onto the wood, but it could happen at any moment.

"Tell everyone the truth, Reed. Tell them what you really are. Because you are forest Fae, aren't you? Your people inhabit the upper reaches of this forest and have for centuries, and the time was finally right for you and your sisters to make a power play. You wanted us all gone. That's why you used glamour to appear human to everyone and even managed to fool Blair and me, so we couldn't pick up on what you are. You found some rogue water sprites who were willing to make a deal—how many years did that take? You placed a barrier around the lake to keep us out and disguise what the water sprites were doing as they tried to break its power, but the lake defended itself! And just as in Salem, you brought about mass hysteria to do your dirty work. It was you who showed Carrie how she could file a lawsuit against me in Wizards' Court, because you know that wizards aren't fond of witches and I'd have a tougher time there."

Reed chuckled, but there was no humor in the sound. "Of course, I did. Did you honestly think that cow would have known what to do? Her husband leaving her made it all that much sweeter and even easier for me to accomplish my task. A few whispers in her ear, a few papers left on her table when she came into the bakery, and she was mine. I would have preferred that you had become my lover. While I'm not into witches," he made a face, "it would have put me in a very convenient position. I would have suffered through it and even made it pleasurable for you. Before I was done, you would have told me the secret of the lake and betrayed your sister witches." His expression darkened when Stasi spat at him. He pulled a handkerchief out of his pocket and wiped off his face. "I will enjoy watching you burn, Anastasia Romanov."

If her hands had been free she would have had them around his neck and tightening by the second. "You're a true piece of work. You thought the worry of the lawsuit would keep Blair and me occupied enough that you could weave your spells and we wouldn't notice until it was too late. What better way to turn the town against us than to use our heritage against us? That way they'd blame us for all that's happened and after our deaths, the people will regain their senses, but they'll still remember the horror of this night and you'll make sure to use that against them." She took a deep breath, reminding herself to be strong and not falter. This would be their last chance. If she lost they would die within minutes. "And that shock will never leave them until they either kill themselves from remorse or they depart from this town because they can no longer stand to be where it happened. And then you'll start to work on the resorts, until you have the mountain back again. There's only one problem. It will never happen." She refused to break eye contact. She meant for him to look away first.

She raised her voice, allowing it to ring out so all would hear her. "Innocent blood will be shed this night! None of you will ever forget what happened here. Dark memories will always be there to haunt you and what you have done will stain that part of you that's pure. Is it worth losing that which makes you human?" There was a murmur in the crowd and Stasi was sure she felt a lightening, a change in the flat black sky. The spell was slipping.

Reed laughed. He made a show of clapping his hands in mockery. "Very nice performance, Stasi. And from one who isn't human, no less. Why don't you three just stand there and take this like three good little witches. The plan is in play and won't be stopped now. All you have to do is die before the lunar eclipse is over and all will be well."

"Oh no, I'm not going down that easy." She bared her teeth. "One I fight. One not fair. Show your true self, lay it bare. If you please!"

Blair's smile blossomed as she echoed the words. "One *we* fight. One not fair. Show your true self. Make it so!"

"One we fight. One not fair. Show your true self. Because I said so, damn it!" Jazz joined in with fervor.

Green and gold light flew out from the three witches and danced about Reed and his sisters. High-pitched voices whispered from the light, repeating the spell Stasi had begun.

"You bitches!" Poppy screamed as her form glimmered with light, then dissolved to be reborn as a woman not more than five feet tall with skin a delicate emerald green and eyes to match. Her hair was a glistening fall of gold curls to her ankles that covered her nude body. Even with the icy wind, she didn't look cold. Rhetta changed into a similar form, but her face showed the same arrogance her human face had displayed.

"This isn't the end," she declared, but her voice was higher-pitched now and she didn't have the power she exuded before.

"They're aliens!" someone screamed.

"They're Fae," Stasi explained. "They live in the forest and obviously they're not happy we're here."

"We were here first!" Rhetta snarled. "You don't belong here. We do!"

Reed, now green-skinned also, but with bark-brown hair, muttered a curse in a strange language, grabbed the lighted torch from Carrie's hand, and lunged with it back toward Stasi. At the same moment, a growling Jake ran through the crowd. His figure flickered in the torch light, and as he leapt toward Reed, his shape changed into the familiar Border collie. He grabbed the man by the throat and shook him as if he was nothing more than an old rag as he pulled him down to the ground. Reed's scream shattered the air as the dog tore his throat out. The torch rolled harmlessly over the snow-covered ground and flickered out with a faint hiss.

"What the Fates?" Blair's jaw dropped as the crowd backed away from the dead Fae lying in the snow. Poppy and Rhetta screamed and abruptly disappeared into thin air when the dog looked their way. Blair looked behind her as the dog climbed up the stacks of wood and began gnawing at the ropes. "Are you saying I've been sleeping with Jake all along? Damn it!"

"They want to burn us at the stake and you're worried about Jake?" Stasi snapped with a combination of relief and anxiety. She wasn't going to feel safe until she was free and could make sure Trev wasn't badly hurt.

Once Blair was free, the dog raced to the back and pushed at Trev, licking his face until he stirred. The dog chewed on Trev's bonds until they shredded enough that he could free himself. Stasi cried with relief to see he was all right. She struggled against her bonds until Blair freed her and they ran to the third post to release Jazz.

Trev staggered to his feet, slugged the dazed-looking man beside Nick, and uttered a spell to break the chains holding Nick prisoner.

Jazz cried out the vampire's name and raced toward him, throwing herself onto his chest and holding him tightly.

"Fuck, Jazz, can't we ever have a quiet evening at home?" he was heard to mutter as he wrapped his arms around her and buried his face in her hair. "No more almost getting killed, ya hear me?"

"Loud and clear, fang boy. Loud and clear." She cupped his face with her hands and kissed him.

Trev met Stasi halfway. She was so relieved he was all right she literally fell into his arms. She gave in to the fear that had blanketed her and burst into the tears she'd held back.

"I thought I'd come to and see you dead," he mumbled against her face.

"They were going to kill you, too." She ran her hands down his arms and across his chest, making sure he was still in one piece. She whispered words that allowed her touch to heal the scrapes and bruises on his skin where his shirt had been torn from his torso.

"What have we done?" Mrs. Benedict sat on a nearby bench and began to cry. Mr. Chalmers sat next to her and handed her his handkerchief before putting an arm around her. Others looked around themselves with a combination of horror and shock.

Blair and Jazz walked over to Stasi. The three witches moved into a tight group hug they were loath to part from any time soon. Irma did a victory dance around them.

"How did this happen?" someone else asked, which began a litany of questions and comments punctuated with tears. "What were we doing?"

"You need to say something to them," Blair whispered in Stasi's ear. "They don't realize what happened. It needs to come from you."

Jazz nodded her agreement. "She's right. It's your show, babe."

Stasi took a deep breath and turned around.

"We have always loved this town and its people," she began. "And once you knew what we were, you never made fun of us or tried to capitalize on it." She dared a brief glance at Agnes, who had the grace to blush and look away. She knew if the mayor's wife could have found a way to bring in business because of the two local witches, she would have done it with a brass band and banners flying. "Tonight was the culmination of what had been going on for months now. It only took a few to fall under the spell of Reed and his sisters and after that you all fell just as easily." She paused, searching her mind for the right thing to say. "As a result, it was easy to target the weak minded." She deliberately aimed her words at Carrie. "To drop a word here and there and start up a hate campaign. I have seen this happen before, and those days were dark and filled with fear. Just as it was now. But we have all been very lucky—the evil was stopped in time." She stopped, as a warming sensation seemed to fill her. She looked up and saw the sky that had been so dark a moment before, start to glow just the tiniest bit as a sliver of the moon appeared above. The others followed the direction of her gaze.

The change in the atmosphere was apparent to all the non-humans.

Stasi closed her eyes and allowed the last of her fear and anger to drain away. When she opened her eyes again, she saw the moon floating gently in the sky and the stars twinkled brightly.

"Time for the healing to begin," she whispered, leaning back against Trev's chest while he stood behind her with his arms wrapped around her.

They saw the dazed-looking residents slowly turn away and begin to move off.

"What's going on?" Trev asked.

"Pod people," Jazz insisted. "We've been dealing with pod people all along." A sudden whirl of cold wind wrapped around them. "Oh shit. Someone else at work here."

Stasi stumbled and as she righted herself, she found herself along with Blair and Jazz standing before the Witches' Council. As always, the three wore lilac hooded robes and their feet were bare on the cold stone floor. Before, the sight of Eurydice had scared the wits out of her, but now she found that she could face her former headmistress head-on. What really surprised her was seeing Trev, Nick, and Jake, returned to human form, standing with them.

"You surprised me this night, young Anastasia," Eurydice spoke, her voice ringing out in the stone hall as she stood behind the ornate table where the other members of the Witches' Council sat. "You have always been a somewhat timid witchling, yet, you didn't hesitate in standing up for yourself when a human dared to go up against you in the Wizards' Court." She cast a quick glance in Trev's direction. Her lips firmed at the sight of the red hearts dancing above his head and the same over Stasi's. "And in the face of a horrific death you spoke not as a witch who could have cursed a town never to forget the horrors of the night, but as one who didn't want them to suffer. And that would have happened if they'd managed to burn the three of you." Her ageless features tightened. A vibrating wave moved through the hall, a display of her matchless power—even the three younger witches together had only a tiny fraction of that kind of power.

"Their only crime was that they were under a Fae spell made even more powerful because of the eclipse. I couldn't blame those people for it, even if I wonder whether the spell didn't bring out what some might truly feel deep inside," Stasi said.

Eurydice turned her attention to Jazz. "And you didn't release one speck of witchflame. I am amazed, Griet of Ardglass. You exhibited great willpower. I didn't know you had it in you."

"No, I just didn't want to hurt anyone who didn't deserve to be hurt," Jazz said candidly, while the others winced.

"And Eilidh equally kept her temper in check." She shared a silent conversation with the other members of the council. "We also thank Wizard Barnes and Nikolai Gregorivich for doing all they could to defend our witchlings, and we especially thank Jacob Harrison for destroying the Fae that sought to destroy three of our own. We are indebted to you for your bravery." She inclined her head in a regal nod.

"I was glad to be of assistance. I only wish my Were blood was more wolf than canine and I could have done more," he replied.

"You did the job, young Were. That is what counts. We have spoken with the Fae, and naturally, they are unhappy with the end results since they feel they were greatly ill-treated when one of their people was killed. They seemed to think it was an unwarranted attack, but after I showed them exactly what happened, they backed off and now apologize for the wrongdoing. The two Fae sisters will be punished. A treaty has been drafted, and they have vowed never to bother your town again. And the Ruling Council has sent out trackers to find the rogue water sprites who tried to defile the lake, so that they may be brought to justice." She turned back to Stasi. "You have proven yourself in ways many of our kind would not. You have always been known for your generous heart and forgiving nature and this occasion has once again proven those qualities. Therefore, we shall do as you wished. The townspeople will not remember the horror of this night. They will only recall a crippling blizzard that closed the roads and disabled their power, and that many were ill during this time. As far as anyone is concerned, the bakery never existed. The lake has also been restored to its good health."

If Stasi didn't know better, she would have thought the stern-featured witch's features had softened just a tiny bit.

"We can also offer you and your friends the same comfort, Anastasia," she spoke kindly. "All of you may have this time taken away and replaced with more pleasurable memories. I am sure with the Wizards' Council permission we can even make the lawsuit disappear, since it should not have been filed to begin with."

Stasi's heart stopped. Did Eurydice mean that Stasi wouldn't remember Trev, and vice versa? It only took one look at the witch's face and she knew that was just what the elder meant.

"Naturally, I can't speak for the others, but I prefer to keep my memories intact," Stasi spoke slowly, not to choose her words carefully, but to make a point. "I won't hold what happened against the people of Moonstone Lake, but if there is a chance this happens again, I want to feel prepared. I don't want to forget anything."

Trev looked at Stasi as he stated, "Nor I."

The other four immediately agreed.

Eurydice nodded. A tiny smile hovered on her lips as if this was the answer she expected.

"What about the time left on her banishment?" Jazz asked. "Stasi deserves to have time off for what she's done out there."

Stasi shook her head. "Only the town matters. The mortals were no match for the evil powers plotting against them. They shouldn't suffer with the memories of what happened. Many of them wouldn't be able to handle what they'd said and done. And I did meddle with Carrie just a wee bit, so let's call it even."

Eurydice nodded. "So be it. As for you, Griet and Eilidh, you threatened an innocent with dire curses…"

"Carrie's not *that* innocent," Jazz muttered, earning a glare.

"You each will receive an additional fifty years for your transgression." A ringing sound in the hall made the pronouncement legal. "Just be grateful we didn't void your probation, young Griet."

Jazz and Blair looked at each other and shrugged.

"The town's back to the way it should be," Blair said. "No one will want to burn us at the stake. Although, for Fates sake, that's so seventeenth century!"

"Yes, I guess that should be enough," Jazz finished. "Still, it wouldn't have hurt for us to receive something good out of all this."

Eurydice turned back to Stasi. "You were the brightest in the class. The one destined to go far," she said softly. "We saw great things for you, Anastasia."

Stasi lifted her chin up another notch. "Perhaps I haven't done what you saw in my destiny, but I have had adventures that I wouldn't have had otherwise. I've seen and done things that were incredible, and they helped shape the witch I am now. I wouldn't lose those memories for anything. And I think it's actually made me a better witch."

"Well-spoken. Just remember something, Anastasia." Eurydice pinned her dark eyes on Stasi. Her emerald pendant winked with brilliant light. "Witches and wizards aren't meant to be."

Stasi flushed, thinking of all she and Trev had done and his confession that he was in love with her.

If Jazz and Nick can prove that witches and vampires can work it out, so can witches and wizards.

And just like that, they found themselves back in the middle of the town square. Except now it was empty of people. The posts and scattered kindling for the fires were gone, and the old-fashioned lampposts shone with soft light. The full moon shone brightly down on them, and the decorations on the buildings gave the town the artistically haunted look it normally had this time of year.

"All is right with the world!" Stasi threw up her hands and spun in a dizzying circle. She laughed as Trev moved forward and caught her up in his arms, continuing the circle.

"Oooof!" Jake bent over, his arms cradling his stomach where had Blair rounded on him and socked him but good.

"You couldn't tell me you're a *Were?* You son of a bitch!" She smacked his shoulder as hard as she could.

"Well, yes, technically, I am," he wheezed, earning a punch on the other shoulder.

"You ate us out of house and home, you shed all over the furniture, you snuck into my bed—stealing all the covers, by the way—and we won't even talk about the fleas last summer!" She continued to pound on him until he straightened up and grabbed her around the waist, hauling her against him and kissing the very breath out of her. She struggled out of his arms and socked him in the shoulder again. "And you saw me *naked!*"

"You saw me naked, too," he argued, ducking and weaving to avoid her fury.

"You were covered with fur! That doesn't count. Damn it, you sat in the middle of my bed and licked your balls! Do you think I'll ever forget that?" Blair was in the middle of a rant she wasn't about to come down from any time soon, but Jake just grinned from ear to ear.

Stasi looked into Trev's eyes, stroking his face with her fingertips. She couldn't stop smiling and she noticed he was doing the same.

"You knew he was a Were, didn't you?"

He nodded. "Nick did too. I couldn't rat Jake out. It was a guy bonding thing while we waited for you three to figure it out. Are you going to whale on me too?"

She shook her head. "No, I'd like to think I'm more a lover than a fighter. Besides, kissing is a lot more fun." She backed up her statement by doing just that, her tongue dipping into his mouth to sweep up his flavor, while she inhaled the scent that was all his.

"I can't believe you didn't tell me he was the dog!" Jazz had her own discussion going with Nick, who took matters in hand by sweeping her toward him for a lengthy kiss that easily shut her up. And since Nick didn't have to worry about breathing, he could kiss Jazz for a long time.

"Hey, you all! Do you know what time it is? Some of us want to sleep. Go party elsewhere!" Grady's grumble echoed throughout the street. "Damn kids."

Stasi looked around and saw Jake steering Blair up the road that led to his cabin while she ranted and raved, berating him for keeping that all-important secret about his furry side. The word neuter even came up a few times until Jake stopped and tossed her over his shoulder and continued on. It didn't stop Blair from yelling at him and pounding his back with her fists.

Stasi drew a breath, preparing herself to look at the remains of their building. When she finally turned around to look she almost fell down in shock.

"All returned to the way it was," she whispered, staring at the building that stood intact and didn't show a hint of fire damage. If she hadn't seen the flames for herself, she would have thought she'd imagined everything. The only difference was the building had been restored to the way it had been before this tiny part of the world had traveled down a darker path.

Suddenly Fergus and Irene appeared, looking just a little more substantial than last time she's seen them—for ghosts anyway. "Thank you, ma'am," Fergus said, nervously rolling the rim of his hat around in his hands. "We're right grateful to you for you what you have done."

"If I do say so myself, you witches do good work," Irma approved, resting her hand on Sirius's head. "Now if you all don't mind I'm going home to watch a movie." She turned to Fergus and said, "Would you like to join me?" He smiled shyly, and then the three ghosts and the dog winked out of sight. "Great," sighed Jazz. "A ghostly film festival."

Jazz kept her arm around Nick as if he needed her strength even though he showed no sign of injuries from the silver chains. Apparently the visit to the Witches' Council had also healed him.

She turned and flashed a smile at Stasi. "But it's Stasi who deserves all the credit. She figured it all out."

"All back to normal." Stasi grabbed Trev's hand and pulled him along.

He held back for a moment. "I bet the road to the resort is cleared now."

She stilled, realizing he was right. "So you want to go back to the resort?" She didn't want to think his admission he loved her was only in the heat of the moment.

He shook his head. "I want *us* to head up there. I'm talking big tub, big bed." He cocked his head toward the other two couples. "Privacy. Chocolate soufflé…"

She was sorely tempted to give in to Trev's suggestion, but her energy level was running high, and she realized this was one time when she wanted to be the alpha instead of allowing Trev to take the lead. But something inside her reared up and roared.

"I can't believe I'm saying this, but I'm sure I can come up with something even better than their chocolate soufflé. So you come with me, wizard." She snagged two fingers in the collar of his sweater, which had also been returned whole and pulled him toward her. "They'll be using Nick's safe room anyway and besides, remember it only takes the right wards," she paused to give him a lengthy and deep kiss he'd never forget, "so that no one will hear you scream when I fuck you so thoroughly you'll forget your own name," she whispered, dragging her teeth lightly over his lower lip and pulling it into her mouth where she nibbled on it. "And that is exactly what I intend to do."

Trev's eyes glazed over with unrestrained lust until they were a glittery blue.

"I have to say there's something very hot about a woman who takes charge." He made it easy for her to pull him down the street then almost stumbled forward when she abruptly stopped in the middle of the road.

"Oh." The word left her lips in a soft breath.

Trev moved to stand behind her and wrapped his arms around her shoulders and rested his chin on top of her head.

Tiny lights in the shape of pumpkins cast orange lights around the display windows in Stasi and Blair's shops.

Blair's shop held two corn sheaves with black crows perched on them and a skeleton sprawled in the middle, while Stasi's sensuous display was complemented by a jaunty black witch's hat set in one corner and a small broom in the other.

Stasi's laughter held tears and joy all mixed up together. "There is no way Eurydice would have put those there."

Trev hugged her tighter. "Maybe she did. You stood up to the Fae without allowing the townspeople to be hurt. You were afraid. I could sense it, but you never allowed it to take over. You didn't permit your anger to fight back when you could have with only a few words. You acted not out of fear or anger, but out of love. And…" he whispered in her ear, "no hiccups. No bubbles."

She reached up and curled her hands around his arms. Her tears trailed down her cheeks and dripped onto his sleeves.

"I didn't hiccup once, did I? And now the fear in the air is gone. The darkness is banished." She looked up to see the full moon now shining bright and the sky filled with stars. "Everyone here will wake up in the morning and not remember a thing."

"You also had that choice."

She shook her head. "No, as I said I wanted to remember." She turned in his arms. "Did you want to forget?"

Trev's smile was as warm in his eyes as on his lips. "Forget that I walked into a shop and met a fiery witch who knocked my socks off? That I hadn't expected to fall in love with her?"

Stasi's smile grew even broader. "This all might be Cupid's doing," she suggested, even though deep down she didn't believe that was all there was to it. She had fought against falling in love with Trev. As Eurydice said, witches and wizards don't go well together, but Stasi knew now that she and Trev were an exception.

"No, I think it was just a little push in the right direction. Come on, let's test those wards," Trev whispered, now being the one to pull her along. "And we'll show everyone that witches and wizards get along very well, indeed. By the way," he paused, "do you think when Eurydice replaced the building she also replaced your cinnamon lip gloss?"

Stasi couldn't help it. She threw her head back and laughed with sheer joy. She hopped into Trev's arms and wrapped her legs around his waist.

"I think we should write Cupid a thank-you note, don't you?"

Epilogue

Fluff & Puff vs. Cupid

"If Jazz finds out we did this we'll be in a lot of trouble," Fluff, a bit more timid than his furry cohort, said as he followed his fellow magickal bunny slipper down the street.

"Naw, she'll understand. The guy messed with Stasi big time."

"It all worked out."

Puff stopped, turning his head from right to left, while his ears lifted to full point. "We wish the land of sweet. It's the land of love we seek," he chanted. "Take us to the creep who does it neat, or else."

A curtain shimmered red and white in front of them and the slippers quickly slid past it and landed on a path paved with smooth, glimmering white stones. Soft music seemed to come out of the air, while on either side of the path, glittering red hearts sprang from the ground. Overhead, the sky was a soft illuminated white with fluffy red hearts for clouds, and the air was faintly scented with cinnamon.

"*Augh!*" The slippers' horror escalated as they recognized the singer. "*Barry Manilow!*"

They gritted their razor-sharp teeth and forged on until the path ended in front of a three-story building shaped like a gigantic heart, complete with a red satin bow. A matching mailbox was set at the end of the pathway with "Cupid, One Heart Drive" written in elegant gold script on the sides.

"Talk about subtle," Fluff grumbled, pausing at the mailbox post. He sniffed the post and tentatively nibbled. "Hmm. Marshmallow." Pretty soon the mailbox was on the ground and the post was resting comfortably in Fluff's tummy, while Puff discovered the mailbox was chocolate.

"A lot of cinnamon out here." Puff used one of his ears to point out a display of cinnamon candies arranged in a heart shape. "Jazz wouldn't want that from Cupid. Just chocolate."

They skittered to the door and pushed it open. The sound of Barry Manilow crooning *Mandy* echoed throughout the entryway as they peeked in the rooms. Another voice joined in lustily from upstairs, clearly belonging to someone who was so tone deaf his singing could shatter glass.

"Cupid's got pretty cool digs," Puff commented, stopping to try out a few chocolate-shaped hearts. "Too bad he's such a jokester."

"Don't let him get out the bow and arrows," Fluff warned him. "I like being single."

"You think I want a million kids running around?" Puff made a gagging sound.

"Same here. I'm too young to be a father. Okay, now that we're here, the plan is we eat everything in sight while he's in the bathtub and then run for it."

On their way out, the slippers gazed at the huge red cinnamon candy heart in the middle of the front yard, exchanged glances, and headed straight for it.

When they left Cupid's realm, the cinnamon candies had been rearranged to spell the words: *Fluff and Puff Were Here.*

More witchy romance by Linda Wisdom
now available from Sourcebooks

50 Ways to Hex Your Lover

Hex Appeal

Read on for a sneak peek…

50 Ways to Hex Your Lover

One

How long are we going to sit here?"

"As long as it takes." Jazz Tremaine shifted in the Thunderbird convertible's bench seat. She loved her 1956 aqua and white classic sports car, but there wasn't much legroom for her five-foot-eight-inch frame.

Nice neighborhood for a stakeout though, with its wide, posh swath of multi-million dollar homes set behind high iron fences and ornate gates. Still, Jazz hoped she wouldn't have to wait all night for Martin "The Sleaze Bag" Reynolds to come home. Her left foot was falling asleep, and that large Diet Coke she'd had with her dinner was warning her that bathroom time would be in her near future.

A scraping sound, a flare of sulfur, and a whiff of tobacco smoke from the passenger seat made Jazz's nose twitch. "Irma, put that damn thing out."

Irma clicked open the ashtray and heaved a put-upon sigh. "I'm bored."

"Then leave," Jazz snapped.

"Ha, ha," Irma snorted. "Very funny."

She sat in the passenger seat wearing her Sunday best, a navy floral-print dress with its delicate lace collar and navy buttons marching down the front. A dainty navy and white spring straw hat decorated with tiny flowers sat squarely on her tightly permed iron-gray hair. White gloves and a navy patent leather handbag completed her perfect 1950s ensemble. No surprise there because Irma had died in the passenger seat of the T-Bird on March 12, 1956.

Irma was the bane of the 700-year-young witch's existence and the sole drawback to the snazzy car she dearly loved. Her 100-percent success rate at eliminating curses had fallen to 99 percent when she'd failed, no matter what she tried, to remove the highly irritating Irma from the car. In the end, Jazz's client refused to pay her, and Jazz ended up with the classic sports car instead; with Irma as an accessory.

"I can make that lamppost disappear with a snap of my fingers." Jazz gestured toward a nearby post standing at the corner and did just that. Another snap of the fingers and the post reappeared. "But with you…" She snapped her fingers in front of Irma, but nothing happened. "With you, nothing. Nada. Zip. No matter how many times I try, you're still here!"

Jazz glared at Irma. Irma glared back at Jazz. The clash of witch temper and ghost tantrum lit the interior of the car with an unearthly silver light; then a gray Mercedes rolled slowly past the T-Bird, and Jazz swung her head away.

"Good," she said. "Martin is home."

The gates to The Sleaze Bag's Spanish-style mansion swung apart. The Mercedes drove past them and up the winding driveway. Jazz pushed her door open and slid out of the T-Bird. She glanced up at the night sky and felt the pull of the slowly waxing moon.

She sighed and fingered the moonstone ring she wore on her right ring finger. The milky blue stone glowed faintly at her touch.

In two weeks she'd drive up to the small town of Moonstone Lake set high up in the Angelus Crest Mountains for the monthly ritual that kept her and her witch sisters centered. The lake and nearby town provided Jazz and two of her fellow banished class-mates a much-needed sanctuary. While Stasia and Blair enjoyed living in the tiny mountain village, Jazz and several of the others preferred the darkness and grit of the city to breathing all that smog-free air.

"You could leave the radio on," Irma called after Jazz in the raspy voice of a long time smoker.

"Bite me," Jazz growled, moving silently across the street toward Martin's house.

She easily blended with the night in her black leather pants, black silk t-shirt, and black, waist-length leather jacket. Her coppery hair hung in a tight single braid down her back. Tonight she was Scary Witch, the better to teach Martin a lesson.

She paused long enough to flick her wrist at the gates, which opened just enough to allow her to slip through before they swung shut again.

Her nose wrinkled against the overpowering scent of heirloom roses lining the driveway. Malibu lights bathed a lawn that had been trimmed with mathematical precision.

"You pay a landscaping service a small fortune to keep the grounds looking perfect, and yet you dare cheat me," Jazz muttered, stopping a short distance from the house. She drew a breath, lifted her hands and murmured, "Resume."

A faint flicker traveled from her fingertips to the house. When the witch light slid through the windows, a woman's shrill, shrieking voice erupted within, so loud Jazz could hear it standing a hundred feet away.

"What have you done to this house?" Martin's harpy ten-years-dead mother-in-law screamed. "There is no way you can tell me my daughter had any hand in the decorating in here! What did you do? Hire one of your bimbos to design this interior like a brothel? Or did the slut do you instead? I told my baby not to marry you! You're a pig, Martin Reynolds! A pig!"

Jazz smiled and sauntered up the driveway to the front door. Figuring Doreen Hatcher's screaming inside would be too loud for Martin to hear the doorbell, she leaned on it long enough to be downright annoying.

"You just can't live without the booze, can you, Martin?" the voice shrieked. "Your liver ought to be pickled by now! Pickled, do you hear me? If not pickled, you should at least be dead from all that alcohol, you drunken slob! If I didn't know I had died from a heart attack I'd think you arranged my death."

Martin Reynolds flung the door open, wide-eyed and grim-lipped, a highball glass in one hand, a cordless phone tucked under his chin.

"Hello, Martin," Jazz purred.

"Jazz! I was just—uh—calling you," he said, stepping quickly backward, unease flashing across his face, though she noticed his forehead didn't move, even if his lips did. She guessed his Botox job had been fairly recent. "Your spell didn't work. You said she would be gone, but she isn't, and she's back with a vengeance. She showed up all of a sudden, just now. I walked in the house and bam, she's here, ten times worse than she was before." He waved his hand toward the other room. "You've got to take care of her."

"Come back here and face me, you coward!" Doreen screamed from the confines of the cookie jar she'd been cursed into before her death.

Martin flinched. Jazz did not flick an eyelash, but she wondered how a man reputed to be a driving force in the television industry could fail to connect her unexpected appearance at his front door with the return of his curse. A curse she'd effectively eliminated—until the sleaze tried to cheat her.

"Maybe she came back," Jazz said, "because you were a bad boy."

Martin looked wary. "I don't know what you mean."

"You know exactly what I mean. You stopped payment on the check you gave me." Jazz stepped into the foyer, plucked from her pocket the check with its giant red Stop Payment stamped across the surface and waved it under Martin's nose. "Not a smart way to do business. Especially with a witch."

"I wouldn't do that!" Martin cried, aghast. "It must have been my wife who ordered the stop payment!"

"Oh, that's right! Blame it on my sweet, precious Lenore!" Doreen's voice cried out. "You are such a worm, Martin Reynolds! You won't even take responsibility for your own mistakes."

"Don't be shy, Doreen," Jazz said. "Please join us."

She waved a hand at the closest wall and Doreen's features—high forehead, hawklike nose, and sharp chin—bulged out of the stucco. Her sightless eyes zeroed in on Martin and he shrieked.

"Did you think you could get rid of me so easily, you slime?"

"You miserable bitch!" Martin threw his highball glass at the wall.

Before it could explode in a shower of glass splinters, Jazz flicked her fingers again. The glass floated down to stand neatly on a nearby table, and Doreen's face instantly shifted to the boldly splashed oil painting over the fireplace. Jazz thought it might be a Picasso; a real one.

"What a cheap painting," Doreen sneered. "Bought this at one of those starving artist sales, didn't you?"

"What the fuck are you doing?" Martin screamed at Jazz and flung a pointing finger at the fireplace. "That's a Picasso!"

"I told you what would happen if you stiffed me, Martin." Jazz shrugged. "I told you the curse would come back ten-fold."

"All right, you win." Martin pulled out a handkerchief and mopped his perspiring brow. "I'll write you another check. Anything to get rid of that miserable old bitch."

"Ah, ah, ah, no B words, and no more checks. Now it's cash." Jazz held out her hand. "Five thousand dollars, please."

"Five grand?" Martin howled. "Our deal was for five hundred."

Jazz smiled. "That was before you cheated me out of my fee, Martin."

"I don't keep that kind of cash here at home."

"Yes, you do. There's twenty-five large in the safe in your office," Jazz said. "The safe your wife knows nothing about. Would you like me to open it for you? I can from here, you know."

"No," Martin snarled, spinning on his heel toward the back of the house. "You wait right here."

"The first number is four!" Jazz called after him, always ready to help.

Then she grinned and headed for the kitchen. A handful of chocolate chip cookies lay scattered on the countertop where Doreen's angry face distorted one side of the cookie jar sitting in the center of the counter.

"Good grief, Doreen. You blew your top." Jazz picked up the lid and helped herself to a cookie from the jar. One bite urged her to take a second one. She could never resist chocolate chip.

"I told her he was no good, but did she listen to me? No," Doreen seethed. "She should've divorced him before the network started canceling his shows. And I'm sure he's hiding money in off-shore banks."

"Too late now." Jazz gave Doreen's Gingerbread Girl decorated lid a sympathetic pat. "Lenore will have to figure that out on her own."

Martin stalked into the kitchen and thrust a packet of bills at Jazz. "Here. Now get rid of the old bitch."

"No name calling, Martin." Jazz moved her fingertips over the money, counting it by touch to make sure the bills totaled five-thousand. Fool witch once, shame on you. Fool witch twice, oozing sores and an eternal rash in private areas.

It was all there. She tucked the cash into the inside pocket of her jacket, glanced at the scowling cookie jar and said, "Be gone."

Doreen's face vanished as Jazz's final word lingered in the air. Martin blinked and his mouth fell open.

"That's it?" He glared at Jazz. "You say two fucking

words and she's gone? No fancy fireworks or arcane rhymes? No waving a wand around?"

"You've been in television too long, Martin." Jazz opened a drawer, pulled out a meat hammer and smashed the cookie jar to smithereens.

"What have you done?" Martin screamed, clutching at his hair. "My wife treasured that damn thing!"

"Blame it on the maid," Jazz said. "Or find one just like it on eBay."

Martin moaned and wiped a hand over his face. His stress etched on his face was warring with his Botox job. "Lenore is going to kill me when she gets home."

"Had to be done, Martin. The cookie jar carried the curse. Now you need to bury the pieces. And you have to bury each piece separately, at least three feet apart. Be sure you say, 'Be gone,' over each one as you cover it with dirt."

Martin gaped at her. "There's a million pieces here!"

"Hm, not that many. Maybe only a thousand, but you'd better get started right away, hadn't you?" Jazz turned to leave, paused in the kitchen doorway and looked back at Martin, staring at the shattered cookie jar. "One more thing, Martin."

"What?" he asked, not bothering to look at her.

"It's never good to cheat people. It only messes up your karma."

When Jazz climbed into the T-Bird, Irma quickly extinguished her forbidden cigarette. "Lands sake, I could hear screaming all the way out here. What did you make this one do?"

"I broke the cookie jar and told him he had to bury each piece at least three feet apart. Good thing he has a lot of property because he's going to need it." Jazz started the engine, sneezed from the cigarette smoke lingering in the car, and pulled the money Martin had given her out of her jacket. "And I charged him five thousand dollars."

"Don't tell me." Irma held up one white-gloved hand. "You're going to give every penny of it to the Save the Witches Fund."

"These are weird times for witches, Irma. I wish the Fund had been around years ago when my sisters and I needed a hand." Jazz pulled away from the curb. "It's not like I need the money. I make enough driving for Dweezil."

"Oh, yes. All Creatures Limo Service." Irma made a face. "I'm sure your mother would be so proud that you grew up to be a taxi driver."

"Stuff it, Irma," Jazz snapped and headed for the freeway.

"I swear, curse elimination always puts you in a bad mood, so let me guess." Irma sniffed, staring up at the freeway signs that whipped past. "We're going to see that alcoholic."

"Nooo," Jazz said. "I am going to see my friend Murphy. You are going to sit in the car, which you've been doing for the last…," Jazz did the math in her head, "fifty-odd years."

"Then let me go in with you sometimes when you do your work," Irma said. "I could help, you know."

"I eliminate curses, Irma, not add to them," Jazz said with a laugh, "You haven't been able to leave the car in fifty years as it is. Plus what would you do in there? Find a bed sheet and wander around flapping your arms?"

"If you gave me a chance, you could find out just what I could do."

Irma stuck her nose in the air and turned her head to look out the side window. A cigarette smoldered between her white-gloved fingers. Jazz had never been able to figure out how a fifty-year-old ghost managed to obtain Lucky Strikes on a regular basis.

Twenty minutes later, Jazz whipped the T-Bird into a parking spot in front of Murphy's Pub. The one-story weathered building near the waterfront had a faded, gilt-lettered sign over the door. No ambiance here. She could hear tinny music coming from the nearby pier, where the amusement park's Ferris wheel glittered with multi-colored lights.

"This is a No Parking zone," Irma announced, a fresh Lucky Strike appearing between her fingers. She sighed and made it disappear when Jazz shot her a warning look.

"Relax, Irma." Jazz pushed her door open. "I'm not lucky enough to have you towed away to a nasty, dirty impound lot." Instead of using a car alarm, she set an illusion spell that allowed anyone without magickal sight to see the car only as a rusting Pontiac instead of the snazzy T-Bird. And anyone who happened to stumble past the spell and still try to steal the car would be in for a nasty surprise. When it last happened in 1980, the hysterical car thief babbled on about the car being filled with snakes. No wonder the police thought he was flying high on drugs.

Fiddles playing Morrison's Jig engulfed Jazz as she stepped inside the pub. The music swept her back in time to the little Irish village where she was born. Memories were so strong, she swore she could almost smell peat burning on the hearth. Seven hundred years ago there had been no pubs, but there were meeting places for the men to gather, drink ale and brag. She was the little girl sent to fetch Da home, cuffed for her efforts as often as not. She shook off the memory as Murphy caught her eye and raised his hand in greeting. She returned the gesture and wove her way between the maze of tables and chairs. The patrons of Murphy's Pub cheerfully ignored the statewide restaurant smoking ban. The two local cops sitting at the end of the bar weren't about to enforce the law when they each had a cigarette in their hands.

"Don't you look like a hot and sexy lady of the night?" Murphy said as she slid into her usual place near the beer taps. He pushed a basket of pretzels toward her and rested his elbows on the bar's surface.

"Thank you, kind sir," Jazz said, letting a hint of Old Ireland creep into her voice.

"So tell me, darlin', you have any whips and chains hiding under that scrap of a jacket?" He leaned across the space between them as if to get a better look.

She picked up the mug and sipped the warm, yeasty ale with a grateful sigh. "You're such a flatterer, Murphy. Is that why the boys in blue are showing up here instead of heading over to one of their usual hangouts?"

His gaze momentarily shifted toward the cops, then came back to Jazz. "Some vamps have come up missing lately, so they're checking all the bars in the area. I told them vamps don't tend to come in here. We don't serve the right kind of refreshment." He chuckled.

"I bet they chose this place because they knew no

vamp would come in here. They just wanted a place where they could kick back and drink," she replied, picking up a handful of pretzels and munching away. In seconds the basket was empty. Murphy replaced it with a filled one.

"They've sure been doing that." He winked at Jazz. "And what brings you to my establishment wearing a hot outfit like that?"

"Getting even with a client who tried to cheat me out of my fee."

"One of Dweezil's clients or a cursed client?"

"Cursed," she replied

"The world was saner before creatures came out of the woodwork," Murphy muttered, nodding acknowledgement at someone's shout for another Guinness. "And according to the boys in blue at the end of the bar, a lot safer."

"But not as exciting." Jazz winked back. "Live and let live, Murphy." She started to say more when she felt a faint stroke of cold trail across the back of her neck. She lifted the mug to her lips and tilted her head back just enough to look in the gilt edged mirror behind the bar. That's when she saw him, sitting at the rear corner table, ready to intercept her gaze in the mirror. Proof positive that a vampire without a reflection is nothing more than an old Bela Lugosi tale.

Nikolai Gregorivich. Tall, dark, and arrogant. Eyes the color of the Irish Sea. Features cold as ice. And a vampire.

Jazz had not seen him in over thirty years. What was he doing here?

White-hot anger settled deep inside and flowed through her veins like lava.

Focus, Jazz, focus.

What in Fate's sake was he doing here? Why wasn't he hanging out at The Crypt down in the warehouse district? There the undead found everything from O Positive to A Negative on tap.

He sure as hell wasn't here to see her. Maybe he was here for the same reason as the two mortal cops were. Nikolai worked as an investigator and enforcer for a vampire security agency. From experience, Jazz knew that vampire cops and mortal cops in the same place didn't always play well together, even if Nikolai seemed to get along better with mortal law enforcement than most of his kind did. A quick glance at the end of the bar assured her the two cops had no idea a vampire was even in the bar.

"Uh, Jazz."

She tore her eyes away from the mirror and saw the mug of ale bubbling in her hand—bubbling like, well, like a witch's cauldron.

"Is there something wrong?" Murphy asked, raising an eyebrow.

Jazz snuffed her temper and smiled, watching the bubbles recede. "Not a thing."

He frowned as he wiped up the liquid and then glanced up at a rumbling sound overhead. "What was that?"

"Probably a low-flying jet," she lied, dialing her temper back a few more notches. At this rate, she'd be sent to witchy anger management. She pushed the mug away. She knew any ale that reached her stomach now would only turn sour. "It's been a long night. I think I'll head on home, Murphy."

"It's not that late," he said with a hint of invitation in his voice.

She smiled and shook her head as she pulled out a twenty and left it on the bar, ignoring Murphy's attempt to push it back toward her. She turned away and headed for the door.

Another boom of thunder rattled the windows as she reached the exit.

"Damn it," Jazz muttered, hurrying outside before her witchy tantrum drew the two cops' attention. "And damn him for invading my territory."

Hex Appeal

Chapter 1

"YOU SHALL PAY, NICK GREGORY. THIS I VOW. YOU shall suffer and scream for a mercy I shall deny you." Jazz's parted lips trailed across Nick's collarbone. She ran the tip of her tongue up the taut lines of his throat while her fingers danced their way down his abs following the line of crisp hair lower still.

"Mercy," Nick whispered as her fingers wrapped around his erection. He lay naked on his bed, legs slightly spread to accommodate Jazz's bare thigh draped over his.

"But we've just begun, darling," she purred, nipping his earlobe just hard enough to cause him to jump in response, then soothed the bite with her tongue. "You must lie there very still while I have my way with you."

"Feel free to do what you will—soon enough it will be my turn." He lowered his voice to a husky growl that made promises she knew he would keep. Her body quivered in anticipation.

But for now, it was her turn and she intended to make the most of it.

Leaning back, she admired the view. Sheer male beauty stretched out beside her. Nick had kept himself in excellent physical condition in life and, as a member of the undead, his well-honed body would never deteriorate. She tangled her fingers in the light dusting of dark brown hair on his chest. She knew many women admired a hair-free chest, but she liked to see a bit there, as long as the man didn't look as if he needed a good chest waxing. No, Nick's was just right. Surrendering to temptation, she lowered her head to nibble on a dark brown nipple that peeked out among the hair. It peaked to a hard nub and brought another groan to his lips.

"Wuss," she teased, dividing her attention between both nipples, alternating with tiny nips of her teeth and soothing licks of her tongue. She glanced up under the cover of her lashes. "Why no nipple rings? So many vamps love them as bling."

Nick made a face. "Not my style. Makes me think it would be too easy to loop a chain through it. Make me a slave."

"Hmmmm," she giggled and hummed as she mouthed her way down to his navel. "The picture that conjures up. . ."

"Seems like you've already conjured something very much up." His eyes followed as she cupped her hand around his straining cock, slowly stroking from root to tip in a rhythm that had him clenching his teeth when her other hand gently cradled the sac beneath.

"I ask that thee render me that which I deserve. Because I say so, damn it!" She finished with her own version of "so mote it be" on a wave of throaty laughter right before she raised her body up over him and settled on him with perfect ease. She straddled his hips, bending her long legs alongside his.

"What? No foreplay?" He grasped her hips, although she needed no help in finding a rhythm. It had been written in their blood ages ago.

She leaned forward and brushed her mouth across his, tickling the seam of his lips and teasing the tips of his fangs, darting out before they could prick the tender skin. "We had foreplay at the movies," she breathed against his mouth. "And during the drive home when I unzipped your jeans and. . ." she deliberately paused for effect, "it's time for the main event, fang boy." She moved in a circular motion, tightening her core to massage him with her inner muscles.

Nick suddenly jackknifed his legs, flipping her onto her back with ease.

"You are so right, mi'lady. But I'll be the ringmaster for this show." He dipped his head, kissing her deeply. The scent of arousal grew thick in the room. He reared back until his cock left her folds. As she whimpered the sorrow of her loss, he thrust forward, filling her once again. With each deepening stroke, she arched up, meeting him as his equal.

Jazz looked up, smiling at the dark intensity of his features.

Her smile faltered a bit when she saw the arousal turn to something else, as his expression sharpened and his eyes turned a burning red. The growl that traveled up his throat turned into a feral hiss. Before she could react, his fangs lengthened and he dipped his head. Pain shot through her as his fangs pierced the sensitive skin of her throat.

Why isn't my blood making him sick? Everyone knows a witch's blood will sicken, and can even kill, a vampire! She wanted to shriek, to fight back, but her heavy limbs refused to obey her commands. Lights danced before her eyes and she feared instead of her blood killing Nick, he would kill her.

Jazz's eyes popped open as she shot up in bed, her hand pressed against the side of her neck where pain still radiated. Nick lay slumbering beside her.

Fear, memory of searing pain, and just plain fury warred inside her. She looked down at the source and let her temper—and fist—loose.

"You son of a whore!" She threw a punch to his bare abs that could easily have broken her hand. Not that she would have noticed. "You bit me!"

"What? What?" Nick scrambled away from her flying fists and fell out of bed. He grasped the covers and stared at her as if he was positive she'd somehow lost her mind. "What in Hades is wrong with you?"

"You bit me!" She slid off the other side of the bed and hurried around the room, keeping her hand pressed against her neck. Pain and anger translated to red and purple sparks flying around her.

"Bit you?" Confusion mingled with being just plain pissed off at being awakened with a punch to the stomach. "I was asleep, damn it!" He hauled himself to his feet and stood there in all his naked glory. For once, Jazz's cold stare warned him that she wasn't admiring the view. He stared at her hand covering her throat but saw no signs of blood or trauma to the skin. He refused to believe he would take her blood without permission, asleep or not. In all their times as lovers he hadn't even given her a hickey. He also kept a close eye on her free hand. The last thing he wanted was witchflame thrown at his favorite part of the body. "Damn it, I didn't bite you!"

With one hand applying firm pressure to her neck, she struggled to pull her jeans on one-handed. "You practically tore out my bloody throat," she snarled, still feeling the ache of her flesh.

Nick crouched slightly, his hands thrust outward. "Will you stop using the word 'bloody'?"

She blinked back the tears that threatened to leak out. "Get out."

"What?" Even with his super hearing, he knew he couldn't have just heard what she said.

She breathed hard as if pushing back tears. Or absolute terror. "I said get out!" She stalked around the room, still keeping him out of reach, snatched up his jeans and T-shirt, and threw them at him. The clothing bounced off his chest and fell back to the floor. "Get out and do not ever come near me again." She refused to look at him as she gathered up her own clothing. "Because if you do I will stake you. I cannot believe you bit me!" Tears and anger made a nasty combination.

Nick's jaw worked furiously. A witch with Celtic origins might have a legendary temper, but so did a vampire with the blood of a Cossack. "This is my room. My apartment."

Jazz froze in the act of pulling her cotton top over her head. She stared at the navy and cream swirled print comforter that had been tossed to the floor, navy sheets that were likewise thrown every which way, and furniture that suited a centuries-old vampire. None of the stark colors that dominated her own suite of rooms. She finished pulling on her top, then picked up her leather tote bag. "Fluff! Puff! Where are you two? You better not have left the apartment!" she shouted when she discovered it was empty of two items. The errant slippers popped into the room and scampered over to her feet.

Sensing the turmoil in the air, and guessing the cause, the fluffy predators snarled and gnashed their razor-sharp teeth at Nick, clearly showing they considered him the enemy in this battle. Jazz quickly stuffed her underwear, the top she'd worn the night before, and a hairbrush into her leather tote bag and slung it over her shoulder. "If Rex sees those man eaters, you'll be permanently banned from the boardwalk along with them," Nick warned, jumping into his jeans as he followed her to the door.

She sniffed at the mention of the boardwalk manager who ruled his kingdom with an iron fist. "He's not the boss of me." She glared at him. "And neither are you."

"Jazz, what in Hades' name is going on? How can you say I took your blood when there's no sign I did! Damn it, show me where I bit you!" Nick was fast on her heels as she raced up the stairs to the building's main floor. Ground-eating strides took her down the hallway to the double glass doors. Nick wasn't worried about the early morning light. His advanced age as a vampire along with heavily tinted glass of the doors helped protect him against the sun. He was confused, and more than a little ticked off, by her accusation. But it was clear Jazz wasn't going to stick around to talk about it.

He gingerly rubbed his palm over his bare abs. If he'd been a mortal man he would probably have had his share of cracked ribs. The heavy glass door almost hit him in the face as she slapped her palm against the surface and pushed it open, sailing through and not looking back. He kept the door open long enough to holler after her, "And why can't you hit like a girl?"

He stared at her retreating figure and realized that wasn't one of his finer moments.

Acknowledgments

Writing is a solitary business, so friends are important. Those friends that understand you best are real treasures to be cherished and I cherish my friends.

My agent, Laurie McLean of the Larsen/Pomada Literary Agency, aka, Batgirl, who's there for me and doesn't bat an eye no matter how off the wall I get.

My editor, Deb Werksman, who loves Jazz and her witch buddies as much as I do. And I thank the Sourcebooks art department who comes up with these awesome covers.

My devoted niece, AshNay, who may not be my niece by blood but definitely from the heart and loves to talk paranormal with me. And my equally devoted nephew Jordan who shares Fluff and Puff with AshNay. Thanks for keeping them occupied guys.

The Witchy Chicks, Yasmine Galenorn, Terese Daly Ramin, Lisa Croll Di Dio, Madelyn Alt, Candace Havens, Kate Austin, Maura Anderson, and Annette Blair. Your support is much appreciated, and I love you all.

About the Author

Linda Wisdom was born and raised in Huntington Beach, California. She majored in Journalism in college, then switched to Fashion Merchandising when she was told there was no future for her in fiction writing. She held a variety of positions ranging from retail sales to executive secretary in advertising and office manager for a personnel agency. Her career began when she sold her first two novels to Silhouette Romance on her wedding anniversary in 1979. Since then she has sold more than seventy novels and one novella to four different publishers. Her books have appeared on various romance and mass market bestseller lists and have been nominated for a number of Romantic Times awards, as well as two-time finalist for the Romance Writers of America Rita Award. She lives with her husband, one dog, one parrot, and a tortoise in Murrieta, California. When Linda first moved to Murrieta there were three romance writers living in the town. At this time, there is just Linda. So far, the police have not suspected her of any wrongdoing.